BERKLEY TITLES BY RAQUEL VASQUEZ GILLILAND

Witch of Wild Things
Lightning in Her Hands

"In her magical, beautiful adult debut, *Witch of Wild Things*, Raquel Vasquez Gilliland absolutely mesmerizes with a richly woven story encompassing family, friendship, and romantic love. The tenderness between Sage and Tennessee truly captured my heart. Perfect for fans of Lisa Kleypas and yet at the same time gorgeously unique, this earthy and luminous book will leave readers spellbound."

—India Holton, national bestselling author of
The League of Gentlewomen Witches

"*Witch of Wild Things* is such a beautiful story of family, friendship, and falling in love. I mean, an anonymous AIM chat relationship from high school, with the boy on the other end now all grown up into a tattooed, plant-loving man? Sisters with a thorny, complicated relationship in need of nourishing? A woman who doesn't see herself as the special, rare flower she is . . . until she does? Raquel Vasquez Gilliland's adult debut is everything I love about romance!"

—Alicia Thompson, national bestselling author of
Love in the Time of Serial Killers

"Raquel Vasquez Gilliland's adult debut is spooky, sexy, and magical. *Witch of Wild Things* is a perfect mix of magical realism and swoony romance, with a fair amount of family drama and love. You'll fall in love with the Flores sisters in this cozy, wonderful novel."

—Elissa Sussman, bestselling author of *Funny You Should Ask*

"*Witch of Wild Things* is a flawless gem. Raquel Vasquez Gilliland's prose is by turns seamless and striking; her storytelling is vulnerable and full of soul. As a Mexican American, reading this novel felt like coming home—it was a song my heart never knew it needed to hear." —Isabel Cañas, author of *The Hacienda*

"Every page sparkles with magic, family, and the lush beauty of wild things."

—Sangu Mandanna, author of
The Very Secret Society of Irregular Witches

"You could cut the tension here with a knife, or should we say, a pair of gardening shears." —*Good Housekeeping*

"A solid, fun novel, full of magic, romance, and characters you can follow along with and root for." —Red Carpet Crash

"Gilliland's adult fiction debut is a beautifully written, entrancing novel that is a must-buy for all collections."

—*Library Journal* (starred review)

"Gilliland mixes magical realism, sisterhood, and, of course, love into a sparkling romance that will sweep readers off their feet."

—*Publishers Weekly* (starred review)

"In a touching and sweet story about moving on from a haunting past, award-winning Mexican American poet, artist, and novelist Gilliland weaves together a complex tale of loss and new beginnings that still manages to be a fun and captivating romance."

—*Booklist*

"Transportive and bursting with heart, *Witch of Wild Things* is a tender masterpiece of magical realism." —*BookPage*

Lightning in Her Hands

Raquel Vasquez Gilliland

BERKLEY ROMANCE
NEW YORK

BERKLEY ROMANCE
Published by Berkley
An imprint of Penguin Random House LLC
penguinrandomhouse.com

Copyright © 2024 by Raquel Vasquez Gilliland
Readers Guide copyright © 2024 by Raquel Vasquez Gilliland
Excerpt from *Witch of Wild Things* copyright © 2023 by Raquel Vasquez Gilliland
Penguin Random House supports copyright. Copyright fuels creativity, encourages diverse
voices, promotes free speech, and creates a vibrant culture. Thank you for buying an authorized
edition of this book and for complying with copyright laws by not reproducing, scanning, or
distributing any part of it in any form without permission. You are supporting writers and
allowing Penguin Random House to continue to publish books for every reader.

BERKLEY and the BERKLEY & B colophon are registered trademarks of
Penguin Random House LLC.

Library of Congress Cataloging-in-Publication Data

Names: Vasquez Gilliland, Raquel, author.
Title: Lightning in her hands / Raquel Vasquez Gilliland.
Description: First edition. | New York: Berkley Romance, 2024.
Identifiers: LCCN 2024000143 (print) | LCCN 2024000144 (ebook) |
ISBN 9780593548592 (trade paperback) | ISBN 9780593548608 (ebook)
Subjects: LCGFT: Romance fiction. | Novels.
Classification: LCC PS3622.A834 L54 2024 (print) |
LCC PS3622.A834 (ebook) | DDC 813/.6—dc23/eng/20240108
LC record available at https://lccn.loc.gov/2024000143
LC ebook record available at https://lccn.loc.gov/2024000144

First Edition: October 2024

Printed in the United States of America
1st Printing

Book design by Daniel Brount

To Donna Cherry,
who showed me the lightning in my hands

here I will give you thunder
shatter your hearts with rain

—BELL HOOKS, "5," APPALACHIAN ELEGY

⚡

Rather than being only a dangerous power,
lightning is considered to be life giving and engendering.

—MARY ELLEN MILLER AND KARL TAUBE,
AN ILLUSTRATED DICTIONARY OF THE GODS AND
SYMBOLS OF ANCIENT MEXICO AND THE MAYA

Lightning
in
Her
Hands

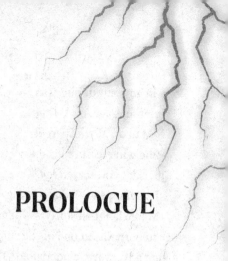

PROLOGUE

MY GREAT-AUNT NADIA SAYS THAT OUR MOTHER ABAN-doned us the way winter comes to Cranberry, Virginia—sudden, deep, leaving everything dusted with tiny splinters of frost.

But Nadia is wrong.

I was little, only five years old, and I awoke in the middle of the night knowing something was off. I wonder, now, if it was anything like Nadia's gift. *Knowing* things she has no reason or right to know. Whatever it was, something told me Mama was in the kitchen and I needed to see her right away.

I tiptoed downstairs in the only home I have ever known, even to this day. The two-story house Nadia bought the day she turned forty, with its strangely angled cupboards filled with books, and windows made of painted-glass butterflies, and an at-tic that whistled in wind so loudly, it always sounded to me like the songs of ghosts.

When I found Mama, she was surrounded with suitcases. In reality, there was no way she could have afforded more than two, but in my mind, she was in a spiral of Samsonite and Globe-Trotter luggage.

"Mama?" I whispered.

She whipped her head toward me with her hand on her heart. "Querida, you scared me."

I swallowed. "What's going on? Are we going to Disney?"

Mama laughed softly. "No, not today." She paused and tapped her fingernails on one of the suitcases. "Today, Mama's going on a long adventure. Understand? I'm going to see some cool things, like real tall mountains with the snow on the tops, and a beach filled with rainbow glass."

By then I was already crying. I must've known what she was saying, underneath all those pretty words. "No, Mama, don't go."

She wrapped an arm around me. "No, no, don't cry, querida. Or else you'll make me cry."

I tried very hard to stop crying, but in my memory, my face remained wet with tears.

Headlights shone in through the windows and Mama jumped up. "That's him," she said, breathless. "He's the one who's going to fix *everything*."

She grabbed the handles to the suitcases and raced to the door. She winked at me. "I won't be long, okay? Tell Nadia—" She paused. "Tell Nadia I left some stuff in my room. Extra diapers, and the snacks you and Sage like, the fruit gummy things, okay?"

She was gone before I could respond, but I was on her heels, faster than the door could slam.

I was always little. I ended up taller than my older sister, Sage, as an adult, but it took a while to get here. From the ages of babyhood to nineteen, I was so small, in pictures I sometimes wondered how I didn't just fly away with all the wild weather I have faced in my life.

That night, I feel like I might have flown a little. The wind was whipping against me, pushing my hair in my eyes. Lightning streaked across the sky, and rain, and then tiny drops of hail, began to fall.

"What is this?" Mama asked, turning toward me as she gestured to the sky. One moment before, all had been clear. The next, an entire thunderstorm swept down upon us as though someone had tapped a cosmic weather button.

She took one look at me and knew where it'd come from.

Our gifts aren't supposed to come until around puberty. But something about my mami breaking my heart that night—it made mine come early.

"Here," Mama said, bending down in front of me. The truck behind her was loud and impatient. I think the man inside revved the engine and I jumped. A crack of thunder made me jump again. "Don't worry," Mama said as I began to wail. "I could use this, right, mamita? I only need just a tiny, little—"

And she took my hand and pinched me.

The second she did, the storm went silent. The rain ceased. The only thing that remained of it was the tiniest bit of lightning in Mama's hand. That must sound ridiculous, I know, but she held a piece of light—*my* light—and it sizzled and glimmered like she had plucked a slice of sun out of the sky.

"You don't need this, do you?" she asked.

I didn't even understand what she was asking, but I shook my head. Even at that age, I knew what she wanted me to say. And I wanted to make her happy. I wanted her to change her mind and stay with us. Stay with *me*.

Mama kissed my nose. "Go inside, Teal." Then she rushed away. She shoved her suitcases in the back seat and hopped in the front of the truck. She disappeared completely into the black behind the headlights—I don't know if it was because of the lightning, or because of her gift. When Mama didn't want to be seen, she simply would not be seen. Eventually they drove away and I watched until the greenish-yellow headlights rounded the end of the street.

This is where my memory dissolves. I must've listened to her. I must've gone inside, to my warm bed, snuggled between Sage and baby Sky. I must've and yet I can't say for sure.

What I do know, all these things I do remember—I've never told anyone, not even Nadia.

But the night my mother left, it wasn't like winter. It was hot. The wind was hot against my teary eyes. The hail was hot against my skin. And in my mother's grasp was the white-hot of lightning she pinched from the palm of my hand, and it burned and burned and burned.

1

WIBTA if I asked my ex best friend to be my plus 1 to my ex's wedding?

posted in r/AITAH by TealLightning ten hours ago

My ex (m34) is getting married this weekend and my date just bailed. I (28f) really don't want to go alone. I want to ask my ex best friend (m26) to be my plus 1.

But this ex best friend stopped speaking to me a while back. My older sister says it's because he's in love with me and I've been leading him on for years and he's just trying to get over me. But there's no way. My sister just got engaged and now she looks at everything with hearts in her eyes.

I miss him so much though. I feel like if he came to the wedding with me, it's a win/win. I'm not alone and we can catch up and it would be just like old times.

My younger sister says I would be the asshole if I did, because he would never be able to say no to me and I need to let his broken heart heal. But he's dated a ton of women who are not me since I last talked with him; clearly he's over his crush, if it was ever there to begin with. Which it wasn't.

Would I be the asshole if I asked him to the wedding?

 |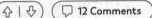

thepoopsmith—YTA

itsholabitch3s—ur the asshole. just leave him alone. god. if he wanted to be friends with u he would be speaking to you rn.

shenanigans007—NTA. Nothing wrong with asking. What's the worst that could happen? Seriously? A girl can't ask a guy to a wedding anymore is that what this is. This world is seriously f**ked up yall I can't even right now with this

raspberrylimeseltzerwater—wait you think it's a win/win because YOU wouldn't be alone and it would be "just like old times" when clearly something went down that must've hurt him and changed everything? you're the assholeeeeeee

iap384771oo1—hey that's a good point. what actually happened last time you spoke to this dude, OP?

TealLightning—Nothing. I was at the bar he was working at and that's when I met my ex actually. That was the night my ex and I first hooked up.

raspberrylimeseltzerwater—something's missing from this story. why does your sister think he has a broken heart? what did u do to hurt him?

TealLightning—Jfc, I didn't do shit to him. So what if we kissed for the first time earlier that week? He knew it meant nothing, I knew it meant nothing. It meant nothing. Doesn't mean he gets to throw away sixteen years of friendship over it.

iap384771oo1—seriously you want him to go to the wedding of the guy you chose after kissing him for the first time? after he's loved you for years??! you're the asshole

raspberrylimeseltzerwater—that's what i thought. we're always missing some part of the story. YTA, OP, sorry not sorry

shenanigans007—yeahhh. yta. you're the f**king asshole bitch I can't even explain how much rn, god this world is so freaking messed up, a guy can't even try to avoid a girl he loves anymore, I just?? you know?

TealLightning—whatever. I'm gonna ask him just to spite y'all. And after that I'm deleting this dumb post.

⚡

I'VE BEEN SITTING IN MY CAR AT THE PARKING LOT OF CRAN-berry Rose Company for almost twenty minutes. My ex, Nate Bowen, owns the place.

But I'm not here to see him.

My sister Sage and her man, Tenn, work here, too. Not here for them, either.

I suck in a breath when a tall, dark-haired Cuban American fellow steps out of the barn, pushing a wheelbarrow full of . . . I'm not sure what. Wood chips?

"Finally," I mutter, and get out of the car.

I push my nerves all the way down as I approach him, until my legs feel steady enough to walk without tripping all over my-self. All morning, my heart has felt like it's grown iridescent, indigo-bunting wings and is vibrating against my rib cage. I couldn't even eat breakfast.

Since when have I ever been nervous to talk to Carter?

Since he melted your boy shorts off with a single kiss last summer, my brain responds.

I close my eyes, and when I open them again, Carter's looking right at me, a line between his furrowed brows. "Teal? What are you doing here?"

I try not to notice the dark clouds in the distance. If I do, they'll get here even faster.

"I'm—" I cough. "Um." I stop when I'm six feet away. I'm close enough to notice the way he looks at me like I'm some kind of a stranger to him now. Like we didn't spend our childhood col-lecting coins for the ice cream truck, eating our Choco Tacos and strawberry shortcakes in the big alder tree behind his mama's old house. Like I didn't call him every time Johnny made me feel like shit, knowing that just Carter's voice would make me feel better about my life, about the fuckup I'd become.

I'm *not* close enough to him for dangerous things. Like to smell his cologne—Polo Green by Ralph Lauren, with its notes of citrus and leather. I'm not close enough to make out the sugar-sweet pink of his full lips. I'm not close enough to remember how they felt around my nipple through my bra—warm and wet and *everything*.

He frowns at me even more deeply. "Sage and Tenn aren't here today. They're working in the field."

"Carter," I say, and my voice breaks and I hate it, I hate it, I *hate* it. Thunder rumbles way too close. I'm running out of time. I always feel like I'm running out of time when it comes to Carter these days.

This time, his eyebrows rise in worry. "Teal, what's wrong? Is it Nadia? Is it—"

"No. Nothing like that." I shake my head firmly and inhale. One-two-three-four in, and out to the count of eight. *Just say it*, I will myself. And I do, in one whole breath, so fast even I can barely understand myself. "Do you wanna go with me to Nate's wedding on Saturday?"

I'm not the asshole, I swear I'm not the asshole. Carter and I might've kissed—*once*—but if it meant something to me? I wouldn't have gone off with Nate just two days later. And if it meant something to him? He wouldn't have slept with every woman under the age of forty-five in Cranberry in the last year.

I just want my childhood best friend back. That's it.

But with the way Carter's jaw tightens, and his eyes narrow—it looks like that's not going to happen anytime soon, if ever. "Weren't you going with Andre Castle?"

"No." Yes. I was, till Andre got sick of my bullshit and

dumped me just yesterday. "Anyway, I just thought we could, you know, go, as friends. And—"

"I already have a date, Teal." Carter's voice is as sharp as the art I saw at the gallery downtown a couple of weeks back, full of glass blown in veins of edges and blades. "And now I have to work."

He dismisses me by angling the wheelbarrow away and marching down the hill toward the garden beds.

⚡

FOR EIGHT YEARS STRAIGHT, MY SISTER SAGE DIDN'T CRY, BE-cause when she did, my other sister, Sky, who we thought was dead, would appear to her as a ghost. Now that Sky is back, alive and well (as well as she could be, considering), Sage is making up for it. It seems like all she does is cry these days. She and Tenn move in together? Weeping-willow-turned-human. She and Tenn get engaged? La Llorona, showing off her artisan-carved engagement ring, with green-gold mushrooms swirling around one giant ivy-hued sapphire.

Sage and I used to have that in common, because I try really hard to not cry, in general. But it's not because the tears call a ghost my way. It's because—

A heavy splatter of cold hits my head.

Another hits my shoulder.

"Dammit," I mutter, glaring up at the sky, where the endless gray clouds have finally caught up with me. I wipe at my eyes violently, willing the salty wet to stay *in*, for the sake of old gods.

I run to my car, followed by a sheet of sleet. It's the end of March and we're supposed to be in the middle of a warm spring.

This is why I don't like to cry.

I lean my head against the driver's door and do the breath

work the therapist taught me, the one who I saw exactly twice after I watched my baby sister fall eighty feet, screaming and screaming and screaming.

In, one-two-three-four. Out to the count of eight.

I thought Mama had taken my gift with her when she pinched that spot of lightning from my palm, but it showed up again, years later, about six months before my first period. But something was *off* with it. Even Nadia, who's seen some shit, didn't know what was all wrong with me.

In all of our known lineage—and I'm talking back and back to Texas, before Texas was even Texas—I am the first Flores woman who can't control my gift.

Sage basically winks at plants and they bloom. Into irises the color of strawberry frozen yogurt, into roses as blue as a cloudless summer sky set over the sea. Sky, her gift is criaturas—animals. She can coax a family of black bears into her lap for a nap. She spends her weekends braiding mountain daisies into her hair, and when she takes a walk, fucking pumpkin-winged house sparrows follow her all over the place, like a flaca, brown Snow White.

If things went right with the development of my gift, I'd be more like my sisters. I'd be able to snap my fingers for a light, warm rain. I'd be able to stop the snow of a blizzard, all with my thoughts and my will.

But what happens, instead, is this: sleet when I cry, rain when I'm depressed, gray storm clouds as dark as night when I'm nervous, endless flashes of lightning when I'm angry, and all kinds of variations between. I thought, for the longest time, that if I pushed down the turbulent emotions, I'd be cured, but that hasn't worked out, either. If I feel nothing—like I did when I was still with Johnny—the sky becomes this flat, overcast gray that's about as cheery as a pile of cinder blocks.

I was happy for about two seconds when Sky came back, before I started worrying about her again. The actual sky burst into rows and rows of rainbows, glimmering into each other like a psychedelic mirage, like somehow a giant, faceted diamond had inexplicably grown around Cranberry. It's the kind of weather event that would've made the news, but only one person got a photo before it disappeared, and as far as I know, they've just been accused of bad Photoshop skills.

There's only one way that I can stop sadness and disappointment and grief, at least for a little while, and I don't even hesitate right now, as I try to push Carter's rejection to the furthest, swampiest part of my brain. I pop in my AirPods, click on my phone's playlist, and turn around and run as fast as I can, toward the dirt road leading away from Cranberry Rose Company.

I run down the hill, where it turns into a paved road, and pass bluish-green fields of tobacco and barley. Every once in a while, a home whizzes by—little distant red farmhouses with white trim and picket fences covered in the hollowed vines of last year's morning glories, which will soon climb up again, dotting the perimeter of the land with blue, violet, and pink-trumpet flowers. The horizon is a curved line of soft hills, the ones Sage has called "mountains" since she was a little kid.

Soon I reach the woods and I veer right at the first trailhead I see. I hop around startled tourists, maps in their hands, jumping over fallen trees and baby boulders. The entire world becomes green, with the first flush of spring leaves surrounding me in electric lime. The wind feels cold against my sweaty skin. I can hardly breathe, but I don't slow, I don't trip, I don't stop.

Not until I reach a babbling brook at the end of the trail. With the rain we've been getting, it's too wide for me to rush through right now. But that's fine, because mission accomplished: I have run so fast and so long that all I can feel is the burn of my lungs and thighs, the pain in my right knee from an old injury. There is no disappointment. No anger. Just physical pain, and the oncoming runner's high that should get me through the rest of this morning. I nudge the voice of Taylor Swift out of my ears and shove the pods in my pockets. Now there's the sound of gurgling water and birdsong. I put my hands on my thighs and bend over, breathing the sweet, moss-smelling air as deeply as I can.

"Teal!"

I straighten and turn around, placing my hand on my chest. My next inhale stutters when I place who the hell is calling me, on a random run, this deep in the woods.

Carter stops six feet away, just like I had done earlier, at the farm. It's like we've both agreed to adhere to an invisible force field. Like maybe he's as wary as I am about the feelings, the memories, that pop up uninvited when we're too close.

His breath is faster than mine, and he bends and coughs. "Jesus Christ," he sputters. He's practically wheezing. "When did you learn to run like that, huh?"

I frown. "You know I've been running."

He coughs, choking on air. When he clears his throat, he says, "I was calling your name. For like, the last two miles."

I huff. "I had my AirPods in." My breath is back to normal. It's the other parts of me—my skin, my belly, my heart, that feel off. Like all my organs have grown fins and gills and are now swimming around inside, making me feel like I didn't *just* find my center with a quick three-mile run. Thunder echoes from far away and I glower at Carter. He's to blame for this. "You followed me all this way? For what? So you can blow me off again?"

He takes a minute to respond. His body has thickened up since we were kids, lined with hard, lean planes. He's in good shape, but I guess he doesn't run. He really needs to work on his endurance. If I were still training at the gym, I'd start him with just ten-minute intervals. In thirty days, he'd be blowing through a 5K. Midyear, a half marathon. But these thoughts are dumb and pointless. I was fired two weeks ago. And Carter, as far as I know, has never set foot in Cranberry Fitness Studio, anyway.

I roll my eyes. "Carter, what the hell do you want?"

He locks eyes with me and takes one sure, steady breath. "I'll go with you."

I freeze and then blink slowly. "To Nate's wedding?" I hate the way my voice squeaks with hope. I'd thought for sure he'd chased me down to finally tell me off for being such a shit friend to him.

He nods. "But then you owe me."

My eyes widen. "Owe you what? Sex?" I don't know why of all the words that can be worded, that's the one that chooses to rush out of my mouth in that moment.

Carter's mouth drops open. "Of course not, Teal! Christ!"

I'm almost offended at how repulsed he sounds. "Well, what do I owe you, then?"

His eyelids shut briefly. I've always thought his eyes were the wildest color I've ever seen outside of a fantasy film. They're brown and so light, they're almost sunflower yellow. They match all the Himalayan salt lamps Sage bought for her place with Tenn. "I can't say right now. It's not a sure thing. So I'll just tell you at the wedding."

"No way." I cross my arms, not missing how his eyes drop to my cleavage for a fraction of a second. I don't have a lot up top— I always joked that Sage stole all the boob genes before Sky and I could get any—but this sports bra is doing me wonders. I'm glad

I wore it today. "I'm not agreeing to anything without knowing what it even is. Do you think I'm stupid or something?"

"Or something," Carter mutters under his breath, running a hand through his hair, his skin lighting up under the dapple of woodland light. Sage explained to me once that white gold always looks warm, which is why it's often plated in rhodium. That's what Carter's skin looks like to me—as smooth and warm as real, unplated white gold. "This is how it's gotta be, Teal. I'll go with you, and you owe me a favor. That's it. That's the best I can do."

If things were like before . . . I could get it out of him. I'd rush up to him, tickle him, climb over his shoulders saying *Please please please tell me, Carter, I'll love you forever.*

But the thought of breaking our invisible force field makes my stomach want to drop all the way to the ground, all the way through it, to the invisible mushroom map Sage and Tenn are always reciting poetry about.

Things aren't like before. And that's on me. Which means it's also on me to fix it.

I close my eyes and picture my list on the dresser, the one I made with my friend Leilani for the new year. Leilani was raised by second-gen hippies and has been on my case to make a vision board for years. The best I could do was a list, which made her do this wild, hair-tossing happy dance.

The first line on that list is *1. Stop being selfish.*

Selfish Teal would've tried to figure out what's in it for her with whatever Carter's propositioning. What it's going to cost her. She would weigh all the options before taking the safest route, even if people were hurt along the way.

I don't want to be her anymore.

"The thing . . . it's not . . ." Carter shoves his hands in his pockets. "I don't even know if I can make this happen right now. I don't even know if I need the favor. I mean—"

"Fine," I announce, before he talks himself out of this.

His eyebrows reach his hairline. "Fine? Really?"

"Yes," I say, making a face. "You don't have to sound so shocked."

"But . . . you just agreed to it without, like—attacking me—"

"What about your date?" I interrupt. "Will it hurt her if you go with me instead?" If I'm going to be Not Selfish Teal, then I gotta think about things like this now. Even about the feelings of a woman I'm pretty sure I'd very much like to punch in the face, for reasons I don't want to investigate right now, or ever.

"No. She won't care." Carter shrugs again and lets out a long breath. We're both silent for a few seconds. "So you're uh—still parked at the farm? Wanna walk back together?"

The question is so absurd, I break into a laugh. I mean, what was I going to do, make him wait here fifteen minutes while I got a head start?

Carter's eyes are on me, unblinking, as his mouth curves into half a smile. He was always weird about making me laugh, even when we were kids. Acting like I broke into song or something, and it was his favorite sound in the whole world.

I push down whatever emotion is trying to ride up now at these thoughts and stomp around him. "Come on, flaco," I say. "You're probably still on the clock, aren't you?"

"Hey, I'm not flaco anymore," he says, jogging beside me, puffing his chest.

"Oh, I know," I mutter.

He leans forward, trying to catch my eye. "What was that?"

"Nothing! Just saying that Sky's the skinny one now."

We hike back to the farm in silence, probably because the pace I set is just short of running. But I'm scared I'm going to open my mouth and mess everything up again. So I just focus on the sun, breaking open through the clouds, steaking toward us until we're both aglow like living gold.

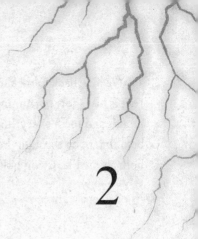

2

CARTER? CARTER *VELASQUEZ?*"

Leilani's voice breaks up, but I hear her incredulity just fine, and it's making me clench my teeth.

"Yup." I run the sponge over the bowl in my hands. My phone's on speaker, angled at me against the window over Nadia's kitchen sink.

"But . . . it's *Carter*. Isn't he, like? You know? He's got nothing going for him? And you've been complaining about him following you around like a puppy dog since I've known you. And now you're *dating* him?"

Carter doesn't have "nothing going for him," but she's not wrong about the rest of it. Carter *like*-liked me for a long time. We were tight when we were little, but when I was sixteen, I got tired of him always being everywhere all the time, those light honey eyes looking at me like I was the whole world when he knew, more than anyone, how broken I was. It wasn't until we thought Sky was gone that Carter and I got close again. And by close, I mean late-night phone calls while Johnny slept, and him leaving me gifts at the gym or Nadia's for my birthday and holidays.

Even then, things remained platonic. Well. Mostly platonic.

"It's not dating. It's just a wedding." *As friends*, I don't add, because I feel like it would sound like I'm protesting too much. Her tone already has me on edge as it is. I swear, I can feel the storm clouds gathering up on the water, marching here to Nadia's like a line of thunderous soldiers.

"Your *ex's* wedding." Leilani still sounds stupidly shocked. For nowhere near the first time in our friendship, I wonder if she's high on some random organic, plant-based microdose.

I narrow my eyes at my phone. "What is your deal, Lani? You're the one who's been on my case to get out of the house and date guys with jobs." The last three guys I'd hung out with were, in order: a musician, an entrepreneur, and a deejay. For these particular men, each of those careers was code for unemployed and couch surfing.

She sighs, exasperated. "I meant, like, guys with real jobs. Not bartenders."

"He doesn't work at Lost Souls anymore."

"Okay, so now he hoists manure at the rose store. Real upgrade there."

"What the fuck, Leilani?" I throw the pot back in the sink with a clatter. "Did you forget that my sister works at that *rose store*, too? And so does her fiancé?"

There's silence for a minute, and then she speaks with a choked-up voice. "I'm sorry, Teal. You're right. I'm just so stressed out lately."

I grab my phone and sit on the table, stretching my legs out. When I glance around, Sky's leaning against the entrance of the kitchen. Her hair is so long, it reaches her waist, and the ends are as gold as Carter's eyes. She narrows her eyes at my phone as she cradles . . . yep. She's cradling a freaking *squirrel*, running her fingers along the bronze fur of its tiny head.

I turn back to my phone. "What's going on? You're stressed about the move?" A few months ago, Leilani purchased what she keeps calling her "dream house," but she hasn't let me see it yet, not till "after renovations." My guess is she's having a giant, cream-colored crocheted swing installed, alongside a greenhouse for all her houseplants, and probably she's waiting on expensive commissions from around the world for earth-tone tapestries to hang on every wall.

"It's—a lot. I'll tell you all about it on Sunday. It's *super* awesome news. You're going to be so excited to hear it!" Her teary voice is gone, replaced by nothing but cheer. It's almost, *almost* like the guilt was an act.

I stifle my sigh as I watch the clouds rolling in from the window. They're not gray like I anticipated—instead they're thick and white with the palest blue shadows. "Okay, girl. I'll see you at the wedding on Saturday, right? And then we'll be able to talk on Sunday." Leilani and I have been renting our own booth at the Cranberry craft fair every year for the last three years. It runs from the first Sunday of spring to the last Sunday of fall. At first, renting a table was just an excuse to drink papaya mimosas from the Lost Souls Lounge table and watch all the hot, local carpenters lugging around their work, but then we started actually selling our own shit. It's why I'm not worried about having just gotten fired. As long as I have my Sundays in the alternative parking lot of Cranberry Library, I'll be able to make ends meet.

There's a pause, and Leilani says, "I just meant, before. You and Sage have *ambition*. You, with the candles, and Sage with her jewelry. You both are like me. We are manifesting our realities.

The whole universe is in motion, and we just don't have time for negativity. There's nothing but love in our lives, right?"

I pinch my mouth shut because Sky is currently holding in a laugh so hard, her eyes are tearing up. As her shoulders shake, I let out a reluctant smile. "Right, Lani. You know what's up."

We hang up after our goodbyes, which includes Leilani wishing me *Blessed be* all weirdly breathless, and as soon as the phone clicks off, Sky's laughter explodes out of her in sputters. "What is *wrong* with her?" she asks after she's caught her breath. "Is she always high? How does she turn every conversation into something about manifesting the universe in motion?"

I shake my head. Usually I can brush off Leilani's idiosyncrasies, but that phone call really annoyed me. She has some nerve, implying that Carter is some kind of loser, like he hasn't been working his ass off since he was fifteen years old, supporting his family any way he could.

"You're mad," Sky says, taking a seat next to me. She has to pull the chair out a lot, to fit her long legs under the table. "Is it because she was a big snob, acting like she was better than Carter and Sage and Tennessee?"

Instead of answering, I work my jaw until I feel a tension headache starting.

Sky tucks the squirrel on her shoulder, where it curls up like a damn cat and falls asleep instantly. "Sage doesn't like her."

"I know," I snap. "But you know what? Lani was the only one who didn't abandon me when—" I stop myself.

Sky smiles sadly. "When I fell off the cliff and became suspended in animation for eight years? Was that the end of your sentence?"

It's as wild as it sounds. Sky fell eighty feet to what should have been her death. They looked for her body for days and days.

I looked for her body for weeks. Months. Even years after, I would take a walk at the bottom of that cliff, my eyes combing the brush for any sign of her—a shoe, ragged and half gnawed-on. A ring, with a sliver of silver shining through a deep black patina. A bone, white, porous, licked clean by some starved scavenger.

I would've settled for a strand of her caramel brown hair curled around blooming dandelions, but I found nothing. And the reason for that is because in the fifteen minutes it took for me to rush down to where she had fallen, Sky was taken. She was taken by these basically unexplainable, immortal beings Nadia calls the "old gods" to a giant, old tree less than a mile away. She was kept inside it in a supernaturally induced coma for *eight years*. Believe me, I know how bananas that explanation is to anyone outside the family. To anyone who wasn't raised to know that the wild earth is autonomous and sometimes chooses startlingly miraculous fates for us.

It's really too bad everyone in town has instead come to the conclusion that we're all freaks, Sky most of all.

When we thought she was gone for real, *everyone* retreated. At the time, Carter's grandfather was in and out of the hospital, and between that and all the jobs he always seems to have, he and I could only chat here and there. I didn't blame him. He tried the best he could, but in the end, I needed more support than what he could offer.

Nadia, my great-aunt, was a wreck. All she did was cry for what felt like decades, so much that I was the one checking in on her several times a day, and never the other way around, ever. But that's Nadia. Her emotions and needs always came before ours.

My grandmother Sonya threw herself into re-renovating her giant, colonial-style, beachside mansion, and pretended like she never even had a third granddaughter to start with.

And Sage? Sage took off and lived in her old red van before finding a job teaching jewelry design in Philly. She chose a van made in 1989 with stained, threadbare upholstery and not one but *two* cracked windows over me.

Is Leilani perfect? No. Is she sometimes really annoying? Yes. But she was there. She was *there*.

I close my eyes and do my counting breath. "Yes," I say on the long exhale. "Sky, I'm sorry. Lani just pissed me off, and I'm nervous about Carter."

Sky raises an eyebrow. "Right. The man you don't have feelings for even though his kiss was so lethal, you ended up dumping Nate Bowen because you couldn't stop thinking about it." She nuzzles the squirrel, who lets out an eerily humanlike sigh of contentment. "The man we told you to not ask to the wedding, because he's so desperately in love with you." Her smile can only be described as that of an evil villain. "*That* man, you mean?"

Now I'm grinding my teeth. At this rate, I'll have a migraine before dinner. "Subject change," I finally grit out. "I need to distract my brain right now. Please."

"Hmm." Sky puts a finger on her chin, tapping. "Oh! Have you ever had your ass eaten?"

It's too bad I'm sipping a cup of tea when she asks. I only *just* avoid spraying the table.

"What," I say, coughing, "the hell, Sky?"

"I'm *curious*. I read about it in one of Nadia's romances and I thought it sounded bewitching."

I snort so loud I can't help but dissolve into giggles. "Bewitching?" I belt out. "Ass-eating sounds bewitching, huh?"

She's laughing, too. "Are you distracted yet?"

"Thoroughly."

"Good." Sky checks her phone. "Oh, don't forget. Spring

equinox tomorrow." She stands, the squirrel still perfectly balanced on her shoulder. "And Leilani Rodriguez is *not* invited."

"But I already invited her!" I say. "She always comes!"

Sky just tilts her head up and gazes down at me, like she's royalty or something. "She can't come until she apologizes to Carter. And I lost years of my life, Teal, so I can call the shots for my first spring equinox in almost a decade. Got it?" Before I can respond, she's already on her way up the stairs, her squirrel friend still knocked out on her shoulder.

I throw my head back and think about saying some kind of prayer to get me through this sudden wave of anxiety. But I'm not really the praying type, so I grab my phone and try to figure out how to white-lie Lani's un-invitation. I don't feel like telling her the truth because I don't want her to actually apologize to Carter and come to Nadia's spring equinox party. Sky's right that Sage hates Leilani. If Leilani does come, Sage'll spend the night making passive-aggressive comments about her and it might piss me off enough to conjure a nasty storm. And if Leilani doesn't come, I might actually have a fun time with just my sisters for once.

Hey, I type. Sorry but the equinox shindig is canceled

I leave out the *for you* at the end of the sentence. That is my version of a white lie.

Omg you're not mad at me are you??!!? She writes back instantly.

I narrow my eyes. Why would I be?

As soon as I hit send, another text comes through. My heart feels like it jumps right out of my mouth when I see it's from Carter. Pick you up at 12:40? On Saturday?

Leilani's next text is as fast as it is unfathomable. No reason, just remember that the universe exhales and inhales, you know?

I send her back a thumbs-up. After a stupid amount of time, I send Carter the same emoji. After that, I'm so jittery, I grab my running shoes even before I hear the distant rumble of thunder, and this time, a creek doesn't stop me, so I keep running for miles and miles.

3

SINCE WE WERE BABIES, SINCE EVEN BEFORE OUR MOTHER took off in an ugly old truck with presumably an ugly-hearted man, Nadia has insisted we celebrate two important events: the spring equinox and Día de Muertos. These dates are more important than any other holiday combined, or at least that's how it feels with the gravity Nadia gives them. And this is a lady who hasn't missed Mass probably since before she was conceived into existence.

"What's with insisting on honoring these two dates?" I once asked her. "Isn't it a little too witchy? Doesn't the Catholic Church think that celebrating any equinox is pagan and that Día de Muertos is some evil ceremony from before our ancestors were saved?"

Nadia just raised one of her skinny, auburn-lined eyebrows at me and said, "Everything the Church believes in has been either made up or stolen, mija. If this were not the case, then the Church would have been there the day this Earth was created." She stuck one of her blunt, bloodred nails in my face. "Pero no. The Church was made up by a group of men, and they took ideas and stories from all the religions that came before and were alongside it." She smirked at the look on my face. I guess I wasn't expecting a real answer, after her dragging me and my sisters, kicking and screaming, to St. Theresa's until we were adults.

That was the moment I realized Nadia wasn't *that* kind of Catholic after all.

Nadia's in the kitchen with Sky right now, and they're beating a couple of cold flans from their glass pie pans onto serving dishes while I light all the prayer candles Nadia had me carry up from the basement. Almost every single one is of Maria Magdalena.

I was never into religion. I was always the kid who frustrated the Sunday school teachers with my incessant questions, like *How could people who lived before Jesus be saved if they never knew Jesus would even exist?* and *Why did God murder innocent babies when he flooded the world for Noah's ark?* I didn't even think I believed in God. Which might sound kind of weird, considering my emotions have controlled the region's weather since I was a child. Not that our family's gifts automatically mean there is a God, but that maybe I should have had a predisposition toward understanding that this world has some serious mysteries working behind it. But I guess, deep down, I assumed there was some rational explanation for our power, even if, to my knowledge, no one had figured out what that explanation might be.

That all changed when we found Sky.

There is no way science can explain how she was kept in a tree outdoors for eight summers and eight winters, and just walked out of it one day with her skeletal and muscular and circulation systems just fine and dandy. I mean, it makes more sense that what she says happened didn't actually happen. Like, maybe a human stole her and kept her in their basement or something. Or that the entire town is right about her—she was a runaway, and now she's back and full of lies about where she had been.

I believe my sister, though. Which means I'm beginning to come close to the fact that there are serious mysteries working behind this world. And even though I don't want it to, I feel hope flaring in my belly as I consider it. As I light the final Mary Magdalene candle, the flame as hot as a curl of lightning in my palm.

Because if God exists, then that means miracles happen.

And if miracles happen, then maybe I can fix whatever is broken inside me.

My eyes turn to the only framed photo Nadia keeps of our mother. She's pregnant with Sage in it, wearing a white dress with horizontal green and violet stripes that flare over her big belly. She was sixteen, but I swear she looks no older than thirteen. She must've been scared out of her mind.

It doesn't make what she did right, though.

Not for the first time, I think about what it would take to find her. To make her give back what she took from me.

"You done with the candles, Teal?" Nadia calls. "We need a little help here."

I leave all the lit-up Magdalenas and find Nadia in the kitchen, trying to pry open a bottle of seltzer water. "We need your muscles," Sky tells me.

I take the bottle and twist, the fizz of carbonation sounding immediately. Just as the top pops off, there's a knock at the door. "Why is Sage knocking?" I mutter, but when I open it, it's not Sage there. It's Sonya. Nadia's sister and our grandmother.

My jaw drops a little. She raises an eyebrow and scowls at me. "Amá," I finally sputter out.

Amá Sonya and I do dinners at her place once a month, and we also meet for brunch every second and third Sundays at this upscale restaurant downtown that offers complimentary glasses of "orange-essence champagne." Of all her grandchildren, she and I are the closest, even if with Amá, "closest" means that she spends more time criticizing me than either of my sisters.

It's not the sight of my grandmother that's shocking. It's the sight of Amá Sonya *here* that has me furrowing my brow.

The last time I saw Sonya at Nadia's, it was after Mama left. Only once. Only then.

"Uhh," I say as she leans on her hip and crosses her arms.

"Uhh," she says, mocking me. I don't take it personally. We all know that Sonya's a bitch. "Aren't you going to let me in? Your own abuela?"

I step aside. "Welcome to our humble abode, Amá."

She snarls as she takes a look around. "It looks . . ." I can tell she is searching for some kind of compliment. "The same." She looks pleased with herself. It must've taken a great deal of effort to not make an offensive comment about the brightness of the yellow walls, or maybe the obscene shine of the olive linoleum floors. Or maybe the fact that it looks like people actually live here.

Amá Sonya's home looks like the inside of a fridge. Like, one of the new ones they have lined up at Best Buy, smelling like cleaner with undertones of new plastic. Only instead of cleaner and plastic, it's built with granite and quartz, and the underlying scent is of Louis Vuitton's Spell on You. That's her style—she acts like she's country-chic, but the truth is she's pure luxe. Right now she's got on a cream tweed skirt-suit that looks custom-made for her small frame. I'm pretty sure it's Chanel. Her pointed stilettos match the outfit exactly, all except for the bloodred sole. She's covered in pearls and diamonds, and she pushes her peachy matte lips out in distaste. I once looked up the price of the lipstick she uses. It's exactly three of my car payments.

She looks just a *little* out of place here, amid Nadia's home-made curtains, vintage dining table, and herbs growing from coffee tins along the windowsills. Not to mention us. Sky's got on old, patched-up bell-bottom jeans and a tank top covered in what is probably real baby eagle feathers. Nadia's adorned herself with one of her floral-patterned cottagecore dresses, almost vibrating with the brightest pinks and oranges imaginable. I'm wearing my usual—matchy-matchy spandex athletic gear in all shades of purple. It's an "I work at the gym" style I still haven't kicked even though it's been weeks since I've set foot in a gym of any kind.

Nadia puts her hands on her hips. "What brings you here, Sonya?"

Amá Sonya huffs. "Can't a woman visit her sister anymore?"

"Ay," Nadia responds. "Que drama."

"Que drama nada. Are we celebrating the return of la luz or what?"

Before Nadia can respond, Sage appears in the doorway. She's got on jeans stained with dirt paired with a neon blue tank top. On her ears are turquoise set in silver, probably handmade by Sage herself. "We're heeeere!" She sings like an opera singer, only terribly off-key. Next to her stands Laurel, her best friend, wearing a white linen wrap dress and the cutest kitten heels, matching her red lipstick exactly. She carries a giant bottle of Patrón in her arms as she greets us.

"Come in," Nadia calls.

Sage stops short when she sees Sonya. "Oh, hey, Amá. I didn't think you'd be here."

Amá throws up her hands as best she can, since a giant Celine satchel probably filled with bars of real gold sits on her forearm. "Everyone thinks the matriarch of this familia would miss a spring equinox."

"Well, you haven't been to one in . . ." Sky begins, but fades out as Sonya levels a glare at her that could freeze hell.

"When's the last time *you* were at an equinox?" Sonya demands of Sky. "In the flesh, mija. Not as a half ghost."

"What Amá means is of course she's been to every equinox ever," Sage says. "We may not have any sort of proof, or memory of it even, but she was there."

"Yeah, she was there all right, just like you, Sage," I mutter, then wince. My MO is to get mad at everyone, especially when things around me get chaotic. For years, Sage was my go-to symbolic punching bag. And once, a literal punching bag. But I'm trying to be better now. *Trying* is the key word.

"What was that?" Sage narrows her eyes my way.

I lower my eyes as my cheeks heat. "Nada."

"Okay!" Laurel says, lifting the tequila again. "Who's ready for a shot?"

Every single one of us answers in the affirmative at the same time. Even Amá, who I have never seen drink anything besides sparkling water sourced from some Swedish mountain, Kona coffee, orange-essenced champagne, or, on very special occasions, extra-dry Manhattans.

Sky and Laurel prepare the drinks as the rest of us settle in the living room. Unlike the kitchen, which is painted marigold yellow and is always bright with sunlight pouring in thick as bright silk through its two enormous windows, the seating room has always been dark. There's only one window facing in from the north, which does nothing to lighten the walls painted a deep forest green. Nadia's filled up the room with all kinds of antique lamps, from brass floor lights glowing with amber, to Tiffany-style, composed of glass shades as colorful as tropical fruit. We only have two lamps on tonight, though. The candles are doing the work of lightning, making everything look like a shade of underwater blue flicked with startling orange and gold highlights. It's like the set of some dark academia film. That or horror.

Nadia begins the celebration by reading her favorite Joy Harjo poem. It's called "Remember." I'm probably not the sort of personality that would take to poetry, but you can't grow up in this house and not have poetry become some part of your emotional body. Nadia didn't read Dr. Seuss to us when we were little ones— she read Linda Hogan and Octavio Paz and Margaret Atwood.

To me, this particular poem is a blessing for someone new to this earth. Or maybe an older person who has been made new in some cosmic way. I hold my breath until Nadia reaches the lines I love and hate the most, on mothers: "You are evidence of / her life, and her mother's, and hers." I have to turn my head away at this part every year, so no one sees my eyes welling up. But it's no use. There's no way anyone misses the way the clouds instantly darken outside, the way rain falls as fast as a heart breaks. Everyone's nice enough to pretend they don't notice.

I throw my shot back the second she reads the last word. "More, please," I say, lifting up my empty glass.

As I sip my second shot, Nadia serves the sangria she'd made the night before. It's her own recipe, made with white wine instead of the traditional red, and she adds just a little seltzer water for "especia." She and Sky had cut up apples, limes, oranges, and strawberries to soak in it overnight. It tastes exactly like summer in Cranberry—thick and bright and sweet.

Laurel jumps up to help Sage cut the flan. One is coconut, the other traditional, with the flavors of vanilla and burnt sugar taking center stage. Soon we're all stuffing our faces. Well, everyone except for Amá, who cuts tiny pieces of her flan with a fork and knife, wincing as she eats, like anyone would believe it's not fucking amazing. I'm convinced Nadia can't produce a subpar flan even if she tried.

This is when the chisme portion of the event begins.

"So, when are you all going to get a man?" Sonya begins, glaring at everyone except for Sage. Not even Laurel, who is not related to us at all, is immune from Sonya's pointed, accusatory gaze.

"You want us to share a man?" Sky asks, completely deadpan, and I almost spit out a large gulp of sangria.

Sonya smacks Sky's knee. "You know what I mean."

"What if we want a woman?" Laurel asks.

Sonya raises her eyebrow, considering. "Just like any man, she better have money." She turns to Nadia. "What about you? When's the last time you've been on a date? A decade? Más? Don't you think it's time to do something other than—" She lifts her hands, as though gesturing to the air explains what she means.

Nadia narrows her eyes. "Other than what, Sonya?" Her voice is dangerous and low.

My sisters and I look at each other in alarm. The last time these two viejitas had a real fight, supposedly Sonya walked away with a bloody nose and Nadia walked away with a poltergeist haunting her. That's Sonya's gift, by the way. Ghosts.

"Teal has a date to Nate's wedding!" Sky announces, pointedly ignoring my wide eyes.

"Who're you going with?" Sage asks. Then she narrows her eyes. "Oh, wait, *no*. Teal. You didn't."

"Didn't what?" asks Laurel.

Sonya tsks disapprovingly at me. "*You* should be the one marrying that Nate Bowen boy. Now *he* has money."

"Did you, though?" Sage asks, ignoring Sonya and pointing at me with her wineglass in her hand. It looks like she hasn't taken a single sip. "Did you seriously ask—"

"Sky refuses to update her wardrobe from the early aughts!" I announce.

"Hey!" Sky glances down at her outfit. "There's nothing wrong with this."

"Not if we're in the year 2006, there isn't," I respond with a smirk.

Sonya wrinkles her nose, then turns to Nadia. "You didn't take her shopping yet? She's been wearing her eight-year-old clothes for all these months?"

"When am I supposed to have time to take her shopping, Sonya? Some of us actually do work for a living."

"I work, Nadia." Sonya's hand is nearly crushing her glass.

"Spying on your neighbors to report them to the HOA doesn't count as work, hermana."

It's like watching a NatGeo doc of two wildcats circling each other as they prepare a battle for dominance. These two need a shiny, glittery distraction to keep them from attacking each other, but I desperately don't want any distraction to include the word *Carter*. "Back to the topic of Sky's ugly clothes." I ignore Sky's cry of offense. "Sky won't let anyone take her shopping, Amá. That's what I was saying before."

Sonya gives me the stinkeye next. "¿Y tú? Why do you always dress like you're about to do a push-up? Haven't we talked about this?"

I groan. "Yes, Amá. We have. Many times." I have a feeling she's going to continue this conversation anyway, and Amá doesn't disappoint.

"To attract a high-quality man, you need to dress con elegancia. No más"—she tosses a hand at my body—"looking like you're competing in the Tour de France."

"I bet all the ladies competing at the Tour de France have high-quality men, Amá."

"You think you're being cute, Teal, pero all that sass will repel a man." Sonya sips her sangria. "Who are you taking to this wedding anyway?"

I inhale too fast and get slightly light-headed. "Jesus. Why does everyone care about my date? Shouldn't we be focused on the dateless?" I glance around "Who are *you* taking, Laurel?"

"I'm taking Alex Ramirez."

"¿Quien?" both old ladies ask.

"She's the sheriff."

Amá frowns thoughtfully. "How much do sheriffs make? It needs to be six figures at least, mija. Or you've got to let her go."

"Carter."

With that one word, we all whip our heads to Sage. Her shot of tequila sits right in front of her, untouched, and Laurel takes it for herself. "Teal's taking Carter Velasquez to the wedding."

"You don't know that for a fact," I say.

"You're not denying it."

"I'm not confirming it, either."

"Ha!" Sage lifts her hands. "That's exactly what all the celebrities say when they're in rehab for meth."

"Is Carter that skinny boy who was in love with you?" Amá asks. "What does his income look like these days?"

Sky is watching me closely. I think she can sense something in me, even before lightning appears in the distance, through the window and over the water like a flicker of a star. I can't help but grit my teeth and tense my jaw. I can't have everyone talking about me and Carter like this. What he and I had . . . our friendship, I mean. It was *precious* to me. And then I broke it. To let everyone dissect it here, now, feels like balancing the most fragile egg on my head and then being forced to perform one of Shakira's viral dances for TikTok. Sky looks at me questioningly and I nod my head.

Sky clears her throat loudly. "Amá Sonya? Have you ever had your ass eaten?"

There is dead silence for several seconds. Laurel and Sage glance at each other with wide-eyed thrill. Nadia is also amused. As for Amá, I have never seen her look so legitimately shocked in my life. Her mouth opens and closes, but not even a breath comes out. "¿Qué es esto?" she finally sputters. "Are you asking me about *ass sex*?"

This is when Laurel, Sage, and Nadia explode. They laugh for so hard and for so long, tears stream down their faces. As they laugh, Amá gets more and more infuriated. "What's so funny?" she's yelling. "Why is my nieta asking about sex of the ass so hilarious to all of you?" Then she points at me. "What is going on with you, Teal? What is with this boy Carter? Why do you all keep changing the subject about him?" She lowers her voice. "Is he on the meth?"

I go from laughing to panic so fast, thunder rumbles the moment I stand up. "Sage hasn't had a single sip of alcohol all night."

Everyone whips their head toward her. She can't hold her poker face for more than a second. She begins to beam, and Nadia gasps. "Sage . . ." she says.

"It's true." Sage slides a hand over her belly. "It's really early, but . . . I'll be nine weeks along on Sunday."

Then we're all screaming. Shrieking, jumping, hugging. Outside, the clouds clear, and long rays of rose gold, peach-pink, and fuchsia stream along the horizon line of the blue topaz sea.

It's the prettiest sunset I've ever seen.

⚡

SAGE AND LAUREL ARE THE FIRST TO LEAVE, WITH SAGE CLAIM-ing exhaustion. I don't doubt it. She's growing a whole new human and all now. She tries to bat Sky away as Sky tries to give her two hugs—one for Sage, and one "for the belly."

Sonya gives us all a dirty look as we all linger at the front door. Or, maybe, that's just kind of how her face is. "Well?" She gestures to Nadia, and then Sage. "What is it? ¿Chico o chica?"

Sage puts her fingers in her ears. "Don't tell me! I don't want to know!"

"It's a boy," Sky says.

"Es la verdad," Nadia confirms.

"You guys!" Sage growls, but then she holds her palms over her still-completely-flat belly. "Really? A boy?"

"Nadia *knows*," Sky explains. "And humans are animals, re-member. I can already hear him!"

Sage bursts into tears. "Oh my God," she says. "I've got to get home and tell Tenn."

"Maybe you could name him Montana," Sky says. "Or Maine! Keep up the theme, you know?"

Sage responds by crying even harder. See what I mean? Ella es la Llorona now, weeping over every dang thing. And now she's pregnant so it can only get worse.

"Let's get you home," Laurel says, wrapping an arm around Sage's shoulder. From there, it takes another fifteen minutes be-fore they're out the door. I just shake my head as my sisters and Laurel keep coming 'round to hug. Latine people and goodbyes.

After that, Sky says she has to check on her woodland friends, so she goes on a short walk. I'm still a little tipsy, so I start my way upstairs but stop and look back at the mess still in the living room. "Stop being selfish," I remind myself, and I begin to pick up platas and glasses.

Nadia and Sonya are muttering in the kitchen. I assume they're just trading farewell insults until I hear one word that stops me in my tracks.

Cora. Sonya's hissing it at Nadia.

Cora. That's our mother's name.

They're talking in fast Spanish, which means I can only understand every third word. I linger in the shadow just outside the kitchen entrance, trying to angle my ear in as much as I can without being seen.

"You're telling me you don't *know?*" Sonya whispers, switching back to English.

Nadia shrugs, then responds in Spanish. It's a question and I think it's something like "Why would she come back now?"

"Es mi hija. She does whatever she wants. There's no sense to any of it. She's always been that way."

"But you didn't even see her, Sonya."

"I'm her mother! I don't need to——"

They both freeze when a cup balanced on a plate in my arms slides, making a disturbingly loud screeching noise. I walk in the kitchen immediately, humming. I stop when I see them both narrowing their eyes at me. "What is it?" I demand.

"Nada." Sonya points her pointy acrylic nail right at my heart. "Next week I am taking both you and Sky shopping. No more of——" She waves a hand over my body. "This."

"Gee, thanks," I respond, but Sonya's out the door before I can finish my sentence.

When I turn around, Nadia's gone, too.

I put the dishes in the sink, my heart beating fast.

A milagro.

This feels like that. Like a miracle is close by.

When I go upstairs, before I wash my face and change into my nightgown, I stop at my dresser. I grab the small carved wood box, curl open its lid. Inside, I keep my most precious jewelry. Big, gold-filled hoops from Nadia that spell *Teal* in a flowing font. A pair of two-carat flawless diamond studs from Amá. The moss agate necklace Sage made for me last year. She carved both herself and Sky an almost-identical necklace with the same stone. "It's us," she'd said when she showed it to me for the first time. The stone captures all the colors of sage, teal, and sky put together.

I don't touch the jewelry, though. Instead I reach for a small, roughly folded-up piece of torn paper. I spread it out, sliding my fingers against it to smooth the wrinkles.

New Year's Resolutions for Teal Flores
1. Stop being selfish.
2. Make it up to Sage.
3. Make it up to Sky.
4. Become best friends with Carter again.

Leilani had made fun of how "negative-energy-filled" these wishes are. "Come on, Teal! There's nothing but love in the world! Focus on *that*."

But *this* is all the shit I'm struggling with. Even tonight, when an opportunity came up to criticize my sister for leaving us, I couldn't help myself. A few years back, when Sage was visiting us when she lived in Philadelphia, I punched Sage in the face for trying to convince me to leave my abusive ex. What kind of sister does that?

And even before all that, almost nine years ago now, I was the one who convinced Sky to tightrope-walk the rusty gate that blocked off the cliff we'd been hiking up. It's not like I thought either of us would ever fall. But because of me, she lost eight years. *Eight. Years.*

If it were up to Leilani, I would've written a list full of expensive self-care options like getting acupuncture, hot-stone massages, and traveling halfway around the world to try, I don't know, some type of hallucinogenic botanical to heal my bipolar disorder. And I'm not saying those wouldn't work for some people, but for me? I needed to clean the mess I'd made, and somehow in the process reshape myself into a good person. A good sister.

Maybe then I'll earn a miracle. The miracle I've been praying for—to heal this half-formed, broken gift inside me. To be able to cry or kick a punching bag in rage without worrying that I was going to hurt someone with a wild lightning storm.

That's my biggest goal. To be totally human, sadness and all, and not have to worry about it one single bit.

4

I'M STILL LITERALLY IN A BRA AND BOY SHORTS, RUNNING LO-
tion on my legs when Sky bursts through my door. "Excuse
me!" I yelp.

She ignores me. "Carter's here."

"What?" I grab my phone. Nate's wedding doesn't start for
almost an hour. "He's twenty minutes early! What for?"

Sky shrugs. "I don't really know Carter, so you tell me what
for." She glances behind her shoulder. "Or you could just ask him
yourself!"

"Teal?" Carter's voice is behind the open door. I squeal and
grab the nearest piece of fabric—a pink towel, still wet from my
shower—and hold it to my torso just before Sky widens the door
to let him in.

"Sky!" I about scream. "I'm naked here!"

Carter makes a choked noise, but Sky just shrugs. "The towel
covers all the important parts." She turns her head toward Carter,
who I am assuming is still behind the door. "You want to talk to
her now?"

"Wait one freaking second, the two of you!" I rush around and throw on a nightgown. It's probably too sheer to be considered decent, but it's not like anyone's giving me time to plan an elegant, conservative outfit here. I take a deep breath. "Okay. Come in."

Sky smiles and winks at me as she pushes the door open. "She's ready to see you now," she tells Carter as she leaves, sounding exactly like a professional receptionist to some fancy lawyer or something. Not like she spends her mornings running with red wolves, which I literally saw her doing just last week.

Carter appears at the doorway and my breath hitches. He's got on a navy blue suit that looks like it was tailored to his exact specifications—his wide chest, his long, lean legs. His shoes are black, shiny leather and look brand spanking new. A silk bow tie just one shade lighter blue than the suit sits at his neck. He's clean shaven, and his edges look wildly crisp, like he got his hair trimmed only yesterday. His gold eyes bore into me with an intensity that makes me feel like I've just had three shots of tequila in a row.

"Hey, Teal," he says, which snaps me out of my ogling. He's going for casual in his tone, but he sounds tense. I know him too well for him to hide that from me.

I turn my head and walk toward my dresser. Facing the mirror on it, I check that my pulling the nightgown over my head in such a chaotic rush didn't smear my makeup. "What's up, Carter?"

He clears his throat and puts his hands in his pockets. I try to act disinterested, organizing some of the makeup brushes thrown around on the top of the dresser, but finally I huff and turn his way. "What is it? What are you here to tell me, that you got cold feet? You don't want to go to the wedding with me anymore?"

The anger in me feels vivid. I cringe, waiting to hear a rumble of thunder in the distance, and breathe in relief when none comes. I'd taken an extra-long run this morning, since I woke up with my nerves feeling like they were raw, as though I'd been peeled open like a birch tree. I'd been up for at least two hours at bedtime, trying to figure out what Carter wanted from me in exchange for being my wedding date. Scenarios flitted in my brain, around and around like the craziest murmuration known to this earth.

Carter requesting a dozen handmade candles he could gift his tías and abuelas. Carter wanting me to leave the country so he wouldn't have to see me ever again. Carter gazing down at me with his wild salt lamp eyes, telling me to rob a bank on his behalf.

The stress got to me even as I slept, with thunder awakening me more than once. As soon as the skinny line of daybreak light hit my window, I'd grabbed my running shoes. I didn't stop for over an hour, and with all those hills I ran up and down I could barely walk home. Even now, my right knee aches, and my muscles feel like they're going to spasm just from me standing here, being pissed at him.

Carter's face is pink and his breath is a little too fast. He's taking too long to answer my questions. I brace myself for all the feelings—disappointment. Grief. Heartbreak. Because that's what he's about to do now, right? He's going to tell me he can't do this. He can't be friends with me ever again. I'd messed everything up to an irreparable state and now I have to deal with the consequences.

He takes two giant steps toward me, until the invisible barrier between us shatters and we're at a dangerous level of closeness. "What I need . . ." He clears his throat. "In order to . . ." He shakes his head hard. "For the favor . . . I mean—" He lifts his right hand, and cupped inside it is a yellow gold ring.

"Teal," he says, his voice breaking. "Sé mi esposa."

My mouth drops open and my knees give. I fall back on my bed with a thump.

Teal. Be my wife.

⚡

THE ROOM GETS FUZZY. MY HANDS TINGLE. I CAN HARDLY breathe.

"Teal?" Carter asks. "Are you—"

"Get out," I respond. It's the only thing I can think of to say, and I make my tone as sharp as I can, which is impressive, given my current state of shock.

He flinches. "Sorry. I did this all wrong."

"If you mean by all wrong that you asked me to marry you in the first place, then yes. All freaking wrong."

"No, I meant. I should have begun with . . . *this* is what I need. The favor, for going to the wedding with you." His cheeks are still flushed. His breath still heavy. "I couldn't—I couldn't ask it afterward. I wanted you to know what you were getting yourself into. So you could decide if you still wanted me or not."

I raise an eyebrow.

He flushes even more. "Wanted me to come with you to the wedding. Obviously."

I push my face into my hands and breathe in, one-two-three-four. Out to the count of eight. "This is really bad timing, Carter," I finally say. "I'm going to bring a thunderstorm to Nate's wedding and ruin it."

"No. You're not." He sits down next to me on the bed and I have to tighten my body so I don't fall into him as the mattress dips. He holds his hand over mine. "Let's do the breath thing together, okay?"

I know he's looking at me. He is seeing all the ways I am flawed and broken and falling apart. But then he begins counting with me—just like he used to when things were bad after Sky fell—and I stop being self-conscious. I just focus on the deep gravel of his voice, how it's almost like a lullaby. After five minutes, when I feel more like myself again, I glance out the window. It's so sunny, it looks like a postcard of a coastal Virginia summer. "Better?" he asks.

I swallow. I don't want to admit how quickly he made everything better, so I stand. "Get out. I need to get dressed. We'll talk more in the car."

The second he leaves, I take a single, shaky breath and focus all my attention on getting ready. The sweetheart neckline turquoise dress, zipped up my right side. The ylang-ylang perfume oil Sage left me when she moved out, spread on my cleavage and wrists and neck. I slip on my high heels, but after trying to stand with my legs in the state they're in, I wince and grab strappy white sandals instead. I open my purse closet—this armoire I installed shelves in—and let myself have one happy moment as I consider my collection.

It's Amá Rosa who got me hooked on handbags. She saw me admiring one of her Chanel baguettes, and the next time I saw her, she had one for me. Of course, she wasn't gracious about it at all. "Now we have to go to brunch, once a month," she'd ordered. I tried to tell her she didn't have to pay me for my time, but she wasn't having any of it. I became her favorite after Sage left. And I think after whatever she went through with my mom, she decided to keep me nearby to spoil me. So now I own three beautiful Chanels, a handful of Chloés, two Louis, and one Cartier satchel. I don't even want to know what any of them cost. I put my foot down when she tried to bring up getting me a Birkin for my twenty-fifth birthday.

I told her I'd sell it, and I would've. As much as I'm obsessed with handbags, I would rather have the eighteen grand.

I don't just have luxe bags. To Amá's great disgrace, I also have embroidered bags from Mexico, and bright, crocheted bags from various department stores, and lots of handmade leather bags from small businesses all over the world. That's actually what I grab right now—a handmade crossbody from Italy, consisting of woven white leather. I transfer my wallet and phone and other essentials, and then I'm good to go.

Carter's downstairs in the kitchen, talking with Nadia over a cup of coffee. He double-takes when I walk in, but I'm slightly annoyed that he just stares right in my eyes and doesn't say a word about my dress or how I look. "You ready?"

"Yup." I walk past him and Nadia to the door, but Nadia beats me there, opening it for me.

"Beautiful weather." Nadia narrows her eyes at me. It's a warning. *Don't call down a thunderstorm. Or a tornado. Don't drown my garden or destroy any homes or kill anyone, okay?* I grit my teeth and make myself hum in response as I hobble out as fast as I can.

Carter rushes around me to open the car door, and once he's inside, I don't even wait till he's done buckling his seat belt.

"So." I turn toward him. "You have to be my wedding date for two hours. And in return, I have to be your wife for the rest of my life. Did I get that right?"

He blows out his hair, hollowing his cheeks as he starts the car. "Not exactly."

I wait for all of five seconds before I huff. "Carter. Any freaking day now."

He runs a hand over his hair. It's too short to stick up or anything, but he still feels rumpled. "It's my abuela Erika. You remember her?"

I snort. "The abuela who accused me of being a loose woman out to ruin her precious, perfect grandson when I first met her at the age of eleven? How could I forget such a lady?"

Nothing I'd said was an exaggeration. Crochety old Erika had taken one look at me and decided I was no good for Carter. To this day, I haven't the faintest idea as to why. Maybe it was 'cause I'd just started wearing a training bra, and at nine, Carter was nowhere near puberty. But it's not like I looked at him—or anyone besides AJ McLean of the Backstreet Boys—like *that*, anyhow. And even in my raunchiest fantasies, all AJ and I did was hold hands and peck one another on the cheeks.

It was Carter's mom's birthday party, and Erika told anyone who'd listen—especially if I was in earshot—what a horrible decision his mom was making, letting him play with the likes of me. It wasn't the first time in my life I'd felt like there was something irreparably wrong with me, but it was the first time anyone had been so direct about pointing it out.

"After Eugenio died—"

I grab Carter's arm. "Abuelo Gene died? Carter, when?"

He keeps his eyes on the road. "Six months ago."

I gasp. "Why didn't you tell me?"

Carter doesn't answer at all. Instead, his jaw clenches, and a wave of something I recognize all too well flashes over his face and arms and fists. Anger.

We weren't talking six months ago. Because I kissed him and then ran into Nate Bowen's arms two nights later.

I turn toward my window, watching as the pines turn to palms the closer we get to the ocean. "I'm just saying. I wish I could've gone to his funeral."

Carter's grandfather Gene was the closest thing he'd ever had to a dad. Heck, he was the closest thing *I'd* ever had to a dad.

Sure, he was married to Erika the nasty old brat, but every day after school, he taught me and C. how to play dominoes, and then he'd take us to the panaderia for flaky pastries filled with guava and sweet cheese. He let us sip café Cubano, even though both of our parental guardians wouldn't have approved. His parental guardian being his mother, and mine being Sage.

He's no longer in this world now. And I had no fucking clue.

I practice my breath work as he keeps going. "He was buried in Cuba." He clears his throat. "Anyway, he left me some money."

"How much money?"

When Carter tells me the amount, I whistle. "Well, congratulations. But I still don't—"

"He didn't officially leave it to me in his will. He left it to Erika to give to me. And she just told me a couple weeks ago that she's not doing it until I get married."

My jaw drops. "Is she serious?"

Carter gives a brusque nod. "As a heart attack." He huffs out a dull laugh. "That's how Gene died. A heart attack." He glances at me for the first time since mentioning it. "No pain. It happened fast." I have to deep-breathe again as Carter makes a U-turn.

Finally we pull into the parking lot of the Beachside Luxury Inn. Two towers that resemble lighthouses stand on either side of the large adobe-esque building in the middle. The roofs are done in bright Spanish tile, the color of mandarin oranges, and the walkways all around the building are set in a tile that matches the deep blue of the ocean. A distant wave of anxiety rushes low in my spine. I take another deep breath. All we're gonna do is watch Nate get married by the ocean, and then we'll go into the ballroom and dance and get drunk off our asses. That's my plan, anyhow. There is no reason to worry about any sort of unexpected, homicidal weather.

"My sisters decided they don't want kids. My cousins are all younger than us, and no one's gotten married, or is even close to it. The oldest of them are doing shit like going to college and backpacking through South America. I think Gene's death scared Erika. She thinks she's gonna go before she gets any great-grandchildren."

I turn my head slowly toward him. "What the hell are you saying? You wanna get me pregnant now, too?"

"No!" He drops his head back and closes his eyes like he's praying for strength. "I'm saying, she wants me to get married. She's requiring it of me to get my money. I'm just speculating why she's making such a big deal of this."

I sigh and glance around. To my side, there's a sliver of beach peeking between buildings. There stands Nate and his bride, and all their people, hanging around with a photographer. "They're still taking photos?" I ask.

"He's marrying a Latina." Carter glances at me from the corner of his eye. "You know how we are."

To most Latines, the time of an event is often a mere sugges-tion. Try telling that to Amá Sonya, though. If I arrive two min-utes early to brunch, she spends the entire appetizer glaring at me while tapping at her diamond-encrusted Rolex. If I'm not there ten minutes early, I'm late.

Carter clears his throat. "You miss him?" His head inclines toward the crowd, who are now jumping, over and over again, with silky indigo bridesmaid dresses whipping in the wind, trying to get the silly shots, I guess.

He's asking about Nate. One year ago, I met him at the Lost Souls Lounge, the only real bar in Cranberry. Carter was work-ing there. I was supposed to be spending the evening with Sage. After about five minutes, I abandoned the both of them to bang

Nate at the entranceway of his downtown apartment. We then grabbed pho for a late dinner, and then I took him to Nadia's, where we screwed two more times—once on the staircase leading to my bedroom, and finally, we made it to my bed.

The truth is, I was using Nate. I realize that now. I used him to stay away from my sister, who I was still so mad at. I used him to stay away from Carter, too.

There's a reason I made that New Year's resolution list.

I'm taking too long to answer Carter's question. I can tell by how tight his arms and spine have gotten. He's not just asking if I miss Nate. He's asking if I wish I were his bride.

I sigh. "No. I don't miss Nate."

He says nothing. I can tell he doesn't believe me. What else can I say, though? If I go on and on about how Nate and I didn't mesh well, he'll think I'm protesting too much. And if I said the real reason I dumped Nate?

Well, I can't say that to him. Not now. Not ever.

"We should get our seats," I say, scrambling out of the car as fast as I can.

5

THE BEACH IS WARM WITH A HINT OF A COOL BREEZE, AND the waves are mild, the color of turquoise, rolling in the pale seafoam. I glance around during the ceremony, spotting Sage and Tenn ahead of us, Laurel and Alex Ramirez next to them, and Nadia and Sky to our left. Just behind them is Leilani and her mom, Helena.

Finally, I relax enough to sit back and watch as Nate exchanges vows with Fern Santos. She's got hair as black as onyx, pinned up with bejeweled pins that sparkle in the sunlight. Her dress is a full-on princess grown, with embroidered lace covering her chest, down to her wrists, becoming a scattering of crystals that waterfall the skirt. Nate wears a black tux with an emerald tie and forest green Converse peeking from the bottom of his trousers. They are both so giddy with nervous joy, I can feel it all the way over here.

He hired her as a social media manager to put Cranberry Rose Company—which he technically owns—firmly in the twenty-first century. I heard the story third- or fourth-hand, but word has it that they hit it off when they met in person only nine months ago. Which was only like two months after he and I broke things off.

I look inside myself for any other feelings about Nate getting married. Any hint of resentment or jealousy or longing. But there isn't any. When the officiant declares them husband and wife, though, his face erupts into a smile so bright, my stomach drops. Not because I want *him*. But because I want *that*. I want someone to want me like that someday. To be wanted so bad that the idea of being with me forever just makes them so happy, it spills over in the biggest smile in the universe.

Carter's to my right and I look at his legs, wondering if that ring is still in his pocket. 'Cause that's what *I* got. Not a man looking at me like I make the world go round. Instead, here's a man so desperate for his inheritance, he wants to use me to get it.

We stand and clap as Nate and Fern run down the aisle, lifting their joined hands in the air. While the officiant explains to everyone where we're all supposed to go next, I elbow Carter's ribs.

"Jesus, your elbow's pointy," he grunts.

"What's in it for me, Carter? 'Cause you being my date to this shindig isn't enough."

I know I said I wanted to be a better person. *Stop being selfish*, that's what I told myself when I accepted this deal without knowing what I was getting into. That said, not being selfish doesn't mean I'm going to let anyone, even Carter, walk all over me. Being a plus-one to a wedding is not equal to being the bride of a wedding.

Not to mention, what I really wanted from this agreement was for Carter and me to repair the friendship we'd lost. The friendship I'd broken. Instead, we're acting like acquaintances who barely like each other. If I have to pretend to marry him, I need way more to get me through a marriage like that, no matter how fake.

People start to stand and chat, with others heading toward the ballroom behind us. Carter and I don't move, except to turn and stare at each other. It's dumb, but I swear I almost gasp when we make eye contact. The bright sun is making his eyes look like yellow crystal flames.

His eyes drop to my mouth for a second. I wonder if I missed a lipstick smear after all. "I can pay you. You'd get a cut."

I scoff. "I don't need money."

Carter shrugs. "Everyone could use money."

As long as billionaires exist, that statement isn't even remotely true. But I don't want to fight with him right now. "How long would we have to be married?"

He shrugs. "Till I get the money. However long it takes for her to give it to me."

"Where would we live?"

Carter shrugs. "My place, I guess."

I furrow my brow. "Where are you living now again?"

Before he can respond, arms from behind wrap around my neck so tight, I can barely breathe. When I glance over, it's Lani and her mom. "Hey!" I stand to give them both proper hugs and cheek kisses.

We all small talk for a few minutes, but then Helena tugs at her arm. "We can't stay for the reception," she tells us. "With everything happening next week, there's no time for fun or wine or dancing."

I shake my head, my eyes going back to Lani. "What's happening next week?"

"The universe in motion!" she exclaims, lifting her arms. Her mom chuckles and we all hug and kiss goodbye. "Tomorrow,"

Leilani tells me before they leave. I think she means it to sound like a promise, but it's almost—almost—a threat.

I turn to Carter, about to comment on how weird that was, but he's turning toward the ballroom. "I need a drink," he barks over his shoulder.

To which I respond, "That's the best idea I've heard all day."

Inside, I wait behind Carter in the line for the bar. I let my eyes drift over the crowd, pretending to act neutral. But what I'm really doing is making sure my ex, Johnny, isn't here. Not that he'd do anything to me. Last spring, Sage scared the shit out of him so thoroughly with her gift, I'm pretty sure he'd leave immediately if he spotted me or her or any of us Flores women here. But generally speaking, he's the last person I ever want to see, ever. Even though we're not together anymore, the idea of being near him sends my nervous system into fight or flight.

He abused me. There's no pretty, nice way to put it. It started with light shoves—just when he was angry, and I happened to be in his way. Except I started noticing that he thought I was in his way *only* when he was angry. Like he coincidentally needed to get to the cupboard behind me for a plate, or to knock me out of the entrance to the bathroom because he needed it first.

The realization of what was really happening came to me too slow. He *wanted* to shove me, so he made damn well sure I was "in the way."

Then he began to push me. At first, against furniture, so I'd hopefully land on something cushioned. But once, he pushed me against the wall so hard, the knot at the back of my head didn't go down for three days. Once, he made sure I didn't have anywhere to land but the cold, hard floor.

The last thing to come was the grabbing, the squeezing, the hitting. They were more infrequent, so Johnny could say things like *Well, at least I don't hit you*. I guess if a man hits a woman only every three or four months, it doesn't count, apparently.

He threatened me by saying he'd ruin me, putting explicit photos of me on the internet for all the world to see if I even thought about dumping him. That's why I didn't leave at first. Not till Sage saved me.

And to add insult to injury, just before the new year, his *cousin* Rhett Miller took over Cranberry Fitness. And the first thing *he* did was lay me off. I mean, yeah, he said they had no choice. They'd had to cut several workers. They needed to get back in the red. Blah, blah, blah.

Did that explain why they fired their most popular fitness trainer?

The problem—of which there are many, mind you—with being a DV survivor is too many people think you're exaggerating or outright lying about what happened. Against all statistical evidence, most people assume the victim is making shit up for fucking fun, because becoming the town outcast—of which there are many—is such a joy to endure.

It was pretty clear what Johnny's cousin thought the first time I met him. He looked me up and down with a snarl and ignored my outstretched hand. I knew I was unemployed right then and there, even though it took another month for it to be official.

I blink out of my thoughts when a drink is shoved in my face. "Oh!" I glance up as I take the glass. Carter looms over me, and he got me a whiskey neat. It's what I always order at the Lounge.

Before I can thank him, he's disappeared into the crowd all around us.

"Well, then," I say, lifting my whiskey to the no one in front of me now. "Cheers."

As soon as I realize that neither Johnny nor anyone else from his stupid family is here, I relax, drink, and dance with Nadia, Sage, Tenn, and Sky, in that order. The whole ballroom is decorated so beautifully, with Cranberry heritage roses and other flowers I don't know just everywhere, a pastel rainbow of petals pinned to the walls and chairs and centerpieces, making everything smell so intoxicating that I can push aside the stressors of this morning for a few songs. But it doesn't take long for them to creep back, one by one, like sneaky little brain goblins.

Carter seems to have disappeared, and I convince myself that he's ditched me. He's changed his mind about everything. That, or I dreamed up the entire proposition. It's preposterous enough to feel like a delusion. Like my mind would've been that creative because I was so desperate to have my childhood best friend back.

"Did you hear me?" Sage is asking, waving a hand in my face. "Earth to Teal."

I shake my head. "No, what did you say again?"

She narrows her eyes at me. "Where did Carter go?"

I shrug. "Who knows?" I say, in probably way too cheery a voice, because Sage simply narrows her eyes even more.

She decides to let it go, and instead, she points to the centerpieces. "Aren't all the dahlias gorgeous? That's what I was asking you before."

They are. I didn't even know they were all the same flower— some were teeny tiny, with tight little petals, and others were enormous, about the size of my face, their petals all loose like ribbons.

Sage sighs. "What I wouldn't give to have these at our wedding."

I furrow my brow. "And why couldn't you? You know, with your gift."

Sage can basically think a flower at a plant and in the next second, it's covered in them. But she shakes her head. "I've noticed I get so tired after using my gift since . . ." She lowers her voice, her hand going protectively to her stomach. "I don't think it's hurting the baby, but I don't want to risk it, either. And this many dahlias . . . that's so much work."

"Can't you order them in?"

Sage snorts and laughs.

"What?" I frown.

"Oh, you were serious." She shakes her head. "This would cost a small fortune. No, forget that. A very large fortune."

I swallow, and maybe it's the whiskey getting to me, but number two of my Become a Good Person New Year's resolutions lingers on my brain. *Make it up to Sage.* The words become larger and larger, like an oncoming spaceship, until it lands and I must speak. "Leave it to me."

Sage widens her eyes at me, and then she shakes her head again. "I'm talking thousands of dollars, Teal. No."

"I said, leave it to me. Consider the flowers handled." I can't help the anger flying up in my tone, that spacecraft zooming away. "When do you need them again?"

"Right." She winces. "September."

"*This* September? I thought the wedding wasn't happening till next year!"

Sage takes a deep breath. "We wanted to do it before the baby came. So we could have an actual honeymoon, just the two of us . . ."

"Right," I say. Sage and Tenn were going to Santo Domingo, to spend time with his family and frolic in the turquoise blue waters. A pang of jealousy thumps through my heart. "Well, no matter. I got the flowers. Take them off your budget."

"Teal."

"I said, for the last time, I got it."

Sage looks hurt by the sharpness of my voice, but she conceals it with a false, bright smile. "Okay. You got it."

I wish I could feel triumphant, but apparently I'm not even the kind of sister who can do a favor without being an asshole about it. I close my eyes. *This* is why I'm trying to be better. Be less selfish. Make it up to the people I love.

"Sorry," I say softly. "I just really want to do this for you."

Sage gives me a look of shock for a moment but covers it with a smile. I guess that's a sign of how often I've apologized our entire lives. This may well be the second or third time ever. "It's no problem, Teal. I just don't want you to go into debt over a few flowers."

"I won't. I promise." And before this conversation gets any weirder, I announce, "I need another drink," and speed away. I stand at the bar, waiting for the bartender to notice me, when a big, bulky body appears in my right periphery.

I turn and glance up. A man in a black suit and a ridiculous jawline stares straight ahead. He's got close-cropped auburn hair and a slightly redder five o'clock shadow dusting that blade-sharp jaw.

"You're Sky's sister, right?" The guy asks the question without glancing my way.

Immediately, my hackles go up. Because if I thought barely anyone believing my past abuse was bad . . . well, Sky has it *way* worse with what she went through last summer and the last eight years all put together. Though all of us have managed to scare off most of the weird people who think Sky's an alien or ex–cult member or something, every now and then someone will try to weasel their way in, trying to find out "the truth."

"Yeah, and what the fuck about it?" I respond.

Now he glances my way, revealing a lightly freckled face and rich blue eyes. "She's been helping my grandfather. William Noemi."

"Oh. You're *Adam*." Now the look I give him is appraising.

When Sky wasn't-quite-dead, she wandered this world, the world of the living, as a ghost. Nadia says it was espanto. This translates to "terror." In this case, Sky's terror when she fell meant a piece of her soul was severed. When Sage and Nadia found her body, that soul went back, I guess, and things are hunky-dory now.

But while Sky was a ghost, she did a lot of snooping. And this snooping made her develop a crush on our neighbor Old Man Noemi's grandson, Adam. Once in a while she'll bring the old man homemade flan or cookies, hoping Adam is back visiting from New York City, I guess, so she can be the small-town lady in a Hallmark film who lures the big-city journalist back for good . . . except this small-town lady is also a witch who is greeted by wildcats and bears when she goes on walks in the woods.

"I'm Teal."

He nods at the empty drink in my hand. "Want another?"

And just at this moment, another figure appears. Carter slides in between me and Adam. "Ready to go?" he grunts out. His tone is so pissed, if it were any louder, he'd be barking at me.

"Nice to meet you, Adam." I say it while glaring at Carter.

Adam grunts something incomprehensible in response, and I hop off the chair, scrambling after Carter. I'm breathless by the time I catch up to him in the parking lot.

"What is wrong with you?" I hiss. "First you leave the reception, only to come back to be an asshole?"

"What about you?" he growls back. "Were you going to text me after you'd gone home with that guy, or just let me figure it out all on my own?"

"Are you seriously slut-shaming me right now?" I have to

tighten my hands into fists so I don't jump over a car to strangle him. "Carter, you've slept with more people in the last six months than I have in my entire life. Calm down with the hypocrisy." It's probably mega-embarrassing to admit that I've been keeping tabs on Carter's dating life that closely, but I'm too pissed off to care right now.

We both open our car doors and thrust ourselves in at the same time. I snap my seat belt on. "And besides. I was there with *you*. I'd never leave with someone else."

Carter snorts in response. I know he's thinking about me rushing home with Nate two days after kissing him. But this isn't the same thing at all.

He sighs and I think he's going to apologize. Instead, he says, "I've only slept with three people in the last six months."

Well, that sentence feels like a knife directly in my gut. "What do you want? For me to stand up and clap? Make an announcement?" I mime speaking into a megaphone. "Everyone, allow me to extend our congratulations to Carter Velasquez, who managed to get his dick wet not once, but three times since October."

The smile he gives me is dry. "No, it's . . . you made it seem like I . . ." He runs a hand over his beard. "I'm sorry, Teal. I was an ass."

I fold my arms. "You were the ass of an ass."

He furrows his brow. "You mean like a donkey?"

"No. If regular asses had asses, that's how you were acting."

He tilts his head as he tries to imagine what the hell I'm describing, and I can't help it. I snort and then I burst into laughter. When I look at him again, he's staring at me like I've presented him with a chest of jewels. I smack his arm.

He rubs his biceps like that actually hurt. "What was that for?"

"Being an ass of an ass." I glance out the window as we settle into silence. "Speaking of sex."

Carter clears his throat.

"How would—if we got married, I mean—"

"I'm not sleeping with you, Teal. That's not part—that would never be part of it."

Disappointment rushes through me and I have no idea why. "But wouldn't you? Need it?"

He cuts me a look that I'm hoping will be full of heat, but it's the opposite. Cold like stone. "I'm never going to sleep with you, Teal."

Well, if the idea of him sleeping with other people was a knife in the gut, the fact that he can't help but be so obviously repulsed at the idea of sleeping with *me* is several dozen knives right in the heart.

It's not that I'm desperate to fall into bed with him. It's more like I can hear my ex Johnny's voice in my head. *No one but me would ever want you.*

I'm not dumb. I know that sentence was a manipulation tactic, designed to make me stay with him, to not consider any other romantic options. He wanted me to believe there would never be any other romantic options.

Still, though, it stung then, and it stings now. Even though it's not what Carter said, I can't help but feel the insult echoing in my body. I try to dislodge it with an angry huff. "Point taken. Jesus. I was talking about you wanting someone else. Because going without sex is hard for some people." It certainly was hard for Johnny. He didn't like to go a single day without it. He insisted it was how men were. *Men need to come*, he'd lecture at me. *But for women, orgasm isn't the point of sex. The point is to make her man happy*. Funny how he didn't include these beliefs in the YouTube videos he uploaded.

"I'm not cheating while we're married. We might not be together, but I'm not cheating." He pulls up in front of Nadia's home and cuts the engine. When he looks at me . . . well, *now* he's heated. His eyes have darkened and his jaw ticks. "Is that what you want? To be able to fuck whoever you want?"

"I wouldn't cheat, either." I cross my arms and glare at him. "I've never cheated and I won't start with a marriage, no matter how fake."

He breathes out a sigh that sounds suspiciously like relief. "So you'll do it."

"We still haven't established what's in it for me, Carter." He didn't even stick around at the wedding to be my date. We didn't share one dance. Not a single reminiscence about our childhood. I blink back tears and sigh an inward groan when the sky darkens with a group of clouds.

"I told you. Money."

"I don't want your money."

We stare at each other until finally Carter gives. "It's a lot of money, Teal. Enough to . . ." He bites his lips. When he releases them, they are unfairly plump. "Enough to get that PI you always wanted. To find your mom."

My breath is frozen in my chest for a moment.

Well. He has me there.

We were thirteen and fifteen when he and I first looked up how much personal investigators cost at Cranberry Library, where we did school research on their internet-connected computers. Both of our jaws had dropped open the second we saw the quotes. I couldn't afford that expense even when I still had my trainer job.

The reminder of me and Carter looking it up brings up a lot more crap I don't want to deal with.

Like the fact that we're not supposed to tell anyone about our gifts, but I blabbed to the two people I had trusted most in the world, Lani and Carter.

Like the fact that of those two people, I trusted only one enough with my theory that my mom had broken my power somehow. And that I wished more than anything I could find her to get it back. And now I'm sitting in a car with him, trying to figure out if I can handle pretending to love him for however long it takes.

"I'll think about it," I finally tell him. I get out of the car too fast to let him respond, and when I'm inside and he drives away, I grab my running shoes and change. Even though I ran too much this morning, I'm doing it again.

6

Should I (fake) marry my former best friend for money?

posted in r/Advice by TealLightning five hours ago

My childhood best friend (m26) just asked me (f28) to marry him. His grandmother won't give him money his grandfather left him unless he's married. He's offered some of this money to me if I marry him.

I haven't been a good friend to him these last few years, not as good as he's been to me. I want to make it up to him and do him this favor.

On the other hand, though, this is a huge commitment. I would live with him. People would think we got married for real. The works, basically.

I don't have a boyfriend or anything, but . . . what if things go wrong?

wunderk1nd33—Did his grandfather not have a will? Because if he did, his grandmother can't legally keep his money from him. Just sayin'

notabeetlewiththumbs—how much money we talkin? 'cause anything less than 20k, nahhhhh

yaeatmeorels3—if you don't have an SO, then why not? You can always become friends again, even if not BEST friends.

pinepinepine—what would go wrong? it's not like marriage is irreversible and you'd be a ruined woman if you divorced him or had it annulled or whatever.

> **TealLightning**—Just scared of ruining the little friendship I have left. This man used to mean the world to me, once upon a time.

> **pinepinepine**—Just don't sleep with him. And you'll be fine.

> **HeroLemon701**—No, DEFINITELY sleep with him. Because fake marriages are my favorite romance trope and this isn't going to work unless you guys fall in love, imho.

> > **TealLightning**—Sleeping together is not a possibility. He'd have to be attracted to me first.

HeroLemon701—So you're saying you're attracted to him? lol?

TealLightning—He's a good-looking guy but he said, and I quote, "I'm never going to sleep with you." So yeah.

HeroLemon701—Wait a minute. What even is this conversation you had? I don't randomly talk to my friends about whether or not we're sleeping together. Which means, there's some attraction both ways, right? Cause why else would you even talk about that?

HeroLemon701—You both have thought about it. Which means if you marry him, the chances of it happening are 100000000%. Add another 1903809820% to that if there's only one bed.

TealLightning—That's . . . not how percentages work. And life isn't a romance novel, friend

HeroLemon701—Just don't come crying to us when you marry your best friend and have the best sex of your life and you think you've fallen in love but you're not sure how to proceed!!!

HeroLemon701—Just kidding. PLEASE come to us when that happens.

HeroLemon701—Seriously, please please update us on this real life romance trope

TealLightning—If that ridiculousness you just described even comes close to happening, I'll literally tag you when I post about it, deal?

HeroLemon701—DEALLLLLL!!!! **cackles in romancelandia**

⚡

THE CRANBERRY CRAFT FESTIVAL IS ALWAYS PEACEFUL UNTIL ten in the morning, when most church services have ended. The rows between the tents and the tables fill with foot traffic, and Lani and I greet everyone who passes by. We field the same questions, over and over again—*Do you really make these yourselves?* and *Why are these prices double what I can find at Target?* Too many people here have never made anything by hand in their lives and it shows.

We each share the table, with my half covered in candles I dipped and poured myself. I was really into it about two years ago—infusing the beeswax with my own blend of essential oil fragrances, and sometimes I would forage in either one of the two state parks here in Cranberry for skeleton leaves to decorate the candles with. But to be honest, I'm burned out on candle making, pun unintended, and I have been for a while. It's the fifth hobby in almost that many years I've put a lot of time and energy into, and I really thought this one would stick. The fact that it hasn't makes me feel like even more of a loser than I already am, especially since Lani's convinced it's my *calling* and *purpose* and *what separates us from the rest of the nine-to-five boring-job world*.

"Got our drinks!" Leilani hands me a peach-hued papaya mimosa—our tradition—and we both sit behind our table, our backs to the sun.

"Did you have fun at the wedding reception?" she asks. She's got her chestnut brown hair dyed with chunks of turquoise tucked under an Indiana Jones–type leather hat. Her maxi dress is navy with a pattern of forget-me-nots, and she has abalone and jade rings on all her fingers, even her thumbs.

"It was nice. Nate and Fern looked happy." I give her a sideways look. "So, are you going to tell me your big news or what?"

"Hold on." She grabs her bag, a patchwork tote she made from sari silks. "Let me show you a few of my new pieces first."

Leilani sews her own bookmarks. I mean, really gorgeous work, made from scraps of fabric she finds at thrift stores. She takes apart old skirts and blouses and lace stockings and refigures them with her sewing machine, making the kind of markers you can slide on the corner of a book as well as the standard long rectangle you can just throw in.

Recently Lani's made this whole new line of bookmarks in which she's taken inspiration from all over the world, with a focus on patterns inspired by Indigenous textiles. I've never said this to her aloud, but I wish she would go back to her old whimsical, floral and spiral-pattern style. But if I actually voiced this opinion, then that means I would be admitting defeat to Sage, who I'm always defending Leilani against. Sage thinks Leilani is a cultural-appropriating spoiled brat. Which . . . sometimes I can see her point of view.

But unlike Sage, Lani was there the last eight years.

"Ta-da!" Leilani pulls out a set of bookmarks. They're a huge departure from anything she's ever made before—in shades of beige and white, with little scraps of gold illustrating symbols I don't recognize. My first thought is that color-and-humor-hating Amá Sonya would *love* these.

"Wow," I say.

"Aren't they great?" She sighs and smiles. "These"—she lifts them up—"are my ticket out of this hellhole." She gestures around with a grimace on her face, as though we were sitting in some kind of postapocalyptic wasteland rather than surrounded by people trying on knitted scarves and snacking on white-chocolate-drizzled popcorn. But Leilani's always hated Cranberry. Or even all of Virginia, for that matter. I've never understood how anyone could judge an entire state based on their infinitesimally tiny viewpoint of the world, but Lani's always been that way. Before Sage met Tenn, she had similar feelings about this area. I guess some people look at a place and can see nothing but their own bad memories reflected back to them in Technicolor.

"What do you mean, your ticket out?" I take one of the bookmarks in my hand, examining it. It's beautiful. But again, it reminds me of Amá Sonya. Specifically, her house. So clean, you could eat off the floor. Perform surgery on the kitchen counter. Everything about it devoid of personality or character. Instead of returning to her old work, Leilani has gone further into the direction of creations distinctly not *her*.

"I mean, my mom's friend in Napa saw these new designs, and guess what? She's signing me on as creative director for her couture accessory company. It's called The Beauty Martyr."

She angles her phone in my face, scrolling through a store shop made up of lampshades, throw pillows, mug coasters, everything the color of white granite with the occasional shimmering minimalist metallic design. All the models are thin, with light-colored skin, able-bodied, traditionally pretty according to Western beauty standards, and they wear nothing but flowing, silky clothes in beige and white.

It's boring as hell.

I force a smile on my face. "That's so great—"

Lani interrupts me by pulling up a photo of a house. "There she is," she breathes, thrusting the image too close to my eyes.

I back up, letting my vision focus. "Your dream home?" I squeal. I can't really tell what it looks like, since the view is aerial.

But it's got a Spanish tile roof, with a pool in the back that over-looks the ocean. It's massive, probably with ten bedrooms or some-thing like that. "But . . ." My voice deflates when I notice that the landscaping looks weird. The property's covered in palm trees, the kind you only see in places that don't get deep frosts in the winter. "You're leaving." When I finally realize what she's telling me, my stomach sinks. My shoulders tighten. My heart begins to beat too fast, too loud.

Leilani grins. "And I have you to thank."

"Me?" I can barely get the word out. Lani doesn't notice.

"Remember how Nadia was doing all that research on your ancestry? And she mentioned those caves they had found in that area of Texas where she thought you guys were from?"

"It was rock art. Not caves."

Leilani shrugs. "Either way, I did some research of my own." She pulls up another image on her phone, one of ancient Indige-nous paintings. People from long ago, people who may have well been the ancestors to us Flores women, ground minerals and used them to paint sacred designs into rocks. I remember Nadia's ex-citement when she first saw them. How some of the paints glit-tered with gold—a sign to our family that a deity is close by. How some of the forms resemble what Nadia says are the old gods.

Lani holds one of her new bookmarks side by side with the phone photo, pulling me away from that memory. "My mom's friend? She saw these and hired me instantly." She smiles and shrugs. "It never would've happened without you, Teal."

I can't keep my eyes from the photo versus the bookmark. It's . . . it's the *same* image. Obviously the materials are different. In the original, mineral paint sits atop a rock somewhere in south-ern Texas. In Leilani's bookmark, it's embroidered with metallic thread. But both designs are of geometric patterns, some formed into what resembles human figures. Or maybe the old ones, like Nadia believes.

I can envision it now. A white woman in California is going to order these from this homogenous Instagram-influencer accessory store, for her book club, also full of white women. They will gush over the design. They will pat themselves on the back for supporting a female artist of color. They probably will assume Leilani is Indigenous herself. Even though she is not. She is a white Latina, with most of her ancestry from France. She has never even been interested in her Puerto Rican heritage.

Just everyone else's.

Thunder rumbles in the distance, as deep and dangerous as a hungry jaguar.

Leilani doesn't hear it. She tosses her hair and puts her phone away. "Like I said, Teal. The universe is in *motion*. This is just the next stage of *love* for me. The unconditional love of this *world*."

Lightning flares across the sky so big and bright, there are a few startled gasps all around us. Even Leilani blinks out of her the-universe-is-only-love stupor. "Yikes, it looks like it's going to rain."

"So when do you leave?" My voice is quiet. I'm trying to count by breaths, but it's hard.

"Aren't you listening to me? That's the big news. That's what's happening this week, that my mom and I were talking about?" She laughs. "I leave on Thursday. I'll be completely moved in by Saturday."

The wind picks up all around us, making the tents' fabric crack like whips. I need to get a handle on this. I begin to deep-breathe again.

Leilani watches me closely. "Why aren't you happy for me?"

"Give me a minute." I gesture to the weather.

"Oh, right." Lani rolls her eyes, which does not help my mood. I turn away from her, desperately pulling the most calming images I can while doing my four-beat-inhales and eight-beat-exhales. I imagine myself on the beach, lying down on a towel while sipping a mojito. Me dancing with my sisters at the wedding.

Carter's hand on mine, as his voice counts with me.

When I open my eyes, the sky has cleared. The dark clouds aren't completely gone, but it doesn't feel like a thunderstorm is upon us anymore.

Leilani's closing a transaction with a customer.

"That was almost bad," the lady says, taking the bag of culturally appropriated bookmarks, gesturing to the receding dark line of clouds.

Lani laughs as the lady turns away, but when she angles her face back toward mine, the laugh, the smile, everything is *gone*, just like that. Her expression is forlorn. "And that, Teal, is why I really need to speak the truth of my heart." She takes my hand in hers and begins speaking slowly, as though I were a small child. "I'm creative director of a thriving company. I got here on my own, without any help. And I just need to cut any and all negative energy from my life now."

I snap my hand back. "What's that supposed to mean?"

She sighs and lifts her hand, pointing at me like that explains everything. "That's what I'm talking about. You with your anger and your"—she lowers her voice—"*bipolar* disorder. You've been dragging me down for years and I didn't make the connection until both my aromatherapist and guardian angel connected the dots for me. They said I'm a hashtag girl boss now, and all my old so-called friends have to go. You see, Saturn is in my *ninth* house. You probably don't know—"

As she explains why the universe has dictated to her that she needs to dump me as a friend, I take the opportunity to think about every red flag I have ignored that has led to my utter astonishment that this is actually happening right now.

How even though Leilani was here for me the last eight years, she was only here in the most superficial way. She'd bring me vegan cake or buy me a series of classes on transcendental meditation. The second I started weeping from my grief over seeing my fucking baby sister fall to her death? Lani'd realize she had a meeting or appointment to run to. If she knew I was having a really bad depressive spell, she'd leave me on read for up to two weeks.

How slowly, over the years, Leilani has become an entirely different person from the one I used to know. She's gone from encouraging me to go to therapy when we were teens to telling me that if only I'd just focus on love, all the bad things in my life would fade away. And if they hadn't yet, that was because I just hadn't tried hard enough.

How Leilani has had everything given to her. Her claim, *I got here on my own, without any help,* is the biggest lie I've heard in a long-ass time. Her parents are millionaires. Everything she has achieved has the underpinnings of extreme financial privilege . . . and she's *never* admitted that. Because then her idea that she's become a self-made woman by the sheer power of the universe's love would pop into a zillion sticky pieces.

Besides the fact that she steals. She steals the gods and the sacred designs of cultures she doesn't belong to in order to make a profit.

I bury my face in my hands. Why hadn't I listened to Sage about Lani? But I already know the answer. It's because of my own damn pride.

"Plus, you know I just didn't want to hurt your feelings on this, because I know that it's your whole family tradition and all—"

I whip my head up, trying to figure out how she's bullying me now, in that way that is so unique to her. Spiritual-washed bully, that's Leilani Rodriguez to a T. It's only taken until now, when it's directed at me so acutely, to see it.

". . . because you just happen to get sad every time the weather's bad. It's . . . no offense, but it's a little narcissistic, you know? Projecting your feelings on the weather?"

"What did you just say?" My voice is low and guarded. The thunder is rolling back in, and I can feel it in a way I've never felt before. Like it's not just on the outside, but also inside me. "You think my and my family's gifts are lies?"

She shakes her head. "Not lies, just metaphors. I mean, come on, Teal. Did you seriously believe that you control the weather?"

Lightning returns to the sky, and it gets so close that Leilani jumps. She clears her throat. "So I just wanted to wish you a really good spring, before I go. I'm sure you're going to have a great life and I wish you all the best. I will pay for our table here till the end of the season, you know, as a parting gift. You've got a lot going for you, Teal, with your little candle-making hobby and—"

I want to hurt her. To somehow help her feel a smidgen of the way she is making me feel right now. I slide my hands under my thighs, pressing in on them until the chair pinches the meat of my hands. If I don't restrain myself, I might punch her like I punched Sage four years ago.

It's not that she doesn't want to be friends anymore. That's not the big deal. I understand that people have the right to be friends or not friends with whoever they want. But does she seriously have to insult me on her way out the door? Does she have to tell me that the one thing I trusted her with, the one thing in my life that has caused me so much suffering, is just in my head?

I need to go, and I can't let her see how mad I am. It's too risky. The urge to knock her out hasn't passed yet. So I paste a saccharine-sweet smile on my face. "Aw, Lani. You didn't have to. And I wish you all the best, too."

She beams. I know this is exactly what she's hoped for—for me to be complacent, to focus on the love of the universe and just find it in my heart to understand. To understand that she's too *full of love* to be cruel, even as she insults me to my face. To understand that she's too *spiritual* to culturally appropriate in her designs, even as she basically copies-and-pastes the work of my ancestors all the way to the bank.

"I gotta run to the bathroom." I wink at her as I leave.

7

HURRICANE WINDS SLICE ALL AROUND ME AS I WALK, AND thunder rumbles again.

"I thought you checked a weather app!" one woman says as she scowls at her husband.

"I did! It said four percent chance of rain!"

With every half-choked gasp of an inhale, the wind gets sharper. With every tear I force back in, thunder rumbles louder. It's going to storm so, so bad if I don't get it together soon.

I'm looking for a place to deep-breathe without anyone bothering me when I run face-first into someone's black shirt. Well, not just the shirt. There's a whole firm torso under there, too, and it startles me enough for the wind to instantly stop, for the thunder to cease midroar.

"Carter?" I can hardly believe it's him. He's never been to the craft fair. Not once.

He's looking down at me, a crease between his eyebrows, his mouth angled into a frown. "Teal? What's happened?"

I start to shrug it off, to say *Nothing, it's fine*, but I can't. I can't ever hide a damn thing because whatever is happening inside is reflecting in the deep black underside of the clouds, the shock white of lightning, the voice of angry thunder. "Leilani just dumped me as a friend," I finally say, not able to make eye contact. "Because I'm . . ." I don't know how to summarize it for him, but I finish the sentence with "bipolar." And I realize that's actually perfect. Bipolar disorder, or the way it shows up for me—deep depressions where I can't get out of bed for days interspersed with impulsive decision-making episodes like random shopping sprees or, I don't know, *literal* rainbows and sunshine, is too real for Leilani, who has carefully constructed a life made out of what she thinks are angel wings but are actually moth balls—toxic and highly flammable.

"She *what*? Because of *what*?" Carter's voice is low, almost a growl. He looks up at the sky and takes my hand.

"Where are we going?"

He doesn't respond. But we don't stop until we reach the oak tree in the middle of the pavilion, its huge, big limbs reaching over us like an umbrella. He pulls my hand until we're both touching the scratchy bark of the tree's trunk.

"Your sister said there's lots of water in trees," he tells me.

"Which sister?"

"Sage. Because she talks to plants, right?"

I nod, with a pathetic little voice in my head wondering if *he* really believes our gifts or not. "Right."

"Listen to the water in the tree, Teal." And then he begins to count.

One-two-three-four, in. And one to eight, out. I close my eyes as his rough voice smooths over me. I try to do what he said, focus on the water in the tree. And you know what? For a split second, I think I can hear it. Feel it. It's like I'm inside a waterfall. Like the water that makes up my body connects to the water in the circulatory system of the tree. But then it's over so quickly, I'm left wondering if I imagined it.

I open my eyes, and the sun shines thick. Not a single dark cloud in the sky. Not a single cloud at all.

Carter turns to me, his eyes as light as sunlight reflecting off a ground cherry. "Now, what do you need?"

I need to listen to my New Year's resolution list. I need to stop being selfish.

But I can't. Not right now, not when what Leilani's done still feels so fresh, it's like the weapon she used to hurt me is still lodged in my body. So I say, "I need revenge."

Carter smiles at me instantly, so genuine and warm that it takes my breath away. "All right."

And then he takes my hand and we're approaching a table. Sitting behind a display of handmade jewelry is Nora Jacoby. She's basically the Cranberry Queen of Gossip.

"Hey, Nora," Carter says.

"Carter Velasquez," Nora stands, grasping her heart. "I haven't seen you here in a dog's age."

"Yeah." He smiles sheepishly. "I've been busy."

"Well, I can see that." Her eyes are on his and my clasped hands, and even though I only know it's going to make her wonder more, I carefully pull my arm away. "Bless your heart, dear. I heard about your grandfather."

Carter clears his throat. "Yeah. That was hard."

Nora makes a pouty face I'm sure she thinks looks like sympathy. "Well, he was a great man."

Carter mumbles something affirmative, then looks at me, then back to Nora. "Say, Nora, if you see Leilani Rodriguez around, could you be a little extra kind to her? She ate way too many jalapeños for breakfast, if you know what I mean."

Nora's eyes are wide and she nearly folds over as she leans toward us. "No, I don't, honey, what do you mean?"

Carter leans in and lowers his voice. "I mean, it was a big mess. She ran out of toilet paper. We had to run and get her some baby wipes."

I snort so loud, it's almost impossible to turn it into a cough, but I manage.

"Ohhhh." Nora looks delighted. "I will be *sure* to be extra kind to her. In fact, I'm going to go ahead and give her some extra Pepto Bismol pills I keep on hand." She starts rummaging through her purse. "Do you think she could use Tums, too?"

At this point, my hands are over my mouth to keep the laugh in.

Carter sighs. "She needs anything you've got, Nora. And if anyone else has stuff to help her, that would be great. To be honest, she might need new clothes, if you catch my drift."

"Oh, bless her heart. Well, you know me. I'll spread the word. I'm going to text her mother to see if she can bring her a change of clothes, too."

When Carter and I turn away, I burst. I can't help it. I laugh so hard, tears fall down my cheeks. I double over. When I finally calm down, I look up, and Carter's so pleased, it makes my heart feel strange.

"Seriously? Telling the whole town Leilani shit her clothes? What are we, in middle school?"

Carter shrugs. "You saying you need more revenge?"

I shake my head. "This feels good for now."

Carter walks me back to my table, where Leilani is surrounded by concerned Southern elder women. One of them is actually holding a package of women's underwear. I bury my face in Carter's chest to keep from laughing too loudly.

When the ladies start to dissipate, Lani looks my way, her face contorted with horror. "Teal," she hisses, pulling me away from Carter. "Why is everyone acting like I'm covered in excrement?"

I make my face as blank as I can. "Aw, Lani. Maybe you didn't focus enough on the love of the universe today."

Her cheeks grow pink and I can see her figuring things out. But I honestly don't care anymore. She's more than welcome to not be my friend, if that's what she wants. But if she thinks she can kick me while she's on her way out the door, she's got another think coming.

"I knew you'd be a child about this," she hisses, gathering up all her things in one angry motion. "I knew it would be too much for you to act like a fully functional adult."

"Wow." I furrow my brow. "That sounds like a lot of negative energy you've got inside you right now. Maybe you should talk to your guardian angel again. Detoxify your aura. Take a break from the *real* world, with all these *real* feelings."

Leilani straightens, her eyes on me full of rage. I know she wants to erupt. She wants to scream and stomp her feet. It would be so good of her to actually let a single negative emotion express itself.

But she can't. That would be too *unspiritual*. Because to Leilana, spirituality is about putting on a mask of pleasantness and pretending nothing ever bothers her. And I am so annoyed with myself for it taking this long for me to see that her entire personality is a fragile shell made up of essential oils, crystals, and variations of the phrase, *There's nothing but love in this world, right?*

So, no, she doesn't express any of her real emotions. But I suppose she's not above revenge, either, because instead she says, "I'm going to cancel our table for the rest of the season. For this." And then she walks away.

I'm consoled by the fact that there's no way she's making it to her Lexus without someone asking her if she's okay since she last shit herself.

⚡

I SIT BACK IN MY CHAIR WITH A SIGH, AND CARTER TAKES LANI'S seat.

"What are you thinking?" he asks.

"I'm thinking there goes my entire income." Lani forgot one of her new ugly bookmarks on our table, and I turn it over and over in my hand as I try to figure this new mess out.

Carter frowns. "What about Cranberry Fitness?"

I shake my head. "That . . . I don't work there anymore." And I'm not in the mood to explain it. I guess Carter senses this because he doesn't ask. I run a hand over my face. "There's no way I can afford to rent a table for the rest of the season." Well, I guess I could, but there's no way I can make enough to cover the rental costs, plus my share of the groceries, plus my car payment and insurance, plus my phone . . .

And the dahlias I promised Sage for her wedding, which she had assured me cost in the thousands. I'm pretty sure she's exaggerating, but even if they were only a few hundred dollars, I wouldn't be able to keep that promise. And I need to.

"I can cover you." Carter says this after a long moment of watching me lose my shit. Figuratively, unlike what everyone thinks is happening to Lani right now.

I have my hands covering my face. I'm glad Carter can't see my expression right now. If he could, he'd know how hard I was trying to not accept his offer.

Old, Selfish Teal would. Without a single moment of hesitation.

I've taken a lot from people offering in good faith. I've taken money and presents from Nadia, even when I knew Sage needed it more. I've let Carter buy every meal and drink we've shared over the years. I've let Amá Sonya try to buy my affections, even though she says all she's doing is trying to make at least one of her granddaughters appear respectable.

And in return, I've turned away and pushed away the people in my life I love the most.

I can't keep doing that. I can't let everyone give me everything I need without offering them a single wholesome thing in return.

Is faking being married wholesome? Maybe objectively not. But Carter needs this. And I want to be able to give him something he needs, too. Not just the other way around.

I pull my hands from my face and tell Carter, "Let's do it."

He sputters. His face, ears, and neck turn a bright pink. "What?" His hands are clutching the table for dear life. "Here?"

I look around. "I mean, we could, but I don't see an ordained minister, do you?"

"Oh. Right." He loosens his fists and runs his fingers through his hair. Then he blinks. "So you—you're serious? You want to get married?"

I nod. "Yeah. I mean, I would still get a cut, right?"

"Yeah. Of course. However much you want, it's yours. And we could rent you a table here, and get that PI for . . . you know."

I shake my head. "I don't know if I need that PI yet. I heard Nadia and Sonya talking the other night? They acted like my mom was in town." I roll my eyes. "Of course they pretended like nothing was going on when they saw me."

And even if I didn't need money for a PI, I sure would want to keep driving my car, using my cell phone, eating, and eventually, figuring out Sage's dahlia situation.

"You really think she's in town?"

"Who knows." I sigh and close my eyes. The sky has turned from bright and blue to overcast. Which matches how I feel exactly—dim, numb. Exhausted. "I'll find out tomorrow. I have to go shopping with Amá and Sky."

"So how about Tuesday, then?" I open my eyes and he's pulling something out of his wallet. "We can meet in the courthouse. You can move into my place by the end of the week."

"Tuesday it is." It's not like I have anything else going on.

Carter takes my left hand and pushes on a ring. I get a little distracted by the feel of his warm skin against mine, so it takes me a second to notice the jewelry. When I do, my jaw drops open.

A line appears between Carter's brow as he takes a big breath. "Do you like it? If you don't, we can change it. It doesn't matter to me. We can get you whatever you want, you know?"

"I—" I tighten my muscles to keep my voice from shaking. "I just can't believe you remembered."

When I was a little girl, I thought Princess Diana had the most gorgeous engagement ring in the universe. Never mind that her husband fucked around, that her marriage wasn't destined to last. I remember cutting out a picture of the diamond-haloed sapphire from a magazine and pinning it to my wall, next to corny pictures of the Backstreet Boys. I was sure AJ was going to get me a ring just like it when he asked me to marry him.

But somehow I ended up with something even better. I mean, I know I've never seen the royal ring up close in real life. But there's *no way* it rivals this one. The gold is impossibly shiny, the diamonds so sparkly, I probably look like I'm cradling a damn disco ball around my finger. The sapphire is lighter than Diana's, a blue that reminds me of the distant ocean, the way it looks from the balcony of Nadia's attic, with the waves in the distance glittering just like the way this giant-ass rock does when I turn my hand in the sunlight.

"It's not as big a sapphire. Di's was twelve carats. This one's only a little over four. And the diamonds around it are smaller. And they're not flawless, but they are ethically mined. I mean, so is the sapphire. It's twelve-carat white gold. Diana's was eighteen—"

I interrupt him by throwing my arms around his neck. "It's the prettiest ring I've ever seen, Carter."

"Yeah?" He's breathless. Probably because I'm almost choking him.

"Yeah."

When I pull back, he's looking at me so closely, I feel frozen. Like the market all around us doesn't exist anymore. Like the whole world has blended into some abstract forms of color, and only Carter and me are the ones in detail.

He takes a shaky breath. "Teal, I—"

"Well, I'll be! Teal Flores, is that an engagement ring on your finger?"

I turn and there is Nora Jacoby. "Oh. Uh—"

"I swear I saw Carter there put something on you. It's a sapphire, isn't it? Good lord, look at the size of that thing!"

Before I know it, my hand is now being yanked by the biggest gossip in town. She wouldn't be around us if we hadn't told her

Lani had a poopy emergency. This is me, instantly reaping what I have sown. "We're trying to keep it a secret for now," I mumble.

Nora grins. "Oh, honey, of course. Of course. I won't tell a soul."

Which means that by the end of the hour, *everyone* will know.

8

Sage: Engaged??! To Carter???!! Teal, when tf were you going to tell us?!

Sky: Can I be your flower girl?

Amá Sonya: **Money comes before marriage, Teal Alegría. NOT after.**

Nadia: I knew it.

My phone's blowing up nonstop. When I park in Nadia's driveway, I pull it out of my purse—a vintage Coach in camel—just to get this over with.

First I assure Amá that Carter has money. I don't go as far as to say that is the whole reason we're doing this, but she is mollified by the time I get off the phone with her. Which for her means she's only mildly condescending and irritated at me.

That's your thing, I text back Nadia as a response to her I

knew it. I swear, that and *I told you so* are her favorite phrases of all time.

Then I get my sisters on a single phone call.

"When? Seriously, when were you going to tell us? I had to hear it from Johanna Ortiz, and act like I knew what she was talking about." Sage sounds equal parts ecstatic and annoyed.

I groan. "We didn't make any decisions until—" I check the clock. "Forty-five minutes ago. I swear. Nora Jacoby happened to see us."

"See you do what?" Sky asks. "Were you two going at it?"

I can't believe that question makes my cheeks heat. Thank the old gods my sisters can't see me right now. "If by going at it, you mean that Carter put a ring on my finger, then yes."

Sage huffs. "I can't believe he didn't come to me for your ring. I could've had it made over the weekend."

"He wanted it to be a surprise."

"I wouldn't have told!"

Sky adds, "I knew he was in love with you, but I didn't know you loved him back."

"Nadia knew, apparently," Sage says dryly.

"Hold on, hold on," I yelp. All this talk about love is bananas. "We're getting ahead of ourselves here."

"*You* got engaged to Carter without anyone knowing you were even together, and *we're* getting ahead of ourselves?" Sage demands.

"Yes. God." I swallow. "He wanted it to be a surprise or whatever, because—" I hesitate. The sham of our marriage has to be a secret, otherwise I'm sure his crochety old grandmother won't give him his money. But I can't lie to my sisters. "It's not a real marriage. We're doing it so he can get an inheritance."

Each of them has about two hundred more questions, one right after the other, and I want to scream by the time I'm done answering them all.

"Doesn't his grandma Erika hate you, though?" That one's from Sage.

"She sure does. Or did. Maybe she doesn't anymore."

"No offense, but when's the last time you ever heard of an old Latina abuela letting go of a grudge?"

I know two old Latina mother figures very well, Nadia and Sonya, and they can't let go of things like a stranger taking the last mango at the store, much less the crap they've done to each other over the years.

"Fine. I'm sure she still hates me. It doesn't matter, though." At least, I hope it doesn't matter.

"So you're moving out?" Sky's voice sounds small. My heart lurches a little. She's only been back for a little while, and then Sky moved in with Tennessee, and now me.

"Temporarily. Yes. But I can come back anytime. I'll spend weekends or even whole weeks at Nadia's. Whenever possible. Or maybe I can get Carter to move in with us."

Sky snorts. "I wouldn't. His house is gorgeous. And right on the water, too?"

I frown, even though neither of them can see me. "Carter doesn't have a house. Carter's never had a house."

Now Sky's laughing hard. "Wow. You guys really need to catch up if you're going to fool Abuela Erika into thinking you fell in love."

"Whatever." This day has been too emotional, and the fact that I didn't know something as basic as the fact that Carter apparently has a house now makes me feel queasy. "I gotta go."

After saying all the goodbyes, I check my messages one last time. And my stomach flips even more.

Nadia: I've known you'd marry him since you were eleven years old.

The way she puts it, like . . . like it's a *love match*. She and Hero-Lemon701 need to get together and talk about IRL romance tropes, apparently. I make a face of disgust.

It's just convenience, I type back. That's all.

Even without seeing her, I can feel that she is making her very annoying *I Know Things You Don't* Face, so I turn my phone off before she, or anyone else, can piss me off further.

$$\not{}$$

I DON'T KNOW WHERE NADIA AND SKY ARE. I DIDN'T ASK ON the phone when I saw that neither of their cars was here. But I'm glad the house is empty. Because there's something shaking inside me, something I can't let anyone see.

I walk up the stairs, practically limping like after a particularly grueling run. Only I haven't run at all. My bones are tired. They ache. And there's an imperceptible trembling in my limbs. If I ran now, I would collapse. I'm sure of it.

Instead, I climb into bed and pull the covers as high, basically up to my eyes.

And then I let those eyes water. I let them sting and glisten till the salt water spills.

It's stupid. It's so stupid but sometimes, I have too bad a day and I can't run it off. I have to cry.

Even as the clouds outside bleed with dark colors right before my eyes, as though someone tapped the sky with deep, dark, dripping watercolors. Indigo. Midnight blue. The deepest moon-light gray.

The wind picks up and it sounds like the howls of wolves. Some of those howls end in a whine, a sound of raw despair, and it makes me cry harder.

I can't believe what happened today. I can't believe Leilani dumped me, just like that.

I know this is the only time I'm going to give myself to cry over her. I'm too bone-tired to try to stuff the feelings inside some interior compartment. So I let my shoulders shake. I wipe my snotty nose on my T-shirt. I gasp and hiccup and just weep and weep.

I told Lani almost ten years ago about my gift. About *our* gifts.

And all this time, she thought I was a delusional narcissist.

I trusted her. I loved her.

And she threw me away like garbage.

I cry for what feels like hours, and the weather cries with me. I almost feel it like a mother. The clouds seeping in through the crack of my window. The fog filling the air of my bedroom, a humid, cool hand upon my shoulder.

I think about what Carter had me do. *Listen to the water in the tree, Teal.* Why did he have me do that? Why did it help?

With these questions in my mind, I fall into a deep, rain-dripped sleep.

9

T HIS." AMÁ SONYA LIFTS A SKIRT SUIT THAT LOOKS LIKE IT'S made of pure silk, in the color of seafoam.

I barely glance up from my phone. We've been shopping with Amá for literal hours. I'm not saying it's the worst thing ever, but if there were a hell, it would look very similar to this scenario: me, having already picked out a few outfits for hopefully job hunting (as well as a few dresses to give to Sage, who missed this trip 'cause of work), all in Amá-approved designers. Amá, not letting us eat lunch until we find clothes for Sky, too. And Sky deciding to be the most indecisive young woman in human history when it comes to her rich-ass grandmother spoiling her with a new wardrobe.

I glance at the skirt suit once more. "That will literally get dirty the moment I sit down for a meal."

"This isn't for eating in, Teal Alegría. It's for meetings. Appointments." She gives me a long glare. "Courthouse weddings."

I keep my sigh inside. "I know you're mad we're doing it at the courthouse—"

"Mad?" Amá grits her teeth and crosses her arms. "Do I look mad to you?" She's baring her fangs like a serpent.

"Uhh—"

"It's just that you're the first grandchild to get married, and you want to do it at the courthouse? Do you know how that looks? Everyone's going to think you're—" She looks around and whispers, "With child."

I can't help rolling my eyes, even though I know that will just make her madder. "Sage is the one who is pregnant."

"Sí, and she will be bursting out of her wedding dress! Getting married in September, giving birth in November! Two grand-daughters pregnant before marriage, what will everyone say?"

"But I'm not pregnant, Amá. You know that, right? I've never even—" I stop myself. I can't believe I was about to tell my elderly grandmother that I've never had sex with the man I'm going to marry tomorrow.

Amá furrows her brow. "Teal? Are you—" She lowers her voice. "Pure?"

It takes a lot of effort to not burst out into laughter. Thankfully, at that moment, Sky stomps out of the fitting room.

Amá gasps. "See?" She points while widening her eyes at me. "*This* is elegance."

Sky crosses her arms as she stands in front of the triptych of mirrors. She's got on a dress Amá chose for her—billowy with long, flared sleeves. The color is a shiny pink. I don't know the brand but I saw the price tag when Amá hurled it into my arms to hand to Sky. It is five thousand fifty dollars. Yes, it looks amazing on Sky. But what any of us would do with a dress that nice, I don't know.

Sky seems to have the same thoughts. She shifts her weight on her feet. "I just don't know where I would wear this."

"To your sister's wedding." Amá shrugs like it's a done deal.

"But this is way fancier than Sage's wedding dress. And, I'm sure, whatever Teal's going to wear."

"That's their problem, not yours."

I wave my hand. "Uh, I'm sitting right here, you know. And no offense, but neither of you are invited to my wedding." Carter and I had decided that over text. I didn't want my family involved more than necessary, seeing that this whole arrangement was a lie. And he didn't want his family there, either, to "avoid drama." Hence, no one but us would be present at our disappointing courthouse nuptials.

Amá just cuts a look at me that says *We'll see about that.* Out loud, she insists, "Your hermana looks like a runway model."

"Agreed. She looks phenomenal. But she also looks miserable."

Sky isn't even listening to us. Her face is pitiful as she folds and unfolds her hands, examining the fabric on her arms.

Amá can't deny that Sky is unhappy. So she gestures to me and says, "Fine. You pick her new wardrobe, since you're so smart."

"Fine." Do I want to be my sister's personal shopper? No. Do I want this to be over with as soon as possible so I can get some lunch? Hell yes. I stand and grab Sky's hand and we disappear into the changing room together.

"What are you doing?" she asks. "I don't need an audience to change."

"Um, just last Saturday you basically invited Carter in my bedroom while I was in my underwear."

"You had a towel on!"

"Whatever. I'm just saying, we need to get it together. Let's find you a bunch of Amá-approved clothes so we can eat, for gods' sake."

Sky sighs as she steps out of the dress and pulls on a tattered pair of too-short boot cut jeans and an even worse-looking giant coral hoodie. As she sits to pull on her white Payless sneakers, I take a long look at her.

When Sky fell at sixteen, she was something like five foot nine with almost no curves to speak of. Now she's almost six feet tall with hips and an enviable round bottom. I mean, I have to squat a *lot* to get what she's got natural.

My baby sister basically had this super traumatic, supernatural coma, and woke up an adult, but she hasn't had any time to really adjust to it. She's always sort of curling in on herself like she doesn't own her limbs. A lot of times it seems like she's flailing, trying to figure out this new body. She's tall, and thin, with rose-bud lips, cheekbones people emulate with contour, and hair that's light chestnut on top and naturally fades to a honey blond at its ends. She literally looks like a young Shakira—not that Shakira really ages—and yet she's still dressed like an insecure teenager from 2009.

And she looks sad as hell.

"Hey," I say softly so that Amá can't hear. Lord knows that woman is a snoop. "What's the matter?"

Sky shrugs. "I'm just hungry like you."

"No, you're upset."

Sky sighs. "I saw Adam at the wedding." She raises an eyebrow at me. "He talked to you, didn't he?"

"Yes." I sit down next to her. "He asked if I was your sister."

Sky looks down. "He didn't ask you out or anything?"

I make a face. "No. Why would he?"

Sky shakes her head. "I . . . His grandpa mentioned he'd be there at the wedding. I was really excited. I wore . . . you know."

Oh, I know. Sky insisted on wearing the dress she had been planning on wearing to prom the year she fell. Nadia had saved it in plastic wrap all these years. It was a knee-length, electric blue halter top with dull, plasticky jewels sewn into the bodice that, for a sixteen-year-old, was cute, but for a grown woman, was . . . kind of a lot. Also, the fact was that dress had been out of style for almost a decade. But none of us said anything—not Sage, Nadia, or even Sonya. 'Cause Sky never got to go to prom. She never will. So if she wanted to wear her prom dress, not one of us was gonna stop her.

"I felt . . . I felt beautiful."

I sense a *but* coming and I really, really want to nip it in the bud. "You were beautiful. You are beautiful."

Sky shakes her head. "Not to Adam."

I narrow my eyes. "Did he say something to you to suggest otherwise?" I'm planning a visit to Old Man Noemi in my mind, to find Adam and to hurt him. Badly.

"No, it wasn't . . ." She sighs again. "So, during the reception, I went outside, and there were . . ." She buries her face in her hands. "Chipmunks. And pigeons. In that little courtyard by the ballroom."

"Go on."

"I was kind of overwhelmed by the loud music, and I wanted to just be in my element, with the criaturas, you know? I had a chipmunk in one hand and a pigeon in the other when . . . when he found me."

I can't help but smile at the image of Adam discovering Sky, wearing a dated prom dress, cuddling two wild animals.

"He stopped short and blinked like he couldn't believe what he was seeing. And then he scolded me. He said I was going to get hurt, because animals like that could have all kinds of diseases." She frowns. "It was his tone. The way a father figure would speak to his twelve-year-old kid. He didn't leave me until he watched me put the animals down."

"You didn't say anything?"

Sky shakes her head. "My voice was stuck in my throat. Here was this guy, who I built up in my head. He's so generous and kind with his grandfather. He's so accomplished—did you know he's employed by the *New York Times*?"

I barely refrain from rolling my eyes. Not only has Sky told me about Adam's work about two hundred times, Adam Noemi has become a kind of legend here in Cranberry. At the Lounge, when there's a lull in conversation, someone will bring up one of his latest articles, or mention that he's currently in Peru with his latest investigative journalism, or some chick will brag about having slept with him last time he was in town. If Cranberry High had a decent football team and one of the players went pro, everyone would be gagging over him. But instead, we have Adam. The amiable, handsome fellow who gets out of the small town with a kind of success most of us only ever see in the movies.

Sky continues, "And he's also, you know. Hot. But with me . . . he saw me as a child and treated me like one, too." She swallowed. "Anyway, when we went in, I pointed you out, because I couldn't think of anything to say. I was like, there's my sister, and when I went to go to you, he said his grandfather was looking for me. And he had totally perked up when he saw you. Because, and I could just tell, so don't tell me I'm making this up, Teal. He saw you as a *woman*. He walked over to you right away with all this *interest*."

"He didn't ask me out, Sky. And I would've never said yes if he had." I would never go with a guy one of my sisters was into. Even if Carter wasn't my date and hadn't asked me to fake-marry him, like, thirty minutes before.

"That's fine. And I believe you. But it's——" She throws up her hands. "I'm a kid to him. I know it ultimately doesn't matter, how a man sees me. But it was still a huge blow to my ego."

Normally, I'd tell her she's right. The way some man sees her doesn't matter. I'd tell her she's beautiful and I'm hungry so let's please buy her some pretty outfits. I would center this on me eating and getting home as soon as possible.

But number three on my resolutions list is *Make it up to Sky*. I'm the reason she's missed eight years. I'm the reason she's feeling this way.

I take a deep breath and hold out my hand. "Give me your phone."

She wrinkles her nose. "Why?"

"Ahora, Sky."

She pulls it from the pocket of her hoodie and drops it in my hand.

I open it up and scroll until I find Pinterest.

"Wait—what are you doing?"

I hold my hand out, blocking her as she tries to get it back. "I want to know what you've been pinning." Sky's only just discovered this app, and I swear she spends more time on that than any other social media.

I smirk as I find an album dedicated to style. "Sky Flores. You are a secret sexy librarian!"

"What? No! Give it back, Teal."

"Look at this. Pencil skirts. Tweed blazers. Lace camisoles." I gasp and look up at her pink face. "Stockings with the seams in the backs!"

"That's nothing. It's just pretty." Finally she snatches her phone back, but I'm all smiles.

Sky already knows what I'm doing. "There's nowhere to wear that stuff. Or this." She jerks her thumb in the direction of the pink Barbie dress Amá had chosen. "I can't even get a job. No one wants to hire the town freak. There's no reason for me to own a pencil skirt to wear at home while catching up on *Gilmore Girls*."

"You are getting a job. Sooner or later. And you need to be ready." I open the changing room door. "Come on. I know your style now, so this should be easy."

Even though Sky is reluctant at first, she soon gets into it as I find whatever I can that matches her Pinterest boards. I find her knitted cardigans and sweater vests, collared shirts and lots of lacey camis. And so many damn pencil skirts. Thankfully Amá thinks pencil skirts are the height of casual-wear sophistication, so she approves all of it. When we finally make it to a restaurant for lunch—at almost dinnertime—Sky's got shopping bags upon shopping bags filled with everything a hot librarian would need, and then some. I insisted she get her first real handbag, too—a Celine carryall-type with leather trim and gold hardware.

"You don't want a bag, too?" Amá had asked.

I almost said yes. I always want another handbag. But I shook my head. "I have all I need." I gave her a kiss on the cheek. "Thank you, Amá."

I swear, the old woman almost smiled. Just almost, though.

She's been like that since—*almost* pleasant to be around. Even me gobbling down a ginormous plate of eggplant Parmesan didn't piss her off like normal. I take a sip of my wine and decide to push my luck by saying, "So, our mother's in town, huh?"

Amá just about growls and looks around. I don't know why. Sky's in the bathroom, and I'm pretty sure my mom's not hiding in this fancy little Italian restaurant. But that's how Amá is. She always thinks people are spying on her, trying to figure out all her dirty laundry. Maybe the ability to see ghosts made her that paranoid, or maybe it was a regular old dose of narcissism. Who knows.

I raise an eyebrow. "Is that a yes?"

Amá shakes her head and gives me an expression I think she intends to come off as bored, but instead she looks a bit constipated. "You know your mother. We haven't seen her in twenty-two years now."

"But I *heard* you and Nadia—"

"You heard *nothing*, Teal Alegría." She glowers at me as though I'd asked her what number facelift she was on and not whether she'd recently spotted the woman who had birthed me. "And if you keep talking like this, I'm returning everything. Even Sky's purchases."

That shut me up. And, to be honest, kind of ruined a fun day.

10

THE FIRST TIME I RAN THE WAY I RUN NOW, AS THOUGH escaping from some enormous, sharp-fanged, soul-eating monster, it was after the search teams had given up on finding Sky's body. I had felt so helpless, so damn *sad* that I didn't think there could be an end to the despair. I've battled with depression since I was a teen, and only a few months before Sky fell, my doctor and I had figured out that the depression came from my being bipolar. She got me on an antidepressant dosage that made riding out those deep, raw moods more doable. But for some reason, the state troopers telling Nadia those words, *Sorry, ma'am, but we've suspended the search indefinitely*, I felt both grief and depression closing in on me at impossible speeds.

I ran upstairs, to bed, which is where I spent most of my depressive episodes. I couldn't breathe. Outside, the weather tossed out choked, spinning clouds that darkened and darkened until they broke. Until the way I felt on the inside reflected exactly how it felt on the outside. I couldn't get out of bed for days, maybe even weeks. Everything—time, meals, showers—became fuzzy in the onslaught of the pain.

That year was the record for Cranberry's yearly rainfall, and most of it happened in the weeks after Sky fell. The valleys flooded, and several homes were destroyed. Nadia's garden was so underwater that she had to wear long rubber boots to get from her car to the porch after work every day.

My doctor upped my prescription dosage again, and that helped some. As in, for weeks there was slight rain as opposed to hurricane-inspired storms, one after the other. But my sister had just died due to my stupidity. No pill was going to cure that grief.

So one day, the day I felt like I couldn't take one second more of that bullshit, I put on some old Nikes, and I rushed out the door.

I ran through the tangible evidence of my emotional body— calf-deep puddles, loud howling wind, fog as sticky as flan. I ran through the woods so that mud splashed up over me. I ran until I felt like my lungs were scarring, my bones shattering, my muscles all cramping, every last one. I might still be running that particular run if I hadn't collapsed, looked up, and seen a sliver of sun breaking through the sky, through the forest canopy, thickened with the soft rain catching the sparkling light. I realized that running *helped*. Just like my prescription, it wasn't a cure—but it somehow carved a hole of sunlight in the sky for the first time in weeks.

I only just told Sky and Sage about my being bipolar a couple of months ago, when they both tried to tell me that the amount of running I do seemed unhealthy. Not going to lie, I was really nervous. The only person I had told about it was Amá Sonya, and she basically pretended like she didn't hear me. But that's kind of how Amá works. If there's some type of information in the air that makes her uncomfortable? It basically doesn't exist.

Luckily both Sage and Sky just asked how they could help, and when I told them I had it handled, they stopped talking to me about how much I run. Maybe the running isn't normal, but it's what's keeping me stable. It's what's keeping the whole of this damn town safe from nonstop hurricanes, too.

I didn't run as much when I worked at Cranberry Fitness—I guess training and doing alternative workouts helped to ease the tide of my emotional turbulence, too. But since I was let go, I think I've done the equivalent of fifteen or twenty marathons in the span of two months.

That's why I groan inwardly when I look at the steps leading to the Cranberry courthouse. I ran for over an hour this morning, as fast and as hard as I could. I couldn't stand in the shower afterward—instead I had to sit down to wash up. And now there's *this*—eighteen concrete steps between me and my new life as a wife. Well, a fake wife. Either way, my nervous system didn't seem to know the difference—hence my need to run until my legs wanted to fall off.

"What is this? Cold feet?"

I turn and groan for real, out loud, as I watch Amá Sonya walk up. She's wearing a belted pale pink suit with cuffed wide legs and a dainty chain belt that may well be real gold. On her wrist is a white snakeskin Dior satchel and her heels are so high, she towers over me even though she's one inch shorter. Her Chanel shades cover more than half her face and I feel like I am speaking to someone wearing a bizarre space helmet. "Seriously?" I ask her. "How did you even find out when I would be here?"

"We abuelas have our ways." She raises her glasses and fixes a long glare on me. "I spent a lot of money on you yesterday. I deserve to witness the first of my grandchildren commit to holy matrimony."

I bite my tongue. I've already explained to her that our relationship isn't transactional, but I guess my actions haven't really been backing that up. I did accept pretty clothes yesterday, didn't I? I decide right then and there I'm not going to allow her to try to buy my love anymore. "Well," I mumble. "I guess we need a witness."

"I wish you had let me *witness* what you had planned on wearing." She lowers her eyes over my outfit as though I'd thrown on a few layers of rotted cheese. "This isn't a beach party. It's your wedding day."

I look down at my Target sundress, white with lace eyelet embroidery in blue. My shoes are sandals—my calves almost leapt out of my skin when I tried to put on heels—and my bag is one of the camel-colored ones I have, handmade from Mexico, the leather tooled into a pattern of vines.

Someone's clears their throat behind us. "Buenos días." We both turn to look up at Carter, who bends to greet Sonya with a cheek kiss, and then he does the same for me. Something about him, old gods know what—the cologne? Beard oil? Deodorant? Either way he smells so good I want to wrap my arms around his neck and keep him where I can just inhale like a total freak.

He looks as handsome as he did for Nate's wedding, in a black suit that emphasizes the V shape of his torso, the thick of his thighs. He looks at me up and down as he pulls away. There's no heat in his eyes, nothing to show that he thinks I look as good as I think he does. His previous words come over me. *We're never going to have sex, Teal.* The reminder helps me to push away the low-level vibe of attraction making me want to do something stupid, like swoon. "Why are you wearing a suit?" I don't intend to make my voice as sharp as it sounds, but I guess I can't help it. I hate feeling even the suggestion that I might want Carter, especially since he's made it so clear the desire is *not* mutual.

"*He's* ready for his wedding," Sonya answers for Carter, her voice approving. "Not like he just walked off a surfboard." She scrunches her nose at my dress again.

"People don't surf in dresses, Amá." I nod toward the big white building looming over us. "Shall we?"

I don't think I've ever been inside the courthouse before. The main room has tall ceilings, wide carved columns, and a mosaic on the wall featuring what looks almost like religious iconography, featuring brown-haired women doing things like brushing their hair and gathering fruit into baskets.

Carter leads us to another room off to the side. It's smaller and reminds me of the post office—shiny, smelling like strong cleaning agents, and a little boring, especially compared to the grand entrance we were just in.

The clerk is a middle-aged brown woman with fine blond curls and perfectly applied brick red lipstick. The ceremony is unremarkable, lasting just over five minutes, with us answering *I do* and *I will* to predictable questions that you hear in all the series and films that show weddings. Finally, the lady gives us a small smile and says, "Now you may kiss the bride." During my research of courthouse weddings the night before, kissing didn't seem to be a requirement, and so I'm a little taken aback.

I look at Carter, who doesn't seem fazed. In fact, he looks downright bored. The look of disinterest on his face at the suggestion of kissing me pisses me off instantly. The last time we kissed—also, incidentally, the first time we kissed—he was so into it, so frazzled by the heat of it, that his hands shook, that he could hardly breathe. How could he go from *that* to *this*—a face without a single emotion—in less than a year?

But I already know the answer to that. I blew it, just like I fuck up all the good things in my life.

I almost jump back when he bends down toward me. The move doesn't escape him, and he pauses, his eyes intent on me, looking at me, searching. I give him a faint nod, and then I smile as big as I can—Amá and this lady need to buy this, after all—and place my arms around his shoulders and meet his lips.

Carter freezes the instant our mouths touch. I feel the way his back muscles tense up under my hands and forearms. My stomach drops—am I really so repulsive?—but one split second before I pull back, he lets out a huff. I would call it a faint moan if I didn't know any better. And then his big hands reach the small of my back and he tugs me closer, angling his head just to the left.

His mouth is still open after that huff, so I tease my tongue in. I can't help it. He looks and smells so damn good that I need to see if his taste matches the rest of him. And of course he does. My entire body heats as his tongue meets mine, so intense and fast that I don't need to tighten my thighs together to know I'm already wet.

He tastes as good as I remember. Better, even. Back after I'd dumped Johnny, after everyone found out about the bruises he'd left on my arm once, with the implied truth of our relationship: that he'd given me a great deal more bruises all over the place in the course of six years. When Carter heard the gossip, he dropped everything—I mean, he *literally* left work in the middle of a shift—and ran to Nadia's to see if I was okay. I broke out the moonshine, and sometime after my tears and him holding my hand, I ended up on top of him, his hands pushing my tank top up over my bra, my hands under his shirt, groping his hips roughly.

Even though we fooled around for all of two minutes, I had never been so turned on in my life.

As though he can sense the memories, too—like they're seeping from my lips to his like a poisoned lipstick—he pulls back, his eyes wide and his breath fast as though he's afraid of something.

Almost a year ago, Carter ended our last and first kiss because he had said I'd had too much to drink. But now I wonder if it was something else. Maybe the fact was that he only kissed me because he felt bad for me. Because now he won't even meet my eyes as the rest of the room—our clerk official, a few random people, the janitor, even Amá—clap in celebration of our holy matrimony.

My heart sinks as I realize that as much as I love his taste, he can't stand mine.

I sternly remind myself that this is for the best. That it would be way better to become best friends with Carter again through this fake marriage than to ruin everything by throwing myself at him over a one-sided, temporary attraction.

11

"YOU TWO NEED TO MEET ME AT NADIA'S. AHORA." THESE are the last words Amá tells me and Carter as she turns away toward her car, her heels clicking on the pavement.

I turn to Carter as he walks me to my car. "You don't have to."

"Of course I do. I'm family now, remember?" He angles a grin at me, one I would almost call giddy. He must be trying to make up for being so visibly disgusted with touching me. "Besides, you know Amá Sonya scares me."

"She's probably going to lecture us about making more money and not doing anything to embarrass her." If I were a hopeful woman, I would think she wanted to talk to Carter to threaten his livelihood if he broke my heart, et cetera, et cetera. But let's face it. This is Amá. The most important things in her life are her wealth and reputation.

"Remember, I spent my childhood living down the street from y'all Flores women. I think I can handle myself." He winks as he pulls open my car door, his eyes bright and twinkling.

I hate the way my stomach feels right now. Like a small bloom of lightning has replaced my nervous system. "If you say so. See you there." I manage a small smile, which for some reason makes Carter's beam fall just a bit.

I don't understand this man. But I guess I don't have to. It's a fake-ass marriage. There's no reason for me to analyze any of my interactions with Carter, whether they make sense or not.

⚡

"OH, SWEET BABY JESUS," I SAY WHEN I PULL UP TO NADIA'S.

The driveway is overflowing with vehicles, half of which I don't recognize. Iridescent white balloons are tied to the mailbox, attached to a hand-painted sign that says,

CARTER AND TEAL!

NEWLYWEDS!

JUST MARRIED!

SOULMATES!

That's all that can really fit on the sign, but under everything, in a scrawl that looks suspiciously like Sky's handwriting, is the added word of *LOVERS!*

I get out of my car, and the scent of tamales and flan and enchiladas hits me, right on top of the distant bass of "Suavemente" by Elvis Crespo.

What I wanted to do after getting married today was get in my room and pack, with nothing for company but a cheap bottle of corner-store wine and leftover angel food cake Nadia brought home from some church function. Not this—having to fake being in love in front of all my relatives with a man who can barely stand to touch me.

They're going to make us kiss. They're going to stomp their feet and raise their glasses and make us kiss, like, the *entire* fiesta.

My face is in my hands when something solid and warm grips my shoulder. "Hey. You okay?"

I look up at Carter. The line is back between his eyebrows, and he looks over me, presumably to check for injuries. But I can't help but notice—or imagine, probably—the way his gaze becomes as slow as molasses when it skirts over my hips, my breasts, my lips.

I close my eyes briefly. "It's fine. I wasn't expecting this." I gesture to the house.

"You didn't think your family was going to use our wedding as an excuse to drink and eat and dance?"

I shake my head and smile. He's right. I should've marked it in my calendar. The family gets together for everything, from baptisms to First Communions to someone getting a new puppy. Everything except Nadia's birthday. But that's just because Nadia likes her birthday to only be us—me and my sisters and her.

"You good?" Carter asks me, pulling my hand away from my face.

I look up at the sky. It's so weird how sometimes I don't really know what I'm feeling unless I examine the weather. I can't ever lie to myself about my emotions—there's always the big, fat truth of it surrounding me, inescapable.

Right now we are surrounded by big, rabbit-tail clouds, overlaid against the blue sky like layers of buttercream icing.

I glance back at Carter. "Yeah. I'm good."

He wraps my hand around the crook of his arm, and my fingers settle over his biceps. "Vamos a celebrar."

⚡

WE MAKE IT INSIDE, WHERE THERE ARE PEOPLE CROWDED IN
the kitchen and living room so tightly, they don't even notice us
at first. Then my cousin Gus spots me, then Carter, and screams,
"She's here!"

Everyone cheers, with a chorus of *Surprise!* weaving in and
out of the noise.

I blink, and my sisters are there, each one grabbing an arm.
"You hate this, don't you?" Sage says in a low voice. There's no
reason for her to try to be quiet, though. She could shout all kinds
of curse words in three different languages and I doubt anyone
but Amá would hear her, and even that would only be because
Amá lives to find reasons to be disgusted with our lack of pro-
priety.

"Don't you?" I ask.

Sage laughs. "Didn't you wonder why I'm having a teeny tiny
wedding? More than half these assholes aren't invited."

"They're going to be there anyway. Mark my words."

As Sage shudders, Sky says, "Well, *I* don't mind."

"That's because everyone adores you. Well, except for Amá,
but she doesn't like anyone," Sage responds.

Sky's silent as Sage pulls us to the staircase. I think a lot of her
enjoyment of being here, now, surrounded by family, is because
everyone here believes her. They know about the old gods, even
if only through the stories by long-gone elders. They don't look
at her like a liar or a freak. They see her as she is—blessed and
beloved and beautiful.

"Where are you doing?" Nadia shouts.

"Sister stuff," Sage responds. "We'll be back down in just five
minutes!"

I furrow my brow. "Seriously, what are we doing? I don't know what *sister stuff* means," I say as we climb to the second floor, straight toward my room. Well, my old room, now.

Sage pushes the door open, and in the middle of my bed are a few presents, each covered with what looks like artisan wrapping paper—olive green with shimmery gold foil, brown packing paper dusted with fine glitter.

I hesitate in reaching for them. "Is this for me?"

"Of course!" Sky clasps her hands together. "Open them!"

I start with the smallest box and gasp when I get it open. Nestled in a black box is a wedding band, constructed of yellow gold carved into a series of twisting, spiraling curls and clouds. I turn it over in my hand and spot, within the swirls, the tiniest sun and eyelash-moon etched on opposite sides.

"Porque tu *regalo* es el clima," Sage explains. "Plus it should fit under your engagement ring perfectly. I threatened Carter for the measurements."

"You made this?" I ask, even though we both already know the answer to the question.

Sage doesn't bother responding. She holds out her hand and removes my engagement ring, placing the band first, then returning the giant Princess Di sapphire. It fits perfectly.

Tears sting at my eyes. "I don't know what to say."

"Don't cry! Open mine next!" Sky pushes the remaining presents toward me.

I rip the beautiful wrapping paper to shreds, open the box, and pull out . . .

"Lingerie." I try to make my incredulity sound sarcastic, rather than weirdly embarrassed, as I lift a black lace bodysuit with material strategically removed from the crotch and bust.

"Come on," Sky says. "Even if the marriage isn't . . . you

know, *real* or whatever. You still should have fun with Carter, right? He's so handsome. He's got really nice legs."

I narrow my eyes at her. "When did you see his legs?"

"Jealous already?" Sage laughs. "Open the rest of them."

I pull out a sheer red teddy, an emerald green nightgown, and the tiniest red bikini I've ever seen. The scraps of fabric for the nipples and vag wouldn't cover a quarter. "I may as well put on some floss. The coverage would be the same."

Sky and Sage laugh. "I have a similar one." Sage raises an eyebrow. "I'm pretty sure it's what got me pregnant. When Tenn saw me . . ." Her cheeks pinken. "Well, let's just say he didn't even take the time to get it off me."

"Because there's nothing to take off!" I yelp, lifting the three pieces of string.

I joke with my sisters some more, and then I thank them both with big hugs. It makes me happy to spend time with them. For too long, we were separate and sad and lonely. Getting them back in my life is the best thing that has ever happened to me.

And yet, when I glance out the window as we go to return to the party, the sky isn't as bright as I wish it were. The clouds are turning into a cold, light gray. And I know exactly what thoughts in the back of my mind are causing it.

Carter won't ever see me in this or any other lingerie. I won't be able to surprise him, to turn him on so thoroughly that he wouldn't even be bothered to take the pieces of lace and string off me before railing me into the next week.

I hear my ex's voice in my head. *No one else would ever want you.*

Even if somehow Carter realized he did find me attractive, and slept with me, he still wouldn't want *me*. The girl whose mother broke her beyond repair. The girl who can drown a whole city in a matter of weeks. The girl who struggled with depression and mania at the same time, and on top of those, a bad, quick temper.

My sisters think Carter has loved me since we were children. But if that's true . . . not even he wants me anymore. I can't help but think that Johnny's words—the things he used to hiss when he gripped me and shoved me around—might be just the tiniest bit true.

Thunder rumbles in the distance and I sigh. Pasting a smile on my face, I return to the party, where everyone demands that Carter and I kiss and kiss and kiss. I make sure the kisses are quick, mostly on the side of his wide, pink mouth, even when my family yells things like "What kind of a kiss is that?"

Carter goes from smiling big to staring at me closely to even outright frowning. It doesn't help when lightning keeps rivering across the sky. It's distant, but it doesn't escape his notice. "You okay?" he mutters near my ear as my relatives force us to dance our first dance as husband and wife. Someone—I don't know who—chose "Nunca es Suficiente" by the Los Ángeles Azules as our song.

"Kiss!" someone shouts again, rapping their fork against a champagne glass.

I can't look Carter in the eye, so I lean toward his neck. "Just a little overwhelmed," I whisper near his ear. Then I kiss the space between his ear and jaw, as light as I can, so everyone around me can stop chanting *kiss, kiss, kiss* for the next thirty fucking seconds.

He tenses so abruptly that he freezes midstep. "Sorry, sorry," he says as I nearly trip. But he lets go of me, even though our song isn't over yet, and says, "Gotta run to the bathroom." And he doesn't mean it figuratively. I mean, he *runs* away from me, disappearing in the hallway under the staircase.

As I watch him go, the clouds outside burst. The rain over the roof and against the windows dulls the sound of the music, of the people surrounding me eating their tamales and flan and sipping their café con leche.

Even though I'd suspected it for a while now, I feel like my fear has now been confirmed.

The man I have married doesn't just *not* want me. He can't *stand* me. He can't stand me so much, I question whether reviving our childhood friendship is even possible.

"Everything good?" Sky asks as she approaches, handing me a glass of what I hope is something very, very strong.

I throw it back without even asking what it is. It burns and I squeeze my eyes shut for a moment. "It doesn't matter," I finally respond.

Because it doesn't. This is just an arrangement. Carter wants his money. I wanted him to be my best friend again, but since that isn't going to work—me getting a PI to find my mom and finally fix me will have to do.

12

B Y FRIDAY, NADIA, MY SISTERS, TENN, AND I ARE ALL IN THE front yard, looking at a dozen or so cardboard boxes sitting neatly in the back of a truck Tenn borrowed from his best friend Abe. "You about ready?" Tenn asks, wiping the sweat off his brow. He looks over my shoulder at Sage, and he gives her a wink I'm sure she's just blushing and swooning over. I roll my eyes, but I can't help my smile. I'm not sure Sage would've stuck around Cranberry if it weren't for Tenn. Plus, he's thoughtful and sweet and easy on the eyes, too. He's going to make an amazing papá to my nephew.

"Yup," I say, and then all the ladies rush to hug me. Nadia and Sky in particular squeeze so tight, I feel like the wind is slowly being knocked out of me. "Jesus, women," I grunt. "It's just a fifteen-minute drive!"

When we all pull back, everyone's wiping their eyes. "Shut up!" I look at the cloudy sky so that the tears can go back in. "Stop crying!"

"You stop crying," Nadia tells me while sniffling. "Here." She shoves a small wicker basket in my hands.

I wrinkle my nose. "What the hell is this?" Inside are weird, dry-looking black things. I would say it's dried herbs, but I don't think I've ever seen Nadia let an herb rot before it was dried.

"Seeds," Nadia tells me. "I had a dream and I *know* you need them."

I roll my eyes, but I'm not really annoyed. Latine women, we're always telling each other about our dreams, our feelings, our *knowings*—to check in, to warn, or even just as an excuse to reconnect. It's a blessing to be loved in this way. Only a fool would think otherwise.

"What in the . . ." Sage says, looking in the basket, and then she grins. Soon that smile turns into a laugh. "Oh my God, *no way.*"

"What?" I glance around. "What in the world?"

Sky shrugs. "I know about as much as you."

I about stomp my foot. "Will someone tell me what's going on?" As the only response, Nadia is now laughing with Sage.

"We better get going," Tenn tells me. He gives Sage a kiss on the mouth and runs a hand over her still-flat belly. "I'll meet you at work."

"See you there." Sage is still laughing, and no matter how many times I ask, neither she nor Nadia will say what these ugly, weird-smelling seeds are.

I can't stay and berate them until they tell me. Nadia and Sage and Tenn all have work, and Sky has a job interview at St. Theresa's, the church Nadia practically raised us at. Carter's got a one-hour window between jobs in which he's expecting me, so he and Tenn can help me get my boxes in his place.

I climb in the truck and wave at my family. "Text me as soon as the interview's done," I call at Sky, who shoots me two thumbs up.

And then we're off. I don't let myself cry, or think, or even speak on the way to Carter's. I don't wonder about his mysterious abode I don't know a damn thing about, even though Sky has been waxing on its beauty pretty much nonstop since the wedding. I don't think about how that address he texted me last night—2848 Sea Green Boulevard—is now my new home.

I just keep telling myself as soon as we find my mom, I'm going to be fixed. I'm going to be whole again. And after that, eventually . . . I'll end up being wanted, too. The way Nate wants Fern, or Tennessee wants Sage.

Eventually, someone will want to marry me for real.

⚡

WHEN CARTER SAID HE LIVED IN THE COMMUNITY CALLED SUN-set View Cabanas, right next to the beach, I assumed his house would look like all the rest—cookie-cutter with beige side paneling and yards covered in lime green European grass up front, with the backyards butting up to the sandy beginning of the shore. The people who live here give their homes a "unique" feel by shopping at Kirkland's and Home Goods, leaning virtually identical *WELCOME* planks next to their front doors, hanging up artificially distressed beach décor proclaiming *Sandy Toes and Salty Kisses* alongside *HOME IS WHERE THE BEACH IS*.

But Carter's house *is* different. Its siding is deepwater blue, for one. The front and back yards are framed by what appears to be a legitimately distressed, tall fence—chipped turquoise paint revealing the warm wood beneath. There is no beachy-themed signage full of cliché ocean proverbs over the tiny porch nor anywhere on the entrance, for that matter. Flanking the camel-colored wood of the front door are massive terra-cotta planters filled with herbs—cilantro, mint, Cuban oregano, and Mexican tarragon. That's it.

The door opens as Tenn and I walk up, each with two boxes in our arms. Carter stands there, looking like he can hardly believe we're here. "You made it."

I want to ask, *Did you really think I wouldn't show? Am I that unreliable?* But instead, I raise my eyebrows and smile and say, "Yep," before hauling my ass inside to deposit the boxes in the front hallway.

It takes us only two more trips to get everything in. I'm catching my breath as Tenn and Carter do that weird man-hug thing where they slap their hands together and then each other's backs as they lean in. Tenn turns to me and pats me on the head. "Congrats, y'all." He lowers his voice as he kisses my cheek. "Anything goes down, you can come stay with me and Sage anytime. Day or night." I can't help but smile at the offer. I don't think anyone thinks I'm in danger with Carter—unlike when I was still with Johnny—but it feels good to know that people still care about me like that.

And then Tenn heads out. He's gone so quickly, I wonder if it's because of how awkward things feel now that I'm here. I put my hands on my hips and survey Carter, who then shoves his hands in his pockets and clears his throat in my direction.

I feel like he wants to say "Welcome" or "Here we are," but he holds back, keeping his expression a really weird mix of uncertain and stormy. He inclines his head past the front hallway, indicating for me to go first. When I do, my jaw drops.

The living area is this wide-open floor plan, the back of which is stuffed with a series of floor-to-ceiling windows that overlook the misty beach. The floors are hardwood, the kitchen open and off to the side, full of smooth, shiny cabinets in aquamarine framing slick, stainless steel appliances that look brand new and untouched. There's an island nook with barstools, a little dining table between that and the couches and love seats that surround a cast-iron fireplace. A large flatscreen is mounted on the wall. The furniture is modern yet rustic, stylish yet comfy.

"Jesus, Carter," I say. "You own this place? Like, not-renting-actually-*own* it?" Even renting would seem impossible to afford.

Carter's jaw tightens. It's driving me crazy that he won't give me anything right now. After I kissed his neck at our wedding, he's been acting so distant and dumb. Is this how it's gonna be? Me trying to act normal while he acts like he hit his head and any kind of relaxed, joyful emotion just fell out of his body? "I bought it myself. With cash."

My jaw drops further. "Your grandmother gave you your money already?"

If he clenches his jaw any more, he's going to get TMJD in the next minute, I swear. "I bought it myself. Abuela Erika hasn't paid me yet."

My jaw drops once again, or maybe even further. Carter . . . he's never been rich, has he? Not *this* rich, at least. He's been working since he was a teenager, making sandwiches and rice bowls, serving at a swanky restaurant uptown, bartending at Lost Souls, and now he works full time at Cranberry Rose, doing what, I'm still not sure.

"I saved money, Teal."

Like that explains it. He'd have to *make* this kind of money to save it first, and I know for a fact that he spent many years using his paychecks to help with his mother's, and later his sisters', bills.

When he sees the look on my face, he adds, "You know Abraham Arellano? He's really good at investing. He can turn a dollar into a fortune." Carter shrugs. "He helped me a few years back, when Mami needed me to cover rent . . . the mentoring sort of all turned into this." He lifts his hands and sighs, like this conversation is boring the shit out of him. "Come on, I'll give you the tour." His tone is flat, like he would rather be eating a bowl of nails, and it's also dismissive. This conversation is over. Time to move on and see where I'll be sleeping for the next year.

I fold my arms over my stomach and clench my own jaw as he points. "Living room, kitchen." He leads me down a hallway next to the kitchen. "Workout room, bathroom, bedroom." He moves fast, too fast for me to really see anything. Still, one detail about this house doesn't escape me, and soon it may as well be a flashing red sign in my head.

"Carter. Why is there only one bed?"

He sighs and runs a hand over the stubble of his chin. He's dressed really casual—gray sweatpants, an old shirt cut into a tank top, the arm holes so big I can see the sides of his chest and some of his abdomen. It's working for me, unfortunately, so I force my gaze to the topic at hand—the bed. The only *one* bed.

"The living room couch turns into a pull-out. So if you're really uncomfortable with—"

"With sharing a bed with my fake husband? Carter, I barely share beds with men I'm actually with."

"You were with Johnny for six years. Didn't you stay at his place all the time?"

"Well, yeah. But not in his bed." Carter stares at me until I explain, "Johnny didn't like how I looked first thing in the morning. I used to spend the night on his couch so I could wake up early and brush my hair and put on makeup."

Carter's fists clench and he closes his eyes briefly. "Please tell me that's not true."

I huff. Now he wants to act like he cares? "Fine. It's a lie. I just lied my face off. Johnny used to love sharing the bed with me. He would just hold me all night. And I never woke up to him needing to have sex with me, whether I wanted to or not."

Carter leans against the wall, his hands still fists. "Jesus. Teal. Is he still at that place on Broadway? I'm going to fucking go over there and—"

"Enough." I can't stand here and listen to Carter go all white knight on me, especially since he's been treating me like shit in his own way since we got married. "I'll sleep on the pull-out. Whatever."

Carter pauses and then lets out a long sigh. "If that's what you want."

"If that's what *I* want?" I can't help but snap back. "*I'm* not the one allergic to being in the same room as you, you know."

Carter's eyes widen in dismay. "What the hell are you talking about, Teal? I have no problem sharing a bed with you. You're the one getting weird about it."

"Hey. I don't have any issues with bed sharing, or dancing, or having to touch and kiss each other for show. I'm perfectly fine with all kinds of affection! I'm Latina, for God's sake!"

I don't even realize I'm yelling until Carter raises his voice back to me. "Fine! So we'll share the damn bed, then!"

"Fine!" I scream back. "We'll sleep next to each other all night, every night." I lower my voice. "But if you so much as wince in my direction if I accidentally get too close to you, I will move to the couch. And if you make a single comment about how my face looks in the morning, I will camp in your backyard. After carving up *your* face with a syringe."

He growls. Like, legit growls, and the hairs on my arms stand straight up, and not in an unpleasant way, either. "You can't camp out there. There are rules about campfires." He turns away, crossing his arms. "And how the hell do you carve someone's face with a syringe, anyway?"

"Shut up." The idiot's trying not to laugh at me and he's failing. I can tell by the way the side of his mouth is squished up like a dried apricot. Plus his shoulders are starting to shake. If I don't leave now, I'm going to laugh next, and then he'll think I'm not being serious about this. Not that I was serious about the syringe threat. I mean the whole rest of it. Because I *am* serious. If Carter tells me any of the things Johnny ever did—how my lips were too dry to kiss, how awful I smelled everywhere, how my hair looked like it belonged to a homeless woman—I wouldn't just sleep in the backyard, I'd legit move out there. Or back to Nadia's. Whichever was more convenient at the time.

So I do the only thing I can think of. I grab my shoes and run.

13

CARTER AND I SURVIVE THAT FIRST NIGHT IN HIS BED WITH me lining up pillows between us like a tall, squishy wall of fortification. No matter what Carter says, I know he doesn't like to get close to me. Whether that's out of fear, disgust, or straight-up hatred, or some combination of the three, that's beyond me. Just, at this point, the last thing my self-esteem needs is my husband, fake or not, dry-heaving after I accidentally touch his calf with my foot.

In the morning, he gives me a Publix gift card and asks if I'd please have dinner ready when he gets home. My immediate first reaction is to laugh in his face. What am I, his fifties housewife now? Should I curl my hair and put on pearls and high heels, too? But then I realize that really, now that we're married, he's kind of got all the power here. This is his house. This whole thing is his agreement. And until I get a job, I'm kind of beholden to all that crap. So I *hmm* in agreement, and he makes a face at me like he doesn't believe I'll do what he asks—I mean, come on, it's dinner, not a request to build him a life-sized, functional sandcastle— which just makes me want to not only cook his dinner but put my whole-ass foot in it, too.

After I grab ingredients, I spend my day halfheartedly look-ing for jobs. It's not that I don't want a job. It's that the whole process of filling out applications, writing cover letters, and send-ing résumés, in the hopes that some asshole will pluck it out of an enormous digital pile of other people's paperwork and offer me an interview—the whole thing makes me kind of want to smash my head out the nearest window and scream.

I unpack my things, which doesn't take all that long, and after that, I'm having a facedown with a crumpled piece of paper I'd placed in front of me at the kitchen table.

New Year's Resolutions for Teal Flores
1. *Stop being selfish.*
2. *Make it up to Sage.*
3. *Make it up to Sky.*
4. *Become best friends with Carter again.*

I haven't made a whole lotta progress on this. I did help Sky shop, and that was fun. But also, a few outfits on her grandmoth-er's dime doesn't exactly absolve, you know, me deleting eight years of her life by being a dumbass. I'm still not sure number four is even possible, so I'm not focusing on that right now.

But *Make it up to Sage*—I already have a plan for that. Sort of.

Opening up my laptop, I begin my search to figure out where I'm going to source all the pretty, pretty dahlias for her Septem-ber wedding.

⚡

CARTER WALKS IN AT SIX ON THE DOT.

If things were like before, when we were still BFFs, I know how he'd be. He'd walk in with a huge smile, the one that makes even my toes feel warm and tingly and weird. He'd say some corny-ass shit like *"Honey,* I'm *home."* He'd greet me with a hug and a peck on the cheek, 'cause that's what Latines do, whether we're dating or not or want each other or not or even know each other or not.

He doesn't do any of that. He pauses as he takes off his shoes in the hallway, and through the reflection of one of the living room mirrors, I see his silhouette. He stands and squares his shoulders and takes a deep breath, like even the idea of looking at me makes him feel like he's being shipped off to war. He turns and walks in, his eyes meeting mine immediately.

Lord, he looks handsome. His face a little brown from the sun, his button-down flannel rumpled from a day of good, manual labor. His jeans snug, his feet bare. Being slightly turned on by a man's hairy feet—that's where I am, I guess. When those feet belong to Carter, at least.

"Uh. Hi." Then his gaze darts everywhere else but me. "You cooked?"

His obvious discomfort pisses me off. But thing is, I've already run too damn much this week. My right knee feels like it's going to crack, it hurts so bad. So all I can do now is suck it up. No outbursts, no lightning storm rampages. Just take a deep breath, in and out, counting, and then I nod. "Uh-huh," I say as brightly as I can. "Why don't you sit and I'll bring you a plate."

"You don't have to—"

Aaaand my patience runs out. "Jesus Christ, Carter, have a fucking seat, will you?"

He closes his mouth and sits, his eyes on me, even more wary now.

And you know what my brain goes to in that moment?

I think about ordering Carter around in a very different circumstance. In bedroom-related circumstances. And I'm not going to lie. It's a turn-on. So much so, that momentarily my anger dampens, and then I realize what my effed-up brain is up to, and I get even *angrier*.

What is *wrong* with me?

I finish topping our dinner—blackened salmon over cacio e pepe, and a side of crispy Brussels sprouts—with a little flourish of chopped flat-leaf parsley and then take our plates to the table.

Thunder rumbles nearby, close enough to make the silverware I've already set on the table ever-so-slightly rattle.

"Looks great," Carter says, and then he digs in. "Holy shit. *Teal.* This is . . . *mmm* . . . so *good.*" The *sounds* he makes. My God. Has he always eaten food the same way most people have orgasms? Or am I just, like, in major need of getting laid?

My brain flashes images to me that are basically X-rated. Images of Carter. Tied to the bed. While I endlessly tease him with my tongue.

"You going to eat?"

I blink and look down at my plate. "Uh. Yeah."

After a few minutes of the both of us eating quietly—me sort of picking at the food, Carter wolfing his down as fast as possible, Carter asks, "You going to tell me what's the matter?"

I stare at him for a moment, my mind blank, because I don't know how to put it into words. *Um, you see, Carter. I just realized I have a new kink featuring you, specifically, on your knees, while I order you to do things like eat me for dinner.* I clear my throat and break eye contact. That image . . . didn't help.

I need to remember why all of this is so dumb. And it all comes down to the fact that Carter doesn't want to touch me. Not like that. And not like anything, it feels. So. Time for a subject change.

"I told Sage I would buy her flowers for her wedding, but it's way too fucking expensive."

"How expensive?"

When I tell him the amount, he winces. "For flowers?"

"Apparently, they are very special flowers. Difficult to import, so they have to be local and shit. And of course she's going to want them to be organically grown."

"How would she know the difference?" I give him a look and he smiles sheepishly. "Right. She could just ask the plants and they would tell her."

"Right."

"Well, once we get Gene's money, you could get them, no problem. I can cover you in the meantime."

I shake my head. "Hell no. No way am I spending that amount on flowers. I'm working on a better and cheaper solution. Besides, I want to use the money for a PI, anyway."

Carter's basically licking his plate clean at this point, so I grab it to serve him more. "So your mom's not in town, then?" he asks.

I snort. "Amá threatened me when I asked her about it. So my guess is something is up. Maybe Mama's here, or maybe she was here recently but isn't anymore . . . who knows. But we're not getting answers from my family." I'd tried to bring up the subject to Nadia, but before I could even get the question out, she raised one mahogany pencil–filled eyebrow at me and said, *I know, Teal, that you're about to ask something that's none of your business, so I suggest you don't.*

Damn, Latine elders with magical powers are unnecessarily difficult.

"Speaking of family . . ." Carter begins, and with that tone, I already know I'm not going to like whatever he's about to say. I set his plate down in front of him and return to my seat, my arms folded over my stomach. "Mine heard about our getting married."

And I'm right. I don't like this one bit. "What do you mean, *heard*?"

He bites his lip and it's so damn hot, I want to smack him. Spank him. Kiss him.

I take a breath and command my brain to stop getting pervy. It doesn't listen.

Luckily, Carter's keen on distracting me enough. "I kind of didn't tell them about . . . you know. Our marriage."

I blink slowly. "And why is that?"

He blinks slowly. "To avoid drama, like I said before."

I stand and point. "You said they weren't invited to the wedding to avoid drama. Not that you'd keep the whole damn marriage a secret from them!"

He frowns and waves a fork around. "Same thing, no?"

"No, it's not the same thing. Which is ridiculous because the whole point of our holy matrimony was so that they would know about it." I huff. "They're going to think that you're hiding me. Like you're ashamed of me."

I know this marriage isn't real. That my accusation doesn't exactly ring true when I'm talking about something fake. How can Carter be ashamed of me when I'm not really his?

And yet I can't stop the emotions—dark, slithering, overwhelming—from rising up inside *and* outside me. Thunder rumbles even closer, so close the windows rattle in their frames. Something horrible inside me whispers one of my greatest fears, straight from the memory of my abusive ex's lips. *No one else would ever want you.*

Not even Carter, in his epically fake way, can pretend that he really wants me.

He frowns at me even deeper, both his jawline and shoulders rigid. "What the hell are you talking about? How could I be ashamed of you?"

I was never good about holding my emotions in. If it didn't come out of my mouth, or through my fists, the sky made sure damn well everyone knew what was happening inside me. Right now, I feel a mix of all three manifestations. My hands are tightened. There's a storm happening outside, because of course there is. Running until I felt like my bones were being ripped inside out earlier today can't help this. Nothing can help this. So I take a deep breath and begin to count. "One. You act like you can't stand the sight of me. Or the touch of me. When I kissed you during our first dance as esposo y esposa, you ran away from me like I stuck a syringe in your neck."

Now he's standing, the anger vibrating off him so visibly, it's like those heat glimmers you see above the road in the summer, like steam is coming off him or something. "What is it with you and syringes?" he nearly shouts.

"Two, you disappeared at Nate's wedding when you were supposed to be my date! Three, you acted like I tried to stab your eyes when I asked you to that wedding in the first place!"

He runs a hand over his head. "Let me guess, stab my eyes with syringes."

I swear I almost let a fist fly over that one. "This isn't funny, Carter! Look, I know I'm a fuckup, okay? I know that. I know no one in their right mind would ever want me. But can't you just, I don't know, pretend? Is it so hard to stay in the damn room when I am supposed to be a wife kissing her husband on their freaking wedding day?"

Carter stomps over to me so fast, I nearly choke on my next inhale of breath. *His* breath is too fast. His eyes too wild. His lips too pink. "I left Nate's wedding because I was trying to keep my distance with you. I was trying to not get my hopes up that you'd marry me. The problem with being near you, and touching you, Teal, it's not that I don't want to. It's the opposite." He laughs, but it's not jovial, it's the laugh you make when you can't believe how dumb you're being. He takes a step closer, and now I can feel his breath on my chest. Inexplicably, stupidly, my nipples tighten, like they know what he's gonna say next. "I left you during our first dance because when you kissed my neck, I got so hard, it fucking *hurt*. And I didn't want everyone to see."

What the hell could I say to that?

Nothing.

I guess that's why instead of saying anything at all, I throw my arms around his shoulders and kiss Carter Velasquez.

14

WHEN CARTER AND I FIRST KISSED, NEARLY ONE YEAR ago . . . it was hot. Although I also initiated that one, he quickly took control, not letting me rip our clothes off pretty much immediately by holding my wrists on the bed, on either side of my head. "Lentamente," he'd whispered, "please, mami." That just made me crazier, kissing him harder, pushing my hands over his stomach, where his muscles undulated under as he tried so hard to not thrust. He wanted to go slow with me, gods know why, but I liked it. Correction: I *loved* it.

I've spent so many stupid nights thinking about it. Wondering how it would have been with him. I bet it wouldn't have been like with Johnny, who always kept his eyes closed tight, thinking about his most recently viewed porno. That isn't conjecture. He literally told me that he had a hard time staying hard if it was "just me."

Nate kept his eyes closed a lot of the time, too, when we were together. It brought me out of the moment. I kept wondering who he was really thinking about.

This wasn't the case with Carter. He kept his glimmering gold eyes wide open, looking me over and over, like I was some kind of goddess made manifest in human form. Like he couldn't believe he'd been given the privilege of touching me. When he pulled my shirt up to my neck, he'd stared at my bra for so long, I thought maybe he didn't like what he was seeing. But then he immediately proved me wrong with his mouth.

I always thought if we had gone all the way, it would have kept on like that. It would have been the closest I'd ever gotten to lovemaking in my whole life.

Now though, what we're doing. It's the complete opposite of lovemaking.

When I basically jumped on him, lips first, he grabbed my ass and whisked me to the counter, where I wrapped my legs around him tight. Our mouths connected the whole time. Like we rehearsed this shit.

We kiss each other like if we don't, we'll drown. He dips his tongue in my mouth, over and over, in tune to his hips, pressing his hot, hard length right where I want it the most.

I'm going to come. I'm going to come and all of our clothes are *still on*.

I moan his name when he breaks the kiss to slide his tongue down the side of my neck, and this does something to him. He jerks his hand from my hip to the open leg of these little shorts I've got on, and his fingers dig their way under my panties. The shock of feeling him there makes me gasp.

"You're so wet," he says, breathless like he can't believe it.

"I'm always wet for you," I respond.

And I don't know why, but me saying that, it's all wrong somehow. He freezes and then slides his fingers from my shorts. He pulls his hips back from mine a few inches as he says, "You shouldn't tell me stuff like that." Before I can respond, he looks into my face and adds, "We shouldn't have done this. This . . . it's a mistake."

And you know what this pendejo does next?

He *leaves*.

He literally runs away from me, grabbing his shoes on his way out the front door. He doesn't look at me as he gruffly calls, "My family will be here for lunch on Tuesday." The next thing I hear is the door slamming and then his car's wheels squealing to who knows where.

All because I told him, what? The truth?

It *is* the truth. Ever since Carter and I first kissed last year, something about that idiot just instantly turns me on. Something about the intense way he watches me, or how stupid nice he is to me.

Or was, rather. What he did just now, leaving me on the counter, breathless, eyes full of tears, a sky full of lightning—this is more than not nice, or mean, even. It's cruel.

I will never forgive him for this.

$$ \frac{\ }{\ } $$

I SPEND WAY TOO MUCH TIME TRYING TO FIGURE OUT THE sleeping situation, since (a) no way in hell am I sharing a bed with that asshole again, and (b), the pull-out he so chivalrously offered feels like it's made from the demolished parts of a greenhouse. I may as well sleep inside a shark's mouth, right over its many layers of teeth, for all the comfort it provides.

I also don't want to go to Nadia's. It feels too much like admitting defeat, not just to myself and to Carter, but also to my family. We've been married for mere days. *Days*. Granted, I'm not exactly known for my relationship expertise, but even I know sleeping elsewhere after just days of marriage, even a fake one, is classified as pathetic. Knowing my luck, one of his family members will see me hauling ass back home, and it will make its way to Abuela Erika, and all of this will have been for naught.

I refuse for all of this to have been for naught.

So I snoop all around Carter's house and find a sleeping bag. I spend half an hour making it up in his gym room. I move my bedside table—the one next to my side of the bed in which I spent exactly a single night—next to it, along with the little lamp, and my stack of books I'm in the middle of, as well as a candle. The carpet in this room is thick so it isn't bad, not really.

I pick up my phone and schedule an appointment for a local PI with good reviews. I register to the local dahlia society's annual tuber sale, happening in only two days. And then I Insta-stalk Leilani, who apparently is having the time of her life, stealing art from nonwhite people and "riding the tide of love with the universe in motion" all over NoCal.

She's also managed to acquire a *whole new face* since moving. When I click on her latest selfie, I swear my jaw drops and rolls out the door like on some kind of old-school cartoon.

Look, I'm not a plastic surgeon, or even a doctor of any kind. But my favorite sort of reality television features cosmetic surgery—*Botched, Nip/Tuck*, you name it and I'm a whore for it. Thus, in my trashy-TV-informed opinion, Lani's had Botox injections on her forehead and eyebrows, filler in her nasolabial folds, and most obvious of all of these, lip injections. The way she's pursed them after slathering on shiny fuchsia lip gloss, it looks like the top lip is about to bust open.

I've got nothing against cosmetic surgery. Amá Sonya has had at least one facelift that I know of, and I'm pretty sure she gets her lips filled routinely. I think she looks elegant. I've even investigated getting a (small) BBL, but the long list of risks didn't seem worth it to me.

That said, Lani has spent her entire life professing that she'll never do anything "fake" with regards to anti-aging, that with her routine of organic essential oil facials and mud and algae baths, she would age gracefully the "natural way." Seeing her face transform in such a short amount of time just reinforces what an asshole hypocrite she is, and it pisses me off enough that I toss my phone halfway across the room before tucking myself in for the night, having had quite enough of the internet for the day.

I fall asleep, and when I wake up, at seven thirty in the morning, thanks to my alarm?

I'm back in bed.

"What the—" I mutter, glancing up. Then I jump up.

The table's back, along with my books, my candle, my phone charger. The long line of pillows in the middle of the bed is there, along with the throw pillows I had collected to make up my gym room bed.

"Carter!" I yell, stomping out. "Carter, what the fuck?"

But the coward is gone.

I swear, I'm so mad I feel like a hurricane is instantaneously going to descend upon our house and rip it to pieces. The sky outside is dark, and wind howls against the windows like angry spirits.

Until I see that the pull-out is made up. Well, messed up. I approach it slowly. I definitely folded it up yesterday, which means Carter undid all that work. Which means Carter spent the night here.

I push my breath out, defeated. The sky clears and sunshine pours through the wall of windows, making everything appear edged in yellow gold. My mood shifted that fast.

He put me in bed. But he knew I didn't want to sleep next to him, so he didn't do that against my will. And I gotta say, that bed is a hell of a lot nicer than carpet, no matter how thick.

I hate how thoughtful that was.

I spend the day digging up sod from the front yard. I have to grow Sage's damn dahlias somewhere. Because yes, I, Teal Flores, a woman who doesn't know the first thing about plants, am going to grow my sister's wedding flowers. And weirdly enough, I don't mind the work of it—of shoveling, at least. Digging through the rough, tight knots of grass roots is kind of like running, only it doesn't make my knee feel like it's breaking into several thousand pieces.

After showering, I look at jobs some more, and then spend a good twenty minutes stressing out over dinner, even though it's only three in the afternoon. Carter didn't ask me to make a meal. But he's expecting it, right? I'm the one staying at home, not working, with access to the nicest kitchen I've ever cooked in. Then again, I really don't feel like cooking for someone who is now making a legitimate habit of running away from me. He can tell me he's attracted to me all he likes, but actions speak louder than words. And right now, his actions have bruised my ego and my feelings and, to be honest, have made my chest feel a bit like someone punched a hole through my sternum.

But also—I don't want to be selfish anymore. Hence New Year's resolution number one.

I decide to call the least selfish person I know to get some advice.

"What's up?" Sage asks. I put her on speakerphone as I prepare a cup of café Cubano on Carter's awesome espresso machine.

"Question. If Tennessee put you on the kitchen counter and fingered you, and then told you it was all a mistake and ran away, and it's been a whole day and you haven't seen or heard from him since, *but* . . . if he did kind of a nice thing while you were sleeping after all that . . . would you cook him dinner?"

I guess Sage was drinking water or something, because the only thing I hear in response is sputtering and coughing.

"Hello?" I ask. "You good, Sage?"

Then Sky's voice is on the phone. "Hey. Did you just say Carter fingered you?"

I close my eyes and stifle a groan. Not that I don't necessarily want Sky to know my problems, but that girl needs to get laid or something. She always focuses on the pervy parts of anyone's business.

"Was he any good at it?" she presses, even though I haven't even answered her first question yet. See, that's exactly what I'm talking about.

There's some fumbling with the phone, and then Sage speaks up, her voice a little hoarse but no longer choking. "You're on speaker now. 'Cause Sky's here. Which you already know." She clears her throat. "So let me get this straight. Your husband put you on the counter, touched you—"

"Fingered her," Sky corrects.

Sage ignores this. "And then he said it was a mistake and took off?"

"Yes."

"And you want to cook him dinner?"

"I'm wondering if I should cook him dinner."

"What are you thinking of making for dinner?" Sky asks.

I shake my head even though neither of them can see me. "I don't know yet! Because I don't know if I should make food in the first place!"

"Well," Sky begins thoughtfully, "did he at least give you an orgasm?"

I sigh. "Is that really relevant?"

"Yes," they both respond at the same time.

"Well, then, no. He left me hot and bothered and disturbed." And some emotion way too close to heartbreak to admit to.

Sage responds first. "Don't cook him dinner. Come out with us."

I scrunch up my nose. "Where are you guys, anyway?"

"Nadia wanted help fixing the wallpaper in her en suite."

"Oh. Ew." I hate home repair crap. If you need help getting ab definition for the summer, I'm your girl. If you need someone to make a few fancy meals, I can do it. Apparently if you need someone to dig up sod, I'm down for that, too. But if you need someone to repair a broken stair, or paint a wall, or clean the gutters, do not call yours truly. I'd very much rather hire anyone to take care of that stuff.

"So right now, stop thinking about Carter," Sage says. "Watch a movie, paint your nails, put on a sheet mask. Then get dressed up and meet us at Evergreen's Brewery for dinner."

I make a face. "That's all the way in Troy!"

"What's the problem, you got a job to get up for in the morning?" That sick burn is from Sky, who adds, "Because I do!"

"What?" I shriek. "You got the job? Why didn't you say anything?"

"I'm telling you now. And we'll celebrate tonight. No excuses."

And then my baby sister hangs up the phone.

"Okay, then," I say as I grab my café and a bottle of nail polish on the way to the sofa.

15

EVERGREEN'S IS RIGHT ON THE CUSP OF CRANBERRY AND Troy, the nearest town to us. It's a bit of a drive, but after Sky called and decided she'd rather we ride all together, so we can roll down the windows of my car and blast the Backstreet Boys' first album, it feels only like ten minutes of late nineties, nostalgic, wind-in-my-hair scream-singing. Do we know, exactly, what all the BSB lyrics even mean? No. But does that mean we're not going to yell/sing the words as we weave through rush hour traffic? Also no.

Evergreen's is one of those rare restaurants where literally every single meal is excellent. It's straight-up Southern comfort food, but everything has a subtle, tasty twist. Like their sweet potato casserole is seasoned with cardamom and orange zest alongside the traditional cinnamon and allspice, and their mac and cheese features an orgasmic topping made up of Creole-spiced kettle-cooked potato chips. The building is pretty big, in the middle of its own parking lot, made up of rustic-style logs and a big deck for people who prefer to eat outside. There's a twenty-minute wait, which we use to get updates on the baby (he's still microscopic in size, Sage hasn't had morning sickness, but she does have an insane, supernatural sense of smell, to the point where she knows the hour someone has last showered).

As soon as we're seated, I turn to Sky and say, "Tell us about the job."

She shrugs her shoulder. "I'd rather hear about you fooling around with your husband."

I make a face. "Um. No. Not drunk enough yet." I take a sip of water. "What is your official job title, anyway?"

Sky clears her throat. "Officially, I am St. Theresa's Catholic Church for Wanderers and Pilgrims' *librarian technician.*"

"No shit," I breathe. "I thought you were going to be in the main office, like, I don't know—answering phones or something." I lightly shove her shoulder. "You see? Our shopping spree has worked out freaking perfect. Now you can dress like the sexy librarian *technician* you are."

Sky shrugs again, but her cheeks are a little pink and she can't hide how pleased she is. "Yeah. The best part about it is most of their library is in the basement."

Sage furrows her brow. "What's so great about the basement?"

Sky lifts her hands with a grin. "No one sees me! So there's no one treating me like the town freak!"

Sage and I share a glance. "Sky," she begins. "You know you're not—"

"I know I'm not a freak, you guys. Well, not any more than you two. I'm just saying. I like being alone. And this job means I'm alone a lot, which I find very agreeable." She turns to me. "Now, tell us about the fingering."

Of course, this is when our server shows up. Who is a young, attractive guy whose diamond-pierced ears are now bright red.

"What can I get you ladies to drink?" he asks without looking any of us in the eyes.

We make our drink and appetizer orders, and this is when my phone buzzes. It's a text from Carter. You okay?

"Ughhh," I groan, flipping my phone around to show my sisters. "You see what I have to deal with here?"

Sage smiles as she leans in to read. "Oh no," she says in a dull tone. "Your husband is concerned over you. What trauma."

I give her a fake glare. "You know what I mean."

"Actually, we don't," Sky says, sipping her water. "You haven't told us anything yet, remember?"

I sigh. "Alcohol, remember? I need alcohol."

"Let's start slowly, then," Sage says. "Why didn't he make you come? Was he just not skilled enough? You weren't into it?"

"That's not exactly starting slowly, but whatever." I shrug. "We were fighting, you know. Screaming at each other and stuff, and then all of a sudden I was on the kitchen counter and his hand was in my underwear."

Our server clears his throat. "Drinks, ladies," he mumbles. Now his cheeks are pinker than Sky's strawberry daiquiri.

"Poor guy," I murmur as I throw back my entire shot of whiskey.

"Don't change the subject," Sky says, snapping her fingers. "Then what happened?"

"I—" Now my cheeks are threatening to become warm. "I told him he always makes me wet."

We're interrupted by our server tossing a plate of sizzling jalapeño poppers on the center of our table and then sprinting away. When I glance back at my sisters, we're all trying so hard to hold our laughter in, we're snorting.

"I think he's doing it on purpose," Sky says, glancing somewhere behind me. "He keeps glancing this way with all his server friends. He's updating them on your story."

I roll my eyes. "Great. Just what I need." I sigh. "Anyway. I told him that he always turns me on, he told me I shouldn't tell him stuff like that, and then he ran away."

"He ran away," Sage repeats.

"I told you that on the phone. Literally out the door. Squealing tires like we were in a sitcom or something."

"You also said he said it was a mistake," Sky adds softly.

I nod. "That, too."

Sage shakes her head. "Carter is a nice guy. Not one of those fake 'nice guys' who are only friends with women to eventually get sex. Like, he's really, sincerely nice."

She's not wrong. If Carter only wanted sex . . . he could've had it by now, is all I'm saying. I raise an eyebrow. "And . . . ?"

"And I'm just reiterating. I don't think he did that to be a villain." She tosses the remaining bit of popper in her mouth. "I think he was protecting his heart."

"Ooh, right. That makes sense," Sky adds. "He's afraid of getting in too deep with his emotions. So he ran. Even though his fingers were literally inside you." She makes a really bizarre motion with her hands, flinging her arm up and pointing her fingers—all five—straight while wiggling them back and forth.

Sage shakes her head. "Nope. No. Not how fingering works."

"This could be fingering!" Sky announces, not exactly quietly. "You all just aren't creative enough."

"Ahem." I'm not surprised our server is back the moment Sky is miming a robotic hand gesture indicating peril and calling it fingering. "Ready to order entrées, ladies?"

I pick the hazelnut-crusted chicken-fried steak, and Sky and Sage both order chicken pot pie. Our server still won't make eye contact, but he is also no longer bright red, so I guess he's recovering.

"No more man talk," I declare after he's out of earshot. "Right now we're celebrating our official librarian of a sister. So let's celebrate."

We eat and laugh for the better part of two hours. Carter texts two more times (Let me know when you're going to be home and We should probably talk). Instead of responding, I order more and more whiskey. Too much more whiskey. By the time I stand up after we pay, the floor is legit spinning under my feet.

Sky holds me up by my arms while Sage digs through my Fendi baguette for the keys. "Looks like I'm driving us back."

"You don't have to do that, Sage," I blubber. "You always do everything for us. Since we were little. You shouldn't have to do everything anymore."

"I want us all to get home in one piece, Teal. So I'm driving."

When we get back in my car, I open the back door and sprawl in. Sky has to help me with my seat belt, but I'm far too gone to be embarrassed.

"You better drink a ton of water when you get home," Sage tells me from the driver's seat. "Or you're going to be sorry tomorrow."

"You're going to be sorry tomorrow!" I shout, pointing out the window. "You're the one who's pregnant."

"Pregnant, not drunk off her ass," Sky says, smirking at me like she finds something hilarious about all this.

"I'm going to text Carter back," I announce, pulling my phone from my bag.

"Oh no you don't," Sky responds, wrestling me for it. It's not a fair fight since my grip is nonexistent right now. "I'll text him for you."

"Tell him I'm so pissed at him. Tell him he's dead to me. But only after he fucks me first." Sage is cracking up. "What's so funny?" I demand. "He didn't finish what he started. I want him to finish it, that's all this is."

"Sure, Jan." She shrugs. "I just think you and Carter are hiding from your feelings in different ways."

"I don't have feelings."

"Whatever you say, Miss It Rains When I'm Sad."

"There." Sky hands me my phone. Though the letters are blurry, I can see she's written Carter, Hey it's Sky. We all went out to dinner and Teal drank too much. Sage is dropping me off at Nadia's, then Teal at your place, and Tenn will pick Sage up so you don't have to worry about Teal's car. Oh, and Teal keeps saying you didn't finish the job . . . Here she inserted an emoji of a hand with the peace sign alongside a winky face. So you better get on that.

"Damn right," I mutter before leaning my head against the window and promptly passing out.

Next thing I know, I'm being pulled out of the car by both Sky and Sage. I blink groggily at them. "Why didn't I get a name that starts with an *S*? Didn't Mama know I'd feel left out?"

"Hey." Carter appears from the shadows, wearing a thin gray shirt and flannel pajama bottoms. It only occurs to me now that we're in his driveway. "I got it."

"No, you don't," I hiss at him. "You proved to me earlier you don't got *it* at all."

Sky erupts into giggles. "She's all yours!"

"Stop laughing at me," I mumble. "I forgot to tell you guys, Mama's in town. I heard all about it from the viejitas."

There's a pause, and somewhere to my left, Sage says in a gasp, "What did you just say?"

"She can barely stand," Carter says, his voice gruff as he lifts me and tosses me over his back. I'm far too gone to argue with him about this, mainly because he feels so good—warm and sturdy and smelling like a mix of salt water and cinnamon sugar. "I'll take it from here."

"I hired a PI," I call as Carter carries me inside. I frown. "Or did I? I can't—"

The door slams shut, and my conversation with my sisters is over.

16

CARTER CARRIES ME THROUGH THE LIVING AREA AND around the kitchen corner to the hallway, and deposits me gently on the bed. "It's bright in here," I grumble.

"There's literally no lights on." I can't tell anything by his bland tone. Is he angry? Resentful? Amused? Before I can ask, he adds, "Be right back."

I groan. I'm still wearing my out-to-dinner clothes. I stand—slowly—and take off my satin crop top, and slide my high-waisted trousers to the floor. When Carter returns, I'm wearing nothing but my black lace push-up bra, decidedly not-matching boy shorts in neon green, and nude slipper socks.

He freezes at the entryway to the room, a large glass of water in his hand. In fact, he stops so suddenly that his hand gets doused, dripping with the water, but he doesn't even notice. His eyes are on me, all over me, and even though he was right, there aren't any lamps on in here, from the window an outdoor light illuminates his face enough that I see the way he swallows thickly. "What are you doing?" he grits out.

"I was uncomfortable." I reach behind as Carter's eyes widen. "And now I'm getting comfortable."

He turns one whole second after my bra falls to the floor, his breath heavy. "Teal . . ."

"Don't you want to?" I ask him. "You wanted to last year at least."

Even though he's facing away from me, his eyes are squeezed shut. "And you're drunk, just like last year. When"—he shakes his head—"*if* something ever happens between us, it can't be like this."

"I wasn't drunk yesterday." Yet another rejection of me—two in twenty-four hours!—is sobering me up quick. I dart over to the dresser and pull out a huge, soft sleep shirt. "And yet you found it prudent to act like I was the most disgusting thing you'd ever touched." I sigh. "I'm dressed. So you can stop acting repulsed now."

I sit on the bed and listen to his soft footfall against the carpet get closer. He nudges the water into my hands. "Drink. Please."

I want to cross my arms and tell him to go away, but I also don't want to wake up puking my guts out tomorrow morning. I sip the water until it's gone, and he takes the glass. After a minute, he returns, sitting next to me. Not close enough to touch, but not exactly as far away as he can, either.

"I don't know if you'll remember this in the morning," he says, his voice gruff and crackly. "But you're the fucking most beautiful girl I've ever seen. No one else comes close. No one else has ever come close."

When he stands I turn my face to him, my eyes wide. Somehow I feel even more naked than when I was only in my underwear a few minutes ago. "No one thinks I'm beautiful." I whisper it.

I know what I look like. Johnny told me all about it often enough. My hips are too narrow and muscular, and my shoulders are too wide and thick. My breasts, just one cup too small, and my ass could be bigger, too, for that matter. My lips and eyes are too narrow and my waist, despite my defined abs, could be smaller. "Not bad," Johnny had said the first time he saw me naked. He was the first man to ever see me naked. And I knew his *not bad* wasn't a compliment. It was telling me about all the flaws of my body, the things that I could never change, the way I could never be enough for him.

Or for anyone. He made sure to tell me that a lot, too. *No one but me would ever want you.*

"Everyone thinks you're beautiful. 'Cause that's what you are." Carter sounds sincere, at least. I can almost believe him.

But that doesn't stop me from turning away from his blazing gaze. I can accept that Carter is physically attracted to me, after yesterday's events. But I guess that means that the rest of me—my personality, namely—is what he is running away from. And I'm not sure which is worse.

I can't respond to him about it. So I say something that's been on my mind—something I haven't had the guts to say till there's a lot of drinks in me. "I wish you had told me about Abuelo Gene, Carter." I take a deep breath and begin counting. On my next exhale, I add, "I loved him, too."

It sounds like he's stopped breathing for a few seconds, and then: "I know, Teal. I should've told you. I'm sorry."

We sit in silence for several long minutes until he clears his throat. "I'll be on the pull-out if you need me."

I nod. And when he's gone, I let myself quietly cry, for five minutes, no more, before falling asleep.

⚡

IF I THOUGHT THIS ROOM WAS BRIGHT LAST NIGHT, WELL, LATE morning, I feel like someone is trying to beat me to death with the bright yellow rays of sunshine leaking in through the windows. And that's after only barely opening a single eye.

"Make it stop," I mumble, pulling my pillow over my face. After a moment, I peek through the cushion to discover that the sun still exists. "Why is it still there?"

"Why is what still there?"

I nearly fall backward, even though I'm lying down, at the sound of Carter's voice in the room. When I pull the pillow away from my face, he's sitting on the edge of the bed. I give his expression, posture, basically his whole vibe a quick assessment. He doesn't look awkward or like he hates me after last night's regrettable series of events. His eyes are warm and bright.

"Why is the sun still there," I respond eventually. "Is what I was asking." My voice sounds like it belongs to a toad that's been unalive for about ten thousand years.

He stands and hands me a glass of water and what appears to be two over-the-counter painkillers.

"Thanks." I down everything in less than a minute.

"How are you feeling?" He's returned to the edge of the bed.

"Not horrible. My head feels like it's being pressed between two bricks that are being wielded by giant yetis. But—" I pause as he laughs. It looks good on him—the laughing, I mean. The way his smile somehow makes this way-too-bright room even brighter, but in the best way. I glance down before he notices I'm staring. "But, yeah. Sorry, I don't know what else I was going to say."

"Well, the Tylenol should help with the yeti-brick thing." He pauses. "Listen. I'm not telling you what to do or anything, but . . ."

"Carter, trust me. I'm not drinking like that again anytime soon."

"Right, I mean, that's good, because remember, that amount of alcohol doesn't mix with your meds."

He's right. It does something to my heart that he's even thought about this. That he cares about my health like that. I want to somehow say what I'm feeling, but instead what comes out is, "I hear you."

He nods and clears his throat. "By the way, your phone alarm has been going off for a while. I think you might've missed something? An event labeled DSATS?"

"What? I missed the DSATS?" I jump up and immediately regret it when my legs buckle beneath me. My right knee in particular is just not up for standing today, I guess. The rug comes at me in hyperspeed before Carter's arms intervene in a big blur of muscles.

"Hey," he says, sitting on the floor and putting me in his lap all casual, like we do this sort of thing all the time. "You okay?"

"It's my knee," I say, flexing the leg out.

"The one you messed up back in high school?"

"Yeah, that's the one."

He reaches down and begins to press his fingers lightly around the bone of my knee. I let out a sigh and lean back on him, because it feels nice. But then he hits the sore spot and I wince, hissing as I smack his hand away.

"You should get that checked out."

"I did. It's a bone spur or two." I move away from his lap so now we're both sitting on the floor, facing one another.

"Um. Okay. So which is it, one bone spur, or two?"

I look directly at the carpet, at my heels squished in the tiny curls of beige. "It's more like three or four."

He's frowning at my knee when he lets out a long huff of a

sigh. "You're running way, way too much, Teal, for having so many bone spurs."

"It's nothing," I respond, and then I remember why I'm on the floor in the first place. "Shit." Glancing at the light, I see that the Dahlia Society Annual Tuber Sale was a good two hours ago. For some reason those idiots thought meeting at seven in the morning was a grand idea, and for some reason, this idiot—as in me— thought drinking her weight in whiskey the night before was also a stroke of brilliance.

"Does the DSATS have anything to do with dahlia roots or whatever?"

I look at him sharply, and then wince when my head feels like one of the yeti bricks smashes extra hard on the left temple. "What do you know about the dahlia tubers? I didn't tell you the plans yesterday," I manage to grunt out. "No one knows about my dahlia tuber plans. Not even my sisters."

He responds by lifting his phone and showing me a text. It's from Tía Nadia, as in the great-aunt who sort of raised me, when Sage wasn't doing the heavy lifting, that is. Tell Teal to not bother with the Dahlia Society tubers. Most of them have gall. Just start with the seeds, otherwise she's wasting her time.

I groan. All-knowing Latine elders and their meddlesome ways. "What's gall?"

Carter slides his thumb over the screen of his phone, lifting it to show me some nasty pictures of plants. I guess gall is some kind of dahlia bacteria. Like, it literally looks like gross alien parasites are growing on them and shit. "I'm going to vomit. Get that away from me."

Carter leans back after he tucks his phone back in his pocket. I hadn't noticed before, but he looks damn good right now, in jeans, a soccer jersey, and scruff growing thick around his soft pink lips. He levels those golden eyes right on me and then I remember that I probably look exactly how I feel—the veins in my eyes too red, my skin and mouth dehydrated, my hair resembling the gnarled roots of some frizzy tree. I turn my face away from him as he keeps talking.

"I have the day off today."

"Okay?"

"You need help planting your seeds."

"My what now?" I touch the tips of my fingers to my forehead. "Right. The seeds." Then I make a face. "Wait, that basket of ugly-looking herbs Nadia gave me are *seeds*? *Dahlia* seeds?" How can something so gorgeous grow from little things that look like something you'd toss in the compost? My next inhale is a little sharp. "I don't even remember where I put those!"

"They're in the gym room closet. They're fine." Carter pushes up to standing, and in the process, for just a moment, I am eye level with the bulge between his legs and even in my yeti-brick state, it does something to me. All those dumb words I said to him last night come tumbling down in my head like yeti anvils. And all the sweet, amazing stuff he said to me does, too.

And just like that, I'm blushing.

"There's breakfast on the stove. Eat and drink a lot of water. We have work to do." Then he walks away, and I'm too hungover to stop myself from ogling his magnificent ass.

⚡

AFTER SHOWERING AND MAKING MYSELF RESEMBLE A NON-massively-hungover human as much as possible, I devour the breakfast Carter made—"hangover hash browns," he called them, and they were somehow exactly what I needed, all crispy and buttery, topped with herbs, cheese, and two poached eggs.

After which we began the work Carter had promised—namely, shoveling compost and manure he "borrowed" from work into the little dahlia bed I dug up from his yard earlier.

"I've been reading about it," he explains to me as we take a water break. It's only been twenty minutes of shoveling from the pile he'd brought over from the farm this morning, and we're both sweaty, with streaks over our clothes and arms of two kinds of shit (manure, being the animal shit, and compost, being basically made up of bug shit, if you also count bacteria and fungus as bugs, which I do). "Dahlias are heavy feeders. So they need all these nutrients to thrive. You can't plant them in this clay and sand mix here in the yard."

"But the grass is doing fine in the clay and sand mix," I say, frowning.

"Grass and dahlias are two very different plants."

"Hmm." But Carter doesn't let me linger with my thoughts. He tosses my shovel back at me and after another thirty minutes, we've incorporated all the various forms of shit, and after that, we top it with a sweet-smelling mulch he says is made of cypress. Bugs that like dahlias don't like the smell of cypress, so it should do some work in keeping them away.

"Why are you helping me with this?" I ask after we're done.

He shrugs. I let my gaze linger on the broadness of his shoulders, but he doesn't seem to notice. "We're married now. We're a team. When I saw Nadia's texts, I figured out what you were doing here, digging up the grass. And I wanted to help you do it right, is all." He glances away from my face. "Speaking of. We need to talk about a game plan for tomorrow."

"Shit." I'd completely forgotten what he'd barked at me when he ran away after the whole kitchen counter shenanigans. "Your family's coming for dinner, was it?"

"Lunch."

I take a deep, deep breath. "And let me guess. Abuela Erika's coming."

Carter laughs. "It was her idea."

I fold my arms over and survey the yard. We've created a flower bed that is about fifteen feet wide and five feet deep. His front yard isn't all that large to begin with, and now most of it is a mixture of dirt, shit, and mulch. But he hasn't complained or made a face or gotten passive-aggressive, like my ex would have, even over something as inconsequential as digging up a flower bed in a yard he never noticed or cared about.

As I watch Carter as he glances over our work, he looks proud.

"So are you going to tell me why you kept me a secret?" I ask finally.

Carter's face turns to me fast, and this time he doesn't deny keeping our marriage from his family. "Erika has gotten . . . worse as she's gotten older. I didn't want to subject you to her until we couldn't hold off any longer."

I clear my throat. "And we have to see her tomorrow, so you can get your money, right?"

It might just be my imagination, but Carter takes a beat to answer. "Yeah. Tomorrow's for the money."

17

MY MEETING WITH THE PRIVATE INVESTIGATOR WAS EX-
actly forty-two minutes, even though I had paid for the
full hour. But to be honest, I wasn't exactly having the best time
so I didn't mind getting out of there a little early.

The guy's name is Gerald Samuels, and he's just this older
white man who kind of reminds me of Jeremy Renner, with an
almost cartoonish droopy face. He smells heavily like laundry de-
tergent and faintly like cigars. I had the impression that he smoked
a lot, and when he wasn't smoking, he was spraying Febreze on
everything around and on him.

I'm in the parking lot, doing my breath work, when Sage calls.

"So, did you and Carter finally get it on?" she asks without
even saying hello first.

I groan. "What do you think?"

"I think I watched that man's eyes gobble you up like you
were his favorite candy, then throw you over your shoulder like a
caveman and take you to bed."

"Where he gave me water and treated me like a gentleman, even after I flashed him."

At this, Sage laughs and I smile, just a teeny bit. "Where are you?" she asks.

"Outside the private investigator's office."

"Right. I wanted to ask you about that. 'Cause Nadia won't tell me a damn thing about Mama being in town."

"I heard her and Amá saying exactly that. Or, Amá was acting like she'd legit seen her, at least." I groan. "How are they so gossipy and private at the same time?"

"I'm sure they're thinking they're protecting us or something."

"Yeah, well, maybe they should have kept her from us before we even had the chance to know her, then."

Sometimes I imagine how it would have been if Mama had never left. Sage wouldn't have taken her place as our mother, and who knows, maybe I wouldn't have struggled so much with my mental health. Maybe Sky and I never would have taken that walk to Cranberry Falls State Park, or if we had, maybe I wouldn't have been fucked up in the head enough to think that walking on top of a railway next to a cliff would be fun. Sky would never have fallen. She never would have been essentially dead for eight whole years, from sixteen to twenty-four.

I rub my eyes. I guess they're still dry and stinging from my hangover.

"So can I ask you something?" Sage's voice is quiet and cautious.

"Sure. Why not."

"Why are you hiring a PI to find her? I mean . . . do you really want to see her that bad?" When I don't respond right away, Sage fills the silence fast. "I'm just saying, if she wanted to see us, to have a relationship with us, she could've done it one million times over by now. The fact that she hasn't . . ." She pauses. "I just don't want you to get hurt, too."

I keep my eyes closed for a long time, and when I open them and focus on the long low orange of the sunlight, draped over the pine and alder trees around me in this almost-empty parking lot, I swear I almost say it. I almost tell someone besides Carter that Mama took something from me. Something essential, something that I need back in order to be whole and lovable again. Something there is little chance of getting back, even with hiring the most reputable PI in town. Because Mama's gift, like, her actual superpower, is hiding. Which of course I can't tell Gerald Samuels about.

Asking even the most successful personal investigator on the planet to find Mama is like asking them to find a needle in a haystack, only the haystack is the size of a small country, and the needle is invisible.

Instead, I sigh out a totally different response. "I know, Sage. I'm not deluding myself. I don't think we're going to have some Hallmark-style mother-daughter reunion. I just want answers."

"Those would be nice," Sage agrees. "Well, let me know if you need any help or if you need to talk about anything."

It's nice to hear those words from her and not have the instinct to rear back and say something nasty. For a long time, I did just that. Every time Sage was nice to me, I would act like a total bitch. I realize now it's 'cause I had a hard time forgiving her for leaving. I can't stand the idea of being alone, really, and that was what happened after I lost both Sky and Sage the same summer. The worst year of my life.

Speaking of the long-lost sister, my phone rings with Sky's name the second I hang up with Sage.

"I have the answer to your problem," she informs me on speakerphone as I drive onto the highway, back to Carter's.

"Which one?" There are so many damn problems she could be referring to.

"You and Carter."

"Again, which problem?"

"The one where there's enough sexual tension between you two, you could stick a spoon in it and eat it with ice cream?"

I smile. It's definitely a sarcastic one. "Yeah?"

"You need to have sex with him."

Now I snort. "Sky, I know you went from sixteen to midtwenties in what was to you the blink of an eye, but you've got to know that's a bit of an obvious solution. One that I haven't exactly not tried." I haven't really tried it, either, but I would call my efforts at sleeping with Carter not-*not* trying.

"I mean, you need to do it at least once and get it out of your systems!"

I stare at the red light in front of me. "Get it out of our systems?"

"Yes! This trope is in, like, a fourth of Nadia's romance novels. They make a sex agreement. They do it at least once."

Oh, Christ. Not another romance novel trope. "And then they get over each other? Is that how those romances end?"

Sky pauses. "Well."

I shake my head. "I appreciate the offer, but I took my bra off in front of Carter last night and he acted like my chest was covered in feathers."

"*Gah!*" she screams. "Why can't you see how much he wants you?"

"It's mainly in the way he runs away from me."

"Just think about it. An agreement to get it out of your systems. Clean. Easy."

I decide it's been time to change the subject. "What about you and Adam Noemi?"

There's a long pause. "What about me and Adam?"

"Well, what trope are you going to use to lure him in? That should be your current focus. And you can't just ask him to eat your ass. He might get the wrong idea."

Sky and I are cracking up by the time I pull into Carter's driveway. "Maybe I want him to get the wrong idea," she muses, then sighs. "But he's back in New York City. I can't ask for an ass-eating anytime soon."

"Road trip!" I announce, and we laugh some more after Sky names it the Get Your Ass Eaten NYC Trip, and then I get out of the car and just stare at Carter's sweet blue house.

Get it out of our systems, huh? Why do I get the feeling Carter *might* be down for that?

"After the Velasquez family lunch," I murmur to myself. One thing at a time.

18

I T TAKES ME ALL MORNING TO DECIDE WHETHER TO COOK FOR
Carter's family, and by the time I decide that I can make my
favorite recipe from childhood—Nadia's famous cheese
enchiladas—I look at the clock and realize all I have time for is
picking up fried chicken, biscuits, and all the fixings from a
nearby Southern food place. This is what Carter had initially
wanted me to do to start with. But I was too nervous to make up
my mind until the clock made it up for me.

I didn't even give myself time to run this morning, which is
probably the worst decision I've made in recent memory. Looking
out the window, though, the sky doesn't reflect my nerves. It's
cloudy with hints of sunshine here and there, peeking through
like cosmic sunflower petals. I wonder if it's 'cause I know Carter
will be here. Knowing that for all his faults, as my husband he'll
have my back, just like he did with Leilani.

"I don't get what's wrong with this," Carter says, popping a
piece of fried okra in his mouth. "Everyone loves soul food."

"But now they're going to judge me for not making a real

effort." I hand him the white porcelain square plates from the cabinets. "Here, help me set the table instead of eating all the food."

"No one's going to judge you, Teal. They're all going to be stuffing their faces with all this deliciousness." As he transfers the biscuits from their packaging to the cute bread basket I found tucked away on top of the fridge, he samples one. As in, a whole-ass, beautiful buttered biscuit is gone in two bites.

I smack his forearm. "Stop that."

He lifts his hands in mock surrender. "I'm just getting my point across."

"You're about to eat everything before they even get here." I sigh as I roll up the cloth napkins I took from Nadia's house. Carter, living the sad, predictable bachelor life, I guess, only had wrinkled brown paper napkins that he regularly stole from Burger King down the street. Lord knows what his family would've said about that. So now we're now the proud thieves of gold-embroidered emerald green napkins that Nadia is definitely going to be pissed about when she finds out they're gone.

I turn to him, my arms crossed. "You know how your family is. The elder women worship the men and boys and criticize the shit out of all the women and girls. And that includes the girls their boys are married to." I'd seen it all firsthand when I visited the Velasquez home as a kid. Nothing Carter's sisters did was ever good enough, from the way they sliced onions to how they mopped the floors. Meanwhile, Carter and his boy cousins could track thick mud through the house, eat with their grubby, bare hands, and be so loud and obnoxious while playing video games that none of us could hear ourselves think, much less talk over . . . and all the mamas and tías and welas would pat their heads and smile, calling them so guapo and strong and innocent.

"Okay, okay," Carter says when I go into extreme detail reminding him of how they were. "You're right. I know it. But—I'm—" He sighs, then takes my hand and pulls me toward him. Half of me wants to run to the other side of the table. The other half wants to close the gap between us with a hug. A kiss. A quick finger-fuck right on the dining room table.

The memory of him running away the last time he had his fingers in me squelches down that thought real quick.

"Abuelo Gene wanted us to be get along and be happy. He was the peacemaker, remember?"

I nod. Gene often defended his granddaughters to his wife and his daughters. He was well aware that there was some type of intergenerational trauma with the women, and although he didn't have the resources to figure out how to heal it, nor did anyone else, he did the best he could. He'd send the girls out to play when they were expected to cook, once again, for the whole family. He'd save them dessert that would otherwise get eaten while they washed the dishes after parties and gatherings. Hell, once he found me crying after Abuela Erika—his wife—had tried her hardest to rip me a new one. He helped me up, dried my tears, and took Carter and me to see *The Matrix*, our first R-rated film. Carter and I spent the rest of that summer pretending we were Neo and Trinity, trying to bend backward and sideways in slow motion to dodge imaginary bad-guy bullets.

Carter runs a hand over his clean-shaven jaw. Whatever aftershave he's got on must be laced with legit pheromones because it's doing illicit things to me. He smells freaking delicious—like the woods and the sea all blended together with something sweet, like honey or cake.

"I know my family is dysfunctional. They have their issues."

"Especially Abuela Erika," I add pointedly.

"Especially her," he agrees. "So yeah, I am expecting some growing pains or whatever, but that'll be over soon enough. But once that's done with, they'll love you." He swallows. "Mom and Gabi already love you. They remember you coming over and out-eating me and all the cousins in guava slices every weekend in the summers."

"You guys always had the best fucking guava," I groan, my stomach grumbling at the memory of it. Carter's mom, Gloria, always squeezed lime over the slices when she served us the fresh fruit. And if she made pastelitos de guayaba, forget about it. We always spoiled our dinners.

"They'll love you, Teal," he repeats, his gaze boring down on me as though I held in my very hands the answers to all the mysteries in the universe. "You're easy to love."

I blink away from our cosmic staring contest. Easy to love, my ass. "Plus we need to put on a good show for Erika so she'll get you your money, right?"

Now Carter's turning away from me, grabbing glasses from the counter. "Right. The money."

"As soon as she gets it to you, I need to get my cut, Carter. I've emptied my bank account on a down payment for that PI."

"Got it," he responds. "I'll get you the money ASAP."

I don't have any time to try and decipher why his tone's gotten so weird and dry, because that's when the doorbell rings.

⚡

CARTER'S FAMILY IS MASSIVE. EVEN WHEN HIS MAMI LIVED IN the three-story Victorian down the street from Nadia's, it felt like there was never enough room. Not everyone could come today, but even with a third of his people elsewhere, his house instantly feels like it was made for Polly Pocket and not actual-sized humans.

Gloria is the first through the door, with a stream of people following behind. "Teal," she says, running to me, wearing a cute, red rose–patterned white sundress. "Oh, I have another daughter!" She then turns to Carter, who opens his arms wide, presumably for a hug. But she instead pulls her shiny black Coach bucket bag off her shoulder and smacks him on the side of the head with it.

"Hey!" Carter yelps as he covers his face. She gets his shoulder next. "Why are you attacking me, Mom?" He looks so aghast, I can't hide my smile. This must be the first time he's been reprimanded by his mom—or any elder woman in his family—in his entire life.

"This is for you not telling us you were getting married—" She smacks his stomach. "And for not inviting us to the wedding." Next is his hip. "And for me to find out from my neighbor? That my own son is now a husband? Do you know how humiliated I felt?"

"Okay, Mom. I think he gets your point," Gabi says, grabbing Gloria's purse-wielding arm to stop her next strike.

Gloria halts and shrugs off Gabi's hand. Next thing I know, she's cupping Carter's face. "My baby boy is married! He has a wife!" And then she kisses both his cheeks and hugs him to her chest, even though he's a good foot and a half taller than her. I'm almost unable to stop myself from rolling my eyes. This is just how it is with the Velasquez family. The mistakes of men are forgettable, to the point where, just a few weeks from now, Gloria, if pressed, would act like she didn't remember any of it—how he'd hidden his wedding, his wife. How she had to hear about it from a neighbor.

And if it had been Gabi, or any of Carter's other sisters? The incident would be brought up at every single gathering, every conversation, even, for the next lifetime or two.

Gabi sees my face and gestures toward her mom and brother with a sarcastic smile. "The baby boy can do no wrong," she says in a low voice as she hugs me and kisses my cheek. "How are you doing, Teal? Or should I say, hermana?" She steps back with a huge smile. "It's been too long."

"Oh, yes, it has. Where's Cristina and Paloma?" I ask, referring to Carter's other sisters.

"Oh, you know. Traveling for this, for that. Work trips, school stuff." She adds under her breath, "Trying to stay away from the madness."

Some of Carter's cousins, aunts, and uncles greet me next. I'm chatting with his tío Rodrigo about my looking for a job when I can feel a shift in the vibes. How the room goes from neutral small talk and lots of familial affection to an awkward accommodation of a thick, underlying tension. People's smiles turn strained. Their eyes widen as they glance to me, then back again.

I glance toward the door, and *shit*. It looks like Abuela Erika has finally joined the party.

19

ABUELA ERIKA KIND OF REMINDS ME OF AMÁ SONYA, ONLY if Sonya decided she wasn't too good for clothes from JCPenney and she was a hell of a lot meaner. I mean, yeah, my grandmother is a bitch. We all know and accept it. But she was worse when we were teens. I think us being the same age as my mom—her daughter—when she moved out did something to Sonya emotionally. But now we get along better. Sure, Sonya mocks my clothing, and she hates my musical taste, and she acts like she'd rather be doing anything else than talk to me when we're together. But she also once offered to buy me a Birkin the same color as my name. I'm pretty sure Erika would rather propel herself through a third-floor glass window than offer to buy me a one-dollar pizza slice from the corner store if I were starving to death.

That said, I wonder how things would have been different if Sonya or Mama had had a son. Based on how my second cousins are treated, the boys versus the girls? The dynamic is very similar to the Velasquez family. Ever since Sky got back from the "dead,"

she's been trying to research our own lineage and she keeps talking about things like *intergenerational trauma* and *colonial inheritance*. I wonder if that is where so much of Latine sexism comes
from. On second thought, maybe Erika and Sonya are more alike
than I know. Sage, Sky, and I were just lucky enough to be all
sisters.

Erika walks past the entryway, her nose in the air, adding half
an inch to her five-foot-two frame. She's a small woman, but she
seems real sturdy somehow. Some elders, their demeanors give
away a type of frailty—the way they slow to go up the steps or
brace themselves before they get up from sitting. Not Erika. She
reminds me of a bull, shoving one of Carter's little cousins out of
the way so she can make her entrance properly.

Erika's hair is short and white, styled to have kind of a poofy
volume. Her makeup is understated except for a coral lip. She's
got on a peach dress, A-line with a long skirt, the neck conservative and square. Pearls adorn her neck and ears. Her shoes are
white slippers, like the kind you see on retail workers, or other
people who are on their feet all day. She's carrying a Michael Kors
handbag, which is basically a rip-off of a gray Saffiano Prada tote.
I don't particularly care about brand knockoffs. Like I said before,
I'll wear a no-name bag one day and a Louis the next. But the fact
that Erika carries something that Sonya would consider not just
disrespectful, but *distasteful*, which is worse to her, makes me feel
a little bloom of petty happiness.

Stop being selfish, I remind myself. I don't even know if she's
the same old asshole as she was back in the day. I mean, sure, her
whole family is terrified of her. One cousin has run into the bathroom to hide, and another is trying to stay unseen behind her
mother. But I'm Carter's wife now. That's gotta mean something
to her, right?

"Hola, Abuela Erika," I say, taking a step toward her. "It's so nice—"

She holds a hand up, her palm open, stopping me in my tracks. "No, no. I'm not interested in greeting you like you didn't ruin my grandson and then trap him into holy matrimony." She looks around and points at Gloria. "I told you, didn't I? I told you when Carter was ten years old that that girl would be the end of him. She would steal him right out from under you. Didn't I say that?"

Everyone's holding their breath. Carter's frozen and I feel a small—okay, a large twinge of disappointment when he doesn't correct her. Which means, like usual, I have to fend for myself.

I inhale deeply. I need to stop being selfish, which means this family get-together can't just be about my feelings, right? Carter wants to fulfill Abuelo Gene's wish, which is peace. So I'm going to try my freaking hardest to be damn peaceful, even if I have no idea how.

"Actually, Erika, you told me that yourself when we first met. Remember? I was eleven, it was Gloria's birthday party. So I can confirm it with my own vivid memory." I smile very sweetly. "And look at us now. You've spoken it all into existence. So powerful." Okay, yes, I am getting sarcastic now, but I swear my tone and face are as sweet as can be. I can tell that no one aside from Carter understands that what I am doing is intentional. *Yes, you called an eleven-year-old child a whore to her face. That's the kind of person you are. So* powerful.

Amá Sonya is going to be so proud when she hears about this. I'm channeling her, after all.

I clap my hands together before she can open her mouth with something stupid and nasty in response. "The food's getting cold. Let's eat."

Luckily the family begins talking at once, racing toward the bowls and containers of food lined up on the counter, and just a smidge of that tension eases. People joke and laugh, and eventually I join Carter at the table. He smiles up at me, and I can't bring myself to genuinely smile in response. I mean, I make an attempt. Erika's watching me so closely, I'd ask her to take a picture (it would last longer! Haha!) if I didn't think it would mess up his chance to get his money.

So yeah, my smile doesn't reach my eyes because damn, I thought Carter would be different. When I told him the crap Erika used to tell me back in the day, he'd play it down. *Oh, she didn't really mean it*, or, *she's extra stressed today. Come on, let's play.* But right now, we're not little kids. We're *adults* and I'm his *wife.*

And the fact that he doesn't notice how pissed off I am just makes me angrier.

"I can't eat this," Erika finally says over the noise. "This food is so unhealthy and fattening, and it has no flavor." She glares at me. "Do wives nowadays no longer cook?"

"I asked her to get this food, Wela," Carter pipes up.

"And she didn't realize that what you really wanted was something homecooked? To make a good impression on your family?"

"It's not what I wanted." Carter's tone is sharp enough to make Erika purse her lips and glare at me. I know exactly what she's thinking, that I somehow coached him into this "disrespect." If I were to crack open her mind and see her thoughts, my guess is that there is a very vivid image of me wearing a witch's hat, stirring a potion that turns well-behaved men into insolent ones.

I give him a smile of gratitude and he puts a hand on my knee. I almost lean into him but I don't want to provoke Erika any more than I already have.

"You know, when I was first married, I didn't know how to make toast. But I learned quick." Gloria grabs another biscuit. "Maybe I can come around and teach you some of Carter's favorite dishes, huh?" She smiles at me so genuinely, it lessens my anger just a touch. Even though she's joining the misogyny chorus, her heart is in the right place.

"I'd love that," I say.

Erika snorts. "You can't teach an old dog new *tricks*." She says *tricks* as though it's well known that I'm a prostitute who specializes in truly outrageous behavior, like sex with goats, or maybe skyscrapers.

When I glance at Carter for support, he's got his head down and is going to town on his food. When our gazes meet again, he gives me a look of pride. Not, like, pride in me or this situation. He's still riding the high of sticking up for me once—just once—so far.

This is what happens when a boy child is praised for doing the bare minimum his entire life. I'm not even sure if he heard his grandmother call me a dog, because he's too busy waiting for me to coo and pat his head for two sentences.

The only person who *sees* me the whole time is his sister Gabi. She winces with every passive and overly aggressive insult and suggestion. If I weren't here, she'd be bearing the brunt of this garbage. I bet no one has ever stood up for her. Not in a real way.

Which means if I want Erika to respect me, I have to keep getting all Amá Sonya on her.

I only vaguely notice how the dark the sky has gotten when I return my attention to the crap she's spewing now.

"There's no reason any woman needs to have muscles," she

scoffs, looking pointedly at my arms but pretending she's just offering a random opinion for no reason. "That's what her man is for."

I try my hardest to think of What Would Amá Sonya Do . . . hmm. Let's try the *I don't know what you mean* route. "Our muscular structure is integral to human health. Without it we would literally die. There's no reason all women need to die." I paste a saccharin-sweet smile on my face as I flex my biceps while grabbing my water.

Erika glares at me. "I *mean* working out all the time, looking like a man. No woman should look like a man."

I barely refrain from rolling my eyes. What would Sonya do, what would Sonya do . . . how about a nice, passive-aggressive compliment. "Erika, I meant to comment on your lovely hairstyle. It reminds me of a great big cone of delicious cotton candy!"

It's weak, as far as insults go. But I had a feeling she would hate the comparison, and her following snarl confirms my suspicions. "Hey!" one of the children says with a giggle. "Abuela Erika's hair *does* look like cotton candy!" A big laugh goes around the table.

Before Erika can respond with something scathing, I laugh and throw my head back. "Beautiful cotton candy!" Sonya loves to smother insults under words like *beautiful*, *sweet*, and *bless your heart*.

"Every woman needs a hairstyle. It's how one stays *respectable*." She narrows her eyes at me and adds, "There's nothing wrong with a boy sowing his oats. But after that, he needs to settle down with a *nice* and *respectable* girl," she exclaims loudly. "Not someone who comes from a gutter family." This last bit, she mumbles under her breath. I swear she *just* holds back from spitting on me.

"Aww, that is such a sweet sentiment." I put my hand on my heart. "And I totally agree. Nice and respectable girls turn into nice and respectable women. The kind of women who are loving and sweet. Not the kind of women who tell children that they would end up as loose as their mother. Right?"

Erika's jaw is slightly dropped. And so are the men's. The women, though. Their eyes gleam with something like glee. I glance at them all and say, "Some vieja actually told me that when I was little. Can you believe it?" I shake my head and sigh. "If it's not something Jesus would do, then it's not something a nice lady would do, am I right?" I raise my glass, because no one is going to argue with me once I bring Jesus into it. "And on that note, I'd like to make a toast." I raise my glass. "To nice women. Who are always kind, whether to Chihuahuas"—because yes, I've seen Erika kick one of her granddaughter's old Chihuahuas before—"to all children"—because although Erika was brutal to me, she didn't like any kids, as far as I could tell—"and most of all, to their daughters and daughters-in-law." I smile as everyone cheers and toasts, led by cousin Gordon, and then I add a little extra something in a low voice especially for her. "Because nice women want relationships with their future great-grandchildren. Right?"

Erika's slams her gaping mouth shut, and then someone gets up to toast me and Carter and all the future Velasquez babies.

If she thought she was going to make me bawl like when I was a child, well. She can see now that she was wrong.

↯

CARTER WALKS EVERYONE OUTSIDE AND I STAY IN, BEGINNING cleanup. "Hey," Gabi says as she joins me, helping to stack dishes and carry them to the sink. "That was something you did there."

She lowers her voice with a grin. "I've never seen her so speechless in my life."

I smile but it doesn't feel as victorious as I'd like. I'm realizing now that I got carried away. That I let the old, selfish Teal through too much. Not that I'll admit that to anyone. I just don't know what to do when I'm cornered like that, when someone is telling me to my face that I'm the one who's ruined their grandson. How does someone get through that gracefully? I don't know. Sage is the least selfish person I know, and I think even she would have conjured some thick vines to smother the vieja.

"We should go out sometime," I tell Gabi as I walk her to the door.

"Yes, you have to show me where you get your purses. Mine is—" She lifts up a bag that, if I had to guess, is a knockoff from a knockoff dollar store. It's so wrinkled, it looks like an old collection of sediment taken from an archaeological site. The deep brown pleather is peeling all over the strap and its bottom, revealing the yellowed lining within.

"Give me your address," I demand, because not only are we going shopping, I'm also sending Gabi something nice as soon as Carter gives me my cut. If he can't get it to me in time, all I'll have to do is describe this purse to Amá and *she'll* give me the money. The idea that this zombie of a handbag exists in Cranberry will be insulting enough for her to cover a Fendi Sunshine Medium Shopper in a tan color, which, looking at Gabi's style, would suit her really well.

After Gabi and I kiss goodbye, I keep the door open as I peek out, looking for Carter. Seems like they're doing the thing that all Latines do, which is hover around their cars for an hour-long farewell that probably will continue once folks starting actually getting in their cars, too.

I'm in the middle of a relieved sigh when a tiny, veiny, pearl-ring-covered hand reaches around me to slam the door shut. It startles me for only a second, but then I put on my game face when I turn around.

Because of course, it's Abuela Erika.

20

You'd think being confronted by a nasty old brat like Erika at close range like this would rattle me more, but I've had plenty of experience from Sonya, who enjoys startling us with intimidation tactics like it's some kind of Latine female elder Olympic sport.

"Yes?" I ask, crossing my arms.

She begins to tell me off in Spanish. Based on her facial expressions, and the way she's waving her arms like an octopus, I'm sure she's calling me all kinds of colorful phrases. But I barely understand my family's Mexican American Spanglish, so this is not having the effect she wants. At a certain point, she stops and narrows her eyes. "You don't even know Spanish?" she hisses at me. "All you know is English?"

"Is the language of one colonizer really better than another's?" I ask.

She ignores me. "Fine. En Inglés, since you're so much better than me." See? What on earth can I say to that nonsense? But she goes on, so I don't need to say a damn thing after all. "I don't know who you think you are, threatening me like that in front of *my* whole family."

My conscience—the Teal I want to be—sprouts up inside me like a hopeful little seedling. I know I can make this better. It's going to be painful but I need to do this for me. "I know." I sigh. "I'm sorry. I shouldn't have threatened you."

All the wind is taken out of her sails. She wasn't expecting that, I'll tell you what. But then she scowls as she brushes my apology off, taking one deep breath to keep on putting me in my place. "All you Flores women are the same. Just because you're witches doesn't mean that you can make everyone do your bidding. I won't stand for it."

Well, now I blink. Does she mean witches like a regular derogatory name for women, or does she mean it like . . . she knows all about our gifts? "What are you talking about, *witches*?"

"You know what I mean, just like Nadia always knew what I meant."

"*Nadia?*" What on earth is happening here? "My tía Nadia? What's she got to do with this?"

Erika, once again, ignores my question. "Your family's specialty is putting men in a . . . how do you say it? A . . ." She snaps her fingers. "Hipnosis."

"Hypnosis?" I ask.

"So you do know Spanish." She narrows her eyes at me.

"It's almost the same word."

She rolls her eyes. "I just wanted to tell you that Carter is too smart for your ways. Right now, I am going to go out there and I am going to weep on his shoulder. And when he comes inside, he will punish you for the ill you have done to me. And that's how you know he will always choose me over you." She raises her head. "Just like how Eugenio chose me over Nadia."

"What?" I gasp. "Abuelo Gene and *Nadia*?" What kind of television novela did I just step into here?

"You are broken, just like her. Just like your mother, and your sisters. Broken," she spits as she swings the door open and stomps out.

Of all the things she said, I really wish she hadn't ended it on *broken*. The word echoes inside me like I contain a murmuration of starlings made of chipped glass. It's the only word I know for sure is true. I *am* broken. I'm trying to fix it, but there's no telling if that's even possible.

As though to prove my point, lightning flashes way too close, followed by thunder so loud, it feels like it's right on my skin like the attack of a wild beast.

$$\lightning$$

CARTER BARGES IN JUST AS I BEGIN WIPING DOWN THE DINING table.

"Seriously?" he says, his voice harsh, like shrapnel sliding over gravel. "I asked you to keep the peace with my family, and you pull passive-aggression all meal, and end it with threatening to keep her great-grandkids away from her?"

I don't have the energy for this. "Yes, Carter. I'm a bitch and a horrible person and Erika is the innocent victim of my asshole ways. You have never painted a more accurate picture."

He crosses his arms and his jaw gets tight. "This wasn't the deal. You were supposed to be neutral, if not pleasant, so that she'd believe we were together. A wife needs to act a certain way, you know?"

Well, he went there. So now I have to go there, too. "Well, Carter," I say, throwing the sponge down. "A husband needs to act a certain way when it comes to his wife. And that doesn't include smiling when his grandmother bullies his wife. So it's a good thing what we have is a fake marriage and that you are a *fake* husband."

He puts a hand on his head and sighs deeply. "I told you that we would have a few growing pains to get through. All you had to do—"

"All I had to do was let her tell me that I ruined you? That I was a shitty wife? That she wanted better for you than me? Seriously, Carter, were we at the same meal? You didn't mention that I would have to suffer abuse from your family in the deal. Maybe you should have said that instead of glossing it over as *growing pains*."

His eyes are like fire right now. "She's a cranky old woman with issues, not an abuser. She loves us."

My mouth drops open. "Jesus, Carter." I feel nauseated and I put a hand on my belly. "I can't believe I thought you'd have my back for this." I shake my head as thunder makes the plates stacked on the counter tremble. "So I had to have my own back. I had to stick up for myself and there's nothing wrong with that, no matter what you or anyone says." I'm choking on the words now but I don't even care. "I didn't ruin you and you and I both know it. I'm not a whore or a slut like she called me when I was a little kid. That shit is called verbal abuse and I encourage you to look it up, since you were raised to think it's synonymous with love." I clear my throat as the tears finally fall down my face. "I *know* what abuse is, Carter. I know what it looks like in *all* its forms."

Outside, the sky has darkened so much, it looks like night has come at four in the afternoon. Wind rushes by the windows with a series of howls that just make me feel sicker.

Carter's face has fallen. "Teal—" It looks like he is going to apologize and I can't let him. I need to hold on to this. I need to remember this, so the next time I feel weakened by my attraction to Carter, I won't get my heart involved. He doesn't have my back. He will let me down and it will hurt so much worse if I'm stupid enough to open my heart up to him even more than it already is.

I point at him, which ceases his sentence. "Absolutely the fuck not." I race toward the bedroom, where I slam the door. I kick off my lilac heels, the ones that match this dress I so carefully picked perfectly, and pace, running my hands through my hair.

"Teal." Carter knocks on the door. "I'm sorry. I'm sorry. Erika was crying all over me and I didn't know what to think. I know she started it—"

I swing open the door where he's frozen, his loose fist up, mid-knock. "You know what she told me before she left?" I take a big, shaky breath. "She said she was going to cry for you, and that you would choose her over me. She planned that shit. She called it. And she and I both knew that she was right."

I'm too upset to even put my shoes on. Instead I race past him, out the back door, through the backyard, through the fence door, until I'm on the beach, barefoot, running into the wildest storm I've seen since I was four years old.

21

THE WAVES ON THE BEACH RUMBLE AND ROAR, ROLLING higher and higher. If a surfer had a death wish, they'd have the time of their life right now, out there on those blue shimmering monsters. Rain slaps against my face and my arms, my chest and legs, all so hard it stings as though hundreds of tiny arrows aim at me straight from the clouds. The sky is a swirling, inky mix of black and indigo, the kind of sky you see in horror movies just before everything goes to hell.

I'm running as fast as I can, maybe even faster than I can, because I can't bear for Carter to catch up to me. If he's even come after me at all. Just this morning, I would have said Carter might've followed me anywhere, especially were I this upset. But now . . . I don't know. Maybe he went back inside to call Erika and now they're gossiping about what a spoiled bitch I am. They're probably founding a club right now, the Teal Haters, and they're planning their inaugural meeting, so they can bond over all the ways I am broken.

It doesn't matter. It's what I keep repeating to myself, every step a word. It. Doesn't. Matter.

This marriage is fake. It doesn't matter. Sure, I wanted to be best friends with Carter again, but that, too, no longer matters. I want to laugh when I think about my plans to get him to fuck me so we could get it out of our systems.

It. Doesn't. Matter.

Shells and rocks whoosh under my feet, and on a couple of steps, I stomp on something sharp. I can't bring myself to care, and instead I increase my speed until it feels like my legs are nothing but blurs, like I'm Sonic from the video game Carter and I used to play when we were little kids.

At about one or two miles, I come upon my first roadblock of jagged, chert-gray rocks, appearing like the open mouth of some giant, ancient creature, its row of fossilized teeth all that's left of it. They're so dark they almost look black in this rainstorm. It would be damn difficult, if not impossible, to climb them. But just the thought of turning around makes me ache, makes me want to weep, and so with grim determination, I slow down to climb, to crawl, to do anything to get myself on the other side of this line of gargantuan fangs.

I'm pretty sure I can hear Carter yelling something like *Teal, what the fuck?* in the distance, so I grab the nearest rock and haul my ass up until I'm balanced right on top of it.

I suck in my breath, my stomach bottoming out as I look down. This is the moment when I realize I'm being an irresponsible ass. Because this, *this*—my feet, slick against the sharp rock, my arms out because the wind is hell-bent on shoving me right back down, the fact that I could so easily fall, and one of those rocks would absolutely pierce my middle, or my spine, or my temple—now I'm the one asking myself, *Teal, what the fuck?*

This is how I watched my sister die. Sure, it wasn't exactly balanced on a sea rock, and she didn't exactly die, but all the same, when I look around, I am there, at Cranberry Falls State Park, looking down at my sister screaming before nothing, nothing, nothing for eight entire years.

I wonder if all the running I do, if it isn't just keeping my worst bipolar symptoms at arm's length. I wonder if I've been running from that day, from that moment, as though it were alive and chasing me, ready to fling eight years' worth of guilt on my shoulders.

I swallow and lower myself until I'm in a crouch, placing my hands on the cold, smooth stone under my feet. Even though it means I have to see Carter's stupid, handsome face, I've got to get back. I need to figure out another way to deal with my mess of a brain. There's no way that climbing over rocks barefoot in the middle of a storm is going to somehow help.

I steady myself so I can slide off and back onto the sand.

And of course . . . this is when lightning strikes.

It's a brilliant and massive map reaching across the sky in all four directions, like hands, only the hands are made up of nothing but an electrical circular system. It makes the sky light up in amber gold, the same color as Carter's eyes, the drops of rain in that glare looking like yellow diamonds falling from the sky.

I don't know when the lightning gets me, the exact moment when I hook up to its vibrating, hot current. All I do know is I look down at my left hand, because it feels strange, kind of like I dipped it into a hole in the wall that led to an alternate universe where everything is thick, where gravity is stronger. And it's alight. I lift my arm and somehow my hand keeps *glowing*, and it glows not yellow nor white, but blue.

And I watch as that blue light stretches in front of me, and just ten or so feet away, it forms into a figure. A little girl, no more than five years old, running after another person lit in blue—a woman.

Goose bumps prick my skin so hard, it's painful. I don't know if it's from being electrocuted or from watching my first great trauma unfold before my eyes in nothing but pure, hot lightning. Probably both.

Farther out, maybe a quarter or a half mile away, there is one more figure. I think it's another woman, and she's not made of lightning. She's real. And she's looking right at me.

Before I can think about it, I stand, leaping forward to the next rock. I don't understand what the hell is happening, but I can't shake the feeling that there is something essential out there, something that is undeniably mine, and I need to get it with the same desperation a selkie would need to find her lost skin before she withers and dies.

When I reach the next boulder, I bite my lips. Just one more. Just one more rock to go, and then I'll make it back onto the sand.

I tentatively place my foot on the smooth, cold black of rock. And when I put my weight there, my heel slips.

And of course. This is when I fall.

⚡

"YOU'RE DAMN LUCKY YOU DIDN'T HIT YOUR HEAD. OR YOUR face. Or lose a limb!"

I roll my eyes and stare out the car window. I shouldn't be rolling my eyes. If I'd just watched Carter run away from me barefoot during a horrible storm, stupidly climb some jagged boulders, and slip and fall while getting struck by lightning, I'd be telling him off, too.

"I get it, sometimes you need to run, that's how you are, but

Teal, we have a treadmill. Do you not know about the treadmill in the gym room? You should by now. I know you have't been here long, but you set up camp in there and everything! You can use it anytime you need to, I would never stop—"

I tune him out as the pain in my ankle intensifies when I shiver. Carter, like some kind of superhero, leapt over two boulders, lifted me up, and carried me all the way back to the house, straight to his car, where he deposited me on the passenger seat. He said he didn't give a damn if I didn't want to go to urgent care, that's where I was going, considering I'd basically been bathed in electricity.

I don't think the lightning hurt me. I know it must sound dumb, but the lightning . . . it felt familiar, when it touched my skin. Kind of how it felt when Carter had me connect to the water in the big oak tree during the craft fair . . . but so much more a vivid, visceral, fuller sensation. The difference between a photo of a cup of coffee and having one in your hands to actually sip its bittersweetness. I *knew* the lightning wouldn't hurt me, because it was as conscious and alive as I was. It reminded me of the stuff I'd always heard Sage and Sky talk about when it came to their gifts. That almost unexplainable sense of connection and belonging— Sage, she feels the cells in the plants speaking to her own cells. Sky feels that same shit with criaturas.

If I didn't know any better, I would say for one small moment, I had that piece back. That essential part of me that Mama stole when I was a little kid.

But now all I feel is pain. Because no, the lightning didn't get me. But my foot getting wedged between those big rocks at an ugly angle sure did.

I'm still wearing the hyacinth-colored dress I'd put on for the lunch with the Velasquez family. It's got long sleeves and a high neck and reaches to my knees. It was a gift from Amá Sonya and I'm pretty sure she had intended for me to wear it to brunch with her, but the lace of its edges make my skin itch, so I'd never even worn it out. I thought for sure the amount of skin it covered might endear me just a smidge to Abuela Erika, but now I know that even if I were dressed in a nun's outfit, with a veil covering my face, a rosary around my neck, and holding hands with Jesus Christ in the flesh, she'd still hate my guts.

Carter and I are both soaked, and the lace itches even more while wet and clinging to me. I full-body shiver again and cry out. Putting on a brave face, I lift my leg up to take a look at my foot. Unfortunately, Carter glances over at the same time.

"Jesus," he hisses. "That looks broken, Teal!"

The ankle is swollen to twice its size and is all black and splotched red on the outer side. When I try to move it, I want to scream.

"No, it doesn't." But my voice isn't convincing at all.

⚡

THE URGENT CARE NURSE TAKES X-RAYS OF MY FOOT AND CON-cludes that it is merely a high-ankle sprain. "One of the worst I've ever seen," Dr. Barringer tells me when he finally comes in; he's an older man with salt-and-pepper hair and the build of a biker, and he can't hide his enthusiasm. I guess he must see a lot of running noses and sore throats and my swollen, bruised ankle is the highlight of his week.

Carter gives him a dirty look as he writes a prescription for painkillers. I guess he doesn't appreciate Dr. Barringer's passion for the severity of my injury.

"Normally I'd just say alternate between Tylenol and Advil for a few days, but you need something a little stronger than that for the first bit. Then alternate the over-the-counter stuff, and keep it elevated, and ice it."

Carter runs a hand over his face. His clothes have dried up some, but they still wrap around parts of him I would rather not be noticing right now—the smooth planes of his pectoral muscles, the cuts of muscle all along his upper back and shoulders. "And what about the lightning strike?" he asks. "Shouldn't you check, I don't know. Her heart or something?"

"Lightning strike?" The doctor lifts his head. "The nurse said you'd made a joke about lightning, but . . ."

"It wasn't a joke. She was literally struck by lightning. I saw it. It was—" Carter takes a shaky breath.

"It wasn't bad," I say quietly.

"It wasn't bad?" Carter says, turning to me. "Teal, you were *struck by lightning*. In what universe can that be classified as *not bad*?"

"Okay, okay." Dr. Barringer stands and he's got a big smile on his face. I guess my being struck by lightning has probably made his whole month, maybe even year. "We don't have the facilities to check her over as thoroughly as necessary for a lightning strike. You'll have to head over to Cranberry Medical Center for that."

I shake my head. "That's not—"

"I insist," he responds, and then, with unsuppressed glee, he goes into a long list of the ways a lightning strike can fuck a human up, including but not limited to organ damage, cardiac arrest, and tissue burns. With each word, Carter's face gets paler and paler until he looks a lot worse than how I feel.

I know the lightning didn't hurt me, but I can't exactly tell them *No, you don't understand. This lightning felt familiar, like a family member, and it was really nice to me*. I can't even say *I'm actually a witch of wild lightning, or according to my great-aunt Nadia I am, so being struck is just one of those things no one needs to worry about.* Dr. Barringer would assume the lightning wrapped around my brain and fried it, and then he'd probably throw an office party over such an exciting turn of medical events.

"Carter," I say once the appointment's done and he hoists me into his arms.

"Don't." His voice is deep and sharp. "We're going to the hospital."

He gets us there in fifteen minutes flat by breaking no less than four different traffic laws on the way. After three hours of waiting and tests, and a hell of a lot more waiting, we're sent home by medical professionals who don't hide the fact that they doubt I was struck at all. 'Cause there's nothing wrong with me. Aside from the high ankle sprain, I mean. Plus the fact that I'm exhausted, and hungry, and my heart feels kind of broken.

I really thought he'd have my back today. I really thought Carter would stand up for me with his family like he did with Lani.

That's the part that makes me want to cry the most. Not the ankle, not the lightning, not even the bizarre, electricity-created reenactment of my mother leaving me when I was five years old. It's Carter and the way he let me down.

He's barely spoken to me more than necessary, and that doesn't change when we get back home. He makes me a grilled cheese and tomato soup (my heart feels stupid when I remember this is what his mother made him and his siblings when they were sick), and he makes sure there's ice on my elevated ankle at all times. He gets me my painkillers and brings me my bedtime clothes, turning his back so I can change, because he refuses to leave me alone. He even brings my toothbrush to me and a bowl to spit in, which seems unnecessarily gross, but when I balk he shakes his head and clenches his jaw and acts like . . . I don't even know. Like he cares? *Now* he cares?

When I lie down in bed, he tucks me in like I'm a little baby. "You don't have to do that. You don't have to do any of this," I mumble.

"Of course I do. I'm . . . I'm your husband."

Okay, so now he wants it to be like that. "Don't say it like that. Like you mean it."

He knows exactly what I'm talking about. "Teal, I'm sorry." His voice sounds so defeated. "While you were getting all those tests done, I looked up what you said. Verbal abuse." His shoulders slump, the small of his back wedged up against my knees. He's so warm and I wish I didn't love it as much as I do. I wish I could somehow stop wanting him in the same way I click off the heat and light of a lamp or take deep breaths to make the rainstorm go away. But I can't. All I can do now is hold my breath because I suspect he's about to make me want him more.

"We've all been raised to never question Abuela Erika, or, when he was alive, Abuelo Gene. When Erika started getting mean, we could all laugh about it later, and almost always Gene was there to balance her. But he's gone now, and . . . and a part of me knew she'd be that disrespectful. That's why I didn't want to tell my family about you. I didn't want her to treat you like that." He turns his body to look at me, and even in the dark, his eyes glow like a wild lightning storm, feral and full of heat. "I won't ever allow it again. I promise you." He glances away. "I already called and told her."

I blink. "Told her what?"

"That if I ever hear about her talking to you that way, I won't speak with her again."

I swallow a gasp. "But, Carter . . . the money."

"Right. Here." He pulls his wallet out of his pocket and hands me a folded check. "I can spot you till she gives me the money . . . or whatever."

"How can you do that? With your investments?"

He stares out the window and clears his throat. "Sí. This is nothing to me. Ta bien, Teal."

I stare at the check. It's two more zeros than I was expecting. "Are you sure, Carter? This is a big cut."

"Consider it another form of apology. I should've been the husband you deserve today. And I wasn't. Like I said, it won't happen again, but maybe that"—he nudges his chin toward the check—"maybe you can use that for something that will, I don't know, comfort you after everything you've gone through." He swallows and when he speaks again, his voice chokes. "When I saw the lightning get you out there . . . Teal. My God, I felt like I was the one who was dying. And when you fell. I thought the worst." He puts a hand on his chest and lets out a shaky chuckle. "Maybe I need to get my heart checked after today."

Next he clears his throat, letting his hand fall into his lap. "There's another thing I looked up. But you've got to let me know if I'm overstepping, all right, and I'll shut the fuck up about it."

I . . . have no idea what he could be talking about. My breath begins to get a little short. Even after all the sweet things he's said and done tonight, I still can't help thinking that he's going to kick me out after I acted like a fool on the rocks. "Yeah? Okay?"

He makes eye contact. "Bipolar disorder."

I shake my head. "Yes? I have it?"

"When you first told me about it, I did a lot of research. I wanted to, you know, figure out how to best support you and stuff. Be a good friend."

My heart feels a bit too full at these words. "That's very sweet. Go on."

"I remembered something I had read earlier." He pulls up his phone. "These are a list of symptoms, the manic states versus the depressive states. And one of the mania ones is 'excessive behaviors with painful consequences.'"

I furrow my brow. "So what the hell are you saying?"

"I don't know, Teal. I just . . . all this running you do sounds like it fits the bill, right?"

My cheeks burn as I look down. This is exactly what Sage and Sky tried to bring up with me earlier this year. That all the running I do isn't "healthy." "So what? Something's got to keep me from drowning the whole world like it's biblical times."

Carter reaches out and touches the tips of his fingers to my chin, lifting my face up. "Remember when I told you that you were the most beautiful girl I'd ever seen? This is *still true*. And I don't just mean your outsides. I mean your insides, as dumb and cliché as that sounds. What you've gone through, and being bipolar on top of it? You're so fucking strong, Teal. I don't want to see you get embarrassed and hang your head, though—" He clears his throat. "I mean, all your feelings are valid and shit. I think you should be proud of yourself, and I just wanted you to be aware of what this running could be, and now that you can't do it for a while, maybe consider other options. Like the breathing, no?"

I was right. I want him now more than ever. And I don't even know if he's being true, if he's actually going to stick to his guns about Erika, if he's going to start acting like my husband. Which is why I can't explain the way my brain immediately goes to my conversation with Sky in the PI's parking lot.

Just get it out of our systems. Right? Right now, fast, before I can think about it too long.

I fling the check onto the nightstand. "Carter," I say, my voice breathless and shaky.

He turns to me fast. "You okay? Was that too much? Or do you need another painkiller?"

I will myself to be brave. To be honest and vulnerable. I swallow, and for all my attempts at bravado, when the words finally come, they're a near whisper. "I want you to make me come."

22

H E STOPS BREATHING FOR SO LONG, I'M ALMOST ALARMED when he finally speaks. "You want me to make you come." His voice is lower and gruff. "Did I hear that right?"

"Yes." I pull the blanket down my body. I'm wearing a giant shirt and plain cotton boy shorts. I wonder if he can see how my nipples pinch in anticipation. If he'll reach for me and feel how wet I already am.

I wasn't lying earlier. I'm always so damn wet for him.

"Why? Why do you want me to do that?" he asks as his eyes linger down my body, at the hint of suggestion under the fabric— breasts, thighs, belly, rising and falling fast with my breath.

"We need to . . . you and I need to get it out of our systems." He frowns in a way that he looks maybe angry, so I go on hurriedly, "I've felt bad almost all day. I just need to feel good for once."

His face closes and my stomach drops. Neither of those reasons are the right response. He tears his gaze from me and I'm certain he's going to say no. He's going to leave me here wet, turned on, and worst of all, feeling pathetically undesirable. *No one else but me would ever want you.* As usual, Johnny's words come barreling down at the worst possible moment.

I reach to pull the blanket over me again, but he grabs my hand, stopping me. "Hands over your head." His voice is hard, as rough as the rocks along the shore, and it makes goose bumps run down my chest, hips, legs. "Grab the headboard like a good girl."

Oh my God. No way that Carter—*Carter*, the nerdy guy who always texted me Good afternoon and Good night back when we were still friends, who stopped fooling around with me one year ago because I'd drunk too much, plus he wanted to take me to *dinner* first?—*no way* he just called me a good girl like that, like if I disobey him, he'll turn me on his lap and smack my ass before fingering me to an orgasm.

"Oh my God," I say as I reach up and clamp my fists on the wood. I'm already trembling.

He lifts my shirt until it reaches my collarbone, and my nipples somehow harden even more. I shut my eyes tight until he commands, "No. Look at me." And I focus back on him just as he lowers his hot mouth to my breast.

"Oh my God." I can't stop saying it. It feels so good. Too good. He teases my nipple with his warm tongue, all the while flicking the other one with his fingers. "Oh my God, oh my *God*." I'm throbbing between my legs. It would take nothing at all to get me there—a slide of his fingers over my underwear, really—but he's not interested in making this quick for me. He prolongs the delicious torture, switching his mouth and fingers between my breasts until I'm begging for him to please *please* touch my clit.

But does he listen to me? No. Instead he kisses under my breasts. He kisses my stomach, then each hip. When I realize his plans as he lowers his broad frame down the bed, I tense. "You don't have to do that. Just use your fingers."

He doesn't break eye contact as he slides my boy shorts down my legs, carefully and tenderly under my bruised ankle. "Teal, I've been wanting to eat you out since I first learned what that even was. You really going to deprive me of it?"

I close my eyes briefly. Is he serious? He can't be. I hate to think about Johnny in this moment, but I can't help it. My ex acted like me sucking him off was a privilege for *me*, and meanwhile him returning the favor was literal torture. He asked me to shower beforehand, and then he would cover me with flavored lube just so he could survive fifteen seconds of licking. I even went to the doctor, convinced there was a reason why he hated the taste of me. When I finally asked him about it, he wrinkled up his nose and said, *No man really enjoys that. Maybe if you didn't get so wet . . .*

And getting wet isn't exactly something I can control. So I asked him to stop eating me out and he joyfully complied.

I shake my head of these thoughts. My worst nightmare is having to repeat that with Carter. I don't want him to go down on me while counting the seconds until he could stop. I honestly can't think of a worse turnoff than that. "But guys don't really like to do that, which I understand. It's—"

"I like it."

I open my eyes to see, even in the dim lightning, the sincerity on his face.

"You do?"

He nods, and then he yanks my legs open, again, taking care with my left foot. I gasp when I feel his hot breath against the slick parts of me. When he gives me a long, hard lick, I moan so loud, it's like nothing exists but my voice and my pleasure for that long moment. "I fucking *love* this," he says, and all my insecurities about my past, about the criticism I'd heard when I asked for this, they all melt away. Along with me, under the wide, hot pressure of Carter's tongue.

"I'm going to come," I say after about two minutes. It's too good. So warm, so—

He then removes his mouth from me.

"Carter, what the hell?" I reach down to pull him back but he leans away from me even more.

"Hands on the headboard or I'll punish you." His voice is stern but there's a ghost of a smile on his face.

"You're already punishing me!" I yelp, but then I fist the wood behind me once more.

Carter smiles. "You wanna come?"

"I need to come so bad." I squirm under his hot gaze. His hands reach my hips to stop me. "I've got my hands on the headboard, all right? Can my reward be an orgasm?"

"Beg. I want to hear you beg again."

I moan, because hearing him demand it is such a wild turn-on.

"Beg me to make you come, Teal."

"Please. Carter, please, please, make me come. Please—"

He lifts my hips—again, gently, glancing back to make sure my foot is still on the pillow—and when he lowers his mouth to me, this time, it's to slip his tongue inside me.

I gasp and my next moan is silent. He's *tongue-fucking* me. I didn't know people did this in real life. While his tongue licks me inside, he reaches up with his fingers, and pinches my clit. Hard. I'm so slippery that what happens is he slides all over me, somehow in all the right ways, and my body arches up as I moan.

I come so hard, I swear I see the Milky Way, swirling in a great cosmic spiral, right here in this bedroom. It's either the longest orgasm in history, or about five of them all rolling into one another. I've never felt anything like it, not even when it's just me and my vibrator, which is pretty much the only way I can come.

I've never believed women when they said it felt like their soul left their bodies during sex. Now I do.

"Oh my God," I whisper because I still can't believe that happened. Carter leans back, his mouth wet and smiling. It's hot. It's so hot I feel another surge of arousal, even so soon after that epic orgasm.

I can't believe how good he is at that, which makes me consider how else he's good. "Do you have a condom?" I ask, not at all hiding my desperation.

Carter's smile at my pleasure, at my seemingly endless orgasm, drops immediately. "We're not doing that, Teal. I told you the other day."

"What?" I almost jump out of my bed, but remembering the pain of my foot, I settle for sitting upright. "What do you mean, we're not doing that? Shouldn't you—" I glance down where he's not even trying to hide how hard he is. His erection should probably be painful by now.

He shakes his head. "This was about making you feel good, remember?"

"But now I can make you feel good."

"No, Teal. This was about you."

That's what I said, wasn't it? That I needed to feel good. But that wasn't really what this was about. It was about us getting it out of our systems. It was about me doing this and being cured of wanting more from Carter, because if I wanted him forever, it would just be painful forever, knowing he couldn't ever want me in return. Knowing he didn't want a broken woman for his for-real wife.

"You . . ." Carter begins. He turns away from me. "I don't think I want you the same way you want me right now."

My heart feels like it's dropped to my belly. It's like he heard all my worst thoughts about us, about me, and decided to confirm them in a single statement. I turn over. "Fine. I'm going to sleep."

He sighs as he stands. "Teal—"

"I'm going to sleep, Carter."

After a few moments, he sighs once more, and then he leaves, shutting the door softly behind him.

⚡

IN THE MORNING, CARTER IS GONE, THE ONLY SIGNS THAT HE had been up the blanket left curled up like a cat on the pull-out, plus the lingering scent of coffee and toast in the kitchen.

For a single, groggy moment, after limping around and not seeing him, I think maybe he has left me. Even though it makes no sense—this is his house, we're still married, where would he go?—but the suspicion hits my stomach like a blade. When I see the note scrawled on the counter, I exhale in embarrassing relief.

> *Gotta work today. Please stay off your foot. Have a bagel or cereal for breakfast and heat up leftovers for lunch. Don't move too much. Don't even THINK about running. Ice and elevation. Don't cook. I'll bring home dinner. —C*

Tears sting at my eyes and I put my arms on the counter, taking some of the weight off my now-dominant foot. Am I always going to think that someone will leave me after a bad day? Will the trauma of Mama abandoning me cling to me forever, like the weight of battered armor I didn't ask for?

I need to find her. I need to fix this, fix my brain, my emotions, *me*.

As the egg bagel toasts, I grab cream cheese, a knife, and my phone. I drag a stool next to the toaster and hit up Gerald Samuels's number.

"Samuels," he says when he picks up.

"Hi, Gerald. It's Teal Flores here. Just calling to see if you had any updates."

His responding sigh tells me even before he uses his words. "So far, my team and I have done a thorough electronic search of your mom. We've used our usual means, but they've turned up very little leads."

The bagel pops out of the toaster, and I push the button down again. Sage thinks I'm some kind of freak because I like all my toasted bread just one shade shy of burnt, but honestly, she uses the toaster more like a warmer than anything else, grabbing the bread after it's been heating for all of five seconds. She may as well pop *her* bagel in the microwave and she thinks *I'm* the freak? "What kind of leads?"

"Well, we've found a marriage certificate dated from 1993. The marriage was annulled only two months later, and the former groom passed away a decade ago."

"What was his name?" I ask as my heart picks up.

"Richard Sanchez."

It doesn't ring any bells, but why would it? It's not like we were ever introduced to any of Mama's boyfriends, not even our fathers. Given the timeline, though, this was probably the man Mama left us for. The impatient jackass in his big truck, revving the engine to hurry up a woman saying goodbye to her daughter for the last time ever. Maybe it makes me a bad person to say it, but I don't feel a single bit sad at learning he's dead.

Gerald lists me other things they've found—a broken deed on a house from years ago, an apartment rented for all of two weeks. I'm halfway done with my bagel when he asks, "Look, this might sound weird, but has your mom ever gone by the name Vivienne?"

I shake my head even though he can't see me. "Uh, no, not to my knowledge."

"It's not a family name or anything?"

I try to remember if Nadia has ever mentioned the name in her long stories about our lineage, but nothing comes up. "Nope."

"We just found a woman who has kind of a stage name or something, Vivienne Cora. Some of her performances and art shows seemed to coincide with your mom's whereabouts over the years. But we can't find Viv's real name—all the galleries she's worked with no longer exist." He grunts out another sigh. "We'll keep going, Teal. Lots of cases start slow, and then one big lead makes things get real hot, real fast."

Inexplicably, I think of the woman at the beach. The one in the distance during the lightning storm. She was on one side of the cackling electricity between us, and I was on the other. A scene drew itself in actual lightning between us—me, a baby, running after Mama, begging her to stay.

What if that woman on the beach was Mama?

Even as the thought comes, I push it away. I have no evidence whatsoever that it could be her. Probably she was just someone who got caught in a bad storm and looked up and witnessed another woman get struck by the most bizarre lightning anyone had ever seen. I don't know anyone who would've been able to tear their eyes away from such a spectacle.

I thank him before hanging up, and then I take some pain pills before limping to wash up and change and sit on my bed, looking out the window in a daze.

The sky is as blue as crushed blueberries swirled into yogurt, with streams of clouds bobbing by, light as meringue topping. The sea is gray like some of Sage's Montana sapphire jewelry, slate blue set into silver. Lots of families have packed themselves on the shoreline, their bathing suits looking like tropical flowers against the more subdued sky, sea, and sand.

It was like the lightning storm never even happened. And what if . . . what if the part where I saw people-shaped lightning *really* didn't happen? Can people hallucinate when they're being electrocuted? I didn't even think to ask Carter if he'd seen it. I was too caught up in the way he slid his tongue inside me, I guess.

My entire body heats at the memory, with my chest and stomach and some . . . lower . . . places tingling as though a hundred Fourth-of-July sparklers were lit too close to my skin. Jesus, Carter is good at oral. I've never been with a guy who was like that before. Johnny obviously was never into it, with him having to cover me in melon-flavored lube just to withstand fifteen seconds of it. And Nate . . . Nate *said* he liked it just fine, but he held his tongue so far away from me that it got cold. And then it felt like he was rubbing a refrigerated sea creature along my clit. Maybe some women are into ice play, but I'm not one of them.

Carter did things to me I didn't even know I wanted. I didn't know it could feel like that. I didn't know any part of a man could feel better than a vibrator.

But what good is knowing that doing me? Carter made it clear that he didn't want me the way I want him. Now all I have is the knowledge of how amazing he is with at least one part of sex, and also the humiliation that he only did it out of pity, not 'cause he really wanted to. *I don't think I want you the same way you want me.*

I bury my face in my hands. I need to get over my husband. Which means I need even more of a distraction than the throb of my ankle.

I limp toward my dresser and pull out my familiar, wrinkled little piece of paper.

New Year's Resolutions for Teal Flores
1. *Stop being selfish.*
2. *Make it up to Sage.*
3. *Make it up to Sky.*
4. *Become best friends with Carter again.*

Honest to God, my lower lip trembles when I reread that last one. I'd written it down with as much optimism I could muster, but the sad truth is I think even all the way back then, I knew becoming best friends with Carter was a pipe dream. Outside, cement gray clouds rush in and I can almost *feel* the dismay emanating from the people on the beach. I do my breath work until I feel . . . not happy, exactly, but some numb place just outside despair. Someplace where the clouds don't leave, but they no longer look heavy and ominous, either.

I take one last counted breath and refocus on the list. Unplugging my phone from its charging cord, I pull up my family text group.

Me: Hey, who wants to meet up for lunch today? My treat

Amá Sonya: You and I have brunch tomorrow, since we missed it last Sunday. Do not forget and do NOT be late.

Me: Is that your way of saying you can't make it today?

Me: . . .

Me: Amá?

Nadia: I'm sure Sonya is too busy volunteering for her HOA today. There are many neighbors out to spy on to report and threaten.

Amá: For your information, Nadia, I am currently at a banquet with the mayor, the large editor from the Cranberry Chronicle, and that young man from that big-time newspaper from the New York City.

Me: the large editor?

Sage: I think she means editor at large.

Sky: Wait, the young man from New York City? Do you mean Adam? Adam Noemi? Do you mean the New York Times when you say "big-time newspaper"? Is he in town again?

For the love of the old gods. I should have just texted one of them at a time. I sigh as my phone explodes with near-constant dings and buzzing for the next five minutes. Yes, Adam Noemi from the *New York Times* is back in town. Yes, she meant editor-at-large but Sonya hates being wrong so she's insisting that everyone is calling her the Large Editor as some kind of inside joke.

Sky: But why? What's Adam doing there with the editor and the mayor?

Amá Sonya: He's leaving the big-time paper for the Chronicle. They are honoring him with the position right now.

Sky: WHAT? WHY?!

Sage: really? leaving the NYT? Why would he do that tho

Amá Sonya: He is a handsome young man, but not too bright. Surely he's making less money here.

Nadia: There has to be another reason. Maybe his grandfather needs more help.

Sky: I spent the day with Old Man Noemi yesterday and he was fit as a fiddle, or so he claimed.

Me: Maybe the Times dropped him. Either way, does anyone want to get lunch today? Please pretty please?

Amá Sonya: Do not forget that we have brunch tomorrow. Do not be late.

Me: I'm going to go ahead and assume that's your version of 'no,' Amá

Nadia: I'm can't because I'm at the church. We're organizing meals to deliver them to the homeless all afternoon.

If we were with each other in person, this would be the point where Amá sucks in her mouth like she's been forced to drink a glass of straight lime juice and then goes into explicit detail on her latest philanthropy work. She can't have Nadia "winning" at anything. But I guess she's busy at the banquet, since she doesn't text again.

Sky: I can after work. I'm here till one if you don't mind it being a late lunch.

Sage: I'm picking her up. I can come too

Me: Good, swing by and pick me up after please? I sprained my ankle and can't drive rn.

Nadia: How did you hurt your ankle TEAL?

I can't even begin to make sense of why only my name is in all caps, so I am going to assume that's a weird elder boomer thing. I wonder if I should tell them everything in response. Well, not everything. I'll definitely leave out last night's tongue situation.

Should I say how Carter's grandmother thinks I'm working directly for el diablo to ruin her grandson? How Carter sided with her, so I ran directly into a lightning storm in which human figures made of electricity were conjured out of thin air? And that's the reason why my ankle is fucked now—because I'm an idiot who can't control her gift and thinks climbing rocks in the rain is a fantastic hobby?

Old Teal—Selfish Teal—would have just laid it all out, expecting lots of attention and advice and maybe some kind of witchy limpia, because that people-made-of-lightning shit is damn creepy as hell and Nadia would surely want to pull it out of me with candles and eggs and an offering to the old gods.

But now *I* want to be the one to help. I want to be the one who is generous and soft and sweet.

So I don't answer Nadia's question. Instead, I type:

Me: After lunch I'm going to buy you a car, Sky.

And then, because I decided to be nice—not a saint—I add:

Me: And Nadia, why didn't you ever tell us that you
banged Eugenio Velasquez?

And then I put my vibrating phone aside and begin to get
ready for lunch.

23

M Y SISTERS AND I DECIDE ON LUNCH AT MOONSHINE Pizza, where they'll give us three free garlic breadsticks with our order. I don't typically indulge in simple carbs this many times in a week, but with everything that's happened in the last forty-eight hours, I order not one, but two Sicilian squares topped with extra Parmesan cheese, and I eat my garlic breadstick first, while waiting in line to pay, dipping it in the complimentary garlic butter they offer by the plastic forks and knives. Because who cares what I smell like when I'm never going to touch Carter, or any man for that matter, again?

"Tell me about your job," I say to Sky as we wait for them to heat up our slices.

Sky's face breaks into the biggest smile I've seen on her in a long time. "Oh, my gosh, Teal. It's so fun. The basement is dark and creepy, like in a horror film, and it's *dusty*. There are little windows at the tops of the walls and you can see the dust motes dancing in them like magic fairy dust!"

I huff out a startled laugh. "No offense, Sky, but literally nothing you've just said I would describe as *fun*."

She grins even bigger in response, and seeing her so happy . . . damn. It makes my chest feel warm and fuzzy, like that one scene in the Grinch film when his heart just about busts out of his chest. "Seriously. It's fun. The books are so old that I have to wear dainty white gloves when I handle them. Right now I am documenting the most damaged ones so we have digital copies of everything before they basically disintegrate."

"Are any of the books cool?" Sage asks between texting Tenn.

"They're okay. Kind of hard to read, 'cause a lot of them have been eaten by little book bugs."

"Ew." I wrinkle my nose. "Well, I suppose dainty little white gloves matches your sexy librarian aesthetic." I nod to her outfit. She's got on a gray button-down tucked into what I'm pretty sure is the tweed Chanel pencil skirt Amá Sonya and I found for her when we had that all-damn-day shopping excursion. Her stockings are black and lacy, and her shoes are adorable-yet-hot Mary Janes.

"I guess," she says, her face turning pink. When we walked in here, nearly every person turned their head to check her out, regardless of their gender. And it wasn't that she's the "town freak." Trust me. I know lusty gazes when I see them, and people are *still* giving her bedroom eyes. She still has no idea how beautiful she is, but my guess is that will come with time.

"So Nadia and Abuelo Gene?" Sage says when we're settled at a table with our food. "Are you for serious about that?"

I raise an eyebrow. "It came from the elder bitch's lips herself."

"Who, Amá?" Sky asks.

I snort. Fair assumption, I suppose. "No, the other elder bitch. Abuela Erika."

"So she still hates you, huh," Sky says.

I shake my head with a sarcastic smile. "The word 'hate' doesn't even begin to touch it. If we were in this same scenario a couple hundred years ago, she'd frame me for witchcraft and toss me in a river herself."

My sisters laugh, but my laugh isn't as robust. It was something in Erika's last words to me. How much even truer they ring now. *You are broken, just like her. Just like your mother, and your sisters. Broken.*

I don't think my sisters are broken. But there sure was something off about Mama . . . and no one can deny my own brand of fucked-up-ness.

"I want to hear Erika's exact words," Sage demands, pointing a breadstick at me.

I can feel the damn blood sinking from my face to my heart, and both Sage and Sky tilt their heads at me in confusion.

"Was it really bad?" Sky asks. "Did she try to curse Nadia as well?"

"Oh." For some reason, my brain malfunctioned, and I thought they were asking about the other crap Erika told me. The stuff I was literally just repeating to myself. I try really hard to make my sigh of relief silent, but there's no way I'm fooling either of these mujeres. I swear, both Sage and Sky have a secondary gift of sussing out people's exact emotions.

"What did you think I was asking, exactly?" Sage asks after she finishes her pizza crust. Normally she goes for plain old four-cheese, but the baby must have ruined her taste buds for the time being, because she is now working on her second piece of bacon, olive, and *pineapple.*

I decide that ignoring her last question in favor of answering her first is the best course of action. "Erika said something like

You Flores women think you're all powerful and you hypnotize men with your evil, stupid magic, but you can't get away with it while I'm around, and blah, blah, Gene chose me over Nadia despite her witchy and wicked ways!"

Sky laughs. "She didn't say it like that, did she?"

I shrug and force a smile. "Look, it may not be verbatim, but that definitely covers the essence of her message."

I check my phone again, where there's been radio silence from Nadia over my asking her about Abuelo Gene.

"So Erika knows, you think?" Sage asks. "About . . . our gifts?" She lowers her voice so that Sky and I can barely hear her.

I shrug. "She seems to know *something* but honestly, I wasn't exaggerating that she thought it involved hypnotizing good men into behaving badly. So she obviously either didn't get any true information, or she twisted it in her vindictive mind." I cross my legs under the table and wince. Damn, I'd forgotten to bring my painkillers and my ankle's already throbbing like a bitch. Car shopping after this is going to suck so bad.

"Do either of you have Advil?" I ask.

Sage murmurs *yes* in response as she digs through her bag. "So you tripped on the beach, huh?" She hands me two Tylenol pills while surveying my leg. But she's not seeing anything un-usual because the lounge pants I wore are low and wide-legged and my comfiest Adidas cover everything else ankle-related. As in, my whole feet.

"Yeah, while running." I don't make eye contact with either of them as I down the pills and push up, holding almost all my weight on my good side. "Let's go, chicas. The car dealership closes at four today."

"Wait," Sky says. "You were serious? About getting me a car? Like . . . *what?*"

"Yes. I am buying you a car. And you know what? Sage, I'm getting you a car, too." It's not really fair that Sage had to save up to buy that raggedy old van that she's still driving over a decade later. I insisted that Nadia buy me a *new* car—and it had to be new, because I was a brat—and I didn't bat an eye when my sister came home with what is basically a warped, paint-chipped metallic rectangle stapled to wheels. There's no way she can drive that for much longer, and it can't be safe for a baby, either.

"So Erika gave you the money?" Sage asks.

"Yes. Sort of." It feels too complicated that Carter gave me an advance on it, but whatever. "Come on, muévete, muévete!" I hurry out, putting too much weight on my bad ankle in the process. Tears sting in my eyes at the pain, but I push on.

Sky chatters about old books and dust motes all the way there, and at the car dealership, both Sage and I push her to make a decision, since she can't seem to manage it even after an hour and a half of looking at the same three cars. "This feels like too expensive a gift," she tells me, but it really isn't. If we were at a Lexus dealership, okay, or even a new car dealership, I'd understand. But these vehicles are all used, and they're working well, and they're all around ten to fifteen grand.

Compared to eight years of her life gone? That's fucking *nothing*.

After only twenty more minutes of hemming and hawing, she chooses a two-year-old Volvo C70—a convertible!—in a shimmering baby blue. She's so excited, she can't stop clapping her hands together like a little kid. "Look! The interior seats are red!" she tells us with several hand claps. "Oh, gosh, it still smells new!" She somehow manages to clap her hands while sticking her whole head through the front passenger-side window.

"What about you?" I turn to Sage, who's watching Sky with a faint, sweet smile on her face.

"Hmm?" She raises her eyebrows as she turns to me.

I gesture to the glare emanating off the vehicles surrounding us for a mile in each direction. "Which one do you want?"

"I don't need a car, Teal."

I scoff. "Uh, yeah, you do. You shouldn't be driving that old garbage anymore."

"Come on." She laughs. "The van isn't garbage! It hasn't broken down once in ten years!"

"The back window is held together with packing tape, Sage."

She sighs and I feel my heart lift, because I am certain she's about to give in. But instead, she says, "I don't need a car because Tenn's giving me one for my birthday."

It's stupid that I'm disappointed by this news. Look, I'm not mad that her awesome, hot, soon-to-be husband is buying her a car. But how else am I supposed to make it up to her? All that crap I put her through, blaming her for Sky's death? Punching her in the face so that she needed stitches? Growing a few dahlias doesn't really cover that. "Are you sure, though? What if Tenn and I put our money together and got you something extra nice?"

She runs her hand over her belly. If you squint, you can make out the first hints of her bump, even though the baby's still the size of a very small marble. "I'm sure."

I run a hand over my face and lean against the car to take my weight off my feet. Sky's inside, adjusting the seat between bouts of hand clapping. The Tylenol took the edge off, but now my good side is sore because it's doing all the work. "What if I got you whatever you needed for the nursery? The crib, the bouncer, the décor. Bookshelves, paint—"

"Teal. We're good on all that. Plus, that's what baby showers are for."

"But—"

"Teal." Her voice is firm. "We're good."

Even though I know she doesn't mean it that way, I feel it like a gut punch. Old Teal would've snapped at her with something hurtful, to try to dull the pain of what seems like Sage's rejection of my goodwill. Instead, I hold my breath. I should be counting it, but whatever. When I finally let it out in an annoyed huff, thunder rumbles in the distance.

"We should get the paperwork done before it storms," I say to Sky, and then I limp toward the main building.

24

T HE RAIN SLAMS HARD AGAINST THE WINDSHIELD OF THE
van, blocking the view with a wall of slick gray. We
should've made it back to Carter's thirty minutes ago, but we're
traveling at a crawl because of the lack of clarity on the beach
highway.

"She loves the car." Sage keeps her eyes on the road as she
says it. "It was good of you to do that."

Sky texted us five minutes ago to say she made it back to Nadia's in one piece. I can't help but faintly smile as I think of the
way she drove out of the dealership parking lot, her honey brown
hair flying straight up through the open top like a troll doll.

"Teal?"

"Yeah?" I won't look at her when she talks. I know I'm being
a bitch, but I need time to get over this. And time to figure out a
way to make things up to her, too. Growing her dahlias just isn't
enough.

"There *is* something you can buy . . . if you want to."

I turn my gaze to her fast. "Sure. Whatever you want." I

wince. "But, like, within reason. I can't afford to buy you a house right now or anything." I frown thoughtfully. "Maybe a down payment for one, though."

Sage laughs as she pulls into Carter's driveway, where his car is already parked. I think I might see him peeking at us through the window, but maybe it's just some weird shadows this hard rain is causing. "You really think I'd ask you to buy me a house?"

"Maybe a down payment," I say defensively, crossing my arms.

Her smile is warm. "Okay, before I tell you what it is, you have to promise me you'll get it. Okay?"

This time my frown is from confusion. "Um. Why would I need to promise that before I buy the damn thing? What the hell is it?"

She shakes her head. "Promise, Teal."

"What is it, Sage? Do you want money for something bad?" I rack my brain. "Debt? Is Tenn addicted to gambling?"

"No!" Now she's cracking up like this is some kind of joke.

"Did you piss off the mafia?"

She snorts as she giggles. "Yeah, that's it. I pissed off the very prevalent presence of mafia organizations we have here in Cranberry, Virginia."

"Well, we're not that far from Philly, or Jersey, or even the city for that matter!"

Her laughter finally calms down enough for her to speak. "No. Not the mafia."

I wait for her to explain it—or even give a hint—but she doesn't back down. We have a miniature staring contest for almost a whole minute before I sigh. "Fine. I promise I'll get the thing. As long as it's not a hit man, I guess." I pause with a thoughtful frown. "Well, depending on who you want dead, I might consider a hit man."

She grabs her purse from under her seat—an old-looking Kate Spade; mental note: buy Sage a new purse, too—and pulls out a folded flyer. She hands it to me with one raised eyebrow.

I know there is a very good chance this isn't mafia-related, but it kind of feels like we're doing some kind of shady deal. I slowly unfold the paper in silence as she watches, fully expecting one of those folded paper snakes to bounce out or some shit. But the only thing that is revealed are letters, words, and when I read them, I glance up at her with an incredulous look on my face.

"A leather-handbag-making class."

Sage raises her eyebrows. "Yes."

"You want to take a leather-handbag-making class?"

She laughs and shakes her head. "No, Teal. You're taking the class."

I scoff. "No, I'm not. Come on, Sage. What was it that you wanted me to get for you?"

She grabs the paper and shakes it around. "This! This is what I wanted. I want you to take this class. For me."

My eyes are still unnaturally big and I can't seem to relax my face in any capacity. "*Why?*"

Sage raises an eyebrow and gives a big sigh, like for all the world, she doesn't understand why *I'm* not understanding. But that's preposterous. I want to make things up to her, and she wants me to accomplish this by my signing up for a useless class?

She counts on her fingers as she responds. "In the last four or five years, you've knitted, crocheted, bound books, and made candles. Am I forgetting anything?"

"Whittling," I mumble, looking out the window.

"Whittling. But none of those stuck. You know why?"

"Because I'm a lazy bitch?" I mean the words to come out like a joke, but instead they are as sour as the strongest synthetically flavored cough syrup.

Sage doesn't miss my tone. "You're not lazy. Or a bitch."

I'm not going to argue with her. I don't want to prove her wrong, even though she's rather enormously and stupidly wrong. Which is the whole reason I'm trying to buy her shit to begin with.

Sage blows air out of her mouth so her cheeks hollow. "Our whole lives, you have loved handbags. Do you remember when we were little, how you carried around those straw Easter baskets? You put Nadia's old credit cards in a sandwich bag, and that was your 'wallet'?"

I snort mirthlessly. "I was just a dumb kid."

"And now, whenever we go anywhere, you should see the way your eyes light up when you check out what people are carrying."

I shrug. "That's just normal curiosity."

"And when we helped you move. My God. I had no idea you owned that many. But you insisted on bringing *every single one* to Carter's."

"A woman needs options," I respond as primly as Amá Sonya would, because that's exactly something she would say.

"Teal." Sage looks at me with big, tea-brown eyes. "Your passion is purses."

My cheeks heat. "No, it's not. And that's a stupid passion. It's shallow and dull. And who cares about handbags that much, anyway?"

A memory comes to me in that moment, back when I was still with Johnny. It was before he had hit me for the first time, but after nearly a year of near-constant emotional and verbal abuse. He had seen me touching a male client at work. And by that, he meant he'd "caught" me "cheating." What had actually happened was I said to the guy, "Hey, is it okay if I put your hand on the right spot on the machine?" because verbal dictation wasn't working on him. And once he said sure, then I did it without thinking. Because that was my *job*. Neither I nor my happily married client gave the action a single blink.

I didn't even know Johnny was there, much less watching. And when he and I went to dinner that night, he acted one hundred percent normal—charming, attentive, and slightly douchey after a couple of drinks. We went to his place after. I'd locked myself in the bathroom to freshen up, because Johnny insisted on daily sex, whether I was into it or not. His nasty temper showed up whenever I denied him anything sexual, which he felt, as a man, he'd had a right to, so best to just get it over with, I'd figured out early on.

And when I got back out, he was holding up a pair of scissors, scissors that were big and orange and ugly and buried in my purse, which was already half shredded.

The Dooney & Bourke small Florentine satchel in the color natural was my first grown-up handbag that I'd saved up for and bought myself. A lot of people don't consider D&B all that fancy or luxe—when Amá had seen my bag for the first time, she scrunched up her nose as though I'd stuffed it with a live turkey— but it was the first purchase I'd made that I was legitimately proud of. Not to mention, the bag was *gorgeous*—smooth, warm brown leather, with fancy matching tassels and all the compartments a girl could need, in a sophisticated yet casual silhouette.

Johnny knew how much I'd loved it. *Silly*, he'd called me when he saw me taking selfies with it to send to Leilani. Come to think of it, Johnny called me *silly* a lot. Once upon a time, I thought it meant he found me enchanting or something. Now I know he meant it like he saw me as a dumb, childish girl.

Anyway, he knew how I felt about that bag, and he decided to punish me for being good at my job by ripping it to pieces.

I lose my temper a lot. I know that's not news or anything. But when I get mad, I tend to yell and scream and generally lose my shit. But I didn't do that with Johnny, not even when he was doing basically the meanest thing anyone had ever done to me. On some level, I must've realized it wasn't safe to be one hundred percent myself around him—especially if that version of myself wasn't smiling, pleasing, giving in to him in any way he demanded, verbally and otherwise.

Instead I cried like a little kid. I wept under his smirking, smiling face, drawing down a torrential, loud rainstorm he didn't even deign to notice. "How could you do that?" I'd asked in a painfully embarrassing, midsob gasp. "*Why* would you do that?"

He laughed. "You're so superficial, Teal. God. It's just a handbag." He picked up the torn bag and put on a high-pitched, effeminate voice. "*Look at me! I'm just a girl who saved too much well-earned money to buy an ugly purse. So I could impress the men I work with like the slut I am.*"

When I blink and return to where I actually am—in Carter's driveway, in Sage's ugly old van, the rain whipping even harder all around—I snap. "Look, Sage, I know what you think you're doing here. You think that you can fix me up and make me whole again, by making me like you. You found jewelry and plant hunting and Tenn and now you're engaged and pregnant and getting your new stupid car to go with your shiny new life. But it's not like that with me." I inhale sharply when lightning cracks way too close to the car, lighting us up in equal parts glowing gold and blue. "I can't be happy until I fix my gift, and I can't fix my gift until I find Mama, and you know her gift means we're *never* going to find her! Which means I am forever unfixable, unlovable, which is why Carter, and you, have always found it so fucking easy to run away from me, am I right?"

I'm too scared to look at her when she breathes, "Teal, no—"

I take a deep breath. Dammit. I'm not supposed to be doing things like blowing up on my sister, one of the few people I'm trying to fix things with! "Look, I know I just said some shit I'm going to regret in about sixty seconds, Sage, and I'm sorry, okay? I just can't stand feeling this way. I can't stand—" I lift a hand, gesturing to the sky. "Let's finish this later," I say. "I need to breathe, you need to get home."

I consider it a victory when I don't slam the door on my way out of the car. Old Teal would've snapped the car damn well in half. That's gotta count for something, right?

25

BY THE TIME I'M INSIDE, I'M SOAKED TO THE BONE AND whimpering in pain. It's been too long since I've taken one of the prescription pain pills.

Carter shoots up out of nowhere like a damn vampire rising from his coffin. "Jesus," I say, startling back on my bad foot. "Fuck, *no*," I add as I tumble to the ground.

Carter grips my arm and hoists me up into his arms before my face can meet the wood floor. "Stop fucking saving me all the time," I mumble into his pec.

"Maybe I like saving you all the time, you ever think about that?"

He sets me on the sofa gently, like I'm something precious and beautiful. It feels like a lie, not just because I'm actually not precious and beautiful, but because as of late, one of his hobbies is to romantically reject me.

"I'll get you a towel." He reappears in about twenty seconds with what looks like half the towels he owns, and he begins wrapping them around me like I'm some orphan he found on the side of the street. And I'm too exhausted—and in too much pain—to stop him.

He clears his throat. "Would it make a single bit of difference if I scolded you for going out while your ankle was this fucked?"

"Nope."

"Thought so." He says it with tenderness. Like he's accepted my stupidity as some dreamy personality trait. He pulls out a glass of water and one of my painkillers, and I down both like they're as important to me as air.

"I got takeout from the Greek place downtown, the one by the pizza places. You like the chicken gyros, right? With extra tzatziki on the side?"

I can't help but give him a weak half smile. "You remembered what I like?"

His eyes on me are the way pure gold looks next to candlelight. "I remember everything, Teal."

It's these kinds of things that make my brain and my heart trip all over each other. Like the way he told me how much he wanted me at our wedding party, how he had to run to hide his apparently massive erection when I kissed his neck. How he ran after me and yelled at me after I climbed the beach rocks, how he grabbed his heart afterward like I'd nearly ripped it in two with my carelessness over my person. The way he kissed my body and ate me out last night, like he was savoring me, like he'd spent a decade waiting to do that and he tried to make it last as long as he could.

So he doesn't want me for real. That's not news to me. I know I'm not supposed to believe my ex's words—*No one would ever want you but me*—but there's a grain of truth there, a grain that's not going to dislodge until I find Mama.

Why not enjoy this marriage, then, while I can? I can leave my heart out of it. All I have to do is remember that *his* heart checked out of wanting me years ago. It's a very effective reminder.

The pain in my ankle has already gone from throbbing to dull, so I turn to him and say, "Can I make you come, Carter?"

He freezes—I think he was about to stand and heat up our dinner—and huffs out a short exhale. "We can't. Sex isn't—"

"I don't want to have sex with you," I say sharply. It's only half a lie. I would love to have sex with Carter, but not if he so obviously doesn't want it. "I want to suck on your cock until you come down my throat, if you're good with that."

He freezes again, only this time his cheeks pinken right before my eyes. When I look down at his lap, there is no denying how my words have affected him. He swallows. "Here?" he says in a bit of a croak.

I get on the ground, on my knees and on my hands, and crawl to him, dragging my injured ankle slightly above the ground. I don't think I look particularly like a jackass. I've got the ab control to make this look natural despite my injury, I think.

He groans. "Jesus, Teal, seeing you like that. All hungry for it. You want to do this for real?"

There are things I know I can't tell him right now. I can't tell him that I have wanted him for so long—even before he came over and kissed me a year ago at Nadia's, when he stopped me because I'd drunk too much moonshine.

And I can't tell him that I broke things off with Nate Bowen, who was arguably the nicest and most polite boyfriend on the planet, because I couldn't stop thinking about that damn kiss.

I can't say these things, so I hope I can somehow convey them with my hands, my mouth, my tongue. I lift up on my knees, wincing just a little when I rest my ankle on the floor.

"You okay?" he says quickly, blinking out of his lusty haze to put a hand on my shoulder. "We should probably just eat, Teal, yeah? You don't—"

He stops when I skim my fingers over his erection through his jeans, and he throws his head back. "God." It comes out as a moan that makes my entire body want to shiver.

I try to wrap my hand around it as best as I can and give it a gentle squeeze. He squirms as he tries to smother his grunt. "I know you want me to suck you off, Carter. So stay *still*"—I grip his hips, hard enough to pinch—"and be *good*, or I'll have to punish you."

I'm throwing his dirty talk right back at him, and he's loving it. He inhales in a grunt as his pupils dilate so much it looks like his eyes are simply rings of gold around fathomless black holes. His breath is already so ragged. "How—how would you punish me?"

I raise an eyebrow and flip my hair back. "I wouldn't let you come."

"You w—" I begin to unbutton his jeans and his voice is completely gone, he is so intent on watching this, like he wants to memorize every moment and won't let anything distract him, not even his own words.

I reach in his boxers and pull him out, all thick and hot and so hard, this must honestly be painful for him. He hisses through his teeth and drops his head back again, shifting his hips.

"I said, *stop moving*." I make my tone strict, like how I'd imagine a woman who was super confident at this would be. "Or I'll lick you"—I bend down and drag my tongue from the base to his tip—"suck you"—I put it all in my mouth, practically, but not quite, down my throat, and tighten around him, releasing him with a wet pop—"and then leave you here in agony."

He is trying so hard not to move, he's already got sweat

beading up on his forehead. "I'm not moving, I'm not moving." He nearly whispers it, his fists clenched at his sides.

It's such a turn-on, being this much in control of his body and his pleasure. Making it into a game for the both of us, a game that feels safe and sexy at the same time, something I had never experienced before Carter went down on me last night.

I try my hardest to make it as good for him as possible. I bob my head over him, getting sloppy until he's moaning loud, and then I focus on the most sensitive spot on the underside of his tip until he's begging me to . . . I'm not sure what. "Please, Teal," he keeps saying. "I'm going to come too fast." It sounds like he doesn't want to come fast, but at the same time, he's begun to lift his hips in a ridiculously hot rhythm, and I'm not sure he's even aware of it.

I release him and shove his pants down. "Spread your legs."

He obeys without question, without hesitation, his erection looking almost angry with its reddened tip. "You were moving," I say accusingly. "You were trying to fuck my mouth!"

"I'm sorry!" he says. "I didn't— I couldn't—"

"So now I get to put my finger wherever I want." I point straight up and wiggle, and unfathomably, the memory of Sky miming getting fingered at the restaurant, using all five fingers, comes to me and I have to suppress the urge to laugh.

I know, I know, I just said if he disobeyed I wouldn't let him come. But I think he and I and all the old gods all know I couldn't do that to Carter. And it's also for my own selfish purposes—I've never seen him come before. I've never made him come before. And I need to do it, to wring it out of him, like I need my next breath.

"You're going to—" His eyes are wide. "I've never—"

"Can I? Put it anywhere I want?" This isn't part of the game, for me to ask, rather than demand, but obviously I need his consent to do this. I've never touched a guy there before—but I've always wanted to. I've read how wild it makes them, how good it feels. And right now, the way he's looking at me like I'm some kind of sex goddess who's just dropped out of the sky, I want to prove it to him. I want to be the best he's ever had, even if this is all he will allow me of him.

He nods. "You can do anything to me. You know that."

Anything but intercourse. Anything but making out. Anything but me telling him how wet he always makes me.

Anything but allowing me in his heart, because he doesn't want me like that.

I shove these thoughts away by returning my mouth to his cock while sliding my hands between and under his legs. It takes a little searching, but I find what I'm looking for, and I don't give myself time to stress about it—I do exactly what I've read in all the magazines, putting pressure at what I hope is the exact right spot.

I think it *is* the exact right spot, because he gasps, "Teal," and instantly comes. "Fuck," he chants over and over, lifting his hips again, in the exact way I'd just scolded him about.

When it's done, and I've swallowed and pulled my hand back from him, he cups my face like I am a precious jewel he discovered completely unexpectedly and he's too scared to be anything but tender and gentle with me. "I'm so sorry. I didn't mean to do it in your mouth . . ."

"It's okay. I wanted it."

He relaxes back, letting his head fall on the sofa. "Christ. Teal. Jesus. Christ."

I laugh because it sounds like it was as good for him as I'd intended. "You liked it?"

He laughs now, his voice husky and deep. "What, did it seem like I would have any complaints? I think you just sucked my soul out of my body. Jesus."

I smile and stand. "Let me clean up and get our food ready."

"I should do that. You need to be off your feet." But he doesn't make a move to get up, his breath still recovering. I think his entire being is still recovering.

"I'm fine to heat up the food. You can get the dishes after." I can't help the grin on my face any more than the balmiest, clearest sky outside, like it hadn't rained at all today, the first stars beginning to show like pinpricks through the deepest indigo-painted sky.

26

Did you make it home? I TEXT SAGE WHILE CARTER AND I finish off our takeout.

Yes. That's all she writes back and I swallow, waiting for another text. About anything. I don't even care if she wants to push the leatherwork class again. But there's just nothing, even after twenty minutes. Finally I add, I really am sorry, Sage. I know it's probably very hard to believe, but I'm trying to be better.

This time she writes back, I can tell, Teal. I'm not mad, okay? I'm just getting busy with Tenn 😉

Ew, I type back quickly, but my shoulders have instantly relaxed.

"Who are you texting?" Carter's got a crease between his eyebrows.

"Sage."

He instantly relaxes. "Did you guys fight or something?"

"What makes you say that?"

He waves an arm in my direction. "You always get the same look on your face when you fight with Sage."

I snort. "Do not."

"Yeah, actually, you do. You sort of scrunch up your nose and grimace like this." He makes a face that resembles something Jim Carrey did in that Grinch movie, and I can't help but laugh.

"Dammit, Carter, you're making my ankle hurt!"

He's staring at me in awe, like always, when he makes me laugh. Like glitter just appeared around me in a swirl, and I was suddenly dressed like Glinda the Good Witch. "How can that hurt your foot?"

"My body shakes when I laugh. If you didn't notice."

"Oh, I noticed." He looks me up and down and I turn away.

I don't know how to flirt with Carter. Which is what I think he's doing. So I swallow and say, "You know why I agreed to marry you? For real?"

Now he's the one swallowing. He shakes his head and finally says, "The money, right?"

I shrug and try to make it look casual. "Partly. But mostly, I wanted to be best friends with you again." My eyes unexpectedly fill with tears when I say it.

"Hey." He lifts from his chair and comes to me fast, kneeling and wrapping his arms around me. I can't help but cry even more, right into his shoulder. "You *are* my best friend. Even when we weren't talking. I thought about you every damn day. I wondered what you were eating for breakfast, what you were doing before bed. If you still wore those perfumes your grandmother got you—"

I laugh into his collarbone. Amá Sonya agrees with Coco Chanel that "a woman who doesn't wear perfume doesn't have a future." When she found out that all I had was a bottle of Pear Crème Brûlée body mist from a cheap lotion store, she marched me into Nordstrom and forced me to choose four perfumes, one for every season. Gucci Bloom for spring, Tom Ford's Soleil

Blanc for summer, Tom Ford Tobacco Vanille in the fall, and for winter, Byredo Vanille Antique. It was winter when she bought them for me, and so I was working at the gym, wearing Vanille Antique when Carter visited me. "Damn, Teal, what are you wearing? It smells . . ." he'd said, then bowed his head toward my neck. It was the first time in our history that Carter had gotten close to me like *that*—something almost bordering on intimacy.

I was filled with so much *want* it frightened me. I wanted him to close the distance. I wanted to feel his lips on my neck, his tongue sliding down my cleavage. So of course, being the scaredy cat I was, I took a big step back and said, "Geez, Carter, ever hear of personal space?" and watched with equal parts guilt and delight as his cheeks turned bright pink.

"I still wear my perfumes," I mumble into his shirt.

"That one, though. You haven't worn that one . . . whatever it was called."

My face flushes. "It's not winter, that's why."

He pulls back with half a smile I don't know what to do with. "I'll be counting the days till winter, then."

I close my eyes. *You shouldn't say stuff like that to me.* It's on the tip of my tongue, but I'm afraid he'll pull away if I say the words aloud.

Luckily he speaks instead. "I'll be your best friend again, Teal. It's what I want, too."

My heart melts and I lean back to look at him. "Really?" I must sound so dumb, so breathless, so desperate. But I wasn't expecting this. For my greatest wish to be mutual.

"Yes." He looks right at me with those gold fire eyes. "I'll start right now." And then he lifts me up, kicking and squealing, turning me around and around, just like when we were teenagers and in one summer, he'd grown a head and a half taller than me and wanted to show off.

He carries me to the back porch and puts me on one of the lawn chairs, and he literally says, "Let's read each other our favorite poems." And you know what? As corny as it sounds, that's exactly what we do. I read to him "Chambered Nautilus" by Linda Hogan and he reads to me "Sometimes a Wild God" by Tom Hirons and then we remember things aloud about our childhood—Abuelo Gene, the dominoes, the guava pastries and sneaky sips of Cuban coffee. Until we're laughing so hard, my eyes are tearing up. Until I'm certain there are a million layers of rainbows in the sky, hidden by the deepest blue velvet in the night sky.

There's the slightest blip in our feel-good vibes when I turn and say to him, "Hey, um. Did you happen to see anything weird in the lightning yesterday?"

He turns to me, that line between his brows there once again. "What do you mean?"

"Like, it took on some weird . . . unexpected . . . forms? Almost like, I don't know. A simulation of some kind?"

He blinks at me and shakes his head. "There for sure could've been. But I was only looking at you, Teal. I didn't look anywhere else."

I nod, trying hard to not show my disappointment, and quickly change the subject, this time to back when I tricked Carter into eating a hot pepper from Nadia's garden, and soon we're laughing all over again. And it doesn't matter. It doesn't matter that I'm all alone in that weird experience. It probably means nothing anyway.

He helps me get ready for bed so I don't put any more weight on my foot than necessary, and he makes sure I have my medicine so I don't wake up in the night from throbbing, sharp pain.

When he goes to the door, to get to the pull-out, I whisper, "Stay," so softly, I'm equally afraid he has and hasn't heard me.

But he freezes and turns to me. "Yeah?"

"Yes."

He pauses. "But . . . not for sex, right?"

I shake my head, ignoring another drop of disappointment in my chest. I wasn't inviting him for sex, but the fact that he is still so against the idea of it feels like another rejection all over again. "No sex."

But then something maybe even better than sex happens. When he gets under the covers, he turns over toward me, draping his heavy arm over my hip, hand on my belly, and then he nudges me until I'm completely wrapped up in him, the way I feel when I'm all alone in the big, dark, safe forest after a long run. He lets out a deep, long sigh and says, "Fuck, I've missed you, Teal. You have no idea."

These words linger in my mind like a lullaby when I fall asleep.

⚡

CARTER WAKES UP EARLY TO MAKE ME BREAKFAST—EGGS AND fried plantains with sliced avocado on the side—and then he claps his hands together. "I took the next few days off, so we can do whatever you want," he tells me with a big smile on his face.

I raise my eyebrows. "The whole week? Really?"

"Yep. I've accrued enough PTO so it doesn't matter. And Nate—" He coughs. "Well, Nate said it was fine."

I finally let myself smile in response to this news. "When did you ask for the week off?"

Carter's cheeks pinken. "This morning." He shrugs and looks off in the distance. "I just . . . you know. I thought we could spend this week doing best friend shenanigans. Like, catching up on old times and stuff."

I'm so moved, I can't speak, so I cover for this with a big bite of plantain.

"I was thinking, today—"

"Dammit!" I rise up, then remember about my foot, and plop back down. "I have brunch with Amá Sonya in two hours. So I can't do anything till after that."

"Oh," Carter says, but he doesn't look at all disappointed. "Two hours gives us enough time, I think . . . for what I have planned today. And maybe I could come with you to brunch after."

I give him a look like he just suggested we should pierce our nipples, ourselves, for funsies. "You. Want to come to brunch. With Sonya."

He shrugs. "She usually gives you a hard time, right? I could be there and buffer things."

And now I'm basically melted butter. "We have to dress up. You know that right?"

He shrugs. "Not a problem at all, Teal."

"And she's probably going to insult us. A lot. But backhandedly. So it sounds like almost a compliment."

"Teal. I grew up with y'all. I know how Sonya is, remember?" He furrows his brow. "Do you not want me to come? That's fine if you'd rather I stay."

"No, I—" I blink a few times when I realize that I'm actually getting emotional. "I just don't know if it's worth your time."

Carter's smile is crooked and his gaze follows me up and down and back up again. "You'll be there. So it'll be worth my time."

I can't think of a single thing to say in response. Instead I clear my throat and say, "But you wanted to take me out first? Like a date?"

Carter nods and winks. "Well, it's not exactly like we're going anywhere. I didn't plan anything elaborate this time . . ."

I wring my hands, the suspense making me want to throw a lightning bolt right at his head. "What is it, then? What best friends shenanigans involves us . . . staying home?" In my memories, there's a jumbling, summery montage of him and me climbing the trees reaching up toward the sky all over Catalina Street, or digging through all of the sofas we could find for loose change for the ice cream truck, or leaving each other secret notes hidden under the rocks of our yards.

Carter's shoulders drop just the slightest bit. "I don't want to let you down."

I raise a playful fist. "Carter Velasquez, if you don't tell me *right now* . . ."

"Fine." He lifts his hands. "Fine." He walks over to the living room, lifting the top off one of the ottomans there, and procures a . . . CD?

"No way," I breathe as he approaches, because no, it's not a CD. It's an old-ass edition of *Mutant League Football*, our favorite video game Abuelo Gene grabbed for us from the thrift store back in the day. Abuelo Gene, poor fellow, thought it was the more popular Madden game. But honestly "mutant" intrigued me far more—I've always loved the X-Men. Hello, Storm? A powerful superhuman who could control the weather? There is no alternative universe in which Teal Flores doesn't love the idea of humans with strange and unusual powers.

Even though this game turned out to be less epically magical mutants, and more of the zombie and alien sorts, Carter and I still had *so* much fun with it.

He stares at me, at my smile and my glee, and freezes, like the sight is too overwhelming to continue movement. "Carter! Put it on!" I shriek.

"Okay, okay, okay, mami," he says, retreating back toward the living area, finagling with cords and video game controllers and whatnot.

I watch him, wanting so bad to bounce up and down but unable to because of not wanting to fall over in agony. "You actually got an old Sega Genesis?"

He gives me a sheepish smile. "They're really cheap on eBay. It was nothing."

The way he calls this nothing, like it isn't everything to me. I half want to cry, I half want to laugh, I half want to rush to Bath & Body Works and buy every Pretty as a Peach body care product they have to help me regulate my emotions.

Instead, I do a few counted breaths. "Do you mind if I get ready for brunch while you do that?" I finally ask.

"Go ahead, mamita. I'll have it ready by the time you're done."

When Carter winks at me, I basically have to run away. Only I can't, so it's more of an extra deranged hobble.

⚡

MUTANT LEAGUE FOOTBALL—OR AT LEAST THE ONE CARTER HAS procured, probably the exact version we used to play—is an old-ass game. It's pixelated, the players are coded to do, like, one of a total of three very awkward-looking actions at a time . . . and yet. Playing it with Carter, it's literally like I'm eleven years old all over again, sitting in Nadia's dark living room. It's just me and Carter and this absurd video game. I don't know how fucked up I am in the head yet, I haven't yet hurt Carter as bad as I eventually will, I haven't made so many mistakes that I barely even know where to begin in repairing them. It's like some type of deep healing, in a way, this nostalgia. Even if it's nostalgia that takes the forms of actual monsters playing football on the screen.

"Jesus, Teal," Carter mutters beside me. "You bribed the ref again? You know I don't like killing him, mujer."

"It's too bad that's the only way to get him to stop," I reply in a singsong voice as my zombie receiver rushes to the end zone. Before he can make it there, a fiery pit opens in the field and devours him whole. "That is *so* unfair!" I moan.

I punch Carter in the shoulder when he cackles at me. "Ow, what was that for?" he yelps.

I gesture to his players, a collection of skeletons wearing only shoulder pads and shoes. "You think they really need that protection?"

"Don't want to dislocate a shoulder." Carter shrugs.

"But they're made of nothing but bones, man! They don't protect their hips or ribs or even their heads, but shoulder pads are the necessity, here?"

And as I'm distracted, Carter has one of his wide receivers rip the ref's head clean off with his bare hands.

I roll my eyes. "That was *needlessly* brutal."

"Babe. You bribed him. You gave me no choice."

"No choice but decapitation," I respond dryly, and then without reason I erupt into giggles. Carter grins at me in return. And then he drops his controller and grabs my hips. "Come here," he murmurs.

"Where?" My voice is breathless and shaky, but he doesn't answer me. He carefully drags me over his lap, until I'm straddling him, my bad ankle thoughtfully tucked against a soft pillow.

When I look down at him, his pupils are blown, the inky black making the honey of his eyes even lighter than normal. He's so hard against my thigh, it's unreal. "I don't remember doing this when we were tweens," I say.

"I wanted to. All the damn time. My mind was so filthy around you." He runs his hands up to my shoulders, then slowly down, cupping my breasts. His pointer fingers run over my nipples.

"Carter," I whimper. "What do you think you're—"

But before I can finish the question, his phone begins to chirp a joyful, electronic melody. "Dammit," he mutters under his breath. "I set an alarm for brunch."

"Right. Brunch." It's like I'm in a trance or something—one fueled entirely by lust—because it takes another few seconds for the words to hit me. "Brunch!" I push myself up on wobbly legs, Carter's arms there to catch me if I fall. "Amá hates it when I'm late."

"We'll be there right on time. Don't worry. I got you."

I want to hate the way his words, his hands, his everything makes me feel so safe. But I can't. So I'm not even going to try.

27

FOR BRUNCH, I DECIDED TO WEAR MY NICEST JEANS, DEEP indigo-stained boyfriend-cut, with ballet slipper shoes. Up top I've got on a silk crewneck the color of peaches and cream, and over that, an earthy brown tweed blazer. Amá is going to kill me for wearing jeans, and she's not going to dig the ballet slippers, either. But I don't want people gawking at my ankle, and there's no way I'm able to wear her preferred shoe choice of towering designer stilettos. I'm carrying the black leather Cartier bag she gave me, plus I put on a solitaire diamond necklace, so hopefully my classy accessories will soften her judgments up a smidgen.

I glance at Carter as he sits in the driver's seat. He's got on a grayish purple dress shirt that is fitted to him in an almost indecent way. I can see the lines of the muscles in his arms, the defined edges of his abdomen. His slacks don't hide his thick thighs and I don't let myself look between his legs, lest I look like there is always only one thing on my mind, even though when it comes to Carter, *that* is on my mind way too much.

I clear my throat.

He looks at me quick. "You okay? You need anything?"

How can two simple, normal questions make me feel so damn emotional? "Yeah, I'm fine. Just not looking forward to this." Brunch with Amá Sonya isn't usually terrible, but I definitely would rather be at home now, continuing what we'd started while playing *Mutant League Football*.

"It'll be fine. We got this." He grins at me and I smile back, my heart feeling like it's somehow grown to fill every part of my body.

If I don't watch myself, I might do something unthinkable. Like fall in love with my husband.

On the way to the bougie, orange-essenced champagne-serving restaurant Amá insists on for brunch every month, I wonder what, exactly, Carter and I are doing. He's taken the week off so we can do best-friendship shenanigans—whatever that means—which is what I wanted from the start. But also? Two nights ago, he went down on me so well, I've had to try to re-create the sensation with my fingers and vibrator twice since, but nothing comes close. Plus, you know. I sucked him off just last night.

And who knows what would've happened just now if his brunch alarm hadn't gone off.

Best friends don't do all that, do they? Not the best friends I've had in my life.

My vibrating phone breaks my thoughts away from the sad trail they keep wanting to go down. I hold back a gasp when I see it's Gerald Samuels.

"Hello?" I ask as soon as I accept the call. "Mr. Samuels? Did you find her?"

"Not yet, Teal," he makes sure to say quickly in his cigar-scratchy voice. "I just wanted to give you an update."

My heart falls as he tells me about another gallery showing

that featured an artist named Vivienne several years ago, and that *this* gallery is still open, which means someone working there may have known whoever the hell this Vivienne was, and blah, blah, blah. The rest of the update goes on like that . . . a credit card opened in Maine. A car sold in Ohio. Nothing concrete, nothing recent.

I knew it was a long shot, but by the time I get off the phone, I feel like I'm never going to find Mama.

"You good?" Carter asks.

I nod, counting my breath the whole while. "I'm fine. The PI is still looking, is all."

He seems to understand I don't want to talk about it and we drive in silence until the restaurant parking lot appears, way too soon for my liking.

Amá Sonya is walking up to the gold-leaf door at the same time we are, so we meet in the middle and Carter opens the door for us after greeting her with a kiss on the cheek. Just like I'd anticipated, she tsks in disapproval when she sees my outfit. "Jeans?" she hisses in my ear, her skinny hand tight on my forearm. "Teal, this isn't the Cheesecake Factory."

"Amá, I messed up my ankle, remember?"

"Sí, which is why you should be in a dress."

"My entire ankle and foot are the colors blue, green, and yellow."

She narrows her eyes at me, like she's weighing the indignity of jeans versus unsightly bruises. Only this woman would consider jeans to be on par with a nasty-looking injury, aesthetically speaking.

She lifts her head and dismisses the conversation. "No matter. We're this way."

She pushes past the hostess with a tight, polite smile, and

Carter and I follow, him holding my arm as I do my little limping dance of a walk.

I stop—so abruptly that Carter nearly trips over me—when I see where she's leading us. *Not* to our usual spot by the large windows overlooking Firefly Mountain. She's taking us to a huge circle table in the darkest corner of the restaurant, where there are already people seated. Nadia, Sage, Sky, and Tenn, to be exact.

"Well?" Amá turns when she sees that I've frozen. "We don't have all afternoon. Ándale, Teal Alegría."

"But—why is everyone here?" I begin walking slowly and turn to Carter. "Did you know about this?"

"Baby, I didn't even know you had brunch today."

I can barely notice the way my body responds to him calling me *baby*—like we were together like that for real, or something—because what the fuck is happening here?

I sit down carefully in the chair Carter pulls out for me, and he sits to my right. Amá is to my left. Sky sits next to Nadia, and Tenn is next to Sage, who is directly across from me, her fingers templed over her chest. She's wearing a black jersey dress with long wide sleeves, and an enormous rainbow moonstone glints at me from the hollow of her throat. She reminds me of an overlord about to pronounce a verdict over someone who's betrayed her.

God, I didn't betray her, did I? I rack my brain. Me not wanting to take a leather class wouldn't result in this bizarre scenario, would it?

"Is this an intervention?" I blurt out before anyone can explain. "Because of the class you wanted me to take?"

"Not exactly," Sage says.

The waiter arrives with five flutes of their orange champagne, and one wineglass of ice water for Sage.

I throw my drink back and down it in two swallows. Beside me, Amá Sonya gasps.

"So I guess the whole family doesn't normally join you for brunch like this?" Carter asks after a few minutes of very awkward silence.

"No, they do not," I respond. "So will someone just get on with it? I'm about to have a panic attack, here."

It's a bit of an exaggeration—there are some dark clouds outside, but it's mostly sunny still—but Carter reaches for my hand under the table anyway. "Breathe, mami," he whispers at my neck. I do what he says, until the clouds lighten softly, so that their dark undersides are now silver.

Sage clears her throat. "Last time we talked—"

"You mean last night."

"Yes, last night. You said something I found very alarming."

I roll my eyes. "I was being dramatic, Sage. My ankle hurt like a bitch"—another gasp from Amá—"and it had been a long day. I was hangry."

"So you didn't mean it when you said you couldn't fix your gift until we found Mama?"

Before the last syllable is out of her mouth, thunder rumbles so loudly, the whole restaurant goes silent for a few tense moments.

Oh *shit*. Did I actually say that aloud? To someone who is not Carter?

I try to backtrack. "I don't actually remember saying anything like—"

"Teal. Mira." Nadia gestures to the windows, where lightning streaks so closely, a few women to our right gasp in unison. "We know you said it. We know it's true. The weather would not look like that otherwise." She exchanges a glance with Amá, who looks like she normally does—equal parts bored and disgusted. "Cora took something from you, didn't she?"

"Breathe," Carter says, squeezing my hand. I listen to the count of his voice, and in only a couple of minutes, the weather calms down enough that people all around us have gone back to their conversations, convincing themselves it didn't go to hurricane level and back again in the span of sixty seconds.

"Damn," Tenn says, looking around, running a hand over the scruff on his chin. "That was wild. I didn't know it was like *that*, with the weather."

Sky snorts. "You should see her when she's mad." Then she turns to me. "I've always wondered, though—what happens, when. You know. You"—she then mouths the word *orgasm*. "Do rainbows come shooting out of you, or—"

"Sky Temple," Amá says, her eyebrows practically to her hairline. "I don't know how you went from an innocent sixteen-year-old to—"

"What do you mean, innocent?" Sky retorts back. "I wasn't a virgin when the old gods took me into their sacred oak tree eight years ago. In fact, I'd totally done it a total of *seven* times."

"Dios mío," Amá says, dropping her head into her hands. "I am glad that you're dressing like a proper woman now, but, Sky, you need to make your mouth match! No man would respect—"

"Hey, everyone, how are we doing today?" The server appears out of nowhere, like a wraith. But he flinches back when he sees the way Amá glares at him.

"I was in the middle of a sentence, young man."

"Ignore her. She's constipated," Nadia says, ignoring Carter's and Sky's snorts and Amá's gasp of indignity. "Would you mind giving us a few minutes?"

The server doesn't even respond verbally. He gives Nadia a short, fast nod and turns and sprints away.

"Back to the topic at hand." Nadia's voice is firm.

But of course Amá isn't finished. "Even Teal was pure when she married Carter," she says, giving meaningful glares not just to Sky but also to Sage's incriminating baby bump. "You two could learn a thing from her on how to keep yourself *without sin*."

Sage is the first to laugh, then me. Carter's shoulders shake as he tries to rein it in.

"What is wrong with all of you," Amá demands, rather than asks. "Is the sacred pureness of the body so hilarious?"

Nadia lets out a short breath. "*Back to the topic at hand*." She looks right into my eyes and I squeeze Carter's hand. "What happened with your mother, Teal? Why do you need her to fix your gift? ¿Qué tomó ella?"

I look down at the table, made of what looks like shimmery dark chocolate milk spilled over white marble. "What does it matter?" I mumble. "It's not like anyone can do anything about it."

"You don't know that," Sonya retorts, her tone indicating the gravest offense.

"Teal." This time it's Sage addressing me. "I know what you've been up to lately. Trying to buy us things, and doing us favors. You think you're not good and that you have to prove that you are somehow." Her eyes fill with tears. "But you *are* good, Teal. You don't have to get us cars—"

"Though the car is awesome," Sky interrupts with a beaming smile.

"Though these things are great. They aren't necessary. You are already worthy." Sage sighs and Tenn wraps his arm around her shoulders, sliding his other hand over her belly. "Which means you are worthy of support. You're worthy enough to tell the people who love you what you need. So tell us. What do you need?"

Damn. My cheeks are all wet now, but for some inexplicable reason, the sky has shifted to a bright, topaz blue, the clouds butter yellow in the sunlight. The weather doesn't match me—or maybe it does. Maybe I'm crying because that's the first time anyone in my whole life has asked me what I need. Not what I want. What I *need*.

"You can tell them," Carter whispers, his breath warm against my ear. "I'm right here, mamita."

I take a shuddering breath and close my eyes, taking one big deep, counted breath. "I was there, when Mama left. I saw her go. I saw the truck . . . the man in the truck come and get her."

"Damn," Tenn says. "That's fucked up, what happened to you all. And for you to see it when you were that little . . ."

My laugh is bitter, and not just because it's salty from my tears. "You don't know the half of it."

"So tell us," Nadia says, her voice smooth and warm and comforting.

Carter has pulled me toward him so that my ass is right up on his thigh. I'm practically sitting in his lap. Sonya keeps glancing at us like he's damn near penetrating me, like she's about to retract the only compliment she's ever given me, about my total lie of purity.

"My gift came for the first time that night. A lightning storm, out of thin air. She—this probably is going to sound dumb and impossible—"

Sky snorts. "Remember who you're talking to here." She points at Nadia—"Psychic"—then Sage—"communicates with plants"— then Amá—"can see ghosts but is in denial about it"—then herself—"and creatures are my brothers from another mother."

"Sky. Temple." Amá's tone is hostile.

"Should I have not said 'mother,' given our conversation? Fine." She taps her chin. "They're my *sisters* from another *mister*."

It probably seems like Sky is being an unempathetic pest, but I know what she's doing. She's giving me a moment to catch my breath. To count my breath, even.

"I get it. Thank you." I smile at her. "Anyway, she pinched a piece of my gift from me. Right from the center of my palm, she took a piece of . . . I don't know. Light. From my body."

"She can't do that without permission," Nadia growls.

I blink back surprise. I was certain no one would have an idea of what I was talking about, but Nadia sounds like she not only has an idea but understands exactly what had happened that night. "She did ask me for permission. I said yes. But I was four. I thought if I said yes to anything she asked for, she might change her mind and stay."

Amá puts her hands over her eyes. "That little conniving *bitch*."

I nearly gasp, hearing the curse come out of her mouth. "Um—"

"She took a piece of your soul, Teal! And *you*." Amá turns to Nadia. "*This* is what you get for trying to teach her the old ways. Going out into the forests to find the footprints of the old ones. Going on, how do you say, soul travels!"

Nadia's hand is over her mouth, her eyes wide. "I didn't think she'd steal from her own daughter."

"Yes? And I never thought she'd leave me, or them, Nadia, but here we are." Amá's voice has gone uncharacteristically shaky, and she takes the fine linen napkin to dab at the corners of her eyes. "What are you all looking at?" she hisses, throwing up a hand that gets dangerously close to slapping the side of my ear. "A piece of pepper got in my eye."

Everyone seems to agree to just let that slide. "Tell them about what you saw in the lightning," Carter says.

"The lightning from your hand?" Sage asks.

This time, our server reappears, on my right side, next to Carter, clearly as far away as he can get from Amá Sonya. "What'll it be, guys?"

Since none of us has had a chance to even look at the menu, I groan. "Um—"

Nadia raises her hand. "I'll have the smoked salmon over the pink salt and pink pepper bagel. Sage"—she points as she goes around the table—"will have the veggie omelet, extra mushrooms and olives, with a side of fresh pineapple for her pregnancy craving, Tenn's getting the maple bacon BLT on sourdough, Carter's having the chicken and waffles with the honey dipping sauce on the side, Teal will get the steamed egg bites with kale and Gruyère cheese, and this one"—Amá is the last—"will get the eggs Benedict over asparagus, with a side of sweet potato fries, which she denies liking but in fact adores." She claps her hands together. "You got all that?"

Our waiter nods and rushes away; meanwhile Carter and Tenn both have their mouths dropped open. "How did she know what I wanted? *I* didn't even know what I wanted, Teal," Carter stage-whispers to me.

"That's her gift." I shrug. It *is* impressive, but I'm a little too emotional to get into it right now.

"Now that that's out of the way," Nadia begins.

"Oh, you just had to show off, didn't you?" Sonya interrupts in a grumble.

Nadia ignores her. "What did you see in the lightning that Cora took, Teal?"

I take a breath. "So . . . actually. You know how I sprained my ankle the other night?"

"Oh my God, I knew it wasn't because you were climbing beach rocks!" Sky gasps. "What happened really? Were you"—she lowers her voice—"having enthusiastic, um, marital interactions—"

"No, I really did mess it up climbing rocks like an idiot. But there was a massive lightning storm—I was running, hoping that would help my, ah, emotions."

Sage narrows her eyes at me. "Wasn't that the day you had Abuela Erika over for dinner?"

I lift my head. "Why, yes. The very one who married Nadia's old sweetheart—"

"Okay, I am saying this only once." Nadia raises her hands like she's trying to stop a fight. "But Eugenio and I were novios when we were in the eighth grade. All we did was send love notes and once, we held hands. I don't know why Erika—"

"Oh, you know Erika," Amá interrupts. "Always a jealous little tramp."

"Amá!" Sky gasps. "'Bitch' *and* 'tramp'? You are letting loose today. Frankly, I'm impressed."

"Anyway!" I shake my head. "Please will someone let me finish this fu—" I glance at Amá, who is scowling at me, despite, like Sky just said, having just said *bitch* and *tramp*. ". . . freaking story? Lightning struck me that night. Only it didn't hurt me—"

"Of course it didn't. You are the witch of wild lightning," Nadia says.

"Right, but there was . . . a person out there. A half mile away. And between me and them, there was blue lightning, and it took the shape of people. A four-year-old running after her mama, and her mama taking a piece of light from her palm . . . you guys, I saw the whole thing, but it was done in lightning. Somehow."

Amá Sonya throws down her napkin. "I knew she was in town."

"So that figure in the distance, that was Mama?" Sky asks.

"Yes," Amá says in response, and then she points right at Nadia. "Didn't I tell you? I don't have to see her to know she's near, I told you this one hundred times!"

"Yes, yes, you were right, Sonya, and I was wrong. Cora is back in Cranberry after all." Nadia leans back and surveys me. "Why didn't you tell us years ago, Teal? About what she stole from you?"

I shrug and look down again. "Nothing could be done. Her gift is to be unseen. Invisible. I've hired a private investigator—"

"Why would you waste your money like that?" Amá yelps.

I sigh and bury my face in my hands, willing the tears back in. I've been crying too much lately. When I lift my head, I take one big breath. "I didn't tell you because I didn't want everyone to know how messed up I was, okay?" I turn to Amá. "And I wasn't pure for my marriage, Amá Sonya. I'm sorry, but I wasn't. Because I was with an abusive dickwad who made me do things I wasn't ready for and didn't want to do! And I didn't tell you about that, either, because I didn't want it to be yet another thing you all would know was wrong with me, okay?" The tears have returned. And this time, the weather matches me—all gray and gloomy. "Not that there's anything wrong with having sex outside of marriage."

"Tell that to Jesus," Amá retorts, but her tone doesn't have the sting it usually does, and her eyes keep roaming over my body like she's looking for some kind of injury.

Our server appears and the next five minutes are dedicated to getting everyone their meals, and devouring our first bites, because everyone's gotten extra hungry during this absurdly long conversation.

"So what do we do now?" Sage asks. "How do we get Teal's soul back to her?"

Nadia smiles. "Cora thinks she outsmarted us. But she set up a trap of her own making." She looks right at me. "She has your soul. Which means there is a connection between the two of you. We find your soul piece, we find Cora. She cannot stay hidden, so long as she has stolen from you."

"That . . . sounds ominous," Sky says.

"We just have to wait until the next full moon," Nadia declares. She glances at her phone. "Which is in . . . oh, two and a half days. Sage, Sky. Clear your schedules."

"I'm participating, too," Amá Sonya declares before demolishing a sweet potato fry.

"Then you can also clear your schedule. Postpone your HOA meeting or Gucci Bingo Night—"

"What's Gucci Bingo Night?" Amá asks, because of course she is interested in whatever the hell that would even be.

"Okay!" I say, holding up my hand. "What are we doing in two and a half days' time? Where are we going to meet? Do I need to prepare anything, or—"

"I'll get all the supplies. I'll text you the rest once I figure it out," Nadia responds, in a tone that indicates that is all the information we're going to get from her at present time.

I turn to Amá. "Do you know what she's up to?"

Amá shrugs. "You know Nadia. It could be anything from dancing naked in the woods to doing despicable things with broomsticks." You'd think she were talking about fucking a broomstick, by the tone of her voice, but no. She waves her arm across the sky, mimicking flight.

Sage, Tenn, and Carter laugh at her, but Sky and I exchange a questioning look. I think of her words to Nadia only minutes ago. *This is what you get for trying to teach her the old ways. Going out into the forests to find the footprints of the old ones. Going on, how do you say, soul travels!*

It's clear we've only gotten half the story with regard to our gifts. And that's bullshit.

28

M Y PHONE VIBRATES WITH A TEXT. IT'S SKY. Meet me
outside before you and Carter leave.

I'm nearly in the car when it pings, and I groan. It takes me
too damn long to get in and out of this vehicle, thanks to my ankle. "Hold on," I say to Carter. "I've got to see Sky about something."

"Want me to come?" he asks as he leans down to help lift me
back up again. Even with everything rolling around in my head
that I've learned in the last hour—the fact that Mom took my
mother-flipping *soul* from me, which, I agree with Amá, that
bitch . . . to the idea that not only can I be fixed, but Nadia also
already knows how to do it . . . to the fact that Sky wasn't a virgin
when she fell? Who the hell was she fucking back then? It couldn't
have been with her boyfriend at the time, whose name I can't even
recall right now, because that boy practically lived at the church
and blushed anytime someone said the word *screw*, even with regard to the Home Depot hardware department. It honestly sounds

like she had more game than me and I was four years older than her and had way more boyfriends.

Back to my point. Even with all the crap in my head, I *still* get goose bumps when Carter's hands are on my arms. I still lean in a little, to smell that sweet salty note on him that makes me so crazy, I keep thinking dumb thoughts like *I want our marriage to be real.*

"No, I think she wants to chat alone for a few minutes. Maybe give me some encouragement or something."

Carter gives me a warm smile. "I'll be right here."

"I know." I smile back at him.

"Teal! Stop hitting on your husband and get your butt over here!" Sky's voice rings out and I laugh, turning to her.

"Okay, okay," I say, stumbling to the side of the parking lot that is lined with tall, pointy evergreen trees. "What's going on?"

She's standing with Sage, and they're both staring at me with equally weird looks on their faces.

I frown. "What is it?" I glance at Sage's belly. "Is the baby okay?"

"Oh, he's fine," Sage says. "Sky just has some interesting . . . *ideas* on some things that have transpired today."

"We need to find Mama ourselves," Sky exclaims, then puts a hand over her own mouth, looking around, presumably for either Amá or Nadia to jump out to stop her. "I mean, we need to find Mama ourselves," she repeats with a whisper.

"But—" I shake my head. "Isn't Nadia the one who, like, knows what she's doing?"

Sky huffs. "First of all, if it weren't for A, Nadia teaching Mama magic to start with, and B, *not* teaching *us* magic to start with, none of this would have happened."

I lift my shoulder. "You're not wrong, but now she can, you know. Make it up to us and fix this."

"I'm just saying," Sky says, throwing her arms about, "that we can totally do it ourselves. We don't even have to wait till the full moon. We won't have Amá Sonya's nasty energy ruining things, and we won't have Nadia there acting like she wasn't a neglectful caretaker to us. It would just be us. Sisters." She lifts the necklace that's wrapped around her neck, the mossy stone glinting in the sunlight. "Sage, sky, and teal. The whole sisterly landscape."

"But what if we mess up?" Sage asks gently. "Teal is right. We don't have the faintest idea of what we're doing."

Sky lowers her voice. "I found a book at work. It's got ancient rituals in it, from the same place in Texas where Nadia says our ancestors are from. In fact, I think this book may have belonged to one of our ancestors. And it has, like, spells in it. Including one on how to find a lost piece of soul."

Goose bumps ripple over my arms, and Sage glances down at her own hands. "Wow, did you guys feel that?"

"I declare," Sky says, putting on an unnatural, regal tone while ignoring Sage, "that if we are all wearing our necklaces that Sage made us, then it's a sign we've got to do it ourselves. A sign from the old gods." She makes her voice drop as dramatically as possible. "That we must do the ritual *tonight*."

Sage laughs. "But you can totally see that I'm already wearing the necklace." And it's true, I hadn't noticed it earlier, because under the big moonstone necklace, the moss agate pendant is being eaten alive by her monstrous pregnancy cleavage.

Sky nods. "Which just leaves Teal. Who, may I add, almost never wears her necklace."

"That's only because I am constantly working out and I don't want to tarnish the silver with my sweat," I respond, putting my hands on my hips.

"So you're saying you're not wearing the necklace," Sage says, lifting her eyebrow.

I sigh and close my eyes briefly. Then I pull the collar of my crewneck and pull up on the chains there. I'm wearing three necklaces, in fact, because I'd read an article about the art of lay-ering from The Beauty Martyr, that white woman homogeneous design store that Leilani's hawking now. And as dumb as Leilani is, and as ugly as everything in that store is, they made me want to layer jewelry. And then I felt humiliated, because why am I taking advice from these assholes anyway, and why am I still internet-stalking Lani anyway, and I threw a crewneck on to hide all of it.

So the necklaces I procure are in this order: a little gold bee that looks like it was pressed in a gold seal of wax, a small, brilliant-cut topaz set into white gold, and lastly . . . moss agate.

Specifically, the moss agate that Sage set into silver and told us the stone represented our sisterhood.

Sky squeals and claps her hands and jumps up and down at once. "See? The old gods want us to do illegal shenanigans again!"

"Wait, who said anything about illegal?" Sage asks, but Sky is already walking away.

"Meet you both at the church at six p.m.!" she calls.

"I can't drive, remember?" I lift my foot up in a big show.

"I'll pick you up th— Oh! Hello, friend." She pauses, looking toward the line of evergreens, where a full-grown raccoon begins to follow her as she heads back to Nadia's waiting car.

"You think she's going to take it home?" Sage smirks at me.

I nod. "I think she's going to fasten it in its own seat belt in the back seat, and tonight Nadia's going to lose her shit when she sees she's sitting next to a raccoon at the dinner table."

"She wants us to meet at dinnertime," Sage reminds me. "I can bring it. Tenn introduced me to this awesome food truck a little while ago."

I blink in surprise. "Oh—okay. Tacos sound good."

Sage leans on her hip. "You thought about taking that class yet?"

I shrug. "Um—"

She puts her hand on my arm. "Just think about it, Teal." She gives me a smile and a wink. "It's not your job to fix everything, you know that, right? You deserve happiness whether you buy me and Sky shit or not."

I look down because I feel like my eyes might water and, dammit, I just don't feel like crying for the millionth time in a row this week. Crying is *exhausting*. "Okay. I hear you. I'll think about it."

⚡

"I'M GOING TO HAVE DINNER WITH MY SISTERS TONIGHT," I TELL Carter, and he nods, giving me a half smile.

"That's good. You mind if we make a stop on the way home?"

"Uh—" I say, thrown off a little. "Sure, that's fine."

"Even if it's kind of a long stop?"

I shake my head. "Why . . . would it be a long stop?" I pause. "Wait. Another best friend thing?"

He glances at me and winks. "You'll see."

"Carter, you've already done too much." But I can't help grinning and wiggling in my seat a little. "You'll spoil me."

This time, he grins. "Maybe I like the idea of spoiling you. You ever think about that?"

Somehow I'm able to smile even wider as I try to figure out where we're headed.

It takes us about ten minutes before we're pulling into the Cranberry Vintage Cinema. I guess back in the seventies, this used to be the big, fancy place people would go to see movies, but now we have a couple of theaters that outshine it by far. So CVC now shows old movies for a serious discount—I'm talking five dollars and under—making all their real money on overpriced snacks.

I gasp when I see what it's showing today. "*The Matrix*?"

He nods, beaming when he sees my own smile.

"The original *Matrix*? The one Abuelo Gene took us to? Not one of the weird sequels that didn't make any sense to me?"

"Yes, Teal. It's the one we saw." He nudges his head toward the theater. "So what do you say? Is this okay for some best friend shenanigans?"

"Yes!" I fling open my car door and about jump out, till I remember one of my ankles isn't working. "Shit."

"Here, here." Carter rushes around and helps me up, one big hand under my arm, along my rib cage, the other at my waist. When he lifts me up, I wrap my arms around his neck, and before my brain can notice, I hug him, hard.

"This is awesome," I whisper.

He laughs into my shoulder, running his hand around my back in a circle. "Baby, you haven't even seen the snacks I brought yet."

"Snacks?"

"Yes, snacks. But we gotta sneak them in your purse, okay?"

Ten minutes later, Carter and I are the only people seated to watch *The Matrix* in this year of our Lord, at two in the afternoon. I pull out the chili-dusted dry mango and the bar of cookies-and-cream chocolate, and meanwhile Carter's already munching on the extra-extra large and extra-extra buttered popcorn he'd insisted on dropping twenty-five dollars on.

"Man, I always wanted popcorn when we went to the theater, but no one could afford it," he says, shoving handfuls into his mouth.

"Don't eat it all!" I say, reaching over for my own share. I close my eyes when I first taste it. "God, I haven't had popcorn in so long. Johnny never let me get it." I snap my mouth shut when I realize the dumb words that have come out of my mouth.

"Why?" Carter asks, which is a perfectly reasonable question.

I shrug. "He was always scared I was going to get fat."

"You?" Carter looks me up and down. "Look, there's nothing wrong with fat. You'd look hot no matter what. But, Teal, you've got more abs than I do! Your body has always been—" He coughs a little. "You've always been thin and cut, you know?"

"I know. But he was—" I shake my head, unwrapping the package of mangoes carefully, so the chile doesn't fly out all over us. I take a deep sigh and say some things that have been on my mind for a while now. "It was like he lived to antagonize me. His whole purpose for existing was to critique any word I said, any move I made. If I wanted popcorn, I better not because I might get fat. If I spent too long on a gym workout, I better stop before I got too muscular. If I wanted to put my hair up, no, he wanted it down because it made me look more feminine, and if it was down, he wanted it up, because it wasn't silky enough to let it loose." I sigh and close my eyes, letting waves of emotion run over me. They're not intense emotions—so I don't have to worry about a lightning storm cutting off the power or something—but they're still visceral. This looming sense of sadness and grief over the years I gave to a man who would never be pleased with anything he had, including me.

For a long time after Johnny, I was numb, because that was what I had to make myself in order to survive that relationship. And it one hundred percent was survival. I've had a few of our former asshole mutual friends come up and say—or strongly imply—that if it was as bad as I made it sound, then why wouldn't I leave?

If you thought leaving a man meant he might murder you . . . wouldn't that give you a goddamn pause?

But no, because beloved, loud Johnny would never be like that. He never shoved me around, never slapped me, never demanded that I have sex with him if I knew what was good for me. Johnny was just so *nice*.

If Sage hadn't threatened him, I know he would've retaliated. He would've made it hurt, to punish me for daring to leave him. I was so angry at her for getting in my business . . . but the truth of the matter was, I was afraid for her. I spent weeks all tense, afraid Johnny would hurt her to get to me. But she must've been very thorough in scaring him. She says she almost choked him to death with a dogwood tree. I thought she was exaggerating at first— because Sage is the best person I know—but then I realized that nothing less would have stopped Johnny. He would *have* to have been scared shitless to leave me alone without having to have the last word, or last hit, or whatever.

"That sounds exhausting," Carter says. "Teal, I'm so sorry you went through that. I wish . . ." He clears his throat and looks away. "I wish I had known. I mean, I knew he wasn't good enough for you. Anyone with eyes knew that. But all that other stuff. You know I would've helped you."

I breathe out a sigh of relief, a sigh I didn't even realize I was holding in. There was no *But why didn't you leave?* from Carter. Of course there isn't. "I didn't want him to hurt anyone I loved."

As soon as the words come out, my heart feels like it might jump out of my throat.

I've always told Carter I loved him. You can't have the same amount of history we do and not, I don't think. But this time . . . I didn't even say it directly, and for some reason, it feels different. It feels like the idea of loving Carter resounds inside me like a bell, ringing through all of my veins and nerves and bones.

"I wouldn't have let him," Carter responds, and that's when the movie begins.

So our conversation ends, and we're snacking on our junk food, watching as Trinity—the absolute badass that she is—runs away from a group of agents while wearing head-to-toe shiny black leather.

But I can't relax. I keep crossing and uncrossing my legs. I tap my fingers on my thighs, on the armrests of my seat.

Because, shit. I think I'm in love with Carter.

29

A T ONE POINT, DURING ONE OF THE SLOWER SCENES IN the movie—when they find out Cypher is a two-timing piece of shit—Carter leans over and whispers to me, "Hey. I know what happened isn't about how you look. But you know . . . I want you to know, okay? That you look like a goddess all the fucking time. First thing in the morning, when you probably think you're messy. You're so gorgeous . . . and whenever you shower, the way your hair gets, and your, you know, glowing skin? After, I mean, not *in* the shower." He coughs a little and even though I can't see him in this dark theater, I know he's blushing. Blushes always look like spilled raspberry sauce on Carter's light skin and I'm sad I'm missing it right now. "After showering, I mean. Of course. And whenever you dress up, sometimes I feel like I can't breathe around you. And when you're just in your pajamas, cleaning . . . you look so pretty when you're by the window and the sunlight makes your hair look like brown metal."

"Bronze?" I ask, my voice a little too froglike and emotional for my liking.

"Yeah, bronze. And I like it when you take your first sip of coffee for the day. Like it's the best thing you've ever tasted. And I . . . yeah. I also like your toes."

"My toes?!"

He laughs. "Yeah, I've always liked them. You paint them so pretty. Remember when you used to wear toe rings?"

I groan, my eyes rolling up into my head. "Those were the early aughts, Carter, you can't judge me for that."

"I'm not judging. I'm telling you I liked them." He is so uninhibited right now, and I can't help but think all the buffers in this place are contributing to that—the dark. The sound. The distraction of sweet and salty snacks. "You could be wearing a dress made out of . . . I don't know. Birds? And I would still think you were the prettiest woman I'd ever seen."

Normally, I'd make a comment on the weird randomness of a dress made of birds, but instead it's like my breath has been punched out of me twice in a row. First, when I had the thought that maybe I was in love with Carter. And now, when I realize that . . . *of course* I'm in love with Carter.

My whole life, Carter has been the one who has seen me without judgment. And not just without judgment, but with unreserved admiration and kindness. He has never judged me, not even when I would call him after another shitty day with Johnny. He believed in my gifts without question from the start, not pretended to believe like Leilani did.

And I think I've always known this. I have always known that deep down, I'm in love with Carter Velasquez. But I've pushed the thoughts and feelings away, just like I've pushed him away, when he got too close to those particular thoughts and feelings.

When we were teenagers, and it was clear he was beginning to get a crush on me. I pushed him away.

When he visited me at work and leaned in to smell my perfume. I pushed him away.

When I was single for the first time in years, and we kissed, and God, the way that kiss made my nerve endings explode, the way it felt like I was being struck by lightning—I can say that now, having actually been struck by lightning—I pushed him away in the worst way possible. By choosing another man right in front of him.

I don't just want to be not Selfish Teal anymore.

I want to be Brave Teal.

I want to not just make it up to the people I love, but I also want to unabashedly love them. And that's what Sage was trying to tell me earlier. To not just love them, but to let them in. To allow them to see the most vulnerable parts of me. To let them care for me and love me, too.

Because I think that Sky was right . . . Carter loves me but he has also been pushing me away, too, because of me constantly doing that to him in the first place. He loves me but he also doesn't want to get hurt by me. I could be wrong, of course—and God, it would hurt so damn much if I am—but right now, I am bursting with the feeling like I am the source of lightning. If I don't tell him . . . if I don't tell him, I will become a storm. I will dissipate into the sky in a flash of white-hot light.

I turn to him. The action scene on right now is brightly lit—Trinity is about to watch Neo dodge bullets—and even though it doesn't escape me that maybe this is kind of a dumb place to do this right now, I open my mouth and say, "Carter. I'm in love with you."

I'm pretty sure that plop is the sound of the extra-extra large popcorn hitting the floor.

"What did you say?" he asks, his voice croaking and gasping.

"I'm in love with you. I've been in love with you since . . . for a while now. And I'm so sorry it's taken me this long to realize it." My eyes are brimming with tears, so I take a deep breath. "And I know I'm broken. I know that . . . I'm probably not your first choice."

"Teal." Carter doesn't know what to do with his hands, so they're all over me, along my arm, my shoulder, till he's cupping my face. "You're not broken. And you've always been my first choice. Since I was nine years old and first moved to Catalina Street and saw you and your sisters roller-skating up and down the street."

I wipe my eyes. "Oh, man. The pink roller skates."

He laughs and says, "Say it again, please. Say you love me, Teal."

"I love you, Carter."

His lips meet mine, clumsily at first, though I'm not sure why—from him not seeing well, or maybe just the intense emotions we both seem to be feeling. But then we get the angle of our faces right and then *everything* is right. Everything. His big lips gliding over mine, me opening my mouth to let his tongue in, our breath getting heavy. I grab at what I think is his pec, or maybe just under, at his rib cage, and his hand slides over my hip, over the juncture of my thighs. He grabs me there, lightly, giving me a squeeze, and I gasp, breaking the kiss to moan as quietly as I can, even though we're the only people here.

"I told myself I wouldn't make love to you until you fell in love with me." His voice is gruff and low and I can feel it somehow vibrating against me through his hand. Or maybe that's because he's gliding his palm against me in a rhythm that makes my eyes want to roll backward.

I try to laugh, but it comes out like a series of erotic groans. "But we . . . but you were fine with oral?"

"I tried so hard to resist you, Teal, but I never could."

I gasp when he rolls his palm in a way that hits me exactly right. "Do you—God—do you have a condom?"

He immediately pulls his hand back from between my thighs, and I am not too embarrassed to whine in disappointment.

"We aren't doing it for the first time in an old-ass movie theater," he responds.

"So you're going to take me to the new one?" I ask, trying to lighten the mood, because it sounds like he's sort of rejecting me again.

His arms wedge under me and I squeak, and then he hoists me into his arms. "Ha. No. We're going to leave right now, actually, and I'm going have you in our bed."

Our bed. In our home. Because Carter Velasquez is my husband.

It's still scary, to think I'm on the verge of having what I have always secretly wanted. But I want to be brave and brave and brave, so I wrap my arms around his neck and, with my lips, find the spot I kissed during our first dance as esposo y esposa.

He hisses in a breath, and I can feel goose bumps forming under my mouth. "That's one of your erogenous spots, isn't it?" I whisper.

"It's . . . something. God. I can't even breathe when you—" And then I do it again, proving him right as he holds his breath in and then shakily lets it out when I'm done. "Damn, Teal. Damn."

We make it back to his place in about five minutes. He kept doing this dumb move of hitting the gas while simultaneously trying to stare at me, like he was in awe of the fact that I was his, seriously his. "Pay attention to the road!" I kept squeaking, watching him blush over as he whipped his head back front-facing.

As soon as we make it through the entryway, I basically jump on him. He catches me, his hands on my ass, leaning me against the wall as we begin kissing with the intensity of a teenage make-out session. He cups my face with one hand, and I hold on to the back of his neck and squeeze. My entire body feels pre- and post-orgasmic at once—warm and tingly, focused only on how I can get ever more closer to Carter.

"Wait," I say suddenly. He freezes, slowly lowering me to the ground. I wince when my left foot hits.

"Are you in too much pain?" he breathes.

I laugh, because even though I *am* in pain, and am probably due for another Advil, the endorphins of him, of his lips and shoulders and hands and everything, are doing a better job of numbing the ache than any pill. "I'm fine. I just wanted to, ah. Change first. If that's okay?"

He furrows his brow and nods. "Okay. Just—"

"I'll let you know when I'm ready for you in the bedroom." And then I limp that way as fast as I can.

Once there, I about rip open the top drawer to my dresser, pulling out socks and bras until I find what I'm looking for. I hold it up in front of me: the barely-there bikini lingerie Sage and Sky gave me on my wedding day. I haven't even tried it on yet, but with something like this, in which the fact it's not supposed to fit is kind of the point, it doesn't matter. I peel off my clothes as clumsily as I can, putting my weight on the dresser and off my foot, and then tie it on.

I burst into laughter when I look at myself in the mirror. The little triangles of the top barely hide my nipples. The bottoms—let's just say I would absolutely be arrested if I wore this to the beach. The backside is a thong, so it hides about as much as the front. There's something about the fact that at first glance, it has the same form as a normal bathing suit, but then all the naughty bits are more or less on display rather than covered. It's ridiculous and hot at the same time.

I open the door to call for Carter, but he's right there, patiently waiting. His eyes drop down my body, and his mouth falls open. "Do you like it?" I ask, putting my hands on my hips and posing as sexily as I can with my weight on one foot. "I was thinking of sunning just a little bit, before sex."

He's staring at my breasts, where I'm pretty sure one of the fabrics has busted off my nipple just by my lifting my arms a little. "What? You sure?"

I snort. "I'm kidding, Carter. This is lingerie."

He stares between my legs, and then he reaches out to touch me there, sliding his fingers where the fabric doesn't even cover, where I am already beyond slick for him. "Good," he says, gruff enough to make me gasp, and then he grabs me to lean on him as he slides one, then two fingers inside me.

"Oh my God," I whimper when he curls his grip right where I need it the most.

He makes me come so fast, I'd be embarrassed if it weren't so good. As soon as it's over, he lifts me and places me on the bed, where he once again just stares at me, as though I were made entirely of pearls and diamonds and whatever other precious stones Sage can't afford to work with yet but spends a lot of time looking at in the lapidary store downtown.

"I love watching you come," he tells me.

"I want you to come now, inside me, please." I tug at his shirt. "Let me see you."

He pulls it over his head and I'm treated to the beautiful expanse of his lean torso. Sitting on his knees, he works his belt and kicks off everything else awkwardly, and I almost giggle until I see his cock, how hard he is, how much I need him inside me.

"You know how long I've wanted to do this?" he asks, grabbing a condom from his side table.

I shake my head.

"Twelve years old. I first learned what sex was from Tito. He had this old *Playboy* he'd found and proceeded to educate me and Marcus."

I laughed. "I'm sure cousin Tito gave a sound sex education."

He smiles at me and it's so big and warm, it takes my breath away. "It was short and to the point. And no mention of how to please a woman, naturally." He lowers his body onto me until we are aligned, my breasts against his chest, his erection against my thigh. "But that night, I jerked off for the first time in the shower and I thought about you."

"You were twelve and I was fourteen."

"Exactly. You were the hot older girl." He leans down to kiss my neck. "Every time I learned something new about sex, from my older cousins or porn or whatever, I'd always imagine it with you."

I feel a frisson of sadness in my chest and swallow as unexpected tears sting my eyes. "What is it, baby?" he whispers. "You want me to stop?"

I shake my head. "No. I just wish my first time had been with you. I wish my head wasn't so far up my ass when it came to my feelings for you."

He kisses me, so slow and syrupy that it makes one of those tears in my eyes fall. "We have now, though, Teal."

He's right. We have now. So I reach down and wiggle until the tip of him is right there, and he whispers *You're sure?* and I whisper back, *Yes*, and then he slides all the way in.

His groan, oh my gosh, it does things to my belly and vag and everywhere else. "You feel so good," he grunts in my ear.

"Muévete," I say, urging his hips on with my hands. He grins and obeys, thrusting his hips soft at first, then getting harder and more urgent.

"How do you like it? How do you want it?" he asks.

I pinch his ass and smile when he yelps. "However you want, Carter."

"But—" He moans when I lift my hips to meet his. "Isn't there a position that gets you off more than the others . . ."

"I don't get off during intercourse."

"Never?"

I shake my head. "Lots of women don't." I try not to sound defensive.

"I know, babe. I want to feel you come on my cock, but that's okay. I'll get you off again however you need it."

What he means by that is, he lifts my legs over his shoulders, until there's friction inside me that actually is pleasurable. And he tries so hard to last as long as he can, but he comes before I do, if I was going to, which I'm not entirely sure I was.

But I sure as hell come when he pulls out of me, slides his body down, and licks me slow and hard until I'm shaking and screaming his name.

30

I DIDN'T WANT TO LEAVE CARTER. I WANTED TO STAY IN BED with him and see how many times we could make each other orgasm, and then lazily eat takeout lounging on the covers, talking and snuggling until we were making out and dry-humping and then for-real humping all over again.

Alas. I had made plans with my sisters. Important ones I can barely remember when Carter kisses me at the door as Sky honks in the driveway. "I'll be right here when you get back," he says with a big smile. "I want to see what other lingerie your sisters got you."

I grin and wink. "One of the pieces is entirely crotchless."

His eyes go a little hazy, like he can't help but imagine it, and then he shuts the front door as I'm opening it. "Changed my mind, cancel on your sisters and go put it on."

I laugh, gently opening the door again. I know he's messing around but damn, I really want to do exactly that. I don't want to think about my sisters and what we're trying to do tonight. I don't want to think about my shitty mother and the way she fucked me up when I was basically a baby. I don't want to think about how, deep down, I don't think it's possible that I can get it back—my soul. That I will remain soul-broken forever.

But Sky honks the horn again, this time for so long, I'm sure the neighbors want to curse us out now.

I sigh and kiss Carter one more time. "I'll be back in an hour, tops." I don't actually know how long it's going to take to get my soul fragment back, but I don't want to give it more than an hour, not when I have guaranteed orgasms at home with my husband.

"I'll be waiting." He gives me one more panty-melting grin, his dark yellow eyes practically twinkling as I make my way out the door with an enormous grin of my own.

"Finally," Sky says when I contort myself to get in her car with minimal pain. She pauses as she looks me over. "Wait a minute. There's something different about you."

My cheeks instantly turn hot. "Um—"

"Are you high?" Sky furrows her brow as she looks me over. "Your eyes are kind of glassy and your *hair* . . ." She wrinkles her nose. "Did you take too much Valium?"

I laugh and shake my head. Sex-obsessed Sky isn't going to guess that I finally banged my husband, and the result was not one but two epic orgasms? "No. I just . . . Carter and I went to the movie theater. Like for a real date. And it was nice." I don't want to share the sex part yet, or the part in which Carter and I declared our love for each other. It feels too new and precious, like something just for us, for however long we need it to be just for us.

"But to be clear, you didn't get high while watching the movie?"

I roll my eyes and point. "No, Sky, and please start driving. I'm starving and I don't want to eat cold tacos."

"Fine."

She doesn't put the top down, but she does roll down all the windows so the salt-thick wind from the sea rushes through. We can't talk, because it's so loud, but I don't care. My hair is going to look like it's made of twigs when this drive is through, but I don't care about that, either. I'm still riding the high of Carter. Specifically, of me being his and him being mine. And how convenient a marriage of convenience turned out to be.

Sky pulls into St. Theresa's Catholic Church for Wanderers and Pilgrims. Even though we spent a hell of a lot of time here our entire childhood, I can't think of this place as mine. It's Nadia's, and now, maybe Sky's, but only because she works there. I've just never been into this stuff like Nadia or Sage, the spiritual parts of religion. Maybe it's my lack of control and connection over my gift . . . or maybe it's just me. I think the old gods stuff is real, if out there, and I mean literally out there—beyond my reach, both physically and mentally. But religion—Mass and church and priests and smelly incense and confession booths—that's always been bullshit to me. Other people can like it and that's fine. Just leave the rest of us alone about it, please.

The worship hall itself is massive, made of white and gray sea stone, the kind you can still see fossils stuck inside if you look close enough, with three tall towers reaching up like witch's claws. On the top of the largest of them is a red cross that lights up from its bottom at night, in a way I've always thought was creepy.

Inside, it's all one floor, those tall walls holding just-as-tall stained glass of images featuring Mary Magdalene and various other figures from Jesus's time, including, naturally, the man himself. The floor is made up of polished black tile, and the harmonics are nuts—you can hear the chisme that viejas are whispering to each other on the other side of the room if you wanted.

Sky doesn't stop at the parking lot in front of the worship hall, though. She goes around, stopping the car when we're right behind it, facing a series of buildings—the two-story gray one in which all the religious and Sunday school classes are taught, the offices for various church-business things, and then . . . the library.

"Damn, I'd forgotten how weird the library looks," I mutter. Someone had the grand idea to put the library in where the old sanctuary used to be. But they didn't exactly remodel it right . . . if at all. It's on the smallish side, made up of white walls peeling to reveal orangey red brick, with two massive red doors cut in front of the entrance like a wide-open mouth. There are always a few crows hanging out on its roof, too, ever since I was a little kid—like they know it's haunted and are trying to warn anyone nearby with their sharp caws.

Sky gives me a huge grin as she grabs her bag. "Isn't it great?"

"Sure, if we're on the set of *Buffy the Vampire Slayer*." I glance at her outfit—a black turtleneck tucked into high-waisted gray slacks, an enormous sunstone silver necklace at her chest, and shiny black, pointed boots. "Actually, you know what? You with the librarian thing you've got going on. You're basically a young, hot female Latina Giles. If Giles were the older version of a tall Shakira."

"That makes no sense, because Giles was rather hot."

I shrug. Point taken. I didn't think it when I watched the show at twelve, but now I can see it, though—the older, kind of awkward guy with the accent and the glasses. Yeah, Giles was hot.

There are two black iron benches facing each other on the walkway leading to the library doors. Sage is sitting on one, already devouring what looks to be her second taco.

"I know you're pregnant and all, but that better not be my taco," I say.

Sage rolls her eyes and digs through the huge plastic bag by her side, and she hands me and Sky a small paper bag each. "Teal, you got three grilled fish tacos with extra guacamole and a side of black bean soup. Sky, you got the fried chicken tacos covered in cilantro and lime crema with a side of maduros."

"How did you know?" Sky gasps, snatching the bag away.

"I asked Nadia. Sometimes her gift comes in handy."

"What did you get?" Sky asks.

"Three four-cheese street-corn tacos with a side of tostones."

"Oh, that sounds good, too. Save me a toston?"

Sage lifts one up—the thing is massive, like, the size of her palm—and tosses it to Sky, who catches it one-handed like she was trained to save delicious fried things from getting ruined on the ground.

Sky and I take the bench facing Sage and dig in. "How much do I owe you?" I ask, but Sage waves me off. That's okay. I'll figure out another way to pay her back.

"So, Sky," Sage says between licking her fingers like a barbarian.

"Yes, Sage."

"Do you have a plan? Like for real? Or are we winging this?"

"I told you, the plan—or spell, if you want to get specific—is in the book. We follow the book. The whole thing is in the book."

I scoff between bites. "Say 'book' one more time please, I don't think she got it."

Sky sticks her tongue out at me before shouting "*Book!*" so loudly, I wish I'd covered my ears for it.

Sage grabs an antibacterial wipe from her purse and cleans her hands. "Well, I'm ready when you are."

I stuff the last bite of taco in just as my phone pings with a text from Gerald Samuels. Just a quick update. No one remembers

Vivienne at the recent gallery. Going to find former employees to question.

I toss my phone back in my bag and remember to chew my taco. "Ready," I say with an entirely too-full mouth. I know Samuels is doing his best, but I don't think he's going to find Mama. At this point, I've got *nothing* to lose. Nada. "I couldn't be more ready, honestly."

"Me too." Sky stands with the rest of us.

We toss the garbage in the trash can near the side of the building, then follow Sky to the front doors.

"I always thought this felt like walking into a vag," Sage muses as Sky pulls out what are I am assuming her work keys.

"Like we're fingers! Fingering the giant church vag!" Sky announces as she opens the door and walks in, making that godforsaken "fingering" motion with her hand lifted high above her head.

"God, I hope no one is in there and could hear that," I mutter while Sage cracks up.

"Nope, it's just us," Sky announces.

"And you sure you're not going to get in trouble for . . . you know. Spellwork after hours?" Sage asks.

Sky shakes her head. "You should see my boss. I'm pretty sure if she caught us, she'd give me a raise."

Sage and I both look at each other and shrug. Whatever that means.

We're all inside now, and it's freezing in here. I shiver and fold my arms over my chest. "Damn, I didn't think I'd need a winter coat."

I haven't spent a ton of time in the church library in my life, but it looks about the same as I remember. Extremely tall bookshelves stuffed with creepy-looking books: check. Small creepy windows that show the dark greenery surrounding the building and nothing else: check. Dark-ass creepy shadows everywhere because of the small creepy windows: check.

Sky leads us to an elevator, which looks like it was installed before elevators were even invented. The doors don't line up right, and when they open, the little yellowed room inside also looks Escher-esque wonky. Like if I look up, I'm going to see our own feet and if I look down, I'll see the tops of our heads or some shit like that.

"Why does it smell like when you solder something in here?" Sage asks.

"I don't know. What does soldering smell like?" Sky says in response.

The doors open before Sage can answer—because hell if I know what soldering smells like—revealing a single-room basement, wide and dark and about one hundred times creepier than the ground floor.

"Jesus," Sage whispers as our footfalls echo around us ominously. "I swear I just felt the presence of, like, sixteen ghosts walking by."

"There was a massacre near here in the late 1700s," Sky responds cheerfully. "That was probably those spirits."

"I was trying to make a joke to lighten the mood, but now sadly, I've made it all worse." Sage puts both hands on her belly, like she's trying to protect the little guy from the seriously now-*very* Buffy vibes. "How can you work down here all day?"

"Oh, it's not that bad," Sky says, leading us around towers of books and tall, half-empty shelves and even an old, enormous trunk made of what looks like pure silver and gold.

I can see where they're both coming from. On one hand, the basement does resemble a catacomb of books rather than a library, with its long, deep blue shadows, bloodred painted walls, and the general feel of underworldly chaos. On the other, there's also this sense of awe that tends to come when I'm in an old place . . . like many people have passed through here, many hands have touched this knob, many feet have twirled around this old-as-hell table. It does feel like there are ghosts here and I wonder how much I would have to bribe Amá Sonya to come and tell us about them through her gift that she likes to deny even exists.

And with the little slants of deep afternoon honey light coming in, and the dance of the tiny dust motes in them, and the coolness of being in a room mostly hidden in the earth, well—considering where Sky has spent most of the last eight years, I can see how she'd feel comfortable here.

"This is my office," Sky says, lifting her arms to show an old desk that looks antique, carved from a red-hued wood with feet shaped like those of a cat's.

"This is a desk shoved into a corner of the basement," Sage responds.

"Like I said. My office."

There's a small desktop computer on the top of her desk, alongside a framed photo of us when we were little, in Nadia's backyard some hot summer. Sage and I were both holding baby Sky at once. We were both in our underwear; Sky was in just a diaper. We're squinting into the sun with big smiles, Nadia's roses and cosmos and marigolds blooming all around us.

I frown, picking it up. I was four here, I'm pretty sure. I stare at my dark eyes and huge baby-teeth grin, my small frame and plump, pink cheeks.

I was a baby. I was a *baby*. My mother stole a piece of her baby's soul and took off without a single fucking word.

I'm not really sure how I rationalized what had happened

before. I guess not knowing what she did, exactly, when she pinched that piece of light from my hand . . . it meant that I could somehow make it so that she was a better person than she was. At one point I even thought that maybe what she took meant she could always find me again somehow. I remember looking out the window of the attic, the one over what would end up being Sage's bed, where I could see Catalina Street all the way down to where it turns, rubbing the middle of my palm, praying to see her. I imagined her walking back, luggage in tow. I imagined running downstairs and jumping in her arms, screaming *Mama, I knew you'd come back for me!*

"You okay?" Sage asks gently.

I nod forcefully and square my shoulders. "I'm ready to find her now."

I'm ready to take back what belongs to me.

31

SAGE, SKY, AND I SIT IN A CIRCLE IN THE MIDDLE OF THE old-ass and creepy-ass church library basement, and between all of us is a lit candle, making everything glow ever so slightly in orange. Sky has put on her pink cat-eye reading glasses and now she's glossing over the spellbook while Sage and I wait.

"How long is this going to take?" I ask, checking my phone.

Sky doesn't answer. Instead, she murmurs to herself as she reads and I look at Sage, who just shrugs.

"Isn't it some shit," Sage says, looking around, "that Nadia trained Mama in the old religion? But not us? I always wondered why she never took us to go find the old gods' footprints."

"She taught us a few things," I say, thinking of all the Nadia sayings I've heard over the years. *There are things older than God. Simple spells are the most powerful. Don't ever reject a gift from a ghost.*

"Very vague things. I knew she was leaving stuff out but whenever I asked her to get specific, she'd shake her head and say it was lost to colonization."

"We need a representation of the old gods," Sky announces.

"Uh . . ." Sage begins, but I raise my hand like I'm in class.

"Thanks to my good-for-nothing ex-best-friend Leilani Rodriguez, I have one right here." I fish in my purse until I find it—the white and gold shimmering bookmark she'd left on the table at the craft fair when she'd huffed away, thinking she was so much better than me because she represses her negative emotions instead of seeing them all across the sky in the form of lightning and clouds and sleet.

Sky smiles. "You finally got rid of her, huh?"

I shrug. "She dumped me, but whatever. I saw with my own eyes what you two kept saying about her."

"She made this?" Sage asks, examining the bookmark. "But this is—"

"Stolen from our ancestors' art? Yes. Yes, it is."

Sage lets out a long breath. "Damn, that girl has some audacity."

I roll my eyes, thinking of the way Lani accused me of being a narcissist because of the very thing I am trying to fix right now. "You have no idea."

"Okay," Sky says. "We have the rep of the old gods. Now we need something that ties the two people together, and something from the earth. And that's it, for materials."

"That's it?" I ask.

"Simple spells are always the most powerful," Sage recites.

"Okay, well, something connecting me and Mama . . ." I sigh and grab the back of my neck. "She left this necklace. Nadia said I could have it when I was fourteen or something like that, so I've been wearing it on occasion for a while now."

"As for something from the earth." Sage digs through her bag now, and pulls out a small baggie of little black speckles. "Saved seeds from the herb spiral at work."

"Okay, let's put them around the candle," Sky says, and Sage and I arrange the objects so they're equidistant and not too close to the flame. "And now, we have to ask the old gods to help us find the soul-stealer."

We all look at one another for a few moments. "You should ask," Sage says to me. "It's your soul."

I close my eyes and shake my head. "I feel stupid."

"Just do it. If nothing happens, we'll just have Nadia perform the ritual in two days or whatever she said earlier."

I glare at the candle and sigh. "Fine." I imagine the last time I felt close to the old gods. For some reason, I anticipate Sky's arrival home after falling to be the thing that should come to me— but no. Weirdly enough, the memory that pops up is when Carter held my hand against the oak tree and told me to sense the water in the tree's circulatory system. That feeling of connection . . . it felt similar to when I was struck by lightning.

Like a part of me was opening up to what I had lost without even knowing I'd lost it. The way I could feel the life of the water in the tree. The way the water itself seemed to be a whole spirit, talking to the water that made up my body . . . and how my body seemed to connect to every single body of water all around me. Every river, every creek, hell, every raindrop, even, that makes up this land. Even the ones long gone, and even the ones that are yet to come. All of that inside me at once, making me feel whole for the first time in a long time.

Now I know that I had briefly connected to a stolen piece of my soul. Which I'm going to get back, dammit. A bit of awkwardness isn't going to stand in my way.

"Old gods," I say, and to my dismay, my voice has the slightest bit of emotion in it. "Um. Please lead me to my lost soul fragment."

We all sit in silence for about thirty seconds, when I throw up my hands. "It didn't work, but that's—"

And then Sky gasps. "Teal! Your hands!"

When I glance at them, they're glowing. They're glowing blue just like at the beach, on the night of wild lightning.

⚡

SAGE AND SKY AND I WATCH, ENRAPTURED, AS THE GLOW OF MY hands pours down, and a line, all crooked and alight, flows out from me and along the floor, leading straight through the wall of the basement.

"We have to follow it!" Sky says excitedly as she blows out the candle and rises to her feet. "It's leading us to Mama!" She wrinkles her nose. "I don't like saying 'Mama,' actually. I'm going to call her Cora now."

"It's leading us to her?" I ask, my voice wavering.

"Yes. Can't you feel it?" Sage murmurs. "Come on. Let's go get her."

We all leap in Sky's car, keeping an eye on the blue line the whole while. It's like my own little GPS connection—wherever I go, the line aligns itself to me, leading me in what hopefully is the quickest way there. "We need to head south," Sky says as she starts the car. And that's what we do.

As the sun lowers itself toward the horizon line, turning the sky into the peachiest pink orange ever, the line spreads out in front of the car, leading us down the highway, past both state parks, toward the downtown beach walk. In fact, it takes us right on the beach strip, and Sage screams, "Left!" in the middle of all the stores and restaurants, leading us to the little parking lot behind one of the art galleries.

"Wait a minute," I murmur, watching the glow of the blue line between my hands and the back entrance to the gallery. "I was here just a couple of months ago. And . . . the PI said that there was a woman who used a name similar to Mama's, an artist . . ."

"She's an artist?" Sage asks, wrinkling her nose.

"We're about to find out, looks like," Sky says, opening her car door.

I do the same, only noticing how much my hands tremble when I climb out of the car. I probably need to take some Tylenol or Advil or whatever is next on the painkiller schedule, but I can barely feel the ache, or even just the regular sensations of my body. Instead, it's like there's not just a line reaching my hands, but also reaching my belly, where it fills me with nothing but fear.

Sky marches right on the blue line to the door. She opens it and holds it for me and Sage, waiting patiently.

"You ready?" Sage asks. She looks nervous, too. A little pale.

"I think so. What about you?"

Sage shrugs. "I'm going in, expecting the worst of her. It's all I'm capable of right now."

I nod. "She stole my soul, Sage. I think it's very realistic to expect the worst."

Sage wraps an arm through mine, and she helps me to the door. Sky keeps it open for us, and she follows behind when we're through.

The gallery is a wide-open single room, a square made up of white-as-snow walls. There is a pale blue marble desk in a corner—where I guess transactions are made—but besides that, there are only staged pieces of art and the posters and papers explaining them.

I walk by one wall hanging titled *The Lightning Bruja* and feel my entire body tingle with apprehension and anger at once.

Vivette Coretta first encountered the sculptures as a result of lightning hitting beach sand in Southern California. The heat of the lightning strike melts the sand into finely textured glass and sand forms. Coretta was enchanted with what she calls "the magic of ocean storms" and began to chase the storms along the beach shores all over the Americas, discovering hundreds of sculptures along the way. "It's a gift," laughs Coretta when asked about how she seems to always be in the right place at the right time. "It's my gift."

"Oh my God," Sage whispers as she reads behind me. "I *literally* can't believe her." Her voice constricts and I don't have to turn around to know that tears stream down her face. "She's not even *trying* to hide the theft."

I glance around at the sculptures themselves. The fulgurites, as one sign declares their official name to be, balance atop plain white stands, made of what looks like glittering quartz and beach sand melded together. Their shape reminds me of an amalgamation of undersea coral and little, pencil-sized lightning, frozen in form. They are beautiful and haunted and messy.

"Teal." I turn to Sky, who stands in front of a door labeled *FOR EMPLOYEES ONLY.* She gestures to where the blue line leads—under the white-painted wood of the door and onward to the other side. "She's in there."

I'm frozen, as still in time as the beautiful and cold sculptures—the result of my stolen gift, my stolen soul piece—all around me.

Sky raises her eyebrows. "Do you need me to open the door?"

I nod immediately.

Sky doesn't hesitate. She throws open the door, and as soon as someone inside says, "Excuse me, this is a private—" Sky throws open her hands and says, "Cora! Do you remember me? It's Sky, your youngest daughter!"

32

I KNOW THAT SKY DOESN'T CARE ABOUT MEETING MAMA, about hearing what she has to say. Sky has never known her, not really, so she doesn't have that sort of hole in her heart. What she's doing is creating an opportunity for me and Sage to gather our bearings and come inside.

The room is similar in taste to the gallery—made up of white porcelain furniture, white walls, two desks pushed up against the only wall with windows facing the walkway of downtown, where between the redbrick buildings across the street the ocean peeks through, right now becoming as dark as indigo while the sun sets.

I'm guessing the director or curator or whoever—a white woman with auburn hair and a confused look on her face—sits behind the desk, and leaning against one of its corners . . . is Mama.

The blue line stops right at her feet, so there is no question it's her. I open my mouth to speak, but nothing comes out. Of all the thoughts fluttering in my mind like a thousand dandelion seeds, the one that settles first is: *She looks different from us and exactly like us at the same time.*

We sisters don't look exactly alike, thanks to our different fathers, but we each inherited something from her—our skin, the color of dark gold, our sharp bone structure, recognizable even on our differently shaped faces. And I guess we each got her smirk—because she smirks at us now, and it feels very familiar, a look I've seen on both Sage and Sky and maybe even in the mirror, when I've had a productive and vindictive day.

Her hair looks dyed to be dark, thanks to the hint of white roots, and lines decorate her skin, mainly crow's feet at her eyes (Sky must've gotten her crinkly smile from her). She's about my height with Sage's curvy body, adorned in a black suit I'm surprised to see her wearing, because it looks slick and expensive and something her mother, Sonya, would approve of. And she and Amá Sonya, from the stories Nadia tells, never did get along.

I'm not sure what I expected to feel, laying eyes on my mother for the first time in over two decades, but for some reason, right now, it's a whole lot of nothing. Like my emotions have vacated the premises because of the intense stress of the moment.

"I didn't know you had a daughter, Viv," the lady behind the desk says, and the way she says *Viv*, like she's super good friends with Mama, makes me snap.

"We're all her daughters," I tell the woman. "She abandoned us when we were babies, and her name isn't Vivienne. It's Cora Flores-Gonzalez, or at least it was about twenty-five years ago."

My mother's expression sharpens when I speak, and the woman—Harriet, I can see her name tag now—looks even more confused, with hurt beginning to color her features. I wonder how long they've been friends. How long she thought she knew this woman—this faker—in front of her.

"Harriet, would you mind giving me a minute with my—" Mama coughs. "My daughters?"

Harriet nods and stands, not sparing any of us a glance on the way out.

As soon as the door shuts behind her, I glare at Mama. "I want it back."

Mama crosses her arms and raises an eyebrow. "I'm sure I don't know what you're talking about." It's scary how much that statement sounds like Amá Sonya.

"Cut the crap, Cora," Sky says, and I blink—I've never heard her sound this mean and demanding before. "We *all* know what she's talking about."

Mama's eyes sheen. "It's been over twenty years . . . and this is the welcome I get from my own children?"

Now Sky narrows her eyes. "You've been in town for how long now? And so far all you've done is made damn well sure we couldn't find you." Sky scrunches her nose. "You were expecting a welcome-back party for that?"

"I've had to work," Mama wails. "I was going to come to you *eventually*—"

"What are you doing in town?" Sage asks. "Why are you even here to begin with?"

Mama shrugs casually even though her face is still contorted as though she's crying. Spoiler: no actual tears are happening right now. "Work. Things have been so difficult. I need to make rent, and since the recession, it's been hard finding a place to show my art. I know I'm always welcome here." She lifts her arms, indicating the gallery. "Unlike, apparently, with *you* three."

Sage's voice is so cutting, I'm surprised we all aren't covered in blood as she speaks, each word a shard of glass. "Did you really think you could leave me to raise them, leave Teal with half of her gift, and leave Sky in diapers, and that we'd what—throw you a party? Worship you at your feet? That's we'd fall over our-selves in gratitude when we finally fucking found you again?"

"I left you with Nadia," Mama hisses. "Don't act like I dropped you off on the streets."

"Nadia housed us and did little else," I tell her. "Sage potty-trained Sky. If you want to know how far Nadia's parenting went."

Mama blinks, then shakes her head. "Nadia wouldn't do that to me."

"Nadia thinks you're shit. Whatever camaraderie you think you had with her doesn't exist," Sky snaps. "Now give Teal's soul piece back, so I can go home and eat s'mores and drink cham-pagne and finish season four of *Gilmore Girls*."

It's the *Gilmore Girls* that does it. The fact that her own daugh-ter would rather be watching a fictional mother and daughter rather than interact with her actual mother bruises Mama's ego enough that she drops the woe-is-me act. She legit snarls as she spits out, "I'm not giving *anything* back. For what? My own daughters don't care about me. My own mother never cared about me."

"Amá Sonya cares about you," Sage says. "She almost cries every time we can manage to get her to talk about you, and then she blames pepper for it."

"She tricked you!" Mama's voice is loud now, and screeching. It triggers some faded memories from when I was small—her yelling at us, at Nadia, at boyfriends on the phone. Somehow I had forgotten how angry and volatile she was. I had romanticized her in my mind, thinking of how she hugged me, of how she hummed to me when I was in her arms, but the truth is . . . she often did these things after she'd hurt me. She *only* did those things after she hurt me.

Mama opens her mouth, continuing on. "Mom is a spoiled bitch—"

"We all know Amá Sonya is a bitch," I say, and she furrows her brow. "You think we're that dumb that we haven't figured that out yet? Now *give it back*."

Mama crosses her arms and lifts her chin. It's amazing, seeing this grown, almost fifty-year-old woman act like a teenager. Nothing is her fault. Everyone is being mean to her. I don't know what shaped her to be this way, but I can't say it doesn't hurt. I wasn't lying when I told Sage I wasn't expecting a Hallmark re-union with her, but that little girl inside me still, the one who ran after her in the storm, who showed up in nothing but lightning in front of me a few nights ago—that girl hoped impossible hopes. And each one is currently being shattered before her eyes.

"I can't," Mama says, allowing her eyes to sheen once more. "It's my only income. I'll be destitute. Would you three really leave me on the streets with nothing to my name but the clothes on my back?"

"Why don't you find a sugar daddy?" Sky asks wryly, her tone bored. "You're very good at that."

Mama rolls her eyes. "I won't stand here and be disrespected by the ones *I* birthed. You owe your *lives* to me. As for you—" She points at me with a sharp deep purple nail. "If she wanted to return to you, she would have by now." She dusts off her shoul-ders. "Before I leave for good—which you know how well I can do, since I'm sure you're aware of my gift—I have a few things I need to make clear." She looks at each of us. "If you all were better-behaved children, I might have stayed. But, Sage, *you*—"

And as she proceeds to insult us, I'm stuck on something she just said. *If she wanted to return to you, she would have by now.*

I've never heard Nadia refer to a soul piece by a pronoun before, but . . . it feels right to say it like that. *She.*

It's not just a fragment of my soul that went to Mama. It's that tiny child, so small the heavy wind of a storm could lift her up . . . *she* went with Mama. She was so scared, she volunteered to leave me with the hopes that her mama would stay, or someday return.

I stare at Mama and in my mind's eye, I see four-year-old me, drawn on the beach in lightning. I can feel her, right now, so close to me. Mama stops midsentence and looks at me. "What do you think you're doing?"

Tears stream down my face. I have no idea what I'm doing, actually. I don't even know if Sky, who's the only one who's read this damn spell, knows what comes next. But I do know this— that little girl is me. She's mine and I'm hers.

I see her step out of Mama and toward me, with equal parts caution and curiosity. Her hair, long and braided. Her eyes, so tired from all the crying. Her skin, as brown as a golden acorn, the one feature I've always loved because it matches the tone of each of my sisters' so perfectly.

She is made of lightning, but she's also made of *me.* I lower myself to my knees. And now I'm at eye level with her. She wants to come back to me, but she's so scared, her whole body trembles. So I open my mouth and tell her—little Teal—this. "You belong to me," I whisper. "You belong to me and I'll take care of you in the ways she never could. You never had a real mother, but I can be that mother for you."

I don't know the first thing about being a mother, but I know that's what I need to be for that child my mother left in the rain.

Mama legit growls like some kind of damn bear, and little Teal gasps and instantly disappears. To add insult to injury, Mama's visage begins to . . . *shatter*. She goes in and out, in and out, like a figure in a video game glitching.

She's trying to superimpose her power over mine. She's trying to disappear before I can become whole.

I'm not going to let that happen.

"I don't know shit about the old gods," I say, "but I am begging them to keep you here till I'm done with you."

And just like that, she stops flickering like a flame. She's firmly in this room, on this polished floor, lit up in fading sunlight from the window and bright fluorescents above.

"Stop it," Mama demands, but it's too late. She lifts her arms, like she's going to push me, maybe—and instead, yellow lightning bursts from her hand. "Make it stop!" she screams.

Sky takes my right hand, and Sage takes my left. "I'm scared," I whisper as my body heats up with light.

"I was scared, too, to step back in," Sky tells me. "But it's the easiest thing in the world. I promise. It's like taking one long, deep breath."

Mama's glowing in blue, and that same form, the one I saw at the beach—she's suddenly here, right in front of me. And Sky's right—it's like *breath*. I pull my left hand from Sage—the one where Mama took my light from me—and I offer it to little me.

It's as easy as an inhale when she returns. When I return to myself.

⚡

"GIVE IT BACK! GIVE IT BACK!" MAMA WAILS, AND THE DOOR bursts open.

"What's going on in here?" Harriet yells.

Then there are hands wrapped around my neck. I turn and see my mother, tightening, frantic, her eyes brown and wild, her hair frizzing. This close to me, I can see how weak she is, how much she has stolen her whole life and how none of it has been enough.

"Get off her!" Sage screams, pulling her back, but Mama won't let go.

"Stop," I say, and when I do, lightning crackles over my whole body. She gasps and releases me as though she was burned. Because she was. I made sure it hurt. Not for revenge, but as a warning.

I take a step toward Mama, and she takes one back. "I am the Witch of Wild Lightning," I tell her. "And until you are ready to apologize for all the wrong you've done to us—all three of us—I am finished with you."

And then I turn and walk out, my sisters right next to me.

33

As I walk out of the gallery, I am completely struck by the intensity of this earth. I can feel *so much*—the way the water inside the trees is the same water gathering in the clouds above us. The way the streetlamps, making everything look a little bit brassy and gold, are a speck of what lightning is, which is a speck of what the sun is. How we are all made up of light and water, sun, stars, oceans.

"Is this what it's like?" I breathe, looking up, up, up. The sky is nearly black, but the last rays of sun illumine the clouds in a dirty apricot glow. I take a breath and more clouds come. I exhale and they push away. I raise my hand and rain flicks onto it, and when I drop it, the air clears of water entirely.

"Yes," Sage says, smiling. "Like you can feel how everything intertwines and touches each other. And how you're a part of that, too."

"How could she take this from me?" I ask again, though there isn't really an answer. It doesn't matter. Because what was lost has now returned.

She returned. *I* returned.

"I don't mean to interrupt your revelations," Sky says to me. "But isn't that Abuela Erika over there?"

I turn, and at the back of a restaurant, at one of the tables under a sea of fairy lights, sits a woman who is indeed Erika. She's glowering at me as though I'd just struck her with lightning. I laugh—I can't help it. Nothing will ruin this for me. I'm no longer broken, like she said. I'm no longer unlovable.

"Ready to go?" Sage asks, wrapping an arm around me.

I nod, and we make our way toward the car. But before we get there, someone stops us, hissing, "Flores brujas!"

I roll my eyes when I see it's Erika walking up. "You." She points at me. Behind her, her dinner companions—older women, probably friends or something—stare wide-eyed. "You think you can keep my grandson from me, and my great-grandchildren and get away with it?"

"Didn't Carter tell you what would happen if you disrespected me again?" I say, and she flinches. I want to feel bad for her, but he set those boundaries. He said he'd never speak to her if she verbally abused me again.

"You got in his head!" she declares. "Why else would he say such horrible things to his grandmother? You and Eugenio." She shakes her head. "I kept that money from him as *long* as I could. Money and women"—she looks over me and my sisters—"Flores women, especially, make men weak!"

"Ma'am, with all due respect, I think you need to get laid." Sky says it so seriously that Erika just blinks at her for a few seconds, speechless, while Sage bursts into laughter.

But I'm stuck on something. "What do you mean, you gave Carter the money? That's the whole reason why—" I break off. *That's why he married me*, I don't say.

"What is this? Now you've messed up my grandson's memory and sense of reason?" Erika gives me another nasty glare. "I waited a whole week. Begging him the whole while to get an annulment. But he kept saying, *No, no, Abuela, I need the inheritance for my new life now.* All that money at once would make him stupid, make him do stupid things like stay married to *you*!"

I blink at her and then I look at Sage. "Carter already has the money? Like, for real? You're not just babbling here?"

"I can't believe he did this to me!" Erika is howling. I'm not even sure she's heard the question.

"She's had a lot to drink." One of her dinner companions has walked up, putting her arm on Erika's shoulder. "Come on, Erika. Let's finish our salmon, no?"

I'm being taken away, too, by both Sky and Sage, who help me into the car. I stare out the window when Sky starts the engine, my mind going over the series of events that have happened since Erika came over to us, rambling like reality had escaped her long ago. Carter, saying his grandmother won't give him the money till he's married. Him letting her walk all over me and me thinking it was because he didn't want to endanger his money.

"Carter already has the money." I tap my fingers against the car door, my heart oddly feeling like it's being ripped apart. "He told me we would just stay married till he got it. And then that would be it. The marriage would be done." I close my eyes tight, cursing under my breath because I think they may be stinging. "We can go our separate ways now. It'll be like we were never married to begin with, I guess."

"Is that really what you want?" Sky asks.

It's immature, but I can only shrug in response. Because no . . . it's not what I want. It's kind of the opposite of what I want, but I'm too scared to be honest in this moment. It feels like there's too much at stake.

Sage breaks my thoughts with her own opinion on the subject. "Teal. I think it's obvious to all of us that you're falling for him. You don't have to end the marriage right now. You can, you know—"

"—stay married to your best friend," Sky finishes.

Stay married to my best friend. I run a hand over my chest. Those words make the whole area feel less like it's breaking and more like everything is actually . . . okay. "I mean. Yeah, that makes sense. Carter told me . . ." My breath catches. Did Carter tell me he loves me back? When I first said those words to him?

I think to that moment. Me being brave and so *proud* of that bravery in the movie theater. He said *I told myself I wouldn't make love to you until you fell in love with me* and *I tried so hard to resist you, Teal, but I never could.* But he didn't exactly say the words *I love you* in return. "He shared that he had feelings for me, too," I finish lamely.

But, honestly . . . did he? It's one thing for him to say he couldn't resist me. That he wouldn't "make love" to me until he knew it wasn't just a fuck to me.

But what about *love*? Is Carter capable of it? Specifically with *me*? Teal Flores. Bad temper. Probable shopping addiction. Runs *way* too much.

Yes, I've gotten my soul back, so there isn't a danger of me attracting tornadoes and hail to Cranberry at the drop of a hat, but . . . ultimately, I'm still *me*. What if Erika is right? That no matter what, I'm irreparably broken?

No one else would ever want you. At the exact worst time, these ugly words bounce into my head, gripping too tight. Not letting go no matter how much I will them to.

"Do you want to go back to, uh, his place?" Sky asks.

Just three minutes ago, before I realized Carter never said he loved me . . . I would've said yes. I would've gone to Carter's place—which I've begun to think of as our place, our home—and told him I knew about the money. And talked it out, confident enough that he would want this. To stay married to me.

But now, even with just those series of insecure thoughts and feelings and memories, I'm so unsure. I feel about as balanced on a skinny fallen tree trunk over a wide, roaring river. All I want is something deeply familiar—a home full of painted glass windows and a sunflower yellow kitchen and an attic filled with the howls of wind-ghosts.

"No," I finally say. "Take me to Nadia's, please."

34

I T'S WEIRD, BEING IN BED IN MY CHILDHOOD ROOM, FEELING
like utter shit, and yet . . . it's *sunny* out. The sunshine is so
bright and yellow, as happy as the line of sunflowers Nadia always
plants by the mailbox, that I honestly feel offended. Dark clouds
do come at my most painful thoughts . . . but then I will them
away. And then they actually dissipate right before my eyes.

I've gotten what I thought I had wanted more than anything
in this universe—my gift, whole, *me*, whole—and yet I couldn't
care less.

I grab my phone for the umpteenth time in fifteen minutes to
see if I have any more responses to my last post. There are a half-
dozen texts from Carter—ranging from Good morning, mi esposa to How are you feeling????? to Hey, call me as soon as you
see this, okay? I'm a little worried.

Last night I told him I wasn't feeling well and that I was going
to spend the night at Nadia's. I feel guilty worrying him, but I'm
stuck. My therapist would say this is the freeze state, triggered by
a previous trauma. And I'm going to guess exactly what the

trauma would be. Mama leaving me, alone, outside this very house, right in the middle of the night.

My deepest fear is that Carter will do the exact same thing to me. I mean . . . of course he won't steal my soul and take off in a big truck with someone else. But what if, now that he has the money, he's just waiting to have a conversation about ending the marriage? About kicking me out?

I don't know if I could survive that.

I fell in love with my fake husband and I don't know what to do

posted in r/OffMyChest by TealLightning four hours ago

I fake married my childhood best friend and I fell in love with him but he didn't say those damn words I LOVE YOU back to me, and I didn't realize it until after he got his money he needed, which is why we married in the first place. Our agreement was that we'd stay married till he got this money and now he has it?? And I don't know what to do? Because what if it's really over now? What if my heart is about to be ridiculously broken by him? Seriously, WHY DO PEOPLE FALL IN LOVE, this is truly THE WORST.

Now I'm moping in my childhood bed like a literal loser, I haven't spoken to him in fifteen hours, I literally feel like my heart has been ripped from my body and someone please just help me, what the hell am I supposed to say to him? I feel like I can't breathe rn

ETA- tagging @HeroLemon701 because you told me I'd fall in love with him if I slept with him like this is a fucking romance novel and it happened, okay, and now you have to tell me how to not feel like every bone in my body is breaking

> **ringalingadingdong**—Why haven't you asked him if he loves you back? Seems like an easy-ass fix to me. Also, lay off the caps next time, would you? Yikes.

>> **TealLightning**—Because, what if he says no? I can't stand another heartbreaking rejection in my life. I've had wayyy too much of that shit. Also, re: all caps: STOP BEING A PRETENTIOUS LOSER, ASSHAT

> **intheravenw00ds**—This is . . . a lot. That is all.

> **coooooookieeeees**—just divorce him. find someone new. no man is worth this bs.

> **HeroLemon701**—Oh my GOOOOOOOOOOOOD NO WAY. THIS IS AMAZING

>> **TealLightning**—Did you not read the part where I feel like I'm being torn to pieces

>> **HeroLemon701**—BECAUSE YOU LOVE HIM THIS IS AMAZING

>> **TealLightning**—this is *literally* the opposite of amazing

HeroLemon701—No it's amazing. You are literally living a romance novel right now and I am so unbearably jealous.

HeroLemon701—BY THE WAY HE LOVES YOU TOO. GIRL JUST TALK TO HIM.

TealLightning—But he didn't say it. What if I go back there and, like, he has all my shit packed up? Technically, our deal is done.

> HeroLemon701—Question. Do you happen to have some traumatic issues with regards to abandonment?
>
> HeroLemon701—It feels like this is just a bit of an overreaction. But that would make sense if TRAUMA
>
> HeroLemon701—Seriously, @ringalingadingdong is a loser for hating all caps (THIS IS A LEGITIMATE HUMAN EXPRESSION, MAN) but he loves you! You need to just ASK him, or, you know, TELL him what you need to hear
>
> TealLightning—Ew. So you're saying I just need to "communicate" and tell him I want him to say he loves me??!!?!?!
>
> Gross.
>
> No.
>
> I don't want to.
>
> HeroLemon701—**cackles in romancelandia**

↯

I STARTLE WHEN THERE'S A KNOCK AT THE DOOR. IT OPENS AND there is Sky, holding her car keys.

"Sky! She didn't say 'come in'!" That's Sage's voice.

"Just go in. You already know what she is doing. Moping around like a pathetic prostitute." That is Amá Sonya. I groan and pull a pillow over my face.

"Amá. She has depression. And it's not 'prostitute,' it's 'sex worker.'" That's Sage again.

"I'm bipolar," I remind her.

Sage lifts a hand. "In the depressive state of bipolar disorder, then."

"She's brokenhearted, too," Sky says.

I'm pretty sure Amá snorts in response. I'm not sure if she believes in mental health disorders or romance; luckily, she doesn't say anything more about either.

"Ask her if we can come in," Nadia whispers.

"Just come in and do whatever you're going to do," I say through the pillow. "As long as it doesn't involve me leaving this room, I mean."

"Too bad!" Sky announces, and I can hear shuffling and grunting and I know that somehow, each of these assholes has squeezed into this tiny bedroom.

I throw the pillow off my head. "What do you want?"

Amá is leaning against my dresser, looking at a Victoria Secret Pure Seduction body spray as though it's labeled *DOG SHIT*. "Where are the perfumes I got you?" If she wrinkled her nose any further, I think it would just fold into her face. "What are you wearing this nonsense for?"

I sigh. "Please, just tell me whatever you all want to tell me so I can get back to what I was doing."

Sage snatches my phone out of my hands. "Which is . . ." She pauses. "Asking for life advice from Reddit."

I push myself up to a sitting position. "Hey! Give that back!"

She holds the phone out of my reach—to be honest, I'm not trying all that hard. I just don't have the motivation. Her thumb slides as she scrolls back, her face one of disbelief. "You've been asking Reddit for advice for the last *twelve years?*"

"Stop scrolling through my shit." I cross my arms and close my eyes as I lean back against my pillow mountain. "It's none of your business."

"It *is* our business," Sage says, her voice getting loud with tears. "Teal, you lock away all of your problems. You never tell us anything, you go to strangers on the internet instead. How are we supposed to help you when you keep everything inside?"

I open my eyes and stare at each of them. They're all looking at me with a little bit of anxiety and a lot of worry. Even Amá Sonya, through her expression of general disgust. "I'm guessing they told you we saw Mama." I'm talking to her and Nadia.

"I heard she's just as I remember." Nadia sighs. She looks right at me. "Teal, I've failed you in a thousand ways. And I'm not going to fail you right now. We're all here because you're in love with that boy, and you've *been* in love with him. Your sisters filled me in on what's happened." She points at me as she continues. "I don't want to anger you, but you're experiencing an overreaction, dear. I've seen the way that boy looks at you. He isn't going to let you go. Not in a million years."

"So we're here to bring you to him." Sky smiles at me, and

then she makes a face. "But you need to shower first. And wear something cute."

"You're here to take me to him?" I sit up and look at Amá Sonya. "Even you?"

Amá Sonya shrugs. "He makes good money, no? All that inheritance."

I slump my shoulders. "But . . ." My voice chokes. Even though Nadia just said the words I wanted to hear, I can't help but let go of this awful insecurity. "What if he doesn't want me anymore?"

Sage sits on the side of the bed and grabs my hand. "Do you love him?"

I shake my head. "It's not about that. It's—"

"Do you love him or not?" Sky repeats the question.

I close my eyes briefly and think of Carter. The way his eyes, his smile, his whole face brightens when I laugh. How nerdy he is, making sure I'm fed and my pain is managed. The way he carried me to the car when I got hurt. How he searched on eBay for the exact copy of *Mutant League Football* we used to play . . . or had us read poetry to one another on the porch, under the cool, blue moonlight. The way he made love to me for the first time, like I was the only thing that existed besides him in this whole universe, with its wild winds and blue lightning and trees made mostly of singing water. "Of course I love him."

"Good. It's settled. Shower, get dressed." Sky announces this, then promptly leaves the room, and everyone follows her. Everyone except for Sage, who lingers, handing me my phone.

"I shouldn't have left you when Sky fell," she says. "I'm sorry, Teal. I should've stayed."

I blink and am dismayed to feel even more tears fall. Now who's the Llorona? "Don't worry about it."

"I'm not worried, I just wanted you to know. How sorry I am." She sits and wipes away my tears, just like she did when I was little, after Mama left. "I'm going to tell you something you're probably not in the mood to hear—don't give me that look, it's nothing bad, I swear."

"Okay . . ."

"I was reading this essay by Ursula K. Le Guin."

"I know her." It's a moot point. We all know her. We grew up with Nadia, surrounded by books written only by women. There was bound to be a Le Guin novel in our childhood a time or two.

Sage nods. "Have you ever heard of *A Space Odyssey*? The film?"

I scrunch my nose. "The one with the gorillas?"

Sage raises a fist. "Yes. Yes! So do you remember what the pivotal moment for those gorillas was? When they used a bone for a weapon—"

"And committed a violent murder? Sure." I stifle a yawn. "I don't know what this has to do with Ursula, though."

"In this essay, she was talking about what complete bullshit that scene was." Sage's eyes are always bright whenever she talks about something that excites her, whether that's bacteria, mycelium, or gemstones. "That our ancestral primates made this great leap in intelligence through the use of a tool to harm. Like it was the first tool of consequence. It's such a—" Sage scrunches her nose. "Such a toxic manly thing to assume."

I blink. "Okay."

"Okay, so you know what she said was likely the first tool of consequence? What tool we needed the most, that it's been found throughout every ancient archaeological site, like, all over the world?"

I shake my head. I can't even venture a guess.

"The container."

"The container," I repeat.

"Yes. The container. The thing people use to gather herbs and foods, to carry water. The container was the pivotal moment. The pivotal tool."

"Okay, like a bowl," I say, trying as hard as I can to keep up.

"A bowl, yes, or . . ." She smiles. "A handbag."

"Oh lord," I say, putting a hand on my head. "Not with the leatherwork class again."

Sage laughs. "Look. I'm just saying this because I want you to know that handbags aren't shallow. They're not superficial. They're the things that women carry that hold their whole world together. They don't just have our currency and our cards, they have snacks, and—"

"Medicine," I supply.

"Medicine, and teas, and hand sanitizer. And more, so much more. Handbags—containers—are important. They're ancient. I wanted you to know this, deeply. In case that was a big part of what was holding you back." She runs her fingers through my hair. "You deserve joy, Teal. Okay?"

I nod. "Okay." I try really hard not to tear up when we hug, and fail . . . but that's okay. I'm trying not to mind people seeing me sad or vulnerable anymore. It's not a weakness, I remind myself.

And when she leaves, I throw off the blankets and do what everyone told me to do. I shower. I dab Victoria's Secret Pure Seduction at my neck and wrists, and I put on a pink sundress and sandals, completing the look with shimmery pink gloss and my hair plaited into one long braid. I hold a hand over my heart and think of the little girl, the piece of my soul, just returned to me. "We got this," I whisper to her. And then I walk downstairs.

MY HEART IS IN MY THROAT WHEN WE PULL DOWN CARTER'S street, and it feels like it's somehow filled up my entire body when I see him outside. He's got a tin watering can in his hands and I am *this* close to bursting into tears when I see what he's doing.

He's watering the dahlias. He's taking care of the flowers I planted for my sister's wedding, even though I was the cruelest bitch in the world to him. "He's too good for me," I say, and all the women around me—we're all squished in Nadia's CR-V—shake their heads.

It's Amá Sonya who responds. "You are better than any man."

"Uh—" Sky says. "That's not quite what—"

"Thanks," I say, because I know what Amá was getting at—sort of—and now my heart is hammering against my rib cage, because Carter has spotted the car. I swallow and open the door.

"Teal?" Carter's staring at me, not even realizing he's probably overwatering the seedlings by now. He looks down and tosses the watering can aside. "What— I mean, how are you fe—"

"Tell him!" Sage commands, and maybe it's something about her being both my big sister and mother figure at once, but I listen to her.

"I'm sorry!" I weep, limping across the driveway.

He gives me an incredulous look. "Sorry for what?"

"I know Erika gave you the money. She told me. And I'm sorry I lied. I wasn't not feeling well. I was hiding at Nadia's because I'm a coward. I was just so scared, you know? Scared you didn't really love me. That you had been lying about your feelings, you know? Because you never said you loved— Not that you have to, I mean—" I shake my head. With my high emotions, my thoughts are getting too jumbled. "But I don't want anyone else.

Ever. I never told you this, but I broke up with Nate for you." I take a deep breath as his eyes widen. "When I was with him, I could only think about you. You've always been the one for me. Even when we were kids, even when I didn't know it. And I understand if I'm too much for you, if you've changed your mind—"

"Are you fucking kidding me?" Carter takes two huge strides, wrapping his arms around me. "I can't change my mind about you, Teal. When you were with those other guys . . . shit, I tried. I tried so hard to stop loving you but it's *impossible*."

I'm weeping hard into his shoulder, but I manage to get the words out. "You really love me? Like, for real?"

"Since I was a little kid. And I've never stopped. Not once in two decades."

Around us, I'm vaguely aware of everyone clapping and whistling. Well, everyone except for Amá Sonya, who probably looks bored as hell, but I don't care. I grab Carter's face and kiss him as the clapping gets louder and Sky, I think, starts hooting.

He breaks the kiss and stares at me with those yellow diamond eyes and I am momentarily breathless. "I'm so glad you're my husband."

"I'm so glad you're my wife."

There is something bizarre happening around us, and I finally glance away from Carter to see that the dahlias are now about as tall as I am, and each and every one is beginning to flower. And they're every color imaginable—pumpkin orange, white swirled with hot pink like raspberry cream fudge, and one violet so saturated it looks as though it's vibrating. From tiny little pompoms to enormous dinner plates the size of my face, some petals round, others as wrinkled and soft as torn tissue paper. I glance at Sage, leaning by the car, who smiles and gives me a thumbs-up. This is her doing, obviously.

"What about the baby?" I call.

"Nadia says it's fine!" she yells back.

And at that moment, something loud and white swoops near my and Carter's heads, and he covers me as he ducks, saying, "Fuck, what the fuck was that?"

I glance over, and landing all around us are *doves*. White doves, to be specific, covering the yard and the driveway with their fluttery wings and coos. Now I look at Sky, who is laughing away. This is *her* doing. Obviously.

"What's next?" I ask my family. "Amá, will you call the ghosts of our ancestors to do a flash mob to a Selena song?"

"Quintanilla or Gomez?" asks Sky.

I shrug. "Both, why not?"

Amá purses her lips and lifts her chin. "I don't know what you are talking about."

"Right. I forgot." I smile as Carter wraps one of his big arms around me and holds me close.

"Why are you crying?" he whispers.

"I just don't know how I got so lucky," I say back.

After everything I've been through—my mother, stealing an integral part of my soul. Me, growing up believing that I could never be loved so long as I was broken, and then Carter proving me so wrong. My whole family proving me so wrong. Above us, the sky breaks into a massive triple rainbow, and the whole scene, with the dahlias, and the doves, is so sickeningly sweet that I grab Carter's hand and all but drag him inside. "Thank you," I shout to my family. "We're going to do unspeakable things to one another now!"

"That's right!" Sky shouts as she makes her way to the car, the doves flying up and away like a collection of oversized dandelion seeds. "Go get your ass eaten!"

Nadia gives me a smile as she walks up the driveway, giving me a peck on the cheek. "She doesn't know it yet, but she's next."

"Next for what? Getting her ass eaten?" I ask.

Nadia pretends to smack my shoulder. "Next for *love*. Now go. Sunday dinner at my house. For both of you."

"We'll be there," Carter answers for me, and when we're through the door, he's kissing me, even before it's shut behind us. "I'm sorry, too," he tells me as his lips glide down my neck. "I should've told you about the money when she gave it to me. And then gotten on my knees and begged you to stay with me as my wife." He leans back to look in my eyes.

I cup my hands around his face. "I get it. You're forgiven." And then I let my hands fall and grasp him where he's hard, hot, and ready for me. He gasps when I say, "You can take me to bed now, esposo."

He winks at me and bends to lift me into his arms. "Sí, esposa."

And that's exactly what he does. And much, much later, after we've spent many hours forgiving each other, and he's snoring softly against my ear as he spoons me, I look out the window and think of that little girl in me. That little soul piece. I imagine holding her tight as I tell her I love her.

I didn't have a good mother, but now I'm going to be a good mother to me. And that starts with doing things I love, things I find exhilarating and scary and exciting.

So when I wiggle out of Carter's arms, I walk to the dresser and open my little wooden box. There, in now slightly smudged ink, is the deeply creased paper with my list of New Year's resolutions.

New Year's Resolutions for Teal Flores
1. *Stop being selfish.*
2. *Make it up to Sage.*

3. *Make it up to Sky.*
4. *Become best friends with Carter again.*

Not being selfish is something I might always work on. I feel like the impulse for most humans is to circumvent pain by smothering it or trying to launch it onto someone else—in other words, being selfish as all hell. But I've been trying my hardest to count my breaths when something pokes at my pain, my trauma. To process things first, then react. And remember that not only am I lovable as I am . . . I'm also forgivable as I am. I can always say *I'm sorry* when I mess up, and that is an incredibly unselfish pattern I'll never let go of again.

Beside the New Year's resolutions list is another folded-up piece of paper. Placing my New Year's resolutions back, I open up the flyer with my phone in my hand, type in the website, and sign up for a handbag leatherworking class.

I've made things up to Sage and Sky. I'm best friends with Carter again.

Now it's time to do each of those things for me.

ACKNOWLEDGMENTS

I knew Teal's book would be difficult to write, because of the three Flores sisters, Teal is most unlike me. She's loud where I am quiet. Teal says what's on her mind, whereas I go over all thoughts from every angle before attempting to reveal them. She's not afraid to show her anger, whereas I tend to push anger down so deep, it settles into my bones until I'm ready to face it with my journal and my therapist.

But Teal's book, I found, was difficult to write not because she's so unlike me, but because her emotional wounds are almost too familiar. I often wept as I was writing, because her healing journey ended up, on some level, becoming transformative for me, too. My deep wish is that it is also transformative to the readers who need it.

Thank you to Elizabeth Bewley. I wouldn't want anyone else to be my publishing partner. You have always been such a champion of my work and I'm so grateful for it.

Thank you to Kristine Swartz, for your valuable input to shape *Lightning in Her Hands* to be as powerful and beautiful as possible. This book could not be as true as it is without you. Thank you, Mary Baker, for your expertise. Thank you to Kristin Cipolla, Jessica Plummer, Hillary Tacuri, Stephanie Felty, and the whole Berkley team, which has been so supportive of my work and getting it out into the world.

Thank you to Carrie May and Sarah Oberrender, for such a gorgeous and visceral cover that matches Teal and Carter's love story so perfectly. Thank you to Amy J. Schneider, who made sure this book was as clean and polished as possible.

Thank you to Eve Hanlin, who answered so many of my questions on farming dahlias one warm summer day in 2022. This was back when I thought Teal would actually care about knowing as much as possible about dahlias when she was growing them, and I should've known she wouldn't—but I'm still so grateful for Eve's knowledge and experience. If you're interested in growing your own dahlias, consider ordering tubers from Gardens by Evelyn.

In October of 2022, I spent two weeks in a cabin in Homer, Alaska, at the Storyknife Writers Retreat, a residency that supports women writers. I was deeply and powerfully changed by the experience. Much, much gratitude to everyone who makes Storyknife possible, especially Erin Coughlin Hollowell. Thank you to my fellow writers who made the experience so beautiful, especially Su-Yee Lin, Ro Alegria, Erin Bow, Debbie Moderow, and Ann Fisher-Wirth. And thank you to the moose, the eagles, the sunsets, and the moonrises; to Alaska, who is so filled with land spirits that are so intact, they walk right next to you when you step outside to breathe the same breath as the blue-white mountains.

Thank you so much to Jil Smith, for your sensitivity read with regards to bipolar disorder. Your training and expertise are so valued, as well as our "buffet"-style Greek lunches, which feed me for days!

Gratitude to my readers, to reviewers, to librarians and teachers and professors who connect with and support my work. I appreciate each of you so much, truly and sincerely from my heart.

Thank you to the members of Romance Book Club—y'all know who you are. Meeting with you has healed me in ways you can't imagine. Thank you for making one of the most difficult years bright and worth reading for.

Thank you to my family, especially Ansel, my son, who loves soccer and music and stories.

Thank you to the ancestors, who have always guided me.

Thank you to the land, who has always sustained me.

Thank you to Story, who existed long before mushrooms and will exist after long after mushrooms. I honor you.

Lightning
in
Her
Hands

Raquel
Vasquez Gilliland

DISCUSSION QUESTIONS

1. It's established early in *Lightning in Her Hands* that Teal and Carter were best friends as children; however, for various reasons, they're no longer friends at the beginning of the book. If Teal and Carter's love story isn't the trope of friends to lovers, what trope do you think they embody? If you think it actually still is friends to lovers, why is that?

2. Teal's magical gift is that the weather bends to her emotions—but she has no control over either of these. If you could choose a Flores sister gift that you could not control, would it be Sage's: influence over plants, Teal's: influence over the weather, or Sky's: influence over animals?

3. Would you consider Teal an unlikable or likable character? Do you think her most unlikable traits stem from

trauma? How can readers hold compassion for a flawed character like Teal?

4. Throughout the book, it's clear that Teal has romantic feelings for Carter but keeps choosing to suppress them over her fear that she is inherently unlovable. Despite her fears, Carter is head-over-heels in love with Teal. When did you know that Carter was in love with Teal? What were some characteristics or behaviors that convinced you of his attraction to her and the depth of his feelings for her?

5. Teal faces stigma with regard to her bipolar disorder internally as well as from her former best friend, Leilani. Why do you think bipolar disorder is one of the more stigmatized mental health conditions? In what ways does reading about characters with bipolar disorder help normalize it?

6. In the first book of the series, *Witch of Wild Things*, Sage sees Amá Sonya as sharp and judgmental. In *Lightning in Her Hands*, Teal definitely still sees her as having these characteristics, but we also see a softer, more vulnerable side to Amá Sonya. Why do you think that Teal is the one who is privy to this version of their grandmother? How do you think Amá Sonya became this way to start with?

7. What were you expecting Teal to find when she followed the line of light to her mother? What did you think Cora would be like? Were you surprised at the turn of events?

Why do you think Cora ended up deflecting all the responsibility of her actions to her daughters?

8. Why do you think it took so long for Teal to accept Carter's obvious love? What were some examples of Carter's patience with Teal's slow realization that not only does he love her but she is completely lovable as she is? What do you think is next for Carter and Teal?

Keep reading for a preview
of Sage's story in

Witch of
Wild Things

Available now!

1

M Y GREAT-AUNT NADIA SAYS IT'S A BAD IDEA TO REJECT
a gift from a ghost.

It's 'cause ghosts like to slide inside all kinds of worlds. They don't just roam the land of the living or the dead. They can show up in our dream worlds to meddle. They can touch the world of shadows and eat the light from your own home, just sucking up the long, thick gold of nightlights and fixtures like dead black holes. "Just ask your prima Cleotilde," Nadia always says, her wine-red acrylic nail in my face as she points. "She once offended the ghost of her abuelo, and boom. Lamps didn't work around her for *years*."

The scariest world that ghosts can touch is the world of gods. The old gods. The ancient gods. The gods we've heard of and the even more numerous gods we haven't. Nadia pours one cup of espresso to these gods every single morning. This woman would rather light St. Theresa's on fire than skip this daily offering.

And if you've got a ghost haunting you, there's no way to tell if one of *these* gods favors *that* ghost. So you offend a ghost? You reject her gift?

You might be offending a god.

Apparently, it's a *really* bad idea to offend gods. That's how you end up with the women in our family and our *gifts*.

This means that when I climb in my janky-ass minivan and see the cup of coffee in the console? Yes, *that* cup of coffee—the mug, a gift from one of my former students, hand thrown and glazed the color of lilacs against a lightning storm. The one steaming with notes of raspberry and a hint of chocolate. The one that I most certainly did *not* place there. The second I smell it—because yeah, I smell it first—I throw myself into my seat and press my face into the steering wheel. "Shit," I say in a long exhale.

I hate gifts from ghosts.

In order to distract myself from the sweet steam swirling around me, I grab my phone, hitting buttons as fast as my fingers can go.

Laurel picks up even before the first ring ends. "Hey! You on your way yet?"

I glance at the back of my van. Every seat is pushed down to make way for half a dozen boxes, triple that in plants, and an antique reading chair. Most of the boxes contain books—I can see a sliver of Joy Harjo's *She Had Some Horses* peeking through cardboard I hadn't bothered to tape shut. It's my favorite of her collections, because it reminds me of the stories Nadia used to tell us when Teal, Sky, and I were tiny enough to squeeze onto one twin bed. I can still hear Nadia's smoky voice filling our room. "In the beginning, there were only gods. Gods and this earth . . ."

Now Teal, Sky, and I will *never* be all together again. I take a shuddering breath as this reality sweeps over me for the millionth time in eight years, like the garnet-sharp winds of a tornado.

There and gone in a moment, but leaving behind painful, devastating destruction. That's how grief works.

"Sage Flores, are you ignoring me?"

I blink and jerk my face toward the console. The coffee is still there. Jerk. "No, of course not. I'm just about on my way. I'm in the van and everything."

"Okay, well, that's a good start. Next step, take your key, you know, the shiny silver thing in your hand right now, and push it through that teeny hole on the side of—"

"Literally giving you my middle finger right now," I say, but I'm laughing.

"Seriously, Sage. You've got this."

I glance up at my apartment—well, I guess it's not mine anymore. It's the third floor up, and the balcony still has dirt on the rails from when I watered my basil plants a little too violently. I take a deep breath, hoping the scent of that basil can calm me.

All I smell is ghost coffee.

"Want me to distract you?"

I put the phone on speaker and place it in the cup holder next to the mug. "Go for it."

"You'll never guess who I saw last night. At Piggly Wiggly of all places."

I sit back in my seat. I get the key in the ignition as I say, "Piggly Wiggly?" I think of who wouldn't be caught dead there. "Amá Sonya?"

Laurel draws out the response long and slow. "Tennessee. Reyes."

It may well be the absolute last name I'd expected her to utter. I think I would've been less shocked if she'd announced it *were* Amá Sonya at Piggly Wiggly, naked as birth, juggling plums in the middle of produce.

My breath's gone way too shallow, my hand gripping the key so tight it's cutting into my fingers. I turn the ignition, hard, but stay in park while clearing my throat. "Tennessee Reyes?" As though there were any other on the planet. "You're certain?"

"It was him, Sage. Trust me."

I close my eyes. "But . . . he moved to Denver and then got off social media and, like—"

"Disappeared off the face of the earth? Yeah. But I guess he's deigned to walk the earth's face once more, because he is in Piggly Wiggly, in Cranberry, Virginia. Or was, as of yesterday."

My heart's finally gone back to a normal rhythm and so I slowly begin reversing the van, angling my head back. "How does he look?" The question's out before I can stop it.

"Oh, gosh. Somehow *better.*"

"Better?" It comes out like a squeak. *Better* doesn't seem possible.

"He's . . . I dunno. He's grown into those legs. And he's got this yummy almost-beard thing happening . . . hold on." Her voice gets distant. "No, hon, of course I'm talking about you! Well, I mean *if* you grew a beard thing!" Laurel sighs. "I think my husband just heard me verbally ogling another man."

Normally I'd laugh and keep up with their teasing each other, but my stomach keeps making stupid, roller-coaster-y loops somehow in my rib cage. Because Tennessee Reyes is back in Cranberry.

Tenn is back in Cranberry.

"Well, that's something." I've made it to the edge of the lot now without hitting any parked vehicles in my emotional state. That's also something.

"Guess that distracted you good, huh? You sound like you've

morphed into some kind of zombie." When I give a flat chuckle in response, Laurel adds, "You okay, Sage?" in a soft voice. I hate that voice. It only comes out when I'm near tears. And to me? The consequences of crying are worse than those of offending gods.

I blink and blink and then respond. "Oh, yeah." I try to make my voice smooth, but it's as useless as ironing linen. "I'm just not looking forward to—you know. Moving back with Nadia." With Teal.

Laurel hears what I don't say. "Maybe she won't be as bad as you remember."

The last time I saw my sister, she cracked my lip open so wide, I needed four stitches. Later she said she didn't mean it—that she'd forgotten she'd worn such a sharp ring that day—but that just tells me that she did mean everything else. As in, the whole situation of her fist in my face.

"Oh, yeah." I finally make a right onto the main road as someone starts honking behind me. "It won't be that bad."

"I'll make you pollo a la plancha the second you get here."

I manage a smile. "Now you're talking."

"Nothing like Cuban comfort food to get settled in." There's a muffled noise in the background. "Ah, I gotta go."

"Tell Jorge I said hi."

"Drive safe and text me the second you get to Nadia's, yeah?"

"Of course. Love you."

"Love you more."

When I merge onto the highway, I do a double take at my reflection in the rearview mirror. My eyes are wide, the brown almost citrine in the sunlight, and my mascara is already smudged even though I applied it less than an hour ago. My hair—a mass of curls I'd braided and pinned up—looks like it's trying to break the hair tie keeping it from reaching down and steering this car without any of my help. I look like a twenty-nine-year-old who is freaking the fuck out.

I *am* a twenty-nine-year-old who is freaking the fuck out.

Why on earth is Tenn back in Cranberry?

I take a deep breath as I veer toward my first exit. It doesn't matter. What happened between us, it was over a decade ago, which feels like a dozen lifetimes by now. And that's exactly where anything between Tenn and me will stay—buried in the memories of seventeen-year-old me, back when I thought heartbreak was the worst thing that could happen to a person.

I have better things to worry about now. I take a long sip of my now lukewarm coffee.

Like ghosts.

2

silvergurl0917: **what haven't you noticed today?**

RainOnATennRoof: Wow

RainOnATennRoof: What didn't you say?

silvergurl0917: **what didn't you laugh at**

RainOnATennRoof: What didn't you do?

silvergurl0917: **what didn't you think about**

silvergurl0917: **. . . you there?**

RainOnATennRoof: You

RainOnATennRoof: I didn't think about you. Until now. :)

RainOnATennRoof: Who is this?

silvergurl0917 has logged off Messenger.

PRESENT

It takes exactly four hours and seventeen minutes to reach Catalina Street in Cranberry. Without even thinking about it, I slow the car down well before Nadia's house, eventually pulling over in front of Old Man Noemi's in-street parking. From here I can see enough. There's the emerald ivy curling over Nadia's place like a clawed, leafy hand. When I crane my neck a little, I make out the glow from her kitchen, through the daisy-patterned curtains she sewed herself when we were little kids.

From here I can look at my new life and think about all the senseless mistakes that led me to this moment.

Sleeping with the department head.

Deciding to never again sleep with the department head.

All that stupidity leading to a very convenient firing under the evergreen excuse of budget cuts.

In my mind's eye, I'm back in Gregory's office, tucked in the basement of the art department at Temple University. It is one big square with no windows, and there are piles of random objects everywhere. I had found the mess charming once, but this day, all I see is trash. A constellation of Skittles peeks out from under his desk. At the very bottom of a pile of abstract expressionists' biographies is a first edition of *For Whom the Bell Tolls*, covered in a thin layer of mold after a coffee spill.

My classroom is right above us—the jewelry studio. It's my favorite place on campus, maybe even in the whole city. It's got a dozen jewelry benches, each one made of rustic, knobbed wood. A wall of windows faces northwest, which means my classes get the most luscious gold afternoon light—the perfect setting for photographing finished pieces. A raw turquoise, blue as photos of the deep sea, bezel set in brass. A silver locket that opens to a faceted Montana sapphire that glows like a lantern made of corn-flowers.

Every day, my students amaze me, but my favorite part of teaching is witnessing the ways they amaze themselves. How they go from *I can't do this* to *Holy shit, I did that.*

And now Greg is taking it all away.

Greg's arms are crossed as he gives me a big, fake sigh. "I tried everything, Sage. It's just . . ." He waves his hands. "You know how it is."

And that's how he dismissed me from the life I'd pulled together from nothing. The one I'd slept in my van for. The one I'd sold basil starts at farmer's markets for. The one I'd stitched and scraped and carved up from the thinnest air, all to get away from the one place I never, ever wanted to live in again.

And now I'm looking right at it.

Cranberry.

My eyes well with tears before I can stop them. "No," I whisper. "No, no, *stop*—"

A single tear makes it to an eyelash, and I violently swipe it away.

But it's too late.

Next to me, in the passenger seat, a figure materializes like the pale curls of coffee steam. It's only one tear, so her edges stay as blurry as a dream. It's only one tear, so the ghost is gone before either of us can say a damn thing.

And what would I say, anyway? *Sorry for killing you? Thanks for the coffee? Leave me alone now, please?*

I take a breath, as deep and long as I can make it, and turn the car back on.

RAQUEL VASQUEZ GILLILAND is a Pura Belpré Award–winning Mexican American poet, novelist, and painter. She received her BA in cultural anthropology from the University of West Florida and her MFA in poetry from the University of Alaska Anchorage. Raquel is most inspired by folklore and seeds and the lineages of all things. When not writing, Raquel tells stories to her plants, and they tell her stories back. *Lightning in Her Hands* is her fourth novel.

VISIT RAQUEL VASQUEZ GILLILAND ONLINE

🅞 RaquelVasquezGilliland_Poet

Ready to find
your next great read?

Let us help.

Visit prh.com/nextread

Penguin
Random
House